The Innkeeper
of Ivy Hill

TALES FROM IVY HILL · BOOK ONE

THE INNKEEPER
OF IVY HILL

JULIE KLASSEN

BETHANYHOUSE
a division of Baker Publishing Group
Minneapolis, Minnesota

Published by Bethany House Publishers
11400 Hampshire Avenue South
Bloomington, Minnesota 55438
www.bethanyhouse.com

Bethany House Publishers is a division of
Baker Publishing Group, Grand Rapids, Michigan

Printed in the United States of America

Library of Congress Cataloging-in-Publication Data
Names: Klassen, Julie, author.
Title: The innkeeper of Ivy Hill / Julie Klassen.
Description: Minneapolis, Minnesota : Bethany House, a division of Baker
    Publishing Group, [2016] | Series: Tales from Ivy Hill ; 1
Identifiers: LCCN 2016017624| ISBN 9780764218149 (hardcover : acid-free paper) |
    ISBN 9780764218132 (softcover)
Subjects: LCSH: Hotelkeepers—Fiction. | Widows—Fiction. | GSAFD: Christian
    fiction. | Love stories.
Classification: LCC PS3611.L37 I56 2016 | DDC 813/.6—dc23
LC record available at https://lccn.loc.gov/2016017624

Unless noted, Scripture quotations are from the King James Version of the Bible.

This is a work of fiction. Names, characters, incidents, and dialogues are products of the author's imagination and are not to be construed as real. Any resemblance to actual events or persons, living or dead, is entirely coincidental.

Cover design by Jennifer Parker
Cover woman photograph by Mike Habermann Photography, LLC
Cover landscape photograph by Trevillion Images/Jill Battaglia
Map illustration by Bek Cruddace Cartography & Illustration

Author represented by Books and Such Literary Agency

16 17 18 19 20 21 22   7 6 5 4 3 2 1

To Stacey,
with fond memories of our girlhood friendship,
and the hours we spent sitting in the gently swaying branches
of the evergreen trees on your grandfather's farm,
sharing our secrets and our dreams.

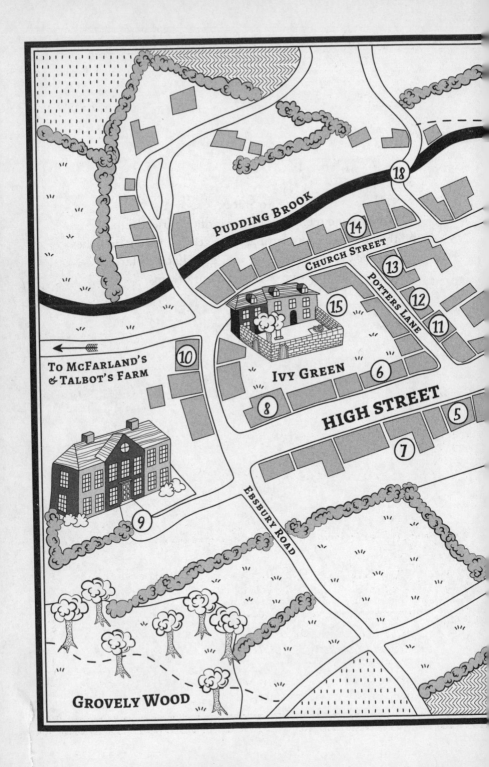

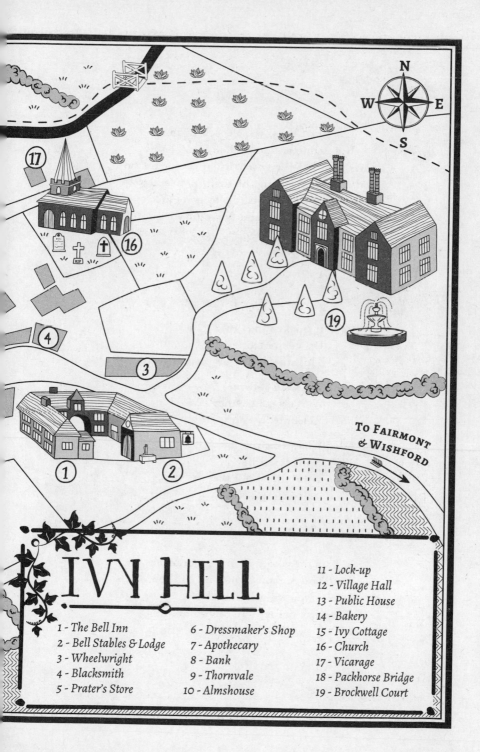

IVY HILL

1 - The Bell Inn
2 - Bell Stables & Lodge
3 - Wheelwright
4 - Blacksmith
5 - Prater's Store

6 - Dressmaker's Shop
7 - Apothecary
8 - Bank
9 - Thornvale
10 - Almshouse

11 - Lock-up
12 - Village Hall
13 - Public House
14 - Bakery
15 - Ivy Cottage
16 - Church
17 - Vicarage
18 - Packhorse Bridge
19 - Brockwell Court

N
W E
S

TO FAIRMONT
& WISHFORD

The Crown was a coaching inn
licensed to a widow called Sarah Smith.
"Mrs. Smith deserves particular commendation
and support, as being the first . . . to add to the
accommodation of visitors by every species of
comfort, neatness, and domestic attention."
—*Powell's Guide*, 1831

The Ivy

It cloaks and climbs
Up steep inclines
This stubborn evergreen disguise.

The walls it twines
With creeping vines
Welcome it, as if to hide.

What treasures lurk
And secrets lie
Within the walls that ivy climbs?
—Anna Paulson

I am the vine; you are the branches.
If you remain in me and I in you,
you will bear much fruit;
apart from me you can do nothing.
—John 15:5 NIV

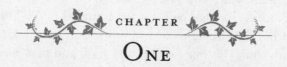

CHAPTER
ONE

May 27, 1820
Ivy Hill, Wiltshire, England

Jane Fairmont Bell sat alone in the keeper's lodge she had once shared with her husband. There she began her solitary breakfast, delivered by a maid from the coaching inn across the drive. Her inn. She still struggled to credit it.

Jane ate in dainty politeness, as though at a formal dinner—or as though her old, eagle-eyed governess sat beside her. In reality, she had eaten alone for a year now. The clink of china and cutlery seemed louder than usual, the courtyard outside strangely quiet for that time of day.

At the thought, she glanced at the nearest window, framed by ivy. The leafy vines had grown unchecked and narrowed the visible glass. She could cut it back, but she liked the privacy it afforded. And how it blocked her view of the often-chaotic coaching inn.

Jane rose and walked into the bedchamber. The view from its window was more peaceful. There, an ivied oak tree and stone wall. And in the distance, if she looked for it, the tall brick chimney stacks of Brockwell Court. The elegant manor might once have been her home, if life had turned out differently. Beyond it lay a patchwork of farms, pastureland, chalk downs, and small villages.

A soft knock interrupted her thoughts. Returning to the sitting room, Jane called, "Come."

Cadi, the young maid who helped her dress and brought her meals, stepped inside, her face cheerful as usual. "Finished your breakfast, I see."

"Yes, thank you." Jane nodded toward the arranged flowers—spring blooms from her own garden combined with a few purchased from the greenhouse. "And would you mind taking these back with you? This one for the entry hall, and that one for the front desk."

"Happily. They're beautiful. You ought to come over and see how they brighten the old place."

"Just set them in their usual places, if you please. I would only be underfoot."

"Not at all. You're the landlady now, and more than welcome."

"Another time, perhaps." Jane had offered to help with the inn early in their marriage, but John insisted her place was here, in the small, separate house he'd built for them. After all, gentlewomen did not "work." After a few attempts, Jane stopped offering. And soon . . . other concerns occupied her mind.

"I am off on an errand this morning," she added.

"An errand?" The girl's gaze shifted from Jane's black bombazine to the long box on the sideboard. "Then . . . might you wear the new gown?"

Jane shook her head. "I am only going to the churchyard."

Cadi sighed, clearly disappointed. "Very well." She carried the vases to the door. "I'll come back for the breakfast tray."

Jane nodded and lifted a deep black bonnet from its peg. She stood before the long mirror to tie its strings, then pulled on her gloves.

A few minutes later, she left the lodge, a clutch of flowers in her hands. As she passed the coach archway that led into the stable yard, movement caught her eye. The farrier stood in the courtyard, burly arms crossed, in conversation with a young postillion who looked to be no more than sixteen. Joe, she believed his name was.

Noticing her pass, the postboy tipped his cap to her, and she sent him a warm smile in return.

The farrier nodded in her direction. "Mrs. Bell."

Jane nodded but did not stop to greet him. There was something about that man. . . . Seeing him always stirred up bad memories. After all, he had been the one to bring John's body back to Ivy Hill.

She continued on, past the front of the inn, before crossing the High Street to avoid the nosy greengrocer arranging his bushels of produce. Thankfully, the rest of the shops were still quiet at this time of morning. She walked up narrow Potters Lane, past the lock-up and village hall, and then turned onto Church Street. At its end, she pushed open the listing gate and stepped into the churchyard, passing ancient tombs and faded headstones until she came to a more recent grave.

John Franklin Bell
Beloved Son & Husband
1788–1819

A visit on the first anniversary of John's death had seemed fitting. But he was not the only loved one she had lost.

Jane stood at that particular spot because it would raise no questions. Anyone seeing her at her husband's grave would walk by without a second look.

She pressed the modest bouquet to her abdomen as though to quell the ache there, and then bent low. She divided the bouquet into six individual flowers—a single pink rose and five white moss roses—and spread them across the grave.

Jane glanced around to make sure no one was watching, then kissed her fingers and touched the headstone. "I'm sorry," she whispered.

The creak of a hinge startled her, and she looked up.

An elderly man emerged from a work shed nearby, pushing a wheelbarrow with shovel handle protruding. He wore a drab coat and flat cap atop scruffy grey hair. The sexton, Jane recognized, who maintained the church grounds and dug the graves. He set the wheelbarrow down and picked up his shovel with gnarled hands.

Suddenly self-conscious, Jane straightened, watching the man from the corner of her eye.

A church door opened and the Reverend Mr. Paley came striding out. Seeing Jane, he diverted from his path and walked toward her.

"Hello, Mrs. Bell. I am sorry to intrude on your private moment, but I wanted to express my condolences. I know this must be a difficult day for you."

"Thank you, Mr. Paley."

The vicar glanced over at the sexton, leaning on his shovel. "Haven't you some work to do, Mr. Ainsworth?"

The old man grunted and began digging up a bramblebush growing between the headstones.

For a moment, Mr. Paley continued to watch the sexton. In a low voice he said to Jane, "That man is one of God's more . . . interesting creations. I've heard him talking to the church mice more than once. He refuses to set traps, so I shall have to do it."

Jane had heard the sexton was odd. Apparently the rumors were true.

The vicar sighed, then gave her a sad smile. "Well. I shall leave you. Please let me know if there is anything I can do. Mrs. Paley and I will be praying for you—today especially."

Jane thanked him again. He bowed and continued on his way.

With a final look at John's grave, Jane left the churchyard with little solace from the visit. Behind her, the gate swung on its hinges. She wished the sexton would repair the latch. It would not stay closed, no matter what she did.

On the walk back, Jane passed the vicarage, public house, and bakery without really seeing them, her head bowed to discourage people from seeking her out. She reached the High Street without having to speak to anyone. The Bell Inn was just across the street. She had almost made it.

To her right, the door to the dressmaker's shop opened and Mrs. Shabner, mantua-maker and milliner, poked her head out.

"Mrs. Bell!"

Jane winced. She had never liked that address. *Mrs. Bell* was John's mother. Hearing it, she squelched the impulse to look around and see if her mother-in-law was standing nearby, a disapproving look on her face.

The dressmaker asked, "What do you think of the new gown? I know you received it, for my girl delivered it to your door herself."

"I did not order a new gown, Mrs. Shabner," Jane replied, gently yet firmly.

"My dear, you have been in full mourning for a year now. You ought to change to half mourning, at least."

The elderly woman wore a frock of bright yellow-and-blue stripes, and a feathered cap. The phrase "Mutton dressed as lamb" whispered through Jane's mind, and she chastised herself for the unkind thought.

"I am sorry, but I don't need a new gown at present."

"Yes, you do, my dear. Look at that old thing. The elbows are worn shiny, and the buttonholes frayed. When I made that, I still had all my teeth."

"You exaggerate."

"Try it on, at least," Mrs. Shabner urged. "I think the lavender will suit you very well. I made it according to your previous measurements, but I shall be happy to alter it as needed. You know my door is always open, though few enough pass through it." She sighed. "I think I shall retire. Or move to Wishford, where my talents would be better appreciated."

The woman was forever threatening to move to Wishford. Jane pressed her eyes closed, stifling a sigh of her own. "If you have another customer in mind for the gown, then, by all means, I shall send it back without delay."

"No, no. You are the only recent widow in town at present. Take your time. But once you try it on, you shall see that I am right."

Jane left her with a wave and crossed the street.

Reaching The Bell, Jane paused, noticing the small *Vacancy* sign hanging by a single chain, the other chain dangling uselessly. A breeze blew up the hill, and the sign slowly revolved on its chain, the word spinning past Jane's eyes again and again.

Vacancy . . . Vacancy . . .

That sign had hung there more often of late. And the word perfectly symbolized how Jane felt.

Empty.

She pulled her gaze away and returned to the refuge of her lodge.

Three days after the somber anniversary of her son's death, Thora Stonehouse Bell sat pressed against a carriage window, the bony shoulder of a young clergyman digging into hers at every turn. On the bench opposite sat an elderly couple, he snoring away, and she fanning herself with a copy of the *Lady's Monthly Museum*.

Thora popped a ginger candy into her mouth to allay her queasy stomach. She offered one to the woman, who listlessly accepted.

The clergyman beside her had put away his New Testament half an hour before, and now read from a traveler's guidebook. Noticing her glance at it, he asked, "Are you a first-time visitor to this area?"

Thora hesitated. It *was* her first trip back—her first time to feel like a visitor in her old home, and probably not a welcome one. "Yes, I suppose I am."

His eyes shone with eagerness. "Then allow me to share what I've read. We are now some ninety miles southwest of London, in Wiltshire, known for its white horses carved into chalk hills, the Salisbury Cathedral, and ancient marvels like Stonehenge. It seems we are in for a treat at our next stop." He ran his finger along the printed page and read, "'The Bell is a fine old coaching inn, licensed to a John Bell and managed expertly by his widowed mother. The Bell accommodates visitors with every species of comfort, neatness, and domestic attention.'"

"Apparently your guidebook is out of date," Thora said dryly. "Better stick to the Scriptures, Parson. Beyond that, you can't believe everything you read."

He gave her a confused look—brow and mouth puckered—but

she did not bother to explain. Instead, she turned away, discouraging further conversation.

She looked out the window, but instead of the passing countryside, memories passed before her eyes and sadness pressed down hard.

Poor John. . . .

Her firstborn had been gone over a year now. The thought lanced her heart. It seemed a lifetime ago that she and Frank and their sons had all lived together under the same roof. She knew where Frank and John were now. Buried in St. Anne's churchyard. But she had little idea where Patrick might be. Her youngest. Her blue-eyed boy. What an angel he had been as a lad. What a disappointment as a man. She wondered what whim he was pursuing now, and if he were in good health and out of trouble. Thora whispered a prayer. It was all she could do for him now.

Very soon she would be back at the coaching inn that had once belonged to her parents, then her husband, then her eldest son, and now her daughter-in-law. She wondered what sort of reception Jane would give her and doubted it would be a warm one. She hoped Talbot, at least, would be glad to see her.

Thora took a deep breath and surveyed her surroundings. The coach crossed the River Wylye bridge, and passed the village of Wishford with its tall, battlemented church tower. Then they began the climb up Ivy Hill, which gave her a fair view of the Salisbury Plain out one window, and Grovely Wood out the other.

Thora could hardly believe she was returning after less than a year away. When she left, she had foolishly imagined she would live with her sister—two independent women together—for the rest of her life. But soon she had seen those impractical dreams fading away.

You can take the woman from the inn, but not the innkeeper from the woman, she mused.

Yet Diana had managed it. Her sister had hated growing up in a coaching inn and had left as soon as she could, never looking back. The same was proving more difficult for Thora.

What would she find upon arrival? She hoped the cook, Mrs. Rooke, had exaggerated in her recent letter, which stated that the place was falling into disrepair without her.

Either way, Thora would not grovel. She would say she had come only for a visit. She would not admit that her future with her sister—and her living situation—had come to an end.

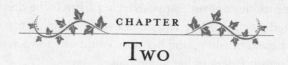

CHAPTER

Two

Cadi nudged the lodge door open with a basket of clothes from the laundress. "Before I forget," she said, "Mr. Bell asked me to remind you that he has a meeting in Wishford this morning."

Jane nodded. She did not recall her brother-in-law mentioning a meeting but was glad to leave business dealings to him.

"And Mrs. Snyder says she's sorry but she cannot get that stain out of your black crepe."

Jane groaned. "Really? Oh no."

"Perhaps it is a sign, ma'am. Do you know, I have never seen you in anything but black? For I came after . . ." The maid's smile faltered for once, and she left her sentence unfinished as she lay the clean nightdresses, shifts, and stockings in the dressing chest.

She then returned to Jane's side. "Mrs. Shabner thinks you ought to have a new gown. Black doesn't flatter your complexion, she says."

Jane rolled her eyes. "Mrs. Shabner will say anything to earn a sale."

"Please try it on, ma'am. For me?"

Jane glanced at the gown box and sighed. "Oh, very well. I'm not going anywhere today. Just this once."

Cadi squealed in pleasure and hurried to help Jane change into the lavender dress.

The twilled sarcenet slid over her stays and petticoats in a smooth ripple of fine fabric. As Cadi stood behind her, doing up the fastenings, Jane studied her reflection in the long mirror. The soft lavender color brightened her somewhat sallow skin and brought out the green in her changeable hazel eyes. The snug ribbon trim beneath her bosom emphasized her figure. The dress made her looked younger. More feminine. Even though her brown hair needed a good brushing and her nose could use powder, it was a definite improvement in her appearance.

"It's beautiful on you, ma'am."

"It is a lovely dress, I own."

"You don't own it yet, but you ought to," Cadi teased. "It suits you so well."

From the road outside came the sound of a horn blast. Jane casually stepped to the window and watched the yellow Mercury turn onto the drive and rumble through the archway. She noticed the coachman in his many-caped coat, the guard on the back, and several outside passengers. And inside the stagecoach, a face pressed near the window. A face Jane recognized with a start. Thora Bell—her eyes locked on Jane.

Panic flowed through her. "I have to change this instant."

"What? Why?"

Jane stepped back, heart pounding, praying Thora had not seen her. Or at least—what she'd been wearing. "I don't want my mother-in-law to see me in this."

Cadi followed her into the bedchamber, face pale. "I'm sorry, ma'am. Had I known she was coming today, I never would have urged you to put it on. You should have said something."

The young woman hurried behind Jane and began undoing the lacings and tiny pearl buttons with trembling fingers.

Jane's hands were not steady either. "I had no idea she was coming. I am as surprised as you are."

Jane told herself Thora would probably go inside the inn first, talk to Mrs. Rooke, and freshen up in her old room before seeking her out—or at least she hoped so.

The lavender fabric slid from her hips, and Jane stepped out of it. Cadi carried the dress into the sitting room and tried to force all that material back into its box.

"Put the lid on," Jane hissed.

Cadi scrambled to comply, then hurried back to help Jane into the black bombazine. But before she could, a sharp knock sounded on the lodge door. Both women gasped. The material shook in Cadi's hands.

"It's too late." Jane swiped up her dressing gown and slid her arms into the sleeves.

"Shall I answer it?" Cadi asked.

"No, you stay here," Jane said. She knew her mother-in-law would not approve of her conscripting one of the staff to open her door for her. Nor did she want Cadi to get into any trouble with Mrs. Rooke.

Smoothing her hair, Jane walked to the door, hoping to appear at ease. She opened it and faced John and Patrick's mother, Mrs. Thora Bell. The woman wore a plain gown of unrelieved black wool. She must have been uncomfortable in it on this warm spring day.

Thora's bonnet was as dark as her look—though the cap underneath was customary white lace. Beneath the cap her black hair showed no hint of grey. She stood of average height, but her confident bearing made her seem taller. Her features, like her figure, were strong. Stern lines framed her mouth and eyes—striking blue eyes that made people look twice.

Those suspicious blue eyes now swept Jane top to toe and back again. "You look terrible."

"Thank you, Thora." Jane forced a smile. "Good to see you as well. We didn't expect you."

"Evidently." Thora surveyed the sitting room, her gaze lingering on the gown box. "I thought I would visit and see how you were getting on."

"I am well. Thank you."

"Are you?" Thora eyed her haphazardly tied dressing gown with raised brows.

"Yes. Won't you come in and sit down?"

"No, thank you. I shan't stay long." Her mother-in-law had never spent more time in the keeper's lodge than absolutely necessary, and had barely set foot in the place since John's death.

Thora asked, "Where is Talbot? I was surprised he did not meet the coach."

"Talbot is gone."

"Gone?" Thora pressed a hand to her chest.

"Not dead," Jane hurried to clarify. "He simply left our employ, about four months ago now."

Thora frowned. "Why would he leave after all this time?"

"He has taken over his family's farm."

"Walter Talbot—farming? I cannot credit it."

"The old homeplace is his now that his brother passed away. And his sister-in-law is quite ill, I understand."

Thora's brow furrowed. "Bill died? I had not heard. Poor Nan. . . ." For a moment she seemed lost in thought, then drew herself up. "Who is managing the inn in Talbot's stead?"

"Well, I recently hired Colin McFarland, but—"

"McFarland?" Thora's face stretched in incredulity. "Why on earth would you do that?"

Jane shrugged. "Mercy told me he needed the work. Asked me to give him a chance to prove himself."

Thora waved an expressive hand. "He'll prove something all right—that it was a mistake to hire him. Besides, he can't be more than, what, nineteen?"

"Four or five and twenty, I believe. And hopefully he will learn in time. In the meanwhile, Patrick is here and helps wherever needed."

Thora blinked. "Patrick is here?"

"Yes. . . . I'm sorry, I assumed he would have written to you."

"How optimistic of you. He has never been one to write letters. You two share that trait, apparently."

Jane ducked her head. "I am sorry. I should have written, I know."

Thora frowned. "I thought Patrick was sailing around the world on a merchant ship."

"He was. He returned a month or so ago."

"Why?"

Jane shrugged. "He heard about John and came back to help. And he is more than welcome."

Jane noticed the woman's gaze fix on something, and turned to see what had caught her attention. A lavender cuff poked its tongue from under the box lid. *Oh no.*

But on second look, Jane realized that was not what had arrested her mother-in-law. Instead, she was staring at the small portrait of John he'd commissioned for Jane as a wedding gift.

Jane picked it up and handed it to her.

Thora took a cursory glance and briskly handed it back. "How young he looks."

Jane regarded the painting. She had almost forgotten how young and handsome John had been when they married. At that age, he had resembled Patrick more than she realized.

Replacing the portrait, Jane asked, "How is your sister?"

"She is well enough, thank you. A bit daft, but otherwise in good health." Thora squared her shoulders. "Well. I shall leave you. I am sorry to hear about Talbot's brother. I shall go and pay my respects soon. That is, assuming I am invited to stay?"

"Of course, Thora. Stay as long as you like." Jane hoped she would not live to regret the offer. She added, "Your old room is much as you left it."

"Is it indeed?" Thora's eyes snapped in disapproval. "What an impractical waste of space."

Thora left her daughter-in-law and crossed the courtyard. A stew of conflicting emotions churned in her stomach, but she determined to show none of them.

The place had certainly not improved in her absence. Nor her relationship with John's wife.

Out front, the vacancy sign hung at an unsightly angle on a single chain. Why had no one repaired it? And why was there any vacancy on a Tuesday—typically a busy day indeed. The inn had needed new paint when she left, and that fact had become more evident—bare wood showed here and there through peeling paint, especially on the window trim. The flowerpots on either side of the door did look well, she begrudgingly acknowledged. Jane's work, no doubt. And the stable yard itself, although too quiet, appeared perfectly neat. That was something. Perhaps Mrs. Rooke had exaggerated when she'd written about the sorry state of the place.

The cook-housekeeper stood waiting for her in the hall, as broad in the hips as her considerable shoulders. "In her boudoir, as usual?"

"Yes."

"At this time of day?" The stout woman tsked.

With Talbot gone, Jane ought to have been greeting coaches and overseeing the staff, not sleeping late or trying on new dresses or whatever she'd been doing.

"She isn't the landlady you were, Mrs. Bell. She's of no earthly use that I can see. Do you know, the butcher reduced my last order, on account of money owed!"

"No."

"Yes," Mrs. Rooke insisted. "You're a sight for sore eyes, I don't mind telling you. Now you understand why I wrote that letter."

Thora nodded. She knew she should not tolerate criticism of her daughter-in-law, but instead gave in to the temptation to add to it. "No wonder the place is falling into disrepair, with no innkeeper to oversee it or welcome guests."

A young maid passing by with an empty basket said, "Mr. Bell has gone to Wishford, madam, or he no doubt would have met your coach."

Mrs. Rooke scowled at the girl. "Get on with your work, Cadi. No need to speak unless spoken to."

The maid hurried up the stairs and out of view.

Thora didn't recognize her. She asked quietly, "What happened to Mary?"

"Ran off with a bag man."

"Ah." Thora turned to the stalwart retainer. "I wonder you did not mention Patrick was back."

The cook lifted a beefy shoulder. "I've no bone to pick with Master Patrick."

"Using my name in vain again, Mrs. Rooke?" Patrick said as he swept inside and removed his hat. He beamed at Thora. "Mamma! I thought I heard your voice. What a surprise."

"Hello, Patrick." Thora stiffly received the kiss he planted on her temple. When he stepped back, she studied her son, relishing the sight of him. How handsome he was—like his father. Taller than she remembered. His dark hair so much like hers. His blue eyes, too. Her heart softened as flickering images of her little boy ran through her mind. His hand in hers. Little arms around her neck. . . . But then she steeled her heart. "What are you doing here?"

Those blue eyes glinted, and he gave a wry grin. "What am I doing here? I grew up here, as you know better than anyone. I've returned to help now that John is gone—and you as well."

He opened the office door and held it for her.

Thora nodded to Mrs. Rooke, then followed him inside. "Why?"

He shrugged easily. "I missed it. Innkeeping is in my blood, after all."

"Like sailing was in your blood a few years ago, and importing before that?"

"Touché, Mamma." He spread his hands, dimples blazing. "But the prodigal has come home."

"This is no longer our home since John died."

Patrick sat at the desk and leaned back in the chair. "Oh, but it is. My sister has made me very welcome."

Thora narrowed her eyes. "What are you after?"

He raised both hands. "Not a blessed thing. Though a bed that doesn't sway with each roll of the sea makes a welcome change, I don't deny."

She searched his face, and he steadily held her gaze. Was he in earnest? She wanted to believe him. "How long have you been here?"

"A month and a half."

"And yet the place is not exactly thriving."

"Not yet. I am still finding my land legs, as it were. And you, Mamma? I thought you were off enjoying life with Aunt Di."

"I was. I am only here . . . for a visit. I heard things were not going well and thought I should call."

He raised a brow. "Your spies alerted you, did they? Mrs. Rooke, no doubt. Or perhaps Blomfield himself?"

Why would the banker write to her? Thora wondered, but she did not reveal her source. Instead she looked around the cluttered office. "What a mess! I still can't believe Talbot left. Tell me she did not force him out."

"Force him out? Jane? Hardly. It was his decision. And why not—he inherited his family's property when his brother died." He added pointedly, "As I once thought I would."

Thora chose to ignore that. "And did you not warn Jane about hiring Colin McFarland?"

Patrick shrugged. "He was already here when I got back. A *fait accompli.*"

"And you said nothing? Don't you remember your father banning McFarlands from The Bell?"

"Liam McFarland, maybe, but that was—what—ten years ago now?"

"Twelve."

"Well, apparently Colin hadn't a sixpence to scratch with, and Jane wanted to give him a chance."

Thora gestured toward the disorganized desk. "And I see how well that is going."

"It's not all his fault," Patrick defended. "Mrs. Rooke said that after Talbot left, no one set foot in this office except to toss more unopened bills on the desk. It seems Colin found it too overwhelming, and let the paperwork continue to pile up. He has been mostly acting as porter and helping in the yard. He has a lot to learn, but he is working hard."

Thora doubted that. She shook her head, lips tight. "A McFarland in The Bell . . . Your father is turning in his grave."

Patrick grimaced at that and rose to his feet. "I will go and let Jane know you're here."

"Warn her, I believe you mean. Don't bother. I have already spoken to her."

"She was no doubt happy to see you."

"Don't be sarcastic. You know she and I have never seen eye to eye. John made it clear she did not want me here."

"Did he? That surprises me."

"It surprised me at the time as well, considering she's never shown any interest in acting as innkeeper or housekeeper herself."

"Perhaps John exaggerated or you misunderstood."

"I hate to think I uprooted myself based on a mere misunderstanding."

"I thought you left because you wanted to experience life beyond these walls at long last?"

"That was part of it. Diana asked me to come. She said she was lonely living alone." *But she is not lonely any longer. . . .*

Patrick crossed his arms and leaned against the doorframe. "How long can you visit? Or do you mean to stay on and help save us from destruction?"

"I trust you exaggerate." Thora looked again around the neglected office with its piles of bills. *But perhaps not.*

Thora inhaled and answered truthfully, "I have yet to decide."

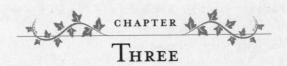

CHAPTER
THREE

Thora entered her old suite of rooms—bedchamber and small sitting room—and for a moment stilled. In some ways she felt as if she had never left. In others, as though years had passed instead of only ten or eleven months. She set down her valise and crossed to the windows to open the shutters. A fine cloud of dust rose as she did so. That was another thing that had changed. Thora had always kept her living quarters spotless.

She stepped to the long mirror to remove her bonnet, and winced at the reflection staring back at her. Her fifty-one years lay on her like a heavy yoke, weighing her down. Her apple cheeks were not as high and full as they once were. Her jawline not as defined. Creases like apostrophes punctuated the space between her brows, and the lines framing her mouth and eyes dug deeper. The ruthless plucking of silver hairs from black had become an increasingly time-consuming task. Her strength and stamina were not what they once were, either. Months of idle living with her sister had made her soft.

And *soft* was not a word anyone had ever used to describe Thora Stonehouse Bell.

Her sister, Diana, was only a few years younger, but looked several more. Diana took pains with her complexion, slathering on the latest creams advertised in *La Belle Assemblée*. Her maid dressed her hair in the latest styles and applied cosmetics deftly—a touch of powder and rouge.

Thora had never fussed with any of it. She'd always been too busy for feminine falderals. Perhaps she should have found the time. Thora turned away from the mirror with a sigh. Over-concern with one's appearance was a waste of time, she told herself. Especially at her age.

For her first fifty years, living in this inn had been the only life she'd known. She had grown up here. Met her husband here. And together they'd run the place after her parents retired and then passed on. She'd raised their sons here. And even after Frank died, Thora had remained to help John fill his father's shoes. It was her duty. But in recent years she'd become increasingly restless.

Her sister had asked her to come and live with her more than once, or at least to visit, but Thora had always been too busy to accept. But after John's unexpected death—and his unexpected will—Thora had finally packed a valise and booked herself on a westbound coach.

Her unmarried sister had inherited a modest townhouse from a spinster aunt, as well as a large enough annuity to live independently and comfortably in Bath.

Thora had at first enjoyed genteel living. She went for long walks around the beautiful city. Took in the entertainments at the theatres and concert halls. And actually read a novel. *Eh*. It wasn't for her. A bit of impractical nonsense in her estimation.

Eventually the extended holiday began to wear on her. She was not bred for idleness. So she started coming up with projects. "Let us put up preserves and pickles for the winter. Why give the grocer so much of your money?" "Don't put that petticoat in the rag bag. With a little careful patching, you could get another year of wear from that." It had taken far less than a year for her to begin wearing on Diana's nerves.

"Thora. Stop bossing me about," she'd say. "I am no longer the little sister in your command."

Thora *was* bossy—she could not deny it. The trait had served her well at the inn. She had managed cook, maids, and head porter with confident ease. But it was harder to manage her tongue.

When her sister began keeping company with a retired sea captain, critical words and warnings immediately sprang to Thora's lips. *"Yes, the man is reasonably respectable. Spend time with him if you like. But don't marry him. Not at your age. Why lose all your independence? Do you not know what happens when women marry? Are you ignorant of the law?"* Thora had made certain her sister knew, whether she wished to be informed or not.

An unmarried woman or a widow had the right to own property and make contracts in her own name. But unless certain settlements were legally arranged ahead of time, when a woman married, everything she owned instantly became the property of her husband. In essence, *she* became the property of her husband. A married woman owned nothing.

It was a lesson Thora had learned when she married Frank Bell. A hard lesson.

But her sister ignored her warnings and agreed to the captain's proposal. Diana's annuity and snug house now belonged to him.

After receiving the letter from Bertha Rooke, Thora had remained in Bath long enough to attend her sister's wedding and then returned to Ivy Hill without further delay.

She had been good at one thing in her life—and that was serving as housekeeper for her family's inn. Would Jane accept her help? She must at least try.

Now here she was, back in her old room at The Bell. But something told Thora there would be no going back to her old life now. If things were as bad as Mrs. Rooke said, perhaps none of them would have a roof over their heads for long.

Thora came face-to-face with Colin McFarland when she walked downstairs the next day. She vaguely recognized him but was taken aback by the man in his midtwenties before her, compared to the adolescent of her memories. He was of average height, with sandy brown hair brushed neatly back. His broad face tapered to a pointy chin. Not a bad-looking man, she allowed. Though she wondered how long it would be until dissipation ruined his looks, as it had ruined his father's.

"So you're Liam McFarland's boy," she began.

He lifted a hand, a spark of sheepish humor in his eyes. "Guilty as charged."

He wore a dark coat, waistcoat, and trousers, and old but well-polished shoes. His collar could have been whiter, but he was surprisingly well kempt. At least he looked the part of a Bell porter.

"Did your father put you up to finding a job here—to see what mischief you could get into?"

A frown creased his face. "I don't know what you mean, Mrs. Bell. I am here to work, and that is all."

"Humpf. We shall see." Thora would indeed see, for she would be watching him.

But first she wanted to talk to Walter Talbot. So she went out into the stable yard and asked Tuffy to hitch a horse to the gig.

The skinny old ostler pulled a face. "That rickety ol' thing, missus? Ain't safe, if you ask me."

Thora sighed. "Very well. I shall walk."

Thankfully, she had donned stout half boots that morning, as well as a bonnet.

The exercise would do her good, she told herself. And if memory served, the walk out to the farm was not too long.

Memory did not serve. Nor did her wool dress. She was warm and itchy well before she arrived. Passing the McFarland place on the way, she wrinkled her nose. As Thora surveyed the dilapidated outbuildings, weedy garden, and rubblestone house, she decided she'd seen better-kept sheep sheds.

Finally reaching Talbot's farm, she let herself in through the wooden gate. Ahead lay a cobbled path to the farmhouse, and to the left, woodshed and barn, then fields and grazing land. She heard the clang of metal upon metal and saw a man bent over near the barn, hammering something. He wore a shirt with rolled-up sleeves, braces, trousers, and work boots. A low tweed cap covered his head. One of the hired men, she guessed. Perhaps Talbot was in the barn, just out of sight. She would try there first. She wasn't ready to knock at the front door, unsure if Talbot's sister-in-law was well enough to answer it herself or if she might be sleeping.

The hired man, bent over his work, did not see her approach. His hat brim shaded his face. She noticed his muscular forearms as he raised the hammer and brought it down in skillful, efficient strokes. The man glanced up and glanced again, the tool stilling in his hands. When he fully lifted his head, she saw his face, and drew up short in surprise.

"Talbot?" She blinked. Walter Talbot had always worn gentleman's attire—coat, waistcoat, trousers, and polished shoes in his role as head porter and manager. Not workman's clothes. She had not seen him in rolled-up shirt sleeves since adolescence, and certainly never with fine linen clinging to sweaty shoulders and chest.

"Hello, Mrs. Bell."

"I didn't recognize you," she said, oddly irritated. "From a distance I thought you must be the hired man."

"He has gone to town for a part. I'm trying to repair this plow blade, but it's as stubborn as . . . my last boss." He set down the tool, pulled a handkerchief from his pocket, and wiped his neck and brow. "Forgive my appearance. I was not expecting guests."

She waved away the apology. "Never mind that. I just returned . . . for a visit . . . and was sorry to hear about Bill."

He nodded, expression pinched. "Me too. I was updating the timetables when word came. I should have been here."

"I was shocked to hear you'd left the inn."

"I didn't like to leave Jane on her own. But the farm is my responsibility now. It's hard labor, though it is good to have the work of my hands mean something."

"Your work at the inn meant something." Thora shook her head. "Just to leave like that, after so many years . . ."

"You left. When it suited you."

The bite in his voice surprised her. She said, "Jane didn't want me there. And she didn't exactly welcome me back with open arms."

"If you came charging in, grim faced and disapproving, I shouldn't wonder."

Thora had a frank relationship with Talbot before, but now she noticed a complete lack of obsequiousness on his part. "I did not charge in . . . exactly. Though of course I was concerned. Word reached me that the place was going to ruin. I had to come."

"Word of that reached you all the way in Bath? From Bertha Rooke, no doubt."

"Yes." Thora went on to tell him what she had learned, about the loss of several coaching lines and the unpaid bills. "Did you know about the inn's . . . difficulties?"

"Not to that extent." He shook his head, lips tight. "But don't blame your daughter-in-law. At least not her alone. I don't mean to speak ill of the dead, but John—"

"Then don't," Thora snapped. "I won't hear a word against him."

Talbot looked down at her sharp tone and kicked at a clod of dirt. "Suit yourself."

"Do you know whom she hired to *try* to replace you . . . ? Colin McFarland."

"Yes, I heard." He lifted his chin and studied her through narrowed eyes. "Don't forget—Colin had nothing to do with that incident on the roof, or all that came after. He was only a lad at the time."

"I know, but he is still Liam McFarland's son." Thora shook her head again. "Coming from where he has . . . How is he to know how to properly maintain a place, let alone how to keep books and timetables and the rest? Patrick is back and trying to help. Had you heard that as well?"

Talbot nodded but offered no comment.

Thora added, "He has his work cut out for him. You would not believe the condition of your desk."

"It isn't my desk any longer. Nor your inn to fret over."

"I know. But the inn is part of me, like one of my children. And a mother never stops fretting over one of her own."

"I can understand that." He looked down in thought, again digging the toe of his boot in the dirt. He offered, "I could come by now and again, and show Colin a few things. If no one would mind."

"Mind? I'd be eternally grateful. And so would Jane, if she is not a complete fool."

"Jane is not a fool. Disinterested, inexperienced, ignorant at worst. Though certainly clever enough, if she wanted to learn."

Thora huffed. "I'll never understand why Jane chased after John if she had no interest in the inn."

"She didn't chase after John. I never saw a man pursue a woman like John pursued Jane Fairmont."

Thora shook her head. "But she was completely unsuited and unsuitable. Well. No one asked my opinion. Nothing new there."

Thora realized she must sound the shrew. Giving way to bitterness was a waste of energy. She inhaled and gentled her voice. "How is Nan bearing up?"

"Not well. She has been ill for a long time, as you know. And Bill's death has laid her very low indeed. Consumption, Dr. Burton says. He calls when he can, but there is little he can do."

"I am sorry to hear it."

He nodded. "Sadie Jones helps care for her. And the parson and Mrs. Paley come out often to pray for her."

Thora asked, "Is it . . . strange . . . living in the same house together with Nan now that your brother is gone?"

"A little at first. But she can't live on her own." He tilted his head and looked at her askance. "Don't tell me you are going to wag your finger at us, like some mean-spirited gossips do? There is nothing improper going on. Good heavens, the woman is an invalid. Sadie has to help her with everything."

Thora said gently, "There was a time you admired Nan."

He lifted his hat and combed agitated fingers through reddish-blond hair. "That was twenty years ago. Before she chose my brother. Now she is like a sister to me. An ailing sister, who needs me."

I need you. The shocking words ran through Thora's mind, but she bit her tongue. Where had *that* come from?

Walter Talbot grimaced and replaced his hat. "I seem to have a knack for admiring women destined to marry other men."

Thora said cynically, "You haven't missed much—except a lot of heartache and frustration. Marriage is more trouble than it's worth."

"I disagree, Thora. In the past, and even now, I miss . . . a great deal."

She looked at him, not certain what he meant. How strange to hear her given name in his low voice after so many years of *Mrs. Bell* or *madam*. But she did not object.

He inhaled and drew himself up. "Would you like to go in and visit Nan? I'm afraid the house is a mess, but—"

"Another time, Talbot. If that's all right. Do greet her for me, and give her my regards."

"Of course."

Was it her imagination, or did he seem relieved she wasn't staying longer?

"Well. Good day, Talbot."

"Good day, Thora. And don't fret too much. I will come by in the next few days and talk with Colin."

"Thank you. Are you sure you have the time?"

"I'll make time."

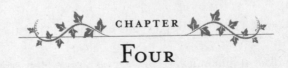

CHAPTER

Four

Jane had just sat down at her pianoforte when a knock sounded. A steady, determined knock. Had Thora returned from her walk already? Jane sighed, anticipating another unpleasant encounter.

Jane rose from the bench and found herself twisting her hands. She forced them to her sides, smoothing her skirts on the way, and opened the door.

It was not Thora. The banker, Mr. Blomfield, stood there. A small man, yet somehow ominous in his black suit of clothes. His hound-dog face was as dreary as a professional mourner's, framed by long, bushy side-whiskers. Jane was not well acquainted with the man. She'd had to sign a few papers when John died, but the lawyer had taken care of most of the distasteful business for her. But she knew who he was. And had a sinking notion she would not enjoy his visit.

He bowed. "Mrs. Bell." He smiled thinly, civility sheathing cool determination. "I regret the intrusion, but as you have not replied to any of the letters I sent, first by post, then by my clerk, asking you to call at the bank, I had no other choice. I have taken the liberty of reserving one of the inn's private parlours and have ordered tea. I shall not leave until you oblige me with half an hour of your time."

Jane nodded gravely. "I am sorry to have inconvenienced you,

Mr. Blomfield. Allow me a few minutes to gather my things"—
wits—"and I shall join you there."

He nodded curtly and turned on his heel.

Jane had not answered the door when a young clerk had attempted to deliver a letter last week. He'd left it on her doorstep.
When he'd departed, she opened it but got no further than the first
paragraph. She had little grasp of—nor stomach for—financial or
legal language. She had laid that letter in the office, atop stacks
of other correspondence related to inn business. She had hoped
Patrick would work his way through them, even if Colin had not.
Yet piles still crowded what had formerly been Walter Talbot's
desk. A larger inn would have employed both a head porter and
booking clerk to manage the lodging and transport sides of the
business. At The Bell, skillful Talbot had managed it all. But he
was gone. And neither she nor, apparently, Colin or Patrick had
assumed his duties.

With trembling fingers Jane put on a black lace cap—hoping
it made her look more mature and capable than she felt—and
followed the man's footsteps to the inn, solemnly answering her
summons.

When she entered the private parlour, the second maid, Alwena,
was setting down a tea tray, and Jane noticed her strained expression. Did she know something Jane didn't? Did all the servants?
Would they eavesdrop?

"Shall I pour?" Alwena asked.

"Yes, thank you," Jane replied, not trusting the steadiness of
her hands.

When the maid left them, Mr. Blomfield positioned spectacles
on his rather thin nose and opened the leather portfolio beside
his teacup. He asked, "Would you like to have anyone else present
during our meeting?"

Jane blinked. "I don't know." Did she really want to face . . .
whatever this was . . . alone? The recently returned Thora went
through her mind, but Jane instantly dismissed the notion. She did
not want her mother-in-law to know how negligent she had been

in dealing with the bank—and everything else as well. She swallowed and suggested, "Should I ask my brother-in-law to join us?"

"If you would like to. Though you are the legally responsible party."

Legally responsible for what? Jane thought with queasy dread. She rose. "Yes, I think I will ask him to join us, if you don't mind. He has far more experience than I do, and has been acting as manager, now that Mr. Talbot has left us."

He nodded, and Jane rose and opened the door. But she had barely closed it behind her when she saw Patrick in the corridor, leaning against the wall. Seeing her, he straightened to his full, lanky height. She was disconcerted and slightly annoyed to find him loitering about, but who was she to complain?

Oblivious to her irritation, he smiled his slow, easy smile. "Thought you might want reinforcements."

In spite of herself, she smiled back. "I would, yes. Mr. Blomfield is here and has news—bad news from the looks of it."

"I thought he might. I saw his grim figure arrive." Patrick gestured for her to precede him back into the parlour.

The banker rose as she entered. He and Patrick met and locked gazes. Something passed between them, Jane saw, but what, she could not identify.

She resumed her chair, and the men sat as well.

Mr. Blomfield began. "I need not remind you, Mr. Bell, that you are present in an advisory capacity only. Mrs. Bell does not require your permission or agreement in any decisions she makes. Understood? She is legal owner of The Bell, per the terms of your brother's will."

"As I am very much aware," Patrick replied evenly.

Jane wasn't sure if she saw resentment in his blue eyes or not. Certainly, Thora had been shocked and displeased when John's last will and testament had been read. The announcement had stirred similar emotions in Jane, but Patrick had not even been there at the time. It wasn't as if he'd been waiting around, hoping to inherit the place. Who could have predicted John would die so young?

For a moment, Mr. Blomfield peered at the pages within the portfolio, and then he interlaced his fingers and looked at her over the top of his spectacles.

"I trust you recall that your husband took out a loan to finance improvements he planned to make on the inn?"

Jane frowned. No, she did not recall that. John had either not mentioned it, or she'd paid little attention, having left business affairs to him.

"Payment on the loan is overdue," Mr. Blomfield went on. "I requested an extension from the partners when Mr. Bell died, and they kindly extended the due date a twelvemonth. But that time has come and gone."

Jane sputtered. "But . . . this is the first I am hearing of it." She glanced at Patrick. Was he as surprised as she was?

"I did send letters, Mrs. Bell," Mr. Blomfield said. "Tactful, discreet letters, I hope. Though in hindsight, perhaps too discreet." He cleared his throat. "You were in mourning at the time. And I thought it inappropriate to demand a meeting. But I can delay no longer. I have been authorized to give you three more months, but no more."

"How much is owed?" Jane asked, clenching her hands.

The banker looked at her skeptically. "Do you not know?"

Jane shook her head.

He asked, "Your husband never mentioned the amount, or showed you a copy of the loan papers?"

"No. As I said, this is the first I am hearing of it."

The banker glanced again at Patrick, who shook his head as well. Then Mr. Blomfield pronounced, "Fifteen thousand pounds."

Jane gaped. Asked him to repeat it. But the sum did not change.

She felt as though she were lurching awake from one of those tedious dreams, hurrying to the coaching inn to meet the stage, only to realize she'd forgotten her valise. Or facing an exacting schoolmistress on the day of the final examination, but having failed to study and unable to answer a single question.

The difference, Jane realized, was that she was wide awake.

She stared at the banker, mind blank, as he asked her question after question. Was the inn profitable? What improvements were underway or future renovations planned? Would she be able to repay the loan by the due date?

Jane forced herself out of her stupefied trance. "I . . . don't know. I was unaware of the loan, or of the seriousness of the situation."

She looked again at Patrick, who watched Blomfield with furrowed brow. He turned and met her questioning gaze. "Business has slowed," he said. "Especially since the new turnpike was completed."

"And our profits?"

"Precious little of late." He ran a hand through his hair. "I don't know exactly. I am still learning my way around the books. I have been back less than two months, remember."

"Can you at least estimate the inn's profits for last month?" Mr. Blomfield asked.

Patrick puffed out his cheeks in a weighty exhale, then named a figure. A dishearteningly low figure.

"You're joking," Jane said.

"I wish I were. But unless something changes, we haven't a hope of paying off that loan in three years' time, let alone three months."

"Things might improve," Jane hedged. She tried to send Patrick a significant look, hoping he would not divulge every detail of their dire circumstances to the man who held their fate in his hands.

But Patrick blithely continued, "I don't see how. Especially now that several coaching lines have chosen to bypass Ivy Hill altogether, as have a handful of carters and wagon drivers. Who knows how many more will follow suit."

Mr. Blomfield spread his hands. "This being the case, I cannot in good conscience go to the partners and ask for a longer extension. You have three months, Mrs. Bell, in which to either pay the loan or to document your plans to make the place profitable. If you are able to prove The Bell a worthwhile investment, I shall ask my partners to come to new terms on the loan. If not, the bank will foreclose and sell the mortgaged property to recoup its losses."

"But . . . ! Surely the inn is worth more than the loan amount."

"At one time, yes. But at its current profitability and condition . . . ? You cannot deny the place has deteriorated in recent years."

Had it? She had barely noticed.

She asked the banker, "Have you any advice?"

"Sell it before we have to." He shut his portfolio with a snap. "If you are able to sell it for more than the amount owing, including interest and late fees, anything remaining would be yours, as John's heir, to do with as you please."

"But then . . ." She bit back the questions tumbling through her mind. *Where would I live? And Patrick? Would a new owner keep on the present staff?*

In the next breath, her thoughts swung in the opposite direction. *I could be free. Leave The Bell and all its clamor and memories and worries behind. . . .* Would she have enough to live on? Where would she go? Might she be able to buy back her former family home, which sat empty and neglected?

"Are you certain you cannot give us more time?" she asked, hating the note of desperation in her voice.

"If I had not already applied for other extensions, perhaps. But as it is, no. Not without solid proof of profitability."

Mr. Blomfield rose. "I regret to be the bearer of such tidings, Mrs. Bell. I have had a long and congenial association with the Bell family, and it pains me to contemplate its end. If I may be of assistance in any other way, please do not hesitate to ask."

The man left, promising—or threatening—to return in three months' time.

Jane rose and numbly followed him out, Patrick beside her. In the corridor they found Mrs. Rooke, making a pretense of dusting the dreary framed prints hanging there, usually neglected.

"You can go back to the kitchen now, Mrs. Rooke," Patrick said with a wry grin. "If you missed anything, I will fill you in later. It shall only cost you a beefsteak."

"Patrick . . ." Jane hissed.

"Oh, Rooke will eventually learn everything anyway."

He waited until the cook-housekeeper huffed and trudged away before adding, "You know there are no secrets within these walls."

"No, I don't know that," Jane insisted.

He cocked his head and looked at her in surprise. "Are there secrets? How delicious . . ."

"Hardly. I'm talking about the money John borrowed. Fifteen thousand pounds! What on earth did he do with it?"

Jane thought of the new suit of clothes, the calling cards, the trips to horse markets and to London to consult with a few architects. But he'd returned after several trips without any new horses, and convinced the renovations the professionals had recommended would be too expensive to carry out, and not yield a significant return on their investment. Jane had nodded along without questioning, relieved his trips would stop, or at least become less frequent. But at the time, she had not known about the loan. What had he spent the rest on?

Patrick looked about him. "He didn't pour it all into the inn, obviously. Might he have hidden it away somewhere?"

That possibility had not occurred to Jane. She had not yet cleared out John's things from the lodge. Would he hide something there or somewhere in the inn? She doubted it.

"Have you seen anything in the books that would account for such a sum?" she asked.

Patrick shook his head. "No. But I hadn't known about the loan until . . . recently. Are you certain you've not run across a copy of the loan papers? Blomfield mentioned John might have a set."

"Not that I know of. You might look in the office, if you like. Though I don't see what good it will do."

Patrick opened the side door for her and followed her outside to escort her back across the drive.

"Don't worry, Jane," Patrick soothed. "We will think of something."

She looked at him dubiously. "Will we?"

"I am here now and shall help you."

"Thank you."

They paused at the lodge door. "By the way," he said. "I rode past Fairmont House yesterday. How sad to see it empty like that."

"Yes . . ."

"Have you ever thought of reclaiming it? This humble little cottage doesn't suit you."

Had Patrick read her mind? The small lodge was certainly not as grand as the house she had grown up in. She shrugged. "I am used to it. Besides, Fairmont is out of reach." She had only a little money of her own.

"Is it? Well, don't worry," he repeated. "We will work something out. If nothing else, perhaps I might take the inn off your hands."

She looked up at him in surprise. "You? Have you a fortune I am unaware of?"

"Not exactly. But I am a man. And . . . pray, do not be offended, but bankers would feel more confident investing in the inn if a man were at the helm. I don't say I agree with them, but it is a fact of life."

"Hmm. You certainly have more experience than I, but you heard Mr. Blomfield. We still have to prove The Bell a worthwhile investment."

"Together we shall." Patrick reached out and ran a hand over her cheek. "Don't worry, little sister. I shall help you."

Jane stilled, surprised by Patrick's display of affection, and struck by the endearment, *little sister*. He had never called her that before. No one had. Jane had no siblings. The words settled over her with a sweet wistfulness.

Movement on the other side of the archway caught Jane's eye. She glanced over, and Patrick turned as well. The farrier stood in the stable yard, watching them.

"There's Locke," Patrick said. "He wants to lodge a complaint against one of the coachmen. We'll talk later, all right?"

She silently nodded and watched as he strode away.

Gabriel Locke stood with a scowl on his face. Was the dark look directed at her, or at Patrick? But a moment later, the expression cleared and he raised a hand to acknowledge Patrick's approach. He did not acknowledge her presence one way or the other. She had probably imagined the dark look. Mr. Blomfield's edict had colored everything in somber tones.

CHAPTER
FIVE

Needing to talk with a trusted friend after the banker's call, Jane went to visit Mercy Grove. Mercy lived with her aunt Matilda in a house called Ivy Cottage, though it was larger and more stately than the term *cottage* evoked. Mercy had grown up there, but after she had come of age, and her brother had embarked on a career that kept him far from home, their father had entrusted the property to his daughter and spinster sister. He and Mrs. Grove preferred to live in London. Now Ivy Cottage housed not only the two women and their few servants, but also a girls' boarding and day school, which Mercy had operated for several years.

When Jane knocked, the Groves' manservant, Mr. Basu, opened the door to her, nodded, and disappeared again in his usual quiet fashion.

A moment later, Mercy walked into the hall, her youngest pupil holding her hand. Mercy greeted Jane warmly, then bent low and urged the little girl to join the others already outside for their afternoon recess. Wordlessly, but without enthusiasm, the girl complied.

Mercy straightened and invited Jane into the sitting room. The two women sat and exchanged pleasantries until Mercy's spry aunt brought in a tea tray.

"Hello, Jane. How good to see you," Matilda Grove said. "We don't have the pleasure of your company often enough. Now, you two enjoy a nice long chat. I'll watch over the girls outside. It's such a lovely day."

"Thank you, Aunt Matty."

When the older woman left them, Mercy poured the tea and passed Jane a plate of anise biscuits as hard as slate. She smiled apologetically and lowered her voice. "Aunt Matty has been baking again. You don't have to eat one. Or dip it in your tea first. I don't want you to chip a tooth."

Mercy Grove was tall, thin, and a year older than Jane. She had an angular face, long nose, small lips, and unremarkable brown hair. She was considered homely, Jane knew. But in her view her friend was lovely, and her kind, intelligent brown eyes were her best feature. When Mercy was younger, her mother had often bemoaned her daughter's height and "unfortunate" figure, worried she would fail to attract a suitor. Mercy was not only taller than many men, but she was small busted, and her gowns hid a disproportionately generous backside. Now that Mercy was nearly thirty years old, her mother had apparently given up her matchmaking attempts at last.

"Have you seen Rachel lately?" Mercy asked.

Jane shook her head, the old ache beneath her breastbone. "Have you?"

"I gather she is staying close to home these days. Last I visited, her father was not doing well at all."

Guilt pricked Jane. She should have visited before now.

Mercy selected a biscuit and inspected it. "It's a long soak in a hot bath for you." She dipped it, then looked up at Jane. "Now, how are things with you?"

Jane explained the situation—the shock of the large loan and the banker's deadline.

Mercy listened intently, then responded, "Oh, Jane. I am sorry to hear it."

"I don't understand what John could have been thinking," Jane said. "Taking out such a sizable loan without telling anyone and risking the inn that way. And now I have to deal with it."

Mercy shook her head, eyes bright with compassion.

Jane went on, "He always insisted he didn't want me to work in the inn. He wanted a genteel wife to keep his home and raise his children to be educated and well-mannered."

Jane sipped and continued, "Of course, back then he had his mother and Talbot to help him manage things. I think John assumed his mother would never leave. Have you heard she has come back for a visit?"

"I did, yes. How is that going?"

"Not well. Things have never been easy between us, and the strain only worsened after John's death. Or more precisely, after his will was read. I know she sees me as a useless failure, in many ways."

"Surely not. Mrs. Bell must have some confidence in your ability, or I doubt she would have left the inn to go and live with her sister."

Jane shrugged. "I imagine she thought Talbot would stay and manage The Bell as long as he lived, such a fixture he'd always been. Not that I begrudge his leaving. He finally has a chance to pour his efforts into something of his own. That must be satisfying."

"Yes, it certainly can be. And now you have a chance to experience that as well."

"Oh, Mercy, I have no idea how to manage a coaching inn. Thankfully Patrick is back and promises to help."

Mercy hesitated. She sipped her tea, then said, "It still surprises me that Patrick Bell returned to Ivy Hill. I thought he was away traveling the world and making his fortune or some such."

"He was. But he heard about John and came back to help."

"Does he mean to stay on?"

"I think so."

Mercy returned her teacup to its saucer. "Be careful, Jane."

"Careful? Why?"

"You know I don't like to speak ill of anyone, but you cannot pretend ignorance of your brother-in-law's reputation."

"As a rake, do you mean? Are you worried about the chambermaids, or our female guests? Certainly not me."

"All of the above."

"Oh, come now. He is practically my brother."

"Hmph."

"What are you driving at? I know he is something of a flatterer, but I am perfectly safe, I assure you."

Mercy opened her mouth, then closed it again and changed tack. "Never mind. I am sure you're right. Besides, who am I to remark upon the wisdom of involving family members in one's vocation?" She tapped a hard biscuit against her teacup for emphasis, and the two women shared a smile.

Jane nibbled a bite of tea-soaked biscuit, then said, "Perhaps Mr. Blomfield is right and I should sell the place before the bank does."

"Oh, Jane. Don't do anything rash. I thought you liked your little lodge?"

"The lodge isn't so bad, but when I learned John had left me the entire inn, it felt like an anchor around my neck. And now, all the more so. I told John when he proposed that I was not cut out for such a life. And that has not changed." Jane was surprised to find frustrated tears welling in her eyes. "Oh, Mercy, he left it to the wrong person!"

Mercy offered her a handkerchief, and Jane dabbed her eyes. "A part of me just wants to . . . go away. Leave talk of business and profits and loans behind me. Live somewhere in solitude and peace, with no coach horns blaring at all hours. No disgruntled staff to contend with . . ." Jane blew her nose. "How my mother would have blanched at the thought of her daughter doing such work!"

Jane glanced at her friend. "Forgive me, Mercy. I don't mean to cast any aspersions on your school. You know I admire what you do here, I hope?"

Mercy nodded. "It is my calling, yes. And I thank God I found it."

Though Jane knew Mercy's mother was not happy about her daughter's chosen career either.

The garden door opened, followed by the clatter of many pairs of half boots on the wooden floor and the chatter of girls' voices.

Jane took a deep breath. "I don't mean to sound ungrateful. I just don't know what to do."

Mercy squeezed her hand. "Then I will pray for you. For wisdom and insight to make the right decision. And for compassion from the bankers."

"That will take a miracle, but thank you."

Jane rose, knowing Mercy needed to return to the schoolroom. Her friend walked her to the door and helped her on with her mantle.

"What funds I have are tied up in the school," Mercy said. "But if I can help you in any other way, please let me know."

"You have helped me already," Jane said with a wobbly smile. "Just by listening."

Jane began the walk back to the inn, no nearer to knowing what she should do. She returned by a different route, taking a shortcut across Ivy Green.

As she approached The Bell, she studied the inn as though for the first time. The listing lamppost. The dingy curtains in the windows. The peeling paint. The faded sign, with its golden letters and bell, needed a fresh coat of paint. The entire exterior did. How many times had she walked past without noticing any of it?

The dire news from the banker had opened her eyes and woken her from her slumber at last.

As she stood there, a tall gentleman in a fashionable green frockcoat and buff trousers approached. A familiar gentleman.

Jane swallowed. "Sir Timothy."

Noticing her there, he drew up short. "Jane . . . em. Mrs. Bell. How good to see you."

Was she imagining things, or did his dark-eyed gaze linger on her black gown? For one irrational moment she wished she were wearing the lavender dress.

Jane stood there awkwardly. Should she walk past with a vague smile, or did he wish to talk?

He cleared this throat and began, "You might like to know that . . ."

Was this the day he would make the long-expected announcement?

At one time, she had expected it every day. But years had passed, and still he had no wife.

". . . my sister has had her season in London with Richard and the Sharingtons and is coming home tomorrow."

"Justina, a season? Heavens. Is she so grown?"

"Eighteen."

Justina had been a late-life child of his parents', and Sir Timothy had been more guardian than brother since their father died, especially as there were more than a dozen years between them. Their middle-born brother, Richard, lived in London, but they rarely saw him.

"It can't be. I feel quite ancient," Jane murmured.

"Imagine how I feel."

If only I could, Jane thought. "Greet her for me."

"I shall, of course, but perhaps you might do so yourself, if . . ." He broke off, glancing at the inn. "I suppose The Bell keeps you rather busy."

Actually, she did very little—so far. She replied vaguely, "Things have been quieter lately."

"Oh? The result of the turnpike, I suppose?" A shadow of a frown crossed his handsome, aristocratic face.

"Yes, but I am sure you are not interested in that."

He sketched a shrug. "As it concerns you and your welfare, I am. And the welfare of Ivy Hill, of course." As magistrate, Sir Timothy Brockwell felt responsible for the village and its citizens.

"I am perfectly well, thank you," Jane assured him with more enthusiasm than she felt. She was relieved he did not press for details about the state of the inn. She did not want to admit her failure. Or for him to feel obliged to offer help. Help she would not accept from him in any case.

The sound of determined, clicking heels caught her attention. His as well. He looked past her, and she turned.

The woman's fashionable bonnet tipped lower than usual, her eyes downcast. Her shoulders were not squared in their usual perfect posture. But there was no mistaking that confident gait.

That small nose peeking out from her brim. That enviable figure in a perfectly tailored blue walking dress. Clearly deep in her own thoughts, her old friend had apparently yet to see them. Then she glanced up, and her gait faltered.

"Hello, Rachel," Jane said gently. Warily.

"Miss Ashford," Sir Timothy added, his expression suddenly somber. He bowed.

Rachel looked from one to the other. "Good day to you both."

She looked ready to continue on, but Sir Timothy said, "I was sorry to hear your father is not well. I hope he is not worse."

"He is, I'm afraid. I was just on my way to the apothecary for more of the lozenges he likes. If you will excuse me."

Sir Timothy's brow puckered. "Could not one of the servants—?"

"Of course they might," she sharply replied. "But I found I needed some air."

"Ah." He nodded in understanding. "No doubt the walk will do you good. A sickbed vigil can be exhausting, I know."

"Yes. But pray do not think I am shirking my duty. I only—"

He raised a palm. "Of course not. I had no intention of implying you were. Do please give your father my regards."

"I shall. Well. I will leave the two of you to your . . ." Rachel's gloved hand gestured vaguely from one to the other.

Uneasiness pinched Jane's stomach. "We happened to pass on the street and were only saying hello," she defended. "Now, I too had better be going. But I will pray for your father. Or . . . I could come and share your vigil, if you like."

Rachel coolly inclined her head. "Thank you, but no need."

Sir Timothy stepped quickly to open the apothecary shop door for her, and Miss Ashford slipped inside.

He watched her go, then turned back to Jane, avoiding her eyes.

Good-bye, Jane whispered in her heart. Again. In the past, she had wondered what might have happened between them if she had not married John. But that was a long time ago.

She did not know the condition of her husband's soul the day he died—if he had been prepared to meet his Maker, and would rise on the last day. But some things, she was quite certain, would never be resurrected.

When the door shut behind her, Rachel Ashford closed her eyes and took a deep breath, the air of the apothecary shop tangy and medicinal—camphor, chamomile, comfrey.

She waited for her heart rate to return to normal. It always beat a little too quickly upon seeing Sir Timothy Brockwell. And seeing him with Jane? That had caused her stomach to knot, and brought back all the old memories of her stymied hopes and soured friendship.

They were only talking, she told herself. She was foolish to let it bother her. Not when she had more important things to worry about—like her ailing father. And what would happen to her after he passed.

Drawing back her shoulders, Rachel stepped to the counter and purchased what she'd come for from Mr. Fothergill, who kindly asked about her father. She assured the apothecary that his remedies and Dr. Burton's treatments kept him fairly comfortable and thanked the man for his concern. But they both knew little could be done to extend her father's life.

When Rachel turned to leave, she paused to look out the front window to make certain Timothy and Jane had left. She did not want a repeat of their awkward encounter.

The three of them had spent a great deal of time together during their adolescence and early adulthood. There had been no awkwardness then. Rachel was a few years younger than Jane, and a late bloomer in the bargain. She knew Timothy had seen her as a child—a pesky little sister, of sorts. He was kind to her but had clearly preferred Jane's company. But all of that had changed the summer after Rachel's coming-out ball. For the better, and then . . . for the worse.

Standing there, an ache of loss washed over Rachel as though it had all happened yesterday instead of eight years ago. She wondered if he hoped for another chance with Jane now that she was a widow. For he had never pursued a second chance with *her*.

Rachel forced leaden legs outside, and back up the High Street. At its end, she crossed Ebsbury Road and cut through the meadow to reach Thornvale more quickly.

Inside the hall, the housekeeper greeted her somberly. "Your father has been asking for you, miss."

Guilt stabbed her. "I'll go right up."

She climbed the stairs, knocked softly, and entered her father's bedchamber.

The room closed in on her as soon as she entered—shutters drawn and windows closed against any chill breeze that might dare enter. Piles of books crowded the side table and formed pillars on the floor. She made her way carefully around them toward the bed. Her father refused to allow the maids to return them to the library. He wanted his favorites near him like old friends. The musty smell of dry leather and yellowed paper hung heavy in air already dank with the sour smells of a sick room. Mamma would never have allowed such clutter while she was alive. But Rachel, like the maids, had given up her protests.

"There you are, my dear." Her father raised a weak hand in greeting. "I wondered what became of you."

"I only went to Fothergill's." She lifted the parcel as proof.

"Ah. See any of our friends while you were out?"

The question reminded Rachel that her father had once been a gregarious and well-liked man.

"I . . . did yes," she replied. "Jane Bell and Sir Timothy send their regards."

"Jane and Timothy?"

"Mm-hmm," she replied distractedly, setting her purchase on the desk beside another packet of Royal English Drops, still full. "And Mr. Fothergill, of course."

Sir William's body was failing, but his eyes were all too clear. She looked away from them.

"May I bring you anything, Papa? Tea? Something to eat?"

"No, thank you. But I had hoped you would read to me again."

She nodded. "I bought the latest *Gentleman's Magazine* last time I was in the High Street. I thought I might read that for a change. Several articles appear rather diverting."

He frowned. "I'm afraid I've lost all interest in current affairs. It's the old books that speak to me now and soothe my soul."

He tried to pick up the thick book on the bed beside him, but the heavy volume trembled in his hands.

She hurried forward. "Here, Papa. Allow me."

"Thank you, Rachel. Will you read it for me? What solace my books give me."

She managed a tight smile. "Of course."

Her father's books gave her no solace at all. In fact, quite the opposite. Sometimes she thought he loved his books more than he loved her. He certainly gave them more of his time and attention.

CHAPTER

SIX

Thora had been standing at the hall window for several minutes, waiting impatiently as Jane talked to Miss Ashford and Sir Timothy Brockwell on the street. Jane had once been one of their set—until she had condescended to marry an innkeeper. By rights, Jane ought to have married Sir Timothy, or someone like him. Everyone had thought she would. Yes, John had been charming and confident and capable. But few had thought he stood a chance of winning the hand of pretty Miss Jane Fairmont, Thora least of all.

Now she wanted to speak to Jane about the news Patrick had confided when she'd returned from Talbot's farm. She thought back, trying to remember what, if anything, John had said about taking out a loan. She knew he had contemplated refurbishments but in the end had decided against it. After all, Thora herself had told him she doubted the investment would yield a good return. And he had listened to her, or so she'd thought. He usually did so—except when choosing a wife. And evidently in this as well. Had Jane asked John to take out a loan anyway? To finance new gowns or a trip abroad, perhaps—or what? Thora doubted whatever Jane had done with the money had been in the inn's best interest. More likely it had served Jane's self-interest.

When Sir Timothy bowed to Jane and walked away, Thora opened the door and waved her inside.

Jane did not look pleased to see her but complied, allowing Thora to lead her into the office.

There, Thora shooed out Colin McFarland with a dismissive wave of her hand. Then she closed the door and started right in. "What are you going to do about the loan?"

Jane sighed. "Patrick told you, did he?"

"Of course he did. You should have told me yourself."

"Mr. Blomfield came only this morning. I have been trying to think. I suppose everyone knows the straits we are in?"

Thora nodded. "Or they will, soon enough."

"And I suppose everyone will blame me, when I have only just learned of the loan myself."

Thora wasn't convinced. "I will go and speak to Arthur Blomfield in person. See if there is anything I can do. Unless you refuse my help?"

"Of course not. I don't pretend to have everything in hand."

That was something, Thora privately acknowledged. It was no doubt difficult for the proud gentleman's daughter to admit she had failed, or how quickly the inn had gone to ruin without Thora or Talbot there to manage it.

Thora walked with determination up the High Street to the stone-and-brick building at its end, the heels of her sturdy half boots clicking sharply with each step. Reaching the door of Blomfield, Waters, and Welch, she let herself in. A young clerk caught chewing a muffin stood abruptly, wiping crumbs from his mouth with the back of his hand.

Thora had known the boy since he was in nappies. "Never mind, Todd, I will announce myself."

"But—"

Pushing open the door marked *A. Blomfield, Esq.*, Thora strode inside.

The banker looked up from his desk, brows high. "Ah! Mrs. Bell. What an unexpected pleasure."

"Is it unexpected, Arthur? When you have given my daughter-in-law a few short months to pay back a massive loan?"

"I . . . didn't even know you were in town. You moved away last year."

"I would have returned sooner had I known the extent of the trouble. I am disappointed you didn't write to me yourself, out of professional courtesy, considering the bank's long relationship with my family."

His Adam's apple rose and fell. "I did not realize you were . . . still involved with the inn."

She could hear the trepidation oozing from the words. *Oh yes*, Thora thought. Arthur Blomfield was afraid of her. Always had been. And he was right to fear a tongue lashing or worse if he dared move against her family's establishment.

"You did not think I would want to know? Have a chance to intervene?"

"Well, I . . . assumed your daughter-in-law or son would inform you, as they saw fit."

"Did you really?"

He touched the knot of his cravat and said weakly, "One doesn't like to meddle in family affairs."

"I have never known you to shy away from a little self-interested meddling, Arthur. In fact, I am disappointed you didn't meddle *before* this dreadful loan was taken out in the first place. I would have thought you would have offered some friendly counsel. Advised against it."

He opened his mouth to defend himself, Thora assumed, but she cut him off. "What's done is done. I have spoken briefly to Jane and Patrick, but I want to hear the particulars from you directly."

He nodded. "If you have spoken to Jane, then you know the amount owing. Overdue now for some time. Regretfully, the bank must pursue recompense if that debt is either not paid in three months time, or if your daughter-in-law cannot prove significant profitability or plans to become so—with which I might apply to the partners for another extension. I gather from speaking with

Patrick that neither is likely to occur, especially without an experienced leader at the helm. I assumed you would not wish to involve yourself."

"Not wish to involve myself? Anything that affects the inn affects me. Always has done and always shall. If nothing else I would want the chance to offer advice or assistance at this critical time."

"But Jane Bell is landlady now—not you."

"Don't you think I know that?" Thora snapped. "But I cannot stand by and do nothing while she brings it to ruin. What was the money used for? I see no improvements. What did she fritter it away on?"

For several moments he looked at her. Opened his mouth, then closed it again. He reached into his lower desk drawer and withdrew a bound document of several pages. He placed his index finger on a specific spot, and slid the document across the desk toward her.

She stepped nearer, bent her head and squinted, recognizing the signature with a frown.

"This is not a new loan, Thora. As you can see, John signed it himself, more than a year before he died. As far as I know, his wife had nothing to do with it. In fact, she seemed surprised to learn of its existence."

"As was I . . ." Thora murmured. Jane had said as much, but Thora had not believed her. Guilt nipped at her, followed by a sinking feeling. *What else did John not tell me?*

She licked dry lips. "Did John specify what he intended to do with the money?"

Again he gestured toward the documents. "It's all there. Plans for refurbishments for the inn, new coach horses, and the like."

"Did you never confer with him? Ask for reports on how the funds were being used?"

Mr. Blomfield shifted. "Not initially. I have had no reason to doubt any of my past dealings with your family. But when the first payment became due, John put me off. He had some plausible excuse—refurbishments still in progress—and I petitioned my partners for an extension, promising payments would be forthcoming, and assuring them the Bells were old and reliable clients. But when the promised payments failed to arrive, I became concerned."

He inhaled, looking up in memory, then continued. "John began avoiding me. Or at least it seemed so to me. Spending more and more time away."

Yes, Thora had been worried about all those trips. But she said, "John was never one to shirk his duty." *Or so I'd thought.*

The banker entwined his fingers on the desk. "I have no wish to speak ill of him, especially now. But nor can I, in all fairness, allow you to lay blame at your daughter-in-law's door. Beyond perhaps procrastination and apathy."

"Those are faults enough."

"Are they?"

Thora studied him through narrowed eyes. "May I ask why you included Patrick in your conversation about this?"

"He was there at Jane's invitation."

"At her invitation, or your suggestion?"

He shrugged. "I may have suggested she might want someone with her to help her navigate the situation."

"Did you write to him while he was away?" she asked.

He shrugged again. "I have kept in touch with Patrick over the years. He has had an investment opportunity or two to present to me from time to time. I . . . may have mentioned my concerns about the inn at some point."

She asked archly, "And I suppose Patrick has made a fortune from these speculations and opportunities, which he has deposited here at Blomfield, Waters, and Welch?"

Arthur Blomfield cleared his throat. "Not as yet. But I view him as a young man of potential. I am persuaded he could do a great deal of good with a place like The Bell. He is brimming with ideas."

Yes, Patrick always had big ideas. Whether he would follow through with them or not was another matter, but she would not malign her son in this man's hearing. Or anyone else's.

"And exactly how is Jane to prove 'significant profitability'?

What sort of plans would convince your partners to grant another extension?"

"Profits increasing at a rate of at least ten percent per annum. Or a sound written plan that includes renovations and new revenue sources that prove convincing in terms of return on investment."

"And if the loan is not repaid or a satisfactory plan submitted in time?"

"Then I will have no choice but to sell the inn, which John used to secure the loan."

"The Bell is worth more than that, and you know it."

"Five years ago, maybe. Even three years ago, before the turnpike was approved. But now . . . ?"

"This is not fair."

"Is it fair that we loaned a sizable sum in good faith and have received not a farthing in repayment in over two years?"

She jutted out her chin. "And who do you think will buy The Bell if it is the poor investment you claim it is?"

"Actually, we have already received one offer to assume the debt in exchange for ownership."

"Assume the debt? Well, yes," she said sarcastically. "Anyone would assume such a debt in exchange for an establishment worth several times that amount. Tell me, who has made this premature offer?"

"I am not at liberty to say."

"The devil you're not. Whose side are you on, Arthur?"

"My dear Mrs. Bell. Our relationship may be of long standing, but I must put the health of my own establishment ahead of any other. Just as you would, were our situations reversed."

She bit back a hot retort. "So. You have decided The Bell hasn't a chance, have you? Well, we shall see about that."

Thora stalked back to The Bell and immediately sought out Patrick. She found him rooting around the office and digging through the desk drawers.

"Can't find a dashed thing in here," he grumbled.

Thora closed the door. "Patrick, I have just been to see Arthur Blomfield. What are you up to?"

"I only want to help."

Suspicion snaked through her. "Help yourself?"

Patrick tucked his chin, looking hurt. "Mamma . . . you misjudge me."

"Do I?" she asked. She hoped that was true.

"Yes. Mr. Blomfield suggested, or at least intimated, that having a man in charge, and an experienced Bell in the bargain, would go a long way to increasing his partners' confidence. He made no promises, but he thinks an extension much more probable if ownership were transferred to me."

"You're the one who wants to assume the debt."

"It is only an idea. You know Jane isn't keen on managing the place herself. I think she'd be relieved to be out from under the responsibility."

"And you think you are equal to it?"

"Why not? I have worked here in one capacity or another since I was a lad—from potboy to porter to booking clerk, I've done it all."

"Not alone."

He rose and put his hands on her shoulders. "I shan't be alone. You shall be with me, ay, Mamma? With my ideas and your experience, we'll resurrect this old place in no time. Give it new life."

She frowned at him. "I had not realized it was dead."

"Not yet. But it will be if we don't make changes while we can."

"What kind of changes? Are you talking about a French chef and foolish falderals as John used to kick about?"

"No. Something more revolutionary."

"Like what?"

He opened his mouth to reply, then thought the better of whatever he'd been about to say. "Still in the thinking stages, Mamma. And of course I will want your advice before I finalize any plans."

"And Jane?" Thora asked.

"Jane is a lovely, kindhearted gentlewoman," Patrick said. "A fine ornament to the place, you can't deny. But do you really think she can offer sound advice or help plan profitable change?"

"I . . . suppose not." Thora was surprised at the stab of disloyalty she felt to agree with Patrick's assessment.

"So are you with me, Mamma?" He pressed her arms affectionately. It was the closest thing to an embrace they had shared since Frank died.

"I haven't heard the plan yet," Thora replied. "When I do, you shall have my answer."

Thora stepped to the door, then turned back.

"By the way, what were you looking for when I came in?"

"The loan papers. Mr. Blomfield mentioned there should be a set around here somewhere."

"Don't bother. I saw the bank's copy and John's signature." Thora glanced at the desk formerly shared by John, Talbot, and even her at times. "Since your brother clearly never wanted me to know about the loan, I doubt he would leave evidence of it here. More likely in the lodge, if he didn't destroy it."

Just as his loan might destroy The Bell, once and for all.

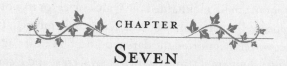

Thora stood at the reception counter the next day, running her finger down the registry for the previous weeks, recognizing the names of a few regulars, but disheartened to see the overnight guest lists far shorter than usual.

A horn sounded out front, announcing the arrival of the morning mail. Thora's heart gave an odd little jump, and anticipation shot through her. *Foolish creature*, she admonished herself. She stepped to the window and watched as Patrick went out to greet the coach. She was pleased to see him up and dressed so early. He looked like his father at that moment—well groomed, handsome, confident. Proud to welcome passengers to his inn, whether for a quick meal, or to stay the night. Thora felt a surge of maternal pride and hoped that Patrick was maturing at last.

In the next breath she reminded herself that even if he were ready to accept responsibility, it would avail nothing, for The Bell was not his inn. It was Jane's. Unless . . . should she support Patrick in his bid to assume the debt for the inn? She would have to think hard on the subject.

Out of old habit, Thora turned toward the office—Talbot's office for so many years. How many times had she turned to him, to ask his opinion on a hundred subjects? But Talbot was not there to ask. Perhaps she would walk back out to the farm and seek his advice.

A thought struck her. Speaking of Talbot, where was his supposed replacement? She glanced at the clock and frowned. Colin was late. She supposed she could expect little more from a McFarland.

Rattling coach wheels drew her attention back out the window. The Devonport mail, nicknamed the Quicksilver for its notorious speed, appeared as smart and sleek as Thora remembered. Gleaming scarlet wheels supported the dark red-and-black carriage, with its passenger door emblazoned with the royal crest and *Devonport London* in gold lettering. On the back perched the guard, the post secured in the boot beneath his feet. Just ahead of him, Thora knew, was the compartment containing the Mortimer blunderbuss to ward off any highwaymen. As the coach rumbled to a stop, the guard withdrew the mailbag and hopped down.

At the front of the vehicle, the Royal Mail coachman faced away from her, in conversation with the ostlers as they unhooked the weary horses, so all she had was a view of the back of his dark head, hat, and benjamin—a tan coat with multiple shoulder capes to sluice off rain. But such clothes were customary of most coachmen. Was it him? Or had he changed routes in the intervening months?

He set aside his long whip and clambered down. She caught a glimpse of his face from beneath his broad hat brim.

Charlie Frazer.

Again that little jolt of anticipation. Again that silent rebuke. There was nothing between them, she reminded herself. He was a flirt—that's all. His handsome face had always split into a grin whenever he saw her, and he would sweep off his hat and press it dramatically over his heart, spouting some blarney about how she stole his breath, and praising her supposed beauty in his low brogue. She knew he probably did the same to landladies all along his route.

And, of course, Thora would wave him off and tell him to hush and stop his foolishness, though inwardly she had liked his attention. Now and again he overdid it and embarrassed her in front of a guest or her son, when John had been alive. But John always chuckled at her discomfiture and offered Charlie a pint, enjoying seeing someone dare to tease her. Charlie was one of the few men who didn't seem put off by her gruff exterior. She had been surprised to miss him while she'd been away. She hadn't thought a great deal about most people, but she had missed Charlie, as well as Talbot, more than she'd anticipated.

Colin McFarland hurried past and sprinted into the yard. He stammered an apology to Patrick before rushing to open the Quicksilver's door.

Thora rolled her eyes.

Passengers began alighting, sleepy and stretching. She watched while Charlie assisted the ostlers in changing the team and then walked around the coach, inspecting the wheels and springs. The relief coachman, a new man she did not know, came out of the stable block, adjusting his neckerchief as he came. The building's upper story held sleeping rooms for visiting coachmen, as well as separate rooms for the inn's horsemen: farrier, ostlers, and postillions.

Thora turned away from the window. She would not stand there like a preening schoolgirl hoping for a compliment on a new dress. It was time to stop dawdling and make herself useful.

She greeted the arriving passengers and showed them into the dining parlour, where Alwena and Cadi would serve the breakfast Mrs. Rooke and her kitchen maid had been up since five to prepare. Then Thora returned to the reception desk.

The side door clicked open. Hearing no sound of its closing, Thora glanced up and saw Charlie Frazer standing in the open doorway, staring at her.

She said, "Close the door before you let in every insect in the county. Close your mouth while you're at it."

He slowly did so, his gaze remaining fixed on her.

"Thora Bell . . ." he murmured, "as I live and breathe . . ."

His deep voice still held a faint Scottish brogue, though he'd lived in England for most of his life.

"Hello, Charlie."

He was a broad-shouldered, stocky man of fifty-odd years. His face was weathered, but he was still handsome. Beneath his coat, he wore a blue neckerchief, striped waistcoat, and low "jockey" boots, a style copied by sporting gentlemen everywhere.

He removed his hat, but said only, "You're back."

"As you see."

No compliments were forthcoming.

He pulled off his gloves. "For how long? Just visiting, or . . . ?"

She had been right to rebuke herself earlier for her foolish expectations. He'd probably forgotten all about her after she left. "I have yet to decide."

He grimaced as though the news did not please him.

She arched one brow. "Sorry to see me?"

"Nae. Not . . . exactly."

What did that mean? "I am glad to see you are still driving the Quicksilver."

"Are you?"

"Yes. We've lost a few stagecoach lines now that the turnpike is finished. I'd hate to think the Royal Mail would follow suit."

"I have'na heard anything about that . . . officially."

Thora noticed him avoid her eyes, but before she could pry out more information, he changed the subject.

"And of course I'm still driving. What did you think I'd be doing? Gone off and become a rich man while you were away? You know better than that."

"Oh come, Charlie. No one charms large gratuities from his passengers like you do."

"Perhaps I once did. But I travel with a dashing new guard now. With his fine horn playing and beautiful voice, he kicks up more tips than I do nowadays." Charlie gestured out the window. The young Royal Mail guard in his official red coat was urging the relief coachman to hurry. "Not that I begrudge him. Best guard I've had since old Murphy. Makes the hours pass more pleasantly, listening to him."

"I am glad you get on well together. It is good to have a useful partner."

"Aye. A good partner is the key to life." He gave her a crooked grin, and she saw a bit of the old Charlie in the mischievous glint in his eyes.

"Charlie. . . ." she admonished lightly with a shake of her head.

He inhaled and said, "It's good to see you, Thora. I have nothing against the new landlady, of course, but she can'na hold a candle to the former."

The compliment pleased her, though Thora tried not to let it show. Her father had been the last man to praise her competence, and the words warmed her and settled deep into her marrow. "Go in and sit down, Charlie. I'll bring you some breakfast."

"Will you join me?"

She hesitated. She had not thought it proper before, when she had served as the inn's housekeeper. But now? "Why not," she said. "I could eat something."

His eyes widened in surprise and pleasure. "I doubt I shall be able to eat a morsel with so much beauty before me."

"Oh, go on with you," she said, with a swat in his general direction.

The old Charlie Frazer was back, and in rare form.

Out in the yard, the guard blew his horn again. Within the dining parlour, harried passengers shoved in final bites of toast or egg, and rose, quickly settling up their bills. Moments later, they streamed back outside to reclaim their seats inside or atop the Quicksilver before it continued on its way southwest to Exeter, Devonport, and points in between.

When the hubbub had died down and the door closed behind the last passenger, Charlie gestured Thora to precede him into the coffee room, where the staff, coachmen, and guards generally ate, separate from the passengers. "After you."

They sat at a small table together, and Thora waved to Alwena. With a curious look between Thora and the coachman, the quiet maid came over to take their orders.

"Coffee for Mr. Frazer, and tea for me please, Alwena. Mrs. Rooke's full breakfast, Charlie?"

"Of course." He patted his stomach, perhaps not quite as trim as it once was.

"Eggs and toast for me," Thora added.

Alwena poured coffee and tea and then left to deliver their orders to the kitchen.

When Thora looked back at Charlie, she found him regarding her closely.

He shook his head. "I still can'na believe the belle of The Bell is back. Or should I say, the angel of The Angel . . . ?"

"Neither. I haven't been the belle of anything in years. And I've *never* been an angel."

"You underestimate your charms."

"And you overestimate yours."

"Tongue still as sharp as ever, I see." Charlie grinned. "Place has'na been the same without you."

"So I see, everywhere I look. That is why I am here."

"To set the place to rights and then return to your sister's?"

Thora cocked her head to the side. "In a hurry to be rid of me?"

"Not at all. It's just . . . I thought you intended to remain in Bath."

"I did, but things change. Have you never hankered for a change? Or thought of what you might do someday after you retire?"

"Retire? I am not so ancient, I assure you, however weathered this old mug of mine looks after years of exposure. I am still strong and young in here"—he patted his chest—"where it counts."

"Yes, very young," she said dryly.

"You question my maturity, Thora? You will not injure me with that. I see no reason to act the dry crust. I would rather enjoy the years I'm given."

He sipped his coffee, then tipped his head to one side to study her face. "I have been considering making a change though. A different route, perhaps."

"Oh, and why is that?"

"A change of scenery. New surroundings—much as you, I imagine, when you left Ivy Hill." His gaze remained steady on her face, and she looked away, taking a long sip of tea, self-conscious under his scrutiny.

"Stop staring at me like that, Charlie. I know you are mapping every one of my wrinkles like a new route."

"Not a bit of it, Thora. You have always been a handsome woman. And always will be. God has blessed you with looks as well as a keen mind."

She snorted. "Blessed is the last thing I feel."

God had taken her husband and son. John had left the inn part and parcel to his genteel wife, who cared not a fig about the place. And she was left with nothing. No home of her own. No security.

He studied her face. "You've borne more than your share of losses, Thora, I know. But is life really so bad?"

She met his gaze. "You are not a woman, Charlie. And can't understand."

CHAPTER

Eight

On Saturday afternoon, Jane filled her water cans at the pump near the paddock. She noticed two stable cats—one grey with black stripes, the other an orange tabby—curled up together in the sun. She took a step toward them, but seeing her, they leapt up and disappeared though a hole in the stable siding. John had barely tolerated the untamed, skittish creatures, but Jane thought it would be pleasant to have one for a pet.

When the cans were full, she carried them to the front of the inn. As she stood there, watering the flowerpots flanking the door, a happy commotion from within drew her attention. She set down the cans and tentatively stepped inside to investigate. Walter Talbot stood in the hall, surrounded by smiling ostlers and chirpy maids, inundating him with questions and greetings. He had surprised everyone by showing up during the afternoon lull, bringing Mrs. Rooke a gift of asparagus picked from his own land. He had not been back to the inn since he'd left it, perhaps to avoid the appearance of checking up on his successor, or too busy on the farm and with his ailing sister-in-law.

Noticing Jane lingering in the doorway, Talbot nodded respectfully to her.

"Thought I might talk with Colin and answer any questions that may have arisen since I left. Only if you don't mind." He looked at the young man. "And only if you think it would be helpful, son." He said it gently and without any suggestion of failure, and Jane admired him for his tact.

"I don't mind at all, Mr. Talbot," Jane said. "It is very kind of you to offer."

Colin nodded his agreement. "That would be very helpful, sir. I would be obliged to you."

"My pleasure. As long as you leave off with the *sir* and call me Talbot, as everyone else does."

"Yes, sir. Em. Mr. Talbot."

The others said their farewells and drifted away, back to their posts. But Jane lingered.

Talbot began, "Now. What can I answer for you?"

Jane noticed his gaze stray to the open office door and the piled desk and empty chair within. Thora had gone to market. She didn't know where Patrick was.

Colin followed his gaze, but then looked toward the stairway instead, asking about the best way to greet guests and see them settled into their rooms.

"An excellent question," Talbot replied with approval. "It is important to make a good first impression."

"Would you mind if I came along?" Jane asked. "I would like to learn as well."

Mr. Talbot gave her a smile of encouragement. "Of course, you are welcome to join us."

They began at the reception counter—a small nook adjacent to the office that also served as the booking desk for coach fares.

Talbot explained how they—he, Frank, and Thora—had done things, but kindly qualified, "I can only demonstrate how we used to do things, but if Mrs. Bell here has asked for any changes, of course her instructions take precedence."

Jane assured him she had not.

After walking them through the use of the registry, the assignment of rooms and keys, and the added services to offer—hot bath, newspapers, coffee, tea, or chocolate delivered to the room, among others—along with their fees, Talbot selected two keys and led the way upstairs. The climb, he explained, was a good opportunity to give mealtimes and ask if the guest required laundry services or boot polishing. He then opened the door to one of the inn's larger rooms with an adjoining sitting room, indicated the features to point out, and then did the same in a more modest room.

Jane had rarely set foot in the guest rooms and was surprised to see a small angelic figure carved into the pediment above each door. "I have never noticed those before. Is there an angel in every room?"

Talbot looked up at the carving in question. "Yes. I've seen them so often over the years, I barely notice them anymore. The angel statue on the roof either."

"Oh, that's right." Jane recalled spotting it as a girl, years ago.

"I've wondered about that as well," Colin added.

"Do you not know?" Talbot looked from one to the other. "I suppose you are both too young to remember. The Bell used to be called The Angel."

"Is that why . . . ?" Colin murmured, his eyes distant in thought.

Jane had heard that bit of history mentioned at some point but had thought little of it at the time. She asked, "How long ago was that?"

Talbot pursed his lips. "Thirty odd years ago now. It was The Angel until Thora married Frank Bell."

"Ah . . ." Jane supposed she should have guessed. "Was the name change her idea or his?"

"I . . . think you shall have to ask Thora that. I was only a fairly new hire at the time, like Colin here." He clapped the younger man's shoulder companionably.

Talbot finished the tour and his instructions, and then they made their way back down to the desk, intending to review the departure and payment routine as well. Thora and Patrick were standing at the office door as they descended the stairs together.

Thora's gaze flicked from Talbot, to Jane and Colin, and back again. "Hello, Talbot."

"Thora. How are you?" He nodded to her son. "Patrick."

"Hello, Talbot ol' boy," Patrick said. "What are you doing here? Thought you'd shaken the dust of this place from your shoes—or should I say work boots?"

"Only stopped in to see how Colin here was getting on."

Patrick raised his brows. "Bit late for that, is it not?"

"Nonsense, Patrick," Thora said. "It's never too late to learn." She slanted a look at Jane. "Is it, Jane?"

Jane felt her neck grow warm. "Of course not."

Perhaps noticing the family tension, Walter Talbot retrieved his hat from the hook near the door. "Well, I had better head back to my place. I shall stop around again, when I have a chance. See if you've thought of other questions."

Colin nodded. "Thank you, sir."

Jane echoed her thanks, and Thora added, "I'll walk you out."

The two older people exited the side door together, and Colin excused himself as well.

Patrick crossed his arms and leaned back against the counter. "It is good to see you here inside the inn, Jane. You give the old place a certain elegance. In fact, why don't you stay and eat dinner with Mamma and me?"

"I . . . couldn't. I am not dressed appropriately. Good heavens, I forgot I was still wearing my gardening apron."

"No matter. We are not formal here. Change if you like, but please do join us for a family dinner. It has been too long."

Jane had never felt much familial feeling for—or from—Patrick or his mother. "I don't know that Thora would want—"

"What wouldn't I want?" Thora asked, returning.

"I was just asking Jane to share a meal with us as a family," Patrick said. "You wouldn't object to that, would you, Mamma?"

"Of course not. We have many things to discuss."

Jane walked back to the lodge to remove her apron, wash her face and hands, and tidy her hair. She dared not summon Cadi to help her change her dress, not at busy dinnertime—and not with Thora waiting. Instead, she made do with adding a black lace fichu around the neckline of her daydress, securing it with a brooch of jet and seed pearls she'd had since her mother died.

Unaccountably nervous, Jane joined Thora and Patrick in the coffee room, where a table had already been laid for the three of them. Patrick rose and pulled out her chair for her, then reclaimed his own seat beside Thora. Handing around the basket of bread, Thora immediately tried to steer the conversation toward the problem of the loan, but Patrick sweetly put her off, saying, "Not tonight, Mamma. For tonight, let us simply enjoy one another's company. Perhaps reminisce about old times."

Thora sniffed and silently spooned her soup. Jane followed suit. And so began a stiff, awkward meal.

Undeterred, Patrick became his charming best, slowly wheedling Thora from her sullen silence with stories from his and John's boyhood.

"John was born a man of business. Did you know, when he was no more than ten, he began extorting sixpence from female guests to 'mouse-proof' their rooms?"

"He didn't!" Thora said, but Jane noticed her indulgent half smile.

"And Jane, I don't suppose your husband ever confessed to the time he and I spied on a glamorous actress who stayed here?"

Jane shook her head, feeling a little uneasy and hoping the story wasn't inappropriate.

Patrick began, "There used to be a hole in the wall between the linen closet and number six. John and I shut ourselves in the closet, planning to watch through the hole while the beautiful Miss Lacey bathed."

"Oh no . . ." Jane murmured.

"We got a good look at a well-turned ankle when all of a sudden a heavily lined eye pressed to the hole, and a voice said, 'And that's the end of your show, boys. Now get to your beds before I call your mother.' Well, that frightened the life out of us, as you can imagine." He winked at Thora.

She frowned and shook her head, though Jane saw a faint sparkle of humor in her eyes.

Patrick added, "I returned to the scene of the crime the following week, I confess, only to find the hole filled. As you never boxed our ears, Mamma, I can only guess Miss Lacey whispered a quiet word to Talbot and he plugged the hole without divulging our secret."

Thora said, "Your father, more likely. He would have laughed it off as harmless boyhood mischief. But Talbot would not have let it pass without a reprimand. He prided himself on The Angel— the *inn*—being a safe place for travelers. Safe from highwaymen, thieves, or," she added dryly, "lascivious boys."

Thora's slip of the tongue reminded Jane of what she'd heard from Talbot. She said, "I saw the carved angels in the guest rooms today. I'd forgotten the inn used to be called The Angel."

"You and most everyone else."

"Don't forget, Mamma," Patrick said. "It has been The Bell since before John and I were born."

"True," Thora said curtly. "Please pass the salt cellar. Mrs. Rooke seems to have forgotten to season the meat again."

Jane watched her mother-in-law's face with interest. She seemed at her ease, but was that a tightening of her jaw? A sharpness in her voice?

Jane chose her words carefully. "The name change must have taken some getting used to. For everyone."

Patrick nodded. "That Bell sign has been hanging out front my entire life, but now and again some old timer will refer to the place, or to Mamma, as The Angel."

"Hush."

"Your parents named it The Angel?" Jane asked.

Thora shook her head. "My great-grandparents."

"Why change it, then?"

Thora's eyes flashed, and her lips tightened.

Jane wished she'd held her tongue. "I'm sorry if it's a sensitive subject. It's none of my business."

"There is nothing to be sorry about, Jane," Thora insisted. "Anything related to The Bell is your business now."

Jane tried to meet her gaze, but Thora looked down, sawing at her meat.

Patrick said casually, "I suppose it was only natural to want to put your own mark on the place when you and Papa took over after your parents retired."

"The Bell is a good, traditional name for an inn," Jane added helpfully. "And considering it was Frank's surname, I suppose it was an obvious choice."

"Yes, quite obvious," Thora muttered sardonically, but did not expand on her answer. "Come, let's finish our food before everything's stone-cold."

After the meal, Thora excused herself rather abruptly, Jane thought, while she and Patrick lingered over coffee. A horn blew outside, startling Jane.

Patrick consulted his pocket watch. "That will be the Southampton to Bristol. I'll go. You stay and finish your coffee."

He rose, folding his table napkin, and she smiled her thanks.

As he left the room, he summoned the porter. "Come, Colin! Cider, and be smart about it."

Doors opened and closed. Carriage wheels crunched on the gravel in the yard. Voices rumbled, and a crusty coachman shouted warnings to the ostlers to take care of *his* horses.

Jane finished her coffee and then wandered back toward the office, pausing to look out the window.

Patrick stood outside, talking to the coachman of the newly arrived stage, while Colin offered passengers cups of cider, since this particular coach did not stop long enough for a meal. A few inside passengers stepped out to stretch or dash to the privy, or leaned down from the roof to accept a cup, but the guard handed down a valise to only one disembarking passenger.

Patrick greeted the man but remained outside, and Colin was

busy accepting coins in return for refreshment, so Jane stepped behind the reception counter to greet the new arrival herself. She hoped she would remember Talbot's instructions.

"Good evening to you, sir," Jane said when he entered. "How may I help you?"

The gentleman, of average height and confident bearing, set down his valise. "I would like a room for a few days, if you please."

That piqued Jane's interest. Most of their guests stayed a single night, on their way somewhere else. But with so many rooms empty, she was not about to complain.

"You are very welcome," she said, hoping not to sound too eager. She opened the registration book and slid the inkpot and quill toward him.

He picked up the pen with clean, well-groomed hands and bent over the registry, scratching away. She took the opportunity to study him. He was in his early to mid-thirties and handsome, with golden-brown hair and side-whiskers. He wore the fine clothes of a gentleman, but there was nothing of the dandy about him. No ostentatious flair to his cravat. No jewelry, quizzing glass, or walking stick. He had good, regular features—a straight nose, full lower lip, and vertical grooves bracketing his mouth.

He glanced up and caught her staring. His soft green eyes shone with humor, and the corner of his mouth quirked in a knowing grin.

Jane looked away quickly, making a show of searching for an available room and selecting a key from the drawer. Then she turned the registry toward herself, ready to add the room number in the appropriate column.

"And how many nights will you be with us?" she asked.

"May I let you know? I am not certain how long."

"Of course. Just let me know when you decide. I will put you in number seven, Mr. . . ." She glanced at the registry, then bent to look closer. She couldn't quite make out the name. James D-something.

He offered, "My friends call me JD."

Jane peered at him, stifling a retort. She reminded herself she was no longer a genteel young lady awaiting a proper introduction. "Well, Mr. *JD*," she said, not quite concealing the disapproval in her voice. "I hope you shall be comfortable here."

He said, "Thank you. And you are?"

"Mrs. Bell."

"Ah. The innkeeper herself."

Jane automatically shook her head, demurring, "That was my husband's title."

"Oh? I thought I read that a Mrs. Bell owned this inn."

Where had he read that? "Well, I suppose I do, officially. Though it is a family business."

"Ah . . ." He nodded out the window in Patrick's direction. "I did meet a Mr. Bell briefly when I arrived, but—"

"My brother-in-law," Jane explained. "My husband passed away last year."

"I see." His gaze ran over her black dress. "I am sorry."

"Thank you." She stepped around the counter, wishing Colin were there to attend to this man.

"Now, right this way. Watch your head." She led the way through the low archway and up the stairs. "Do you have friends or family here in Ivy Hill?" she asked casually.

"I am here on business." His tone was polite but did not invite further inquiry.

"Oh?"

"Um-hm."

When he did not expand on his two-syllable answer, she decided it would be rude to probe further.

"Be careful of this step," she warned. "It needs looking after. And the handrail is a little loose here. Pray, don't lean on it."

Reaching the half landing, Jane noticed the patterned paper coming away from the wall, and a large spider web draping the candle chandelier above them. She'd noticed neither before. But suddenly, with this well-dressed gentleman behind her, every cobweb and crack in the plaster seemed to shout of neglect. She also felt self-conscious, wondering if her backside was at the man's eye level as she climbed the stairs. She hoped he wasn't looking. She ought to have suggested he precede her.

She reached number seven and inserted the key, disconcerted to find her hand not quite steady. How foolish. The door refused to give. "A little sticky, I'm afraid."

"Allow me."

She stepped aside, and he gave a well-placed shove with his shoulder and the door gave and swung wide.

"After you," she insisted.

Inside, she pointed out the basin and towels, described the location of the outside privy, and reiterated mealtimes. "I'll ask Alwena to bring hot water. If you need any clothes washed, she'll take them to the laundress for you. Anything else you need while you're here, just let us know."

"I will certainly do that, Mrs. Bell."

Jane knew she should leave but found herself lingering. "The floor slants a bit; please watch your step."

"It's not too bad," he said affably. "When was the inn built?"

"I don't know exactly, but it is over a hundred years old." She gave a sheepish little chuckle. "And probably looks it."

"I don't know . . ." he mused. "She isn't in her first blush of youth, I grant you. But she has good bones. She's still a beauty."

Jane looked over and was disconcerted to find the man's gaze resting on her. Surely he did not mean . . . ? She swallowed and reached for the door latch, backing across the threshold. "I shall leave you to get settled. Enjoy your stay."

He smiled, and the grooves in his cheeks deepened. "I believe I shall."

CHAPTER

NINE

The pews of St. Anne's held most of the usual parishioners that Sunday morning, though Jane noticed one particular person missing. She and Thora sat together near the middle of the nave, two widows in black. Patrick had volunteered to stay at the inn and watch over things. They had left him in the coffee room, ensconced with a freshly brewed pot of tea and the London newspapers.

In the front row sat Sir Timothy, his sister, Justina, and their mother, Lady Brockwell. Across the aisle was the box pew where Rachel had usually sat by herself in the months since her father's illness kept him home. But today the Ashford pew was empty. Two rows behind it sat the Miss Groves and their pupils. Though not titled, the Grove family enjoyed esteem and respect as one of the founding families of the village.

Growing up, Jane had attended church with her parents in neighboring Wishford, as Fairmont House lay a few miles out in the country, about midway between Wishford and Ivy Hill. And it was just as well, Jane had often thought. Because in Wishford, her family had enjoyed a position of honor among the gentry. How awkward it would have been to have to give up her prominent pew and move several rows back after marrying John Bell.

Jane's gaze returned to the Brockwell family pew. A sliver of

Sir Timothy's profile was visible from where she sat. She noticed a few more silver hairs in his side-whiskers and nape. He was only thirty, but she remembered his father had possessed a full head of silver hair by the time he was forty. She wondered why grey hair on men was handsome, while on most women, merely a telltale sign of middle age. It was not fair, Jane thought idly, that men grew more distinguished, while women just grew older. She wondered if Timothy ever looked at her, taken aback to see his childhood friend already a widow—and not a young one. She could hardly believe she was nearing thirty herself.

Mr. Paley was in fine mettle that morning, his sermon-making energetic, his prayers earnest. Finally, he led the congregation in the closing hymn, while Mr. Erickson played the pipe organ tucked out of sight at the rear of the nave. The organ was a recent addition to St. Anne's, of which they were all inordinately proud.

After the service concluded, Jane waited until Mr. Paley and his family, and those in the front pews, had passed down the aisle before following suit.

"I'm going to talk to Mercy," she whispered to Thora, who was stoically bearing the greetings and curious questions of several women who had just learned of her return.

Ahead of Jane, the Miss Groves shepherded their half-dozen charges through the vestibule and entry porch. A chorus of dutiful "Thank you, Parson" and "Good day, Mr. Paley" heralded their exit.

Jane waited her turn to thank the vicar, then hurried to catch up with Mercy, already walking away down the churchyard path.

"Hello, Mercy," Jane began, lengthening her stride to keep up with her taller friend. She then turned to smile at the young pupil holding Mercy's hand. "Hello, Alice."

The girl shyly ducked her head.

Mercy smiled at Jane, then said, "It was nice to see Thora in church again. But strange not to see Rachel in her usual pew."

"Yes. I saw her on the High Street the other day. She mentioned her father has taken a turn for the worse."

Mercy sighed. "I am sorry to hear it. I shall have to visit again. We could go together, if you would like?"

"Oh, that's all right. You go on your own. I don't think my presence would be a comfort."

"Are you sure? You two were once so close."

"I'm sure."

Nearby, Mercy's aunt greeted the dressmaker, Mrs. Shabner, near her own age. The two women linked arms and chatted easily as they strolled up Church Street. The students hurried ahead of them. Young Alice, however, remained at Mercy's side, clinging to her teacher's hand.

"Girls! Slow down," Mercy called. "It is the Sabbath, after all." In a quiet aside to Jane, Mercy said, "And we don't want another reprimand from Lady Brockwell."

Reaching the intersection with Potters Lane, the pupils huddled at the bakery window, pointing and exclaiming over the treasures within. Jane and Mercy reached them, and through the glass, Jane saw breads, iced biscuits, and a tiered cake decorated with piped icing and pastel flowers.

"Girls. Don't press your noses to the glass or Mrs. Craddock shall have to clean it in the morning." When they remained, Mercy repeated, "Girls. Come away." She added under her breath, "Before Aunt Matty sees and takes it into her head to bake again . . ."

Too late. Matilda Grove excused herself from the dressmaker and hurried to join the girls at the bakery window. "Ohhh! Look at those sugar flowers. All the colors of spring. I wonder how they tint the sugar like that. Well, girls, pick something that captures your fancy, and I shall attempt to create it in our own kitchen! What say you?"

The older girls exchanged knowing looks, while the younger ones oohed and aahed and pointed to the tiered cake.

"The cake it is!"

Mercy sighed.

"Poor Mercy," Jane teased.

"Let's go home the long way, girls!" Mercy called to them, then turned back to Jane. "Walk with us? It is such a lovely day. And the Brockwell Court gardens must be in glorious bloom by now. The girls could use the exercise, and I the air."

"So could I, come to think of it, after the long service."

So instead of continuing on Church Street, they turned up narrow Steeple Lane, past several cottages, then crossed the packhorse bridge over Pudding Brook. Soon they were walking along a green slope dotted with sheep and a few cows, with a farmhouse and barn in the distance.

Seeing a quartet of lambs leaping and frolicking, the girls hurried to get closer to the adorable, nimble creatures. Matilda Grove followed, chasing after the lambs as though a girl herself. Jane and Mercy shared a bemused look and burst into laughter.

Then Mercy turned to the little girl still clutching her hand. "Go on, Alice," she urged. "Go see the lambs."

She gave the girl a gentle nudge, and after a reassuring glance at Mercy over her shoulder, Alice hurried to join the others.

"She's very attached to you," Jane observed.

"Yes," Mercy replied on a sigh, part wistful, part worried.

"Has she no family of her own?"

Mercy hesitated. "Not . . . close family. Her mother died a few months ago."

"How sad. And her father?"

"He has been gone for years, I understand. A merchant marine who died at sea."

"Then who pays for Alice's school fees and room and board?"

Mercy bit her lip and made no reply.

"Mercy . . ." Jane admonished. "I don't pretend to have much experience, but even I know that's not the way to manage a business."

Her friend lifted her chin. "I believe every child, girl or boy, should be educated, regardless of family or financial circumstances."

"Very noble. But can you afford it?"

Mercy shrugged. "Most of my pupils have relatives who pay

their fees. But my heart is with those without homes of their own. When last I visited my parents in London and saw all those street urchins . . . I wished I could cart them up and bring them all here."

"You cannot rescue them all."

"I suppose not."

They reached Brockwell Court and walked along the bridleway, admiring the manor's gardens, yew houses, and topiaries. The grounds had changed little since those long ago days when Jane had been a frequent guest there.

"Why don't you join us for dinner?" Mercy suggested. "Mrs. Timmons put on a Sunday roast and Auntie baked more of her, em, *special* biscuits."

Jane smiled. "As tempting as that sounds, no thank you." She plucked at the heavy, warm fabric of her dress. "I think I shall return to my lonely little lodge, get out of these dreary widow's weeds, and take a solitary Sunday afternoon nap."

Mercy regarded her, then said gently, "Don't feel too sorry for yourself, Jane. Remember, you *had* a husband—a man who loved you and pursued you. More than one man who pursued you, if memory serves."

Jane winced. "I'm sorry, Mercy. That was thoughtless of me. But at least you have your girls."

"They are not mine. Not really." She looked off into the distance. "None shall ever call me Mamma."

Jane reached out and squeezed Mercy's long fingers. Voice hoarse, she whispered, "We have that in common."

CHAPTER

TEN

The next afternoon, Jane put a small dish of kipper, left over from breakfast, on her doorstep, hoping to lure one of the stable cats to her door. She waited, and after several minutes, the grey-and-black tabby came slinking over warily from the yard. He slowed as he neared, hesitant at seeing her in the open doorway.

Jane bent low. "It's all right. I mean you no harm."

The cat sniffed and, unable to resist the fishy aroma, crept atop the step. As he began nibbling the fish, Jane slowly reached out to try and pet him, but the cat darted back through the archway to the safety of the stables.

Jane rose with a sigh. Ah well. It was a start.

Retrieving the two vases of flowers she had arranged earlier, Jane carried them across the yard to the inn, to see if she could be useful, and she admitted to herself, curious to see the man called JD again. After putting one vase of flowers on the hall table, and the second on the desk, she glanced into the dining parlour and saw him sitting at a small corner table, set apart from the passengers of the recently arrived stagecoach. As Jane lingered there, the guard entered only long enough to call out a ten-minute warning. Inside the dining parlour, passengers grumbled. One tried to snag Alwena's arm as she hurried past with a teapot.

Jane glanced around the tables. Only bread and butter had

been served so far. The short layover was ticking away, and the passengers were growing impatient.

Jane took a deep breath for courage as she walked down the passage and paused in the kitchen doorway. Inside, the cook stood at her leisure at the worktable, sipping tea.

Jane said, "Mrs. Rooke, the passengers must leave in a few minutes and have yet to be served. What is the delay?"

"Just making sure the soup is plenty hot."

Jane crossed the threshold only far enough to peer inside the open pot, surprised to see its contents steaming and gurgling away. "It is more than hot enough."

"That is a matter of opinion. Thora Bell always insisted on serving it piping hot."

"Too hot to eat?" Jane challenged.

"Precisely."

Realization swept through Jane. The delay was intentional! At that moment, Thora walked past the kitchen door, and drew up short at the foreign sight of Jane in Mrs. Rooke's kitchen.

Seeing her, Jane gestured toward the pot in exasperation. "Thora! You approve of this?"

"I'm sorry if your delicate sensibilities are offended, Jane," Thora coolly replied. "It is the way we've always done things—the way most inns do things. And with finances as they are, you should be thanking Mrs. Rooke instead of standing there the picture of moral outrage."

Alwena entered, helped Mrs. Rooke ladle bowls of steaming soup, and placed them on a tray.

Aiming a glare at Jane, the cook said to the maid, "Here, Alwena. Serve these."

Jane followed the maid back to the dining parlour. Tension eased as a bowl was set before each hungry customer.

"This soup is much too hot," one matron immediately complained.

"It will cool, by and by," Jane soothed, pasting on a smile.

A gentleman pulled out his pocket watch. "We're to depart soon. You had better bring us the rest of our meal now."

Jane swallowed. "I will see what I can do."

The guard called another warning, "South Way passengers. Time to take your seats. The coach leaves in five minutes."

Again people grumbled. Others tried to drink their soup, blowing and sipping and wincing.

Finally, Alwena brought in the meat and potatoes, but the guard outside blew the final warning. Passengers rose, fumbling for shillings to settle their bills, muttering about the poor service, and hurrying outside, leaving almost as hungry as they arrived, no doubt.

As the dining parlour emptied, Alwena hurried around, picking up bowls of barely touched soup which, Jane surmised, would be dumped back into the pot.

She glanced over and found JD still sitting at his corner table alone, watching her. Slowly, patiently, stirring his soup.

He waited until Alwena left the room with her tray, then said, "That's the oldest trick in the book, you know."

"What is?" Jane said, feeling defensive and embarrassed on The Bell's behalf.

His eyes glinted. "Oh come, you know very well. Passengers have a limited time. Inns take their orders and their money, then serve scalding soup too hot to drink and delay serving the rest of the meal until the guard blows his horn. Then they serve the uneaten food to the next passengers. I noticed your maid didn't collect their money first, though. That could have cost you. The customers might have refused to pay, given the circumstances, and then what would you do?"

"It wasn't my idea. My mother-in-law just told me it is the way most inns do things, so apparently passengers expect little better."

He nodded. "It was the way many *used* to do things, yes. But times are changing. Gone are the days when hostelries could provide poor service and expect customers to keep coming. Word gets around you know—it travels up and down the line with the coaches. Private lines want satisfied customers. Enough complain about one inn, they'll change their route and stop at another. Now that the turnpike has drawn off some of your traffic, you can't afford to alienate those still coming to The Bell."

"You seem to know a great deal about it."

He shrugged. "I visit many hostelries in my line of work."

"Perhaps you could repeat what you said to my mother-in-law. She insists old ways are the best."

"Then I doubt she would listen to me," he said with a good-natured smile. "Or anyone else for that matter."

Jane cocked her head to one side and regarded him thoughtfully. "But you believe *I* will listen?"

"Yes, I think so. You are young and not steeped in tradition or stuck in old ruts. Life and business are about change, Mrs. Bell. We must embrace change or die."

"That sounds rather radical. May I quote you?"

"By all means." He gestured toward the chair opposite his. "Will you join me?"

She hesitated. "I . . . had better not, but thank you for the offer."

He rose and pulled out the chair for her. "Come, Mrs. Bell. Look around you. I am your only customer at present. You won't suffer me to eat alone, I hope?"

"I eat alone regularly and have suffered no ill effects, I assure you."

"Not even . . . loneliness?"

"Not at all. I enjoy solitude." *Is that true?* Jane asked herself.

"I would think solitude a rare thing in a coaching inn."

"You would think so, yes." Jane stood there, vacillating, then said, "Just give me one minute."

In the kitchen, she found Thora helping Cadi empty the last of the soup bowls, while Alwena and Mrs. Rooke returned meat and potatoes to the warming cabinet.

"Thora, our overnight guest has asked me to join him in the dining parlour. I tried to refuse, but he insists that—"

"Why refuse?" Thora broke in. "John and his father often sat down with well-heeled guests, to make sure everything was to their satisfaction."

Jane was surprised Thora would encourage her to eat with the man. But she *was* curious to hear what else JD had learned from successful inns during the course of his work.

"If you say so. Cadi, no need to bring a tray to the lodge this afternoon."

"Very well, ma'am."

Jane returned to the dining parlour, allowed the man to push in her chair for her, then unfolded a table napkin over her lap. Cadi brought out another plate for her, and Jane did not miss the sparkle of interest in the girl's eyes, seeing romance where there was none.

"Do you enjoy life in a coaching inn, Mrs. Bell?" JD began.

She picked up knife and fork and sliced into the roast. "Why do you ask?"

"You don't appear to enjoy it."

"I hope my enjoyment or lack thereof does not detract from your stay, Mr. JD," she replied, her tone more tart than she intended.

A slow smile spread over his face. "It's James Drake, by the way, if you prefer not to call me JD." He watched her reaction.

"Thank you, Mr. Drake." Did he expect her to recognize the name? She did not.

She took a small bite, then continued, "I never planned to work here in the inn myself. But with my husband gone . . ." She allowed the sentence to trail away, then admitted, "Some say I ought to sell out."

"Oh? And what do you say?"

"I don't know. All I know for certain is that we must find a way to increase profits."

He sipped, then set down his glass. "Would you mind some advice?"

"Not at all."

He nodded thoughtfully. "Your rates are low compared to other inns on the route. You could raise them a shilling, maybe even half a crown, without affecting demand."

"Really? That is not a suggestion most paying guests would offer."

He shrugged easily. "I am not often a paying guest."

"Oh? You receive free lodging in return for your valuable advice, I suppose?"

He chuckled. "Not at all. I reside in a small hotel of my own."

Surprise flashed through Jane, followed by unease. "I see. You might have said so earlier. And where is this hotel of yours?"

"Southampton."

"I am surprised you can get away."

He waved a dismissive hand. "I employ a capable manager and housekeeper."

"And what other advice would you offer? If The Bell were yours, what would you do?"

He inhaled and paused to collect his thoughts. "Hire an excellent cook. Perhaps even French. Offer fine dining in this room, as well as in private parlours for wealthy patrons. Charge a pretty penny for it, too. But also offer inexpensive, basic food—stew, bread, meat pies—ready to be served at a moment's notice in the coffee room for those with smaller purses or little time. How many private parlours have you?"

"Three. But I gather they are infrequently used. I'm afraid one has become little more than a storage room. And I've noticed our potboy sneaking a nap in the other."

He smiled, then went on. "So, either court the patronage of wealthy travelers by attaining the high standards of a private posting house, or if that seems improbable given the turnpike and your regular customer base, I'd suggest opening up at least one of those unused rooms and expanding this dining parlour. Perhaps add a few high-backed booths for privacy for those who want it. Then convert the second unused parlour into a washroom for gentlemen who would appreciate a place for a quick wash and shave, even if they are not staying the night. Charge a modest fee for soap and towels."

He wiped his mouth with a table napkin, then continued, "Cultivate a reputation for dependable service, excellent food, clean rooms, and comfortable beds. Frequent travelers will thank you for it, return, and tell their friends. Word will get back to the owners of the stagecoach lines, and The Bell is certain to maintain or even expand business."

"My goodness. Is that all?" Jane replied, incredulity coloring her voice.

"Not quite. You need a large, professionally painted sign kept in good repair. It's the best advertising you've got and tells customers what to expect inside."

Jane winced at the thought of the paint peeling from The Bell sign and that dismal vacancy placard dangling from it. "You've certainly given this some thought," she acknowledged.

Again that easy shrug. "It is my business, after all."

Cadi returned on the pretense of refilling their glasses, but Jane wasn't fooled. Little eavesdropper, that one.

"Well," Jane said. "Perhaps in a town like Southampton, people expect and are willing to pay for such niceties, but here in little Ivy Hill . . . ?"

"You would be surprised, I think. Don't forget that coaching lines bring people through your doors from far and wide. Coach travel is expensive, so it is primarily used by people of means. People who are coming to expect or at least appreciate a higher level of service, speed, and comfort, not only in the vehicles themselves but also in the hostelries along the way."

Jane considered this, then asked, "Would you mind terribly if I asked my mother-in-law and brother-in-law to join us? I'd like them to hear your opinion from you directly. I'm afraid they won't credit it, coming from me."

He looked at her steadily. "You may of course ask them to join us. But . . . do you work for them, or they for you?"

Jane ducked her head. "On paper the inn is mine, yes. But Patrick grew up here. And so did Thora, for that matter. The inn has been in their family for generations. So their opinions matter to me."

"I see. You are wise not to discount the experience and wisdom of your elders, Mrs. Bell, but don't discount your own thoughts and opinions either. You are intelligent and educated. I can see that. You have a mind of your own and should not hesitate to use it."

Jane felt her cheeks heat at his praise, and pleasure warmed her. John had often flattered her beauty, but she could not recall the last time anyone had praised her intelligence.

Someone strode into the dining parlour. Jane glanced over, and her face heated anew to be found dining tête-à-tête with a man she barely knew.

Sir Timothy Brockwell drew up short at the sight of the two of them sitting alone together.

"Jane, I . . . Forgive me, I did not mean to intrude."

Jane forced a smile and kept her tone casual. "Not at all, Sir Timothy. We were just discussing possible improvements to the inn." Jane turned politely to her companion. "Sir Timothy Brockwell, may I present Mr. James Drake. Mr. Drake, my old friend, Sir Timothy."

James nodded. "How do you do, sir."

"Drake . . . ?" Sir Timothy echoed. "Any relation to the Hain-Drakes?"

James opened his mouth. Closed it, then said modestly, "Only distantly."

"Ah."

Jane explained, "Mr. Drake owns a hotel in Southampton."

"The Drake Arms?" Sir Timothy said. "I have dined there myself. An excellent establishment. You are to be congratulated."

"You are very kind. But all the credit goes to my chef, I assure you."

Sir Timothy turned to her. "Jane, I have only come to ask if we might prevail upon you to join us for dinner tomorrow. Justina was saying only this morning that you haven't been to the manor in ages."

"That is thoughtful of her. Do greet her for me. But I'm afraid I shall find it difficult to get away."

"Of course. We only thought now that . . . Well. Never mind. You let Justina know when you have an hour or two free. I know she would like to see you. And now, I shall trespass upon your time no longer. Good day to you both." He bowed briefly, turned, and strode from the room.

Jane stared after him until his boot falls no longer reverberated the floorboards and the door had shut behind him.

She felt Mr. Drake's gaze upon her. He said quietly, "You've disappointed him, I think."

No, Jane thought. *He disappointed me. . . .*

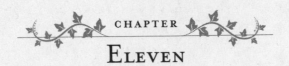

CHAPTER
ELEVEN

Jane saved another dish of kipper the next day, and this time set it just inside the lodge door. Sure enough, the grey-and-black-striped cat came running from the stables and leapt atop the step.

Jane stood quietly in the open doorway. The cat sniffed and, lured by the promising smell, slowly crept over the threshold. As he began nibbling, then wolfing down the treat, Jane bent and traced a finger along his back. The cat growled low in its throat, but when she did not try to take away the food, the growling stopped, and Jane took pleasure in stroking his soft fur.

The cat allowed her to rub his head, then darted back out the door. Perhaps next time he would stay longer.

She straightened and watched as he loped away.

"Tell me you're not feeding the stable cats."

Startled, Jane looked up to find the farrier, Mr. Locke, frowning at her from the drive, fists on hips.

Caught. Red-handed.

"Only this one. Why?" she said, feeling defensive. What was wrong with giving a cat a little fish?

"They are supposed to be mousers. Not pets."

"Why can't he be both?"

"He will become too fat and content to chase mice."

"Has the stable been overrun?"

"Not yet."

"Good." She was about to close her door but noticed he remained where he was. "Was there something else?"

"Haven't heard you playing your pianoforte lately. We miss it, the postboys, ostlers, and I."

She looked at him sharply. "You can hear me play from the stables?"

"Not during busy times, but during the afternoon lull or when the yard quiets down after dinner."

Embarrassment pricked Jane. "I wish I'd known. I would not have played during quiet times."

"Why? It's a pleasure to hear you. Don't stop because I erred in mentioning it. Tuffy and Tall Ted would never forgive me."

"Tuffy and Tall Ted?" she asked. "Are those horses?"

"No! Ostlers." He chuckled, a rare grin brightening his face, already shadowed with whiskers.

"Oh."

"An understandable misapprehension," he assured her. "I won't mention it."

"Thank you. I will play again . . . but I have been busy lately."

"So I've noticed."

Did his tone convey surprise, or disapproval, or what? His expression was difficult to decipher as well.

"By the way," he added. "I saw Patrick go into the inn with Mr. Gordon a short while ago. He's the local property agent, I believe. Some important meeting, perhaps?"

"Oh." Jane did not want to admit that she was unaware of—or being left out of—any such meeting. "Yes, thank you," she murmured. "Excuse me."

She crossed the courtyard to the inn. Inside, she pushed open the office door, interrupting Patrick and the agent in earnest conversation. "Hello. What is going on?"

Patrick smiled. "Hello, Jane. Mr. Gordon was just telling me about a potential buyer interested in The Bell. Since you were not here, he gave the details to me."

"I was only in the lodge. You might have sent for me."

"I did not wish to bother you."

"If it relates to The Bell I think I ought to be involved." Jane turned to the agent. "I am sorry, Mr. Gordon, but I am afraid I must ask you to repeat yourself."

"That's all right, Mrs. Bell. Happy to do it."

"Just one moment, if you please. I would like Thora to hear this as well." Jane excused herself, and found Thora in the coffee room, where she sat with Charlie Frazer over a pot of tea.

"Forgive the intrusion, Thora, Mr. Frazer. Thora, might I ask you to join us in the office, please?"

Thora rose immediately. "Of course. Excuse me, Charlie."

When they returned to the office, Patrick gave Thora his chair and dragged in another for Jane.

Then Mr. Gordon began, "As Patrick said, I've received an offer on the inn from a potential buyer. Knowing of the bank's interest in the place, I considered taking the offer to Blomfield, but I thought I would see if you were interested first."

Thora sent Patrick an irritated glance. "Does everyone know the bank is threatening to sell the inn out from under us?"

"Not everyone," Mr. Gordon replied before Patrick could. "But as I have conducted such sales for the bank in the past, I was of course informed."

"Well, the bank doesn't own The Bell yet," Thora snapped.

Jane added more gently, "So we appreciate your coming here first, Mr. Gordon."

He nodded. "I would be happy to deal with you directly, Mrs. Bell, for my usual fee. But I can only give you two days to decide."

"Two days? What is the hurry?"

Patrick smirked. "Maybe Gordon here is worried his buyer might take a closer look at this old place and change his mind."

"No," the agent said. "But the buyer is considering other properties as well."

"What price was offered?" Jane asked.

He named it.

Thora scowled. "That is far too low."

Patrick tilted his head. "Gordon, since you're here, I wonder if you might tell us the asking price on Fairmont House—just out of curiosity, of course."

Fairmont House was not entailed, and after Jane married, her father had surprised everyone by selling it to a retired admiral. But the old mariner had died soon after, and his heir had no interest in some remote country estate, so he'd put it up for sale. But no one bought it.

Mr. Gordon named a figure.

Jane shook her head. "That is less than Father originally sold it for, but still well beyond my means." Even if she could buy it, Jane knew she could never afford the maintenance on the place.

Mr. Gordon rose. "Well, I will await your answer."

After the agent took his leave, Jane turned to Patrick in puzzlement.

"Why did you ask about Fairmont House? The only way I could buy it is if I sold the inn to someone else at a very good price. Is that what you want?"

"I was thinking of you, Jane. I know you will never be happy here at The Bell. Do you deny it?"

Jane felt Thora's scrutiny, and barely resisted the urge to squirm. "I . . . don't know."

"Well, I do," Patrick insisted. "And I'd like to see you happily settled in Fairmont or somewhere like it. And who knows, if you sell the inn, the new owner might want a competent manager and keep me on."

It was possible, Jane realized. Thora, however, looked less than convinced.

Thora watched Patrick's expression. What was he up to? Was he really trying to help Jane? Thora hated the nagging suspicion that trickled through her as she looked at her son. Was she setting him up for failure by always expecting the worst from him—or were her concerns justified?

Patrick had given her reasons not to trust him in the past.

The sneaking, the lying, the manipulation . . . had it ended, or only just begun? Her heart ached for her son. He was so much like his father that it was tempting to lay the blame at Frank's door, but she knew she had not been a perfect mother by any means. She had married so young and had little idea how to raise hardworking, responsible children. Yet John had turned out all right for the most part, had he not?

Thora shifted on her seat. She wanted to give Patrick a fair chance. She wanted to believe that he had changed. But the old suspicion kept gnawing away at her.

Why had he been meeting with Mr. Gordon alone? And what were he and Arthur Blomfield cooking up together?

Oh, God, please don't let him be involved in anything illegal or immoral. . . . Merciful Father, please protect him, keep him on the right path. And give me wisdom, Almighty God, for I have never known what to do where Patrick is concerned, and all the more now.

CHAPTER
TWELVE

A week had passed since the banker revealed the overdue loan, and Jane had not yet decided what to do about it. Wanting a change of scenery to clear her thoughts—and secretly longing to see Fairmont House again—Jane went out to the stables the next day, steeling herself to speak to Mr. Locke. Inside, she found their farrier shoeing an old nag.

"May I borrow a horse?" Jane asked him.

"Of course," Mr. Locke said. "They're your horses, after all."

"Perhaps, but I would not want to leave the ostlers short for changes. Any decent riding mounts among the coach horses?"

"There's always old Ruby here," he said, a slight quirk to his mouth. "Slow and stubborn, but safe."

"If she is the only one available, then she will do."

He looked up and studied her, eyes glinting speculatively. "Are you an experienced horsewoman, Mrs. Bell?"

"I . . . was. Though I have not ridden much in years. And not at all this last year."

He looked again toward the nag.

Jane quickly added, "I had my own horse growing up, a spirited Thoroughbred called Hermione. I all but lived on her back when I wasn't forced to remain in the schoolroom."

One dark brow rose. "A Thoroughbred?"

She nodded. "A descendant of Trumpator."

He pursed his lips, either impressed or doubtful. "You don't say."

"I do. In fact, Papa made good use of that information when he sold her the week after my wedding."

"I'm sorry."

She shrugged. "She no doubt fetched him a good price. I suppose he thought I would be too busy being a wife and mother to ride. But I missed her. I wished I'd asked him who bought her, but I did not."

He narrowed his eyes in thought. "That being the case, perhaps you would do me a favor."

"What favor?" she asked warily.

"We are boarding a horse for a gentleman who is away from home at present. You might exercise him for me."

"Which gentleman? Would I know him?" Jane asked, thinking of James Drake, but then recalled that he'd arrived by coach.

"Not likely," Mr. Locke said. "He's from Pewsey Vale."

"Will the horse take a sidesaddle?" Jane asked.

"It is not his preference, but he is very well-trained."

"Well then, let's have a look at him."

Locke led the way deeper into the stable building and stopped at one of its many stalls. Inside stood a tall chestnut with a white blaze on his forehead. The horse regarded her with intelligent dark eyes.

"This is Sultan."

"He's a beauty," Jane breathed, feeling excitement and a thread of trepidation. She hoped she could handle him.

Half an hour later, dressed in her old riding habit—thankfully in a muted Devonshire brown—Jane returned to the stables. The horse jigged a bit when Mr. Locke helped her mount onto the sidesaddle, but after a few turns around the paddock, he settled into his stride.

"He's wonderful!" she called.

In reply, Mr. Locke opened the gate. "Don't go far. Not on your own."

"I won't. Only to Wishford and back."

Jane rode off on the spirited Sultan, down the hill and along the Wishford Road. Her nerves subsided and pleasure overtook her. Ah, the exhilarating freedom of riding horseback. How she had missed it. She looked around her as she rode, relishing the beauty of a Wiltshire spring day—green hedges, honeysuckle bushes blooming pink and white, and fields dotted with yellow buttercups.

After five or ten minutes, she signaled the horse across the new roadway. As she passed through the familiar gate to Fairmont House, she heard the telltale call of a cuckoo bird.

Jane halted Sultan on the half-circle drive and gazed up at the house where she had been born and lived the first two decades of her life. How strange to see its low wall and gate so near to the new turnpike, instead of the country lane that had formerly marked its approach. Weeds grew up among the pea gravel of the drive, and the lawn sprouted tall grass headed with seeds. The hedges had outgrown their shape and symmetry for lack of trimming. The house itself looked better, but one of the front windows had a long crack and another a pockmark spidering from its center. Had some vandal thrown a stone? Anger filled her, and Jane reminded herself yet again that her family no longer owned the house and hadn't for years. It should not bother her if it lay abandoned and decaying or abused.

But it did.

Everywhere she looked, she saw memories captured in amber resin. There the lawn where she and her friends had played battledore and shuttlecock. There the flower garden her mother had loved. And up there, beyond the second level of windows, the room that had been hers—that had held her dolls and books and dreams.

Jane rode around to the rear of the house, lifting a swaying pine bough and ducking her head to pass beneath. The sharp sweet smell of pine brought back the memory of her and Rachel climbing these trees as girls, sitting in their upper branches, and talking about their dreams for the future—whom they would marry and how many children they would have. Jane had always wanted a large family, but dreams did not always come true.

She looked toward the stables, where she had spent so many hours grooming Hermione. And then at the pond behind the house, where Timothy had tried to teach her to fish. And the path through the woods, where they had so often ridden together.

How long ago it all seemed. But in the next breath, it seemed like only a few weeks had passed, for how clearly she could remember his good-natured teasing about his riding superiority, and challenges to race. The exhilaration of cantering across the countryside on her beloved horse, her friend at her side. She had thought then, with the naïveté of youth, that life would always be so happy and carefree. That she and Timothy would be close forever. And that she could predict how the future would unfold. How wrong she had been. She would never have foreseen her current situation. Not in a hundred years. Perhaps she should not have so hastily declined his recent invitation.

"Woolgathering?" a voice said, interrupting her reverie.

She whipped her head around, surprised to see the very man of her thoughts sitting at his ease atop his own horse. He wore a crooked grin, his hat pulled low. His hands, encased in fine leather gloves, held the reins with casual competence. In his fashionable riding coat and polished Hessians, he was the picture of a well-turned-out country squire.

"Reminiscing," she admitted.

He looked up at the dim windows. "It's sad to see it empty, is it not?"

"Yes."

"Well then. You must be glad about the news of an interested buyer at last."

She sucked in a breath. "For Fairmont House? I did not know."

He lifted a cautioning hand. "It is just something I heard in passing. I could be wrong."

Mixed emotions flooded Jane. She should be glad, but she was not quite ready to relinquish the impractical dream of somehow buying the place back one day.

Sir Timothy gestured toward the wooded path. "Shall we ride together? For old time's sake?"

Jane shook off her illogical disappointment and looked at him. She knew she probably shouldn't but didn't want to refuse another invitation from her old friend. She smiled. "Why not?"

When she returned to the stables, Mr. Locke was waiting for her.

"You were gone a long time. I was starting to worry."

"I am sorry. I happened into an old friend."

"Did the horse give you any trouble?"

"None at all. He's marvelous. My compliments to his owner." Locke grinned. "I shall pass them along."

He reached up and put his hands on her waist to help her dismount. Caught unaware, she grasped his shoulders—his broad, muscular shoulders. As soon as her feet touched the ground, she snatched back her hands.

His grin faded and he was all seriousness again. "Mrs. Bell, I hope you don't mind. But I have heard about the situation you find yourself in with the bank."

She huffed in exasperation. "Does everyone know?"

"I believe most of us do, yes. But I feel the need to caution you."

"*You* need to caution me?" she asked snappishly. "What do you know about it?"

"Please, do not be offended. I have no intention of meddling, but I feel it my duty to make you aware of something."

"What are you talking about?"

He hesitated. "I understand that you are considering allowing John's brother to assume the debt in exchange for the inn."

She lifted her chin. "That is one possibility. Why?"

"I wonder if you have asked Patrick what he plans to do with the place?"

"What do you mean? The Bell is a coaching inn, as you know very well."

"Yes, it has been these many years. But I understand that he has something very different in mind for the property should he become its owner."

This was news to Jane. "What, exactly?"

"I have heard talk of a private gentleman's club, like those in London. Or dividing the building into private residences and renting them out like townhouses."

"A gentleman's club in Ivy Hill? Private dwellings? You must have heard wrong."

"And if I did not?"

"Well, I admit the idea of a gentleman's club sounds outlandish, but I see no harm in townhouses . . ."

Gabriel shook his head. "Think about it, Mrs. Bell. Like it or not, the future of the inn not only affects you and Patrick and Thora Bell. It affects everyone."

"You're worried about your job."

"Not my job. Dozens of jobs. Maybe more. Townhouses would require few stable hands. A groom, maybe, but no ostlers or postillions. No porter or clerk. Residents would probably engage their own servants. So Patrick would employ few domestic staff, unless he keeps the kitchen open."

"I see . . ." Jane murmured, thoughts whirling.

"And that's only the top of the carrot. This coaching inn provides employment and trade not only to those who live and work within its walls, but also to many others in Ivy Hill."

For a moment, Jane stared at him, measuring his words. Then she drew herself up. "Well. You have given me a great deal to think about, Mr. Locke. I hope I do not discover it is all scurrilous rumor."

"I hope you do. In this instance, I would be relieved to be wrong."

Jane went and found Patrick in the office and lost no time in raising the matter.

"Is it true you are thinking of converting The Bell into a private club or residences?"

Patrick shrugged. "Maybe. If you don't sell it to someone else. And why not?" he defended, leaning back in his chair. "Wealthy gentlemen who can afford to travel by mail or post chaise would not hesitate to pay more for exclusive accommodations. A place to eat fine dinners, play cards or billiards, and socialize with their peers instead of rubbing elbows with every sailor, joiner, and traveling peddler we cater to at present."

He leaned forward and pressed her hand. "Don't look at me like that, Jane. It's only an idea I've been kicking around. Assuming you are not going to sell The Bell to some stranger, I am trying to think of ways to change with the times and save the old place."

Jane shook her head. "I don't like the idea of a club. I'm not keen on townhouses, either. Would you really divide up the building? End its days as a wayside inn?"

"Imagine how much less work it would be! Far fewer staff to pay, and no more empty rooms! Think of it. Regular income, fewer expenses. How could it fail to increase profits?"

"But wouldn't many jobs be lost?"

"Some would be lost, yes, though not all. Don't worry, Jane. I wouldn't do anything without your consent. But we have to do something to increase profits and pay back that loan. Unless . . . have you decided to accept Gordon's offer, low as it is? Or found money hidden away among John's stockings?"

"No, I'm afraid not." But nor had she looked. In a place as small as the lodge, she deemed it highly improbable that John could have hidden anything larger than a few coins without her noticing by now. And why would he do so?

"What about the loan papers Mr. Blomfield referred to?" Patrick asked. "I can't find them in here."

Jane sighed. "Gone, along with the missing money, I imagine."

Patrick rose and stepped around the desk, lowering his voice. "Jane, I've been thinking. If you allow me to assume the debt in exchange for ownership, I will make sure you have a home here for as long as you want. Nothing would really need to change for you. You could go on living in the lodge as you do now. Free from the burdens of inn management."

She regarded him doubtfully. "You didn't offer before, when you were trying to persuade me to move elsewhere."

"True, but that was before I realized Fairmont House or some-where like it was out of reach. Unless, perhaps, you marry again."

"Goodness. I have no thought of that at present. John has barely been gone a year." She considered, then asked, "But wouldn't you want to live in the keeper's lodge, as would be your due as owner?"

"Oh, someday, perhaps, were I to marry. But I have no thought of that at present either. For now, we could go on much as we have been these last few months, you in the lodge and me here, but with a few changes in responsibilities and legalities barely noticeable to others."

The idea was mildly tempting in some ways. Especially if hand-ing the reins to Patrick ensured an extension on the loan and The Bell's future. But there was no guarantee of that. And if the bank ended up selling the inn out from under them anyway, she would lose any share of the proceeds as well as the lodge.

"I don't think so, Patrick." She gave him a wry grin. "But thank you for offering to allow me to live in my own house."

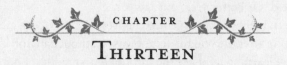

CHAPTER

Thirteen

Jane didn't speak to Mr. Locke again until the next morning. As she crossed the courtyard, she saw him giving instructions to ostlers brushing down a weary team just released from their traces. Noticing her, he stepped away to address her.

Without preamble, he asked, "Did Patrick deny his plans?"

"No. He is simply weighing his options were he to take over the place. Mr. Blomfield suggested that his partners would be more willing to extend credit to him than to me."

"I don't trust Mr. Blomfield."

"Why not?"

Locke shrugged. "A friend of mine did business with him once. And only once."

"What happened?"

"I only have it secondhand, so I'd rather not say. What about your marriage settlement?" he asked abruptly. "That's not tied up in Blomfield's bank, is it?"

"My . . . settlement?" Jane tried to cover her surprise. "What would you know about that?"

"John mentioned it to me once. He was offended that your father insisted upon one, as if John could not provide for you himself."

Jane frowned. "You seem to know more about my personal affairs than I do." She heard her caustic tone but made no effort to curb it. Even though she knew the real source of her annoyance lay with her father, who had not included her in those discussions and had never valued her opinion on anything beyond menu planning.

Mr. Locke said apologetically, "I don't know anything for certain. I'm only recalling what John told me. You should talk to Blomfield. Or better yet, your lawyer."

Jane thought back and gentled her voice. "Mr. Coine mentioned something after the will reading. I was so stunned by John's death, and then learning he'd left the inn solely to me, that I don't recall the details. But I assume any portion John agreed to settle on me in the case of his death has been superseded by the fact that he left me the inn in total."

"You may be right," Locke acknowledged. "Is this Mr. Coine local?"

"His office is in Wishford."

"I've made some repairs to the old gig in the carriage house, and I'd like to see how she handles. I have business at the Wishford bank this afternoon, as it happens, and could give you a ride."

"Inn business or personal business?" Jane challenged.

"Personal." His dark eyes glinted. "But don't worry, I shall work late tonight to make up for the time off."

"Yes, you shall," she said with hauteur. This glorified blacksmith was far too casual with her.

Jane walked inside the inn, exchanged greetings with Mr. Drake in passing, and then found her mother-in-law in the office. Thora looked up from her newspaper when Jane entered.

"Thora, will you watch over things this afternoon? Patrick has gone to the brewer's but should return soon. I am going into Wishford to see my lawyer."

Thora straightened and removed her spectacles. "I will, yes. Is something the matter?"

"Not that I know of. I just have a few questions for him."

"How will you get there?"

"Mr. Locke will drive me. He says he has business in Wishford anyway."

"What sort of business has our farrier in Wishford?"

"Something at the bank."

"And what is wrong with the bank here in Ivy Hill?"

"Apparently he doesn't trust Mr. Blomfield."

Thora humphed. "That I do understand."

Jane hesitated, then asked, "Thora, do you know anything about the marriage settlement between my father and John?"

"Not much. John didn't discuss it with me. Probably guessed I would not approve of any money being funneled away from the inn."

"I did bring a dowry into our marriage, you know," Jane said tartly.

"Yes, that was something."

Perhaps Jane should not have mentioned the settlement after all. There was no point in arguing about money that probably did not exist. "Well, I don't know if there is anything left to discuss or not. Mr. Locke merely suggested I confirm one way or another."

"Is not a jointure a *portion* of a husband's property?" Thora pointed out. "You were left the *entire* inn, Jane. What more could there be? I wouldn't get your hopes up."

"I'm sure you're right. I just want to ask."

Thora raised a hand in a "suit yourself" gesture and went back to her newspaper.

Later that afternoon, Jane stepped into the yard, dark carriage dress and bonnet in place, reticule on her wrist.

Gabriel Locke and an ostler stood beside the gig, waiting. "I reinforced the axle and secured the loose wheel as best I could. I think it will hold."

"And if it doesn't?"

"Then we shall have a nice long walk." He offered her a hand, and she hesitated only a moment before placing her gloved hand in his. With a firm grip, he helped her up, and then rounded the horse to climb in on the opposite side. A lanky ostler Locke introduced as Tall Ted held the reins. As soon as Gabriel was seated, the young man handed them over and tipped his cap to Jane.

"You will be back for the four o'clock?" Ted asked, a little worry line between his brows.

"I will be, Lord and axle willing. But you and Tuffy know what to do. I have every confidence in you."

"Thanks, Gable. That makes one of us."

Mr. Locke acknowledged his words with a nod, then lifted the reins and urged the horse to walk on.

As they rumbled through the archway, he said, "Ruby here is an old girl, but a steady one. Let's see how she does. It's either this or the caddy butcher."

"Oh, I hope it doesn't come to that. She may not be a prime bit of blood, but she's sweet."

"Just don't turn away from her, or she'll nip you in the backside."

Jane felt her face heat at the thought. "I shall remember that."

"Forgive me. I suppose that was an impolite thing to say to a lady."

"I would rather have the warning than the consequence."

He urged Ruby down the Wishford road. She seemed more interested in the weeds and grass of the verge, but with a steady, skillful grip and click of his tongue, Mr. Locke kept the old nag on course.

"Not exactly neck-or-nothing, hmm?" he murmured.

"No, you shall win no races today, Mr. Locke."

Beside her, the man seemed to stiffen. What had she said? Did he fancy himself a crack-whip? Or was she sitting too close and making him uncomfortable? Jane inched over a little farther on the narrow bench.

Reaching the outskirts of Wishford, Jane tried not to let nostalgia overtake her. Growing up, she and her parents frequented Wishford's shops as well as attending its church. Wishford had a lovely village green, bustling businesses, and well-kept homes. The scenic River Wylye curved around the town, bringing beauty as well as trade by narrow boat.

Jane had encountered resentment from some Ivy Hill residents when she had married John. Not only because she—a gentleman's daughter—had married an innkeeper, but also because many considered her a citizen of Wishford and assumed she would look down her nose at them. She and Rachel—and to a lesser extent, Mercy—already knew one another. The Brockwells, Winspears, Ashfords, Fairmonts, Bingleys, and Groves had made up the area's leading families. They had dined together. Invited one another to their Christmas parties, Twelfth Night celebrations, and coming-out balls. Their similar status superseded the less-relevant fact of which village his or her house happened to be nearer. But the distinction was far more marked by others.

Over the course of Jane's years in Ivy Hill, she had come to understand and even share her neighbor's resentment of Wishford residents, who viewed their town as more prestigious than its humble sister squatting upon her hill. Even so, Jane could not deny Wishford's charms.

Mr. Locke turned the horse up the High Street and halted Ruby with a low "Whoa, girl." He tied off the reins and hopped down, coming around to offer Jane a hand. "I shall return and wait for you here when I finish my errand. I shouldn't be long. But no need to hurry. We have plenty of time."

She nodded her understanding and stepped onto the paved walkway in front of the law office and neighboring flower shop, the smell of sweet peas and lilies fragrant in the air. She watched Mr. Locke drive away and turn the corner but lingered a moment to admire the vibrant blooms. As she stood there, curiosity nipped at her. Her questions for the lawyer could wait a few minutes longer. Jane walked toward South Street, just out for a short stroll to stretch before going inside—that was what she would tell Locke if he happened to see her.

She paused at the corner jeweler's shop, pretending to look into her reticule for something, and then glanced around the corner. There at the bank, Mr. Locke again halted Ruby. An adolescent hurried forward and took the reins, all smiles. Locke hopped down, said something to the lad that made his grin widen, and tossed him a silver coin.

"Thank you, sir!"

A clerk opened the door and welcomed Gabriel inside. Jane walked closer, paused again at the bank windows to adjust her reticule, and glanced surreptitiously inside. She was in time to see a well-dressed older gentleman greet Mr. Locke, hand extended. Locke shook it, and the man gestured him into his office with a pat on his shoulder. Jane could not imagine dour Mr. Blomfield treating any client so warmly. Perhaps she ought to consider changing banks.

The lad, clerk, and banker were obviously acquainted with Mr. Locke, so he had clearly come here more than a few times before. *Man must set his own hours*, she sarcastically thought. She had not paid any attention to his comings and goings until recently—until she had been made to care about the inn and those who worked there. But she might have to begin doing so.

"May I help you, ma'am?" the lad holding Ruby called.

Guiltily, she stepped back. "I . . . am a friend of Mr. Locke's. Can you tell me if he has been a client here long?"

The lad shrugged. "Half a year, I reckon."

"But you seem so well acquainted."

He grinned. "He's a generous fellow."

"Ah, that explains it." Jane returned the lad's grin. But *did* it explain it?

Jane walked back to the law offices and let herself in. A bespectacled clerk looked up as she entered and rose to his feet. Heavyset, ruddy-cheeked Mr. Coine was just stepping from his office, head bent over a sheaf of papers. He looked up and hesitated midstride.

"Mrs. Bell! I did not expect you. Tell me I am not forgetting an appointment."

"No, Mr. Coine. I had a few questions for you, if it is not inconvenient."

"Not at all." He handed the papers to the clerk and gestured toward his office. "Come in, come in. May I offer you some refreshment?"

"Nothing for me, thank you."

She sat in the offered chair and he sat behind his desk. He moved aside a stack of papers, entwined his fingers, and leaned forward. "Now. How may I help you?"

"What can you tell me about the, em, marriage settlement my father and husband arranged?"

He spread his hands. "Whatever you like. I mentioned it after the will reading, did I not? Pray, tell me I did not neglect to do so."

"I'm sure you did everything properly, but I confess, I remember little you said after hearing I'd inherited the entire inn."

"Ah . . ." Mr. Coine nodded his understanding. "And you were busy with wedding preparations when we drew up the original terms."

Jane nodded. She had signed some papers before the nuptials but had paid them little heed—her mind full of the ceremony, the wedding breakfast, and the trip to follow.

"Forgive me, Mr. Coine, but could you reiterate the details?"

"Of course. The amount of two thousand pounds was settled upon you in case of your widowhood. Your father thought it sufficient that, if need be, you could live comfortably, though simply, off the interest. The way prices have risen in recent years, that may have been optimistic. But a nice nest egg, all the same."

"But John left me the inn in total. Surely I don't still receive any sort of jointure?"

"This money was not John's—it came from your father. It was a portion of your dowry set aside for your future. Your father insisted. What would become of you in the event of John's death if the inn burned down, or was bequeathed to someone else, or failed financially?"

Jane's heart thudded hard. She and her father had never been close, and she had resented so many things he had done—selling her horse, selling their home and its contents without so much as a by your leave, and then that final betrayal. But now she realized that he had considered her welfare after all. Perhaps Jane should have thanked her father instead of resenting him. But it was too late now.

When she said nothing for several moments, Mr. Coine continued, "Because you did not inquire then or since, I assumed you planned not to touch those funds at present, but to save the money for your retirement or—"

"My dotage?"

"Well, something like that, yes."

The amount was not nearly enough to pay off the loan, or to buy Fairmont. Would it be possible to live off the interest, as her father thought, if invested wisely?

Jane asked, "What rate of interest might I reasonably expect?"

"Depends on the market and how the funds were invested—bank annuities or bonds, the navy five percents, stocks . . . I would estimate four percent per annum. You would have to talk with the bank."

Could she live on eighty pounds a year on her own somewhere? It would mean no horse or carriage and only a servant or two—perhaps a kindly married couple—to do the plucking and wood chopping and fires. But might it be done? She doubted it. She would have to ask Mercy to help her estimate living expenses.

"Who invested the funds for my father? The banker here in Wishford?"

Mr. Coine frowned. "No. Your father chose Mr. Blomfield, since you would be living in Ivy Hill."

Jane reared her head back. "Mr. Coine, I don't know if you are well acquainted with him, but—"

He lifted a palm. "I am not privy to his dealings, Mrs. Bell. I have met him and his partners in Salisbury, but we are not close colleagues."

"Well then, I should tell you that recently Mr. Blomfield made me aware of a large debt owed his bank—an outstanding loan John took out without my knowledge."

The man grimaced. "I am sorry to hear it."

Jane nodded. "So, am I correct in assuming I no longer have any right to the two thousand, since I owe the bank that much and thousands more?"

"No, Jane. This settlement is not subject to your husband's

debts. It was set aside out of your portion for your sole and separate use. You could use that money toward the debt, if you wish, but that is your decision, not the bank's."

"In that case, it surprises me that Mr. Blomfield made no mention of these funds."

"That is surprising."

Jane sat in thought, dark suspicions brewing.

But Mr. Coine conjectured reasonably, "Perhaps he simply assumed you would not wish to use personal funds to deal with business debts."

"Perhaps. But I believe I had better pay a call on Mr. Blomfield and ask him myself."

The lawyer nodded. "No doubt you will find everything in order. But if you have any problems, do not hesitate to return. Or send word and I shall come to you, at your convenience."

"Thank you, Mr. Coine. I shall."

Mr. Locke was waiting beside the gig when Jane exited the law office. He helped her in, and in a matter of minutes they were on their way back out of Wishford, passing a meadow and beginning the ascent up the hill.

"What did you learn?" he began conversationally.

She sent him a wry look. "That you are very inquisitive."

He urged Ruby to more speed up the incline. "I could say the same of you, you know."

She glanced over at him, and he smiled. "I saw you outside the bank."

Her prepared excuses evaporated under his knowing smirk. "It is a public street. And you don't have anything to hide, I trust?"

When he made no answer, she went on, "I also learned that you are surprisingly well known in Wishford. And that your banker seems a far more cheerful character than my own."

Gabriel Locke chuckled. "Yes, Matthews is a good man. I like him a great deal. Trust him, too." He glanced over at her again. "And the settlement?"

"It is as you said. My father settled money on me before I married. He intended it as a nest egg for the future, should the worst happen, though I doubt the amount sufficient to support me for long. That is, assuming . . ."

"Assuming what?"

"Nothing. I will just feel more confident about its existence after I speak with Mr. Blomfield again. He and his partners supposedly invested the funds on my father's behalf. But he has never mentioned it to me."

Jane wasn't sure why she was telling this to Mr. Locke, when he already distrusted the banker. She supposed she hoped he would say, *"Of course the money is still there. I wouldn't worry if I were you."*

Instead he said, "Shall I take you there directly?"

"No. I shall go myself later. I should see if Thora needs anything first."

He nodded and at the crest of the hill turned Ruby into The Bell courtyard.

The settlement of money in her name, if it existed, glimmered on the horizon like an oasis. It seemed to represent her last chance at independence—freedom from the burden of trying to save an inn she'd never wanted.

CHAPTER

Fourteen

Finding everything under control at The Bell, Jane walked to the bank, arriving just before closing time. She resolved to remain civil, and hopefully avoid angering the man who would decide The Bell's fate.

"Hello, Mr. Blomfield. I am here about my settlement."

The man stilled, his small eyes flat as he looked at her. "Oh?"

"I must say I am surprised you did not think to mention it before, knowing of our financial difficulties."

He casually raised his hands, but his expression and posture were anything but relaxed. "You did not ask."

She said, "I am asking now. What is the present balance?"

"I would have to check."

"Then please do." Jane sat down, though he'd not invited her to do so.

He shrugged. "If memory serves, perhaps a thousand pounds."

Jane frowned. "But Mr. Coine said two thousand."

"Did he?"

"Yes, I spoke to him in Wishford earlier today."

Mr. Blomfield leaned back in his chair. "That may have been the original amount, but that was eight years ago."

"So would it not have accumulated interest?"

"On the contrary. We have endured many difficult years and wars and shortages. Not to mention market crashes and bank failures."

"Are you saying the amount may have actually . . . decreased?" Jane's chest tightened.

"That is exactly what I am saying."

No wonder he had not mentioned the settlement. Jane said, "Mr. Coine thought I could count on four percent?"

"That might have been the case were it all in government annuities, but your father entrusted that money to us, and we preferred a diversified approach."

She took a deep breath, trying to remain calm. "But why would you invest a woman's settlement in some risky venture?"

"Investments are never without risk, Mrs. Bell. As my partners and I know all too well." He gave her a significant look.

Jane forced her chin up. "In any case, I would like to know the present value. Please check, Mr. Blomfield. I shall wait."

He spread his hands. "What is the sudden hurry? Have you decided to live on your own and let Patrick Bell assume the debt? Or to sell the inn and buy another property?"

"I have not decided anything, Mr. Blomfield. How can I, when you refuse to give me the information I ask for?"

"Pray do not upset yourself, you—"

"I do not upset myself. You do. Shall I return with Mr. Coine? He kindly offered to intercede if I discovered any problems with the funds."

"No need to inconvenience Alfred Coine," Mr. Blomfield said with a sour twist on his lips. He rose. "I am sure we can settle this satisfactorily on our own. Please wait here, Mrs. Bell. I shall return as soon as may be."

He returned ten minutes later with a ledger. Opened it, then pronounced, "I must remind you of the nature of this firm. People deposit money, which my partners and I invest in the hopes of earning a profitable rate of return. However, due to a few unfortunate investments, especially one particular loan"—here he coughed twice—"instead of a return, the account has lost money. The value is now just over one thousand."

One thousand . . . Not enough to invest in a government annuity and live off the interest. Not enough to support herself for the long term.

He formed a smug smile. "That amount, added to the profit from the inn if you sell, would make a tidy sum all told. Shall I speak to Mr. Gordon on your behalf about proceeding with the sale . . . ?"

Jane shook her head. "I may be female, Mr. Blomfield, but I am not stupid. I will not sell the inn for far less than it is worth. You may convey *that* to Mr. Gordon on my behalf."

"Then will you put the settlement toward the loan?"

"No. But I would like every penny of it in ready cash or bank draft."

"But . . ." His face reddened, and the cords in his neck protruded. "Mrs. Bell, that is not how this works. It is not as though I have all that money sitting in a vault in the back room. Some of it is tied up in loans and Consols and other stock. Nor is withdrawing such a sum advisable. Most ladies in your situation invest the principal and spend only the interest."

"What interest? The investment has lost money. Apparently, I would be wise to withdraw the rest before more is lost."

"Then I will help you transfer the remainder into a secure little annuity."

"No, thank you. I would rather entrust it to the bank in Wishford. Mr. Matthews seems very obliging."

"You have met him?" The banker's composure began to crumble at last.

"He seems a most personable man," Jane replied. Let Blomfield think she'd been in Wishford to meet the banker.

She rose. "I will give you until the end of the month to produce the full amount." She hoped he didn't hear her voice tremble. "If you fail, I shall send Mr. Coine to retrieve it for me. Good day, Mr. Blomfield," she said, and took her leave before he could object further.

The next day, Jane went looking for Mr. Drake, hoping to talk with him again. He was still lodging at The Bell, as far as she knew, but she had not seen him since the day before. Nor was he in any of the public rooms now. She asked Colin, and he reported that he had seen the man go out that morning but had not yet returned.

The vicar's wife stopped by and asked if Jane would be willing to bring flowers for the pulpit a week from Sunday. One of the older women in the rotation had recently resigned her place. Jane agreed. She could easily manage a vase of flowers at this time of year.

Mrs. Paley thanked her and bustled out as quickly as she'd bustled in, no doubt off to attend to a dozen other parish duties.

After she left, Jane spent an hour in her small garden behind the lodge, removing spent flower heads, weeding, and watering in preparation for the following week.

Late that afternoon, Jane returned to the inn. She glanced into the taproom and saw Mr. Drake sitting at his ease, pint at his elbow, talking companionably with the barman, Bobbin, while the potboy gathered up the glasses and tankards left here and there on tables.

Bobbin screwed up his face, gazing upward at the beamed ceiling. "Miss Payne . . . ?" he said. "No, can't say the name sounds familiar. But then, I don't mix much with ladies."

Bobbin looked over and noticed her in the hall. "Ah. There's Mrs. Bell. Ma'am, do you know of a Miss Payne hereabouts?"

"I don't believe so, no."

Mr. Drake turned toward her and rose. "Good afternoon, Mrs. Bell."

"Good afternoon. I am sorry to interrupt."

Mr. Drake smiled warmly. "Not at all. We were only passing the time."

Jane said, "Perhaps if you tell me Miss Payne's given name, I might—"

James waved away her offer. "Never mind. We have happier tidings to discuss."

"Oh?"

A pair of militia officers entered, and while Bobbin took their orders, Mr. Drake gestured toward a quiet inglenook. "Come and have a drink with me, Jane. Help me celebrate."

"Celebrate what?"

He spread his arms. "You are looking at the new owner of the Fairmont."

Jane gaped. "*You* bought Fairmont House?" Her heart thudded.

"I hope you aren't displeased."

"I . . . don't know what to think." She sank onto the high-backed bench. "What about your hotel in Southampton?"

He took a seat opposite. "I will keep that as well. I have a capable manager, as I mentioned."

Jane's mind spun and clattered to a jarring conclusion. "You were the man who put an offer on The Bell! Quite a low offer, as a matter of fact."

"I did, yes. I admit I came here with that purpose in mind. When I saw the plans for the turnpike, I guessed the inn might be acquired at a good price. But after becoming acquainted with its charming landlady, I retracted my offer."

"After I refused it, I think you mean. I told Mr. Blomfield yesterday I would not sell at such a low price."

"Good for you." He nodded approvingly. "But by then I'd already set my sights elsewhere. I considered buying land and having a place purpose-built. But it seemed unlikely such an investment would yield quickly. So I decided instead to convert an existing property with all the stately elegance and fine architectural details so often overlooked in modern buildings. It will still take time and expense, especially with the place sitting empty so long. But in the end, I believe it shall be worth it, especially considering its advantageous location."

"Wait. . . . Are you saying you plan to make Fairmont House . . . a hotel?"

"Of course. What did you think I meant to do with it?"

"Live in it, like a normal person."

He chuckled. "There's no profit in that. Besides, I already have a perfectly good suite of rooms in Southampton if I simply wanted a dwelling."

"But . . . but . . ." she sputtered. "It's a manor house. With a long history. Meant for a family . . ."

"Mrs. Bell. Jane." His brow furrowed. "I am surprised at your reaction. The agent mentioned you had grown up there and hated to see the place rot. I thought you'd be relieved."

"Relieved? To see my family home become a hostelry for strangers?"

"But your family sold it years ago. I had no idea you still felt any claim to the place."

"I . . ." Jane ducked her head, knowing how illogical and futile her feelings were. If her father could have foreseen the future, would he still have sold the house so abruptly?

"Had you intentions for the property?" he asked.

She lifted her chin. "I had thought I might buy it back one day."

He sobered. "Did you? I had no idea. I am sorry. I shall go to Mr. Gordon and retract, if possible."

"No. Don't. Thank you, but don't do that. I am being utterly foolish. Reclaiming the place was only a girlish dream. I haven't the means to do so, nor likely ever shall. Please, forget I protested." She managed a smile. "I wish you happy in your new venture."

He regarded her steadily, then murmured, "Brave Jane."

Another realization struck her. "Oh no! You will not only own my old home, you will also be my new competition! You mean to steal business from us, don't you, *JD*?"

"Oh come, Jane. You are not afraid of a little healthy competition, are you?"

"Afraid is exactly what I am. You know we are struggling already."

"I also know you've lost several coaching lines and have never enjoyed much post-chaise traffic. I hope to gain the lines you've lost and court private post travelers as well. A place like the Fairmont would appeal to the upper crust, you must admit."

Jane could not deny it. She said sarcastically, "And of course you will turn away any of our current customers."

"Jane. Keep your customers satisfied and they shall have no cause to stray. Once the novelty wears off at any rate." He winked at her.

"If we have any customers left by that point! When will you open?"

"I'm not sure. I need to meet with an architect and hire a builder. But I shall keep you apprised."

She regarded him curiously. "Will you? Why?"

"I see no reason why we cannot be collegial, even friendly competitors."

"Do you not? Your optimism is inspiring."

"Why, thank you. I do what I can." He smiled, which emphasized the deep grooves on either side of his mouth, masculine and appealing.

"I shall remove to the Fairmont as soon as I am able," he added. "I plan to reside there while I oversee construction of new stables as well as repairs in other parts of the house. By the way, I'm acquainted with a builder in Salisbury, but if you can recommend a good local man, I would be much obliged."

"The Kingsley brothers build most things around here—from my little lodge to the conservatory at Thornvale. Everyone speaks highly of them."

"Excellent. Thank you."

Something niggled at Jane. "I have to ask—why here, of all places? We're not the only village threatened by the turnpike. There must be better places to open a hotel."

"I have my reasons."

She opened her mouth to respond, but before she could pry further, he tapped a finger to her nose. "Personal reasons."

On Sunday, Jane walked out of church beside Mercy, while Aunt Matilda went on ahead with their pupils. Rachel had been absent again that morning, no doubt home at her father's bedside. Mr. Paley had prayed for Sir William during the service. Apparently, he was weakening by the day, though remained in good spirits, and still enjoyed his favorite books.

Jane thought of her own father. And as they walked, she told Mercy about the settlement he had arranged and admitted that perhaps she had somewhat misjudged him.

"I am glad to hear it, Jane. I know he did some things that hurt you, but I hope this will help you forgive him."

Forgive him? Jane thought, lapsing into silence. *For the house, and Hermione, and betraying Mamma's memory?* Besides, he was no longer there to forgive.

"So . . . will you join us?" Mercy asked, apparently for the second time.

"Hm?"

"The Ladies Tea and Knitting Society meets tomorrow night."

"The Ladies Tea and Knitting Society?" Jane repeated dubiously. "I don't know, Mercy."

"Oh, do come, Jane. I think you will find it . . . edifying."

"Heavens. That sounds serious."

"It is, but pleasant too."

"I haven't knitted in years. I can sew, but—"

"You don't need to knit. It is more of a symbol. Though some bring needlework to pass the time."

"To pass the time? How boring are these meetings?"

"Not boring at all. But some ladies like to keep their hands busy while we discuss problems and ideas. Besides, with the price of textiles, there is never a shortage of mending to do."

"What sort of problems? Women's troubles?"

Mercy laughed. "No. Business problems, mostly."

"What sort of business are you talking about?" Jane asked, growing increasingly wary.

"All sorts. The fact is, we are a group of women managing businesses of one kind or another, though we keep that aspect rather quiet. Tends to make men uncomfortable. Some women too."

"So the knitting is merely a guise?"

"Basically," Mercy agreed, eyes twinkling.

"What about the tea?" Jane asked. "Is that a guise as well?"

"Heavens no. Tea is mandatory. What would a clutch of women do without tea? We take turns providing it to share the expense. Thankfully, it has come down in price, though still dear."

Jane said, "There can't be many women in business in a village the size of Ivy Hill."

"You might be surprised. Our attendance usually numbers from eight to ten. Not every woman wishes to join us. And some attend only occasionally when they can spare the time. Aunt Matty watches the girls for me so I can get away. Just come to one meeting and see what you think."

"Oh, very well," Jane said. "Though I don't consider myself a woman in business." *Not yet, at any rate.*

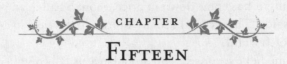

Chapter

Fifteen

On Monday evening, the Ladies Tea and Knitting Society met in a small room in the village hall. A dozen chairs were set up facing one end of the room, while at the back, Mercy scooped tea into a pot and waited for the kettle to boil on a corner stove.

"Can I do anything?" Jane asked.

"Yes, arrange these biscuits on a plate, if you please."

Jane did so, happy to keep her hands busy and focus her attention on something other than her nervous stomach as women began to enter, some chatting to each other as they came, others slipping in quietly as though to avoid drawing attention. All sent curious looks her way.

The dressmaker, Mrs. Shabner, Jane knew. And the laundress, Mrs. Snyder. She had also briefly met Mrs. Burlingame, who carted goods to and from outlying businesses. She recognized other faces as well but could not put names to all.

Jane stood there, feeling out of place as Mercy made the introductions, including the nature of each woman's trade. Jane would not remember all the names but was surprised to learn the variety of businesses with women at their helms. There was a wax-and-tallow chandler, a poulteress, a house-and-sign painter, and a piano tuner, among others.

Jane looked around as more women entered the room. How

strange to find herself at a social gathering with people she had previously only seen or spoken to from across a service counter— not viewed as her social equals. How did they view her? In the tightening of Mrs. Barton's mouth, Jane thought she detected a trace of censure or perhaps only incredulity. Could she blame her? When Jane had treated her with condescension—though hopefully not rudeness—when they'd last spoken about an order of cheese? Mrs. Bushby, gardener, florist, and greenhouse proprietor, gave her a small smile of acknowledgment. She and Jane had talked often of plants and seeds, and Jane bought hothouse flowers for the cemetery and sometimes the inn when her own garden was not yet in bloom.

Were these women aware of The Bell's financial problems? The poulteress probably was. She recently came to the door to collect what she was owed, but, unable to pay the bill, Mrs. Rooke sent her away empty-handed.

And worse, Jane wondered if the laundress remembered the last time she had spoken to her in private, asking if she might help remove the stubborn stains from her favorite nightdress. Bloodstains.

"I have to say, I am surprised to see you here," Mrs. Barton, the dairywoman, spoke up. "Thora Bell I could understand, though she has never joined us. But I don't know that we are fine enough for the likes of the former Miss Fairmont."

"Bridget!" Mercy admonished.

The ruddy-faced woman held up her palm. "I mean no disrespect, but we've always been honest here, and I'd hate to see that change now."

Mercy glanced at Jane, and seeing her make no attempt to speak for herself, gently replied, "You may not be aware, Bridget. But Jane is the owner of The Bell, and has been since her husband died."

"Well, having one's name on a deed doesn't always indicate who's doing the work, does it, girls?"

Around the room, heads nodded and knowing looks were exchanged.

Mercy went on, "I thought we might be able to help Jane. Some of you know The Bell is facing difficulties. And Jane must soon decide whether to take on the management of the inn to make it profitable, or sell. But for tonight—her first meeting—I thought we would allow her to simply observe and ask questions if she likes, but feel no pressure to participate until she feels comfortable."

Murmurs of assent arose, punctuated by a few grumbles, and the meeting commenced.

The first topic raised was the overcrowding of market stalls and the bias of the village council to assign the better stalls to men, whether they resided in Ivy Hill or not. Mercy offered to speak to Sir Timothy on their behalf, to see if he might sway the council to be more fair to Ivy Hill's merchants—be they men or women.

"What's next?" she asked.

The poulteress, Miss Featherstone, rose. "I was going to ask your advice about what to do when a customer don't pay, but as Mrs. Bell is here tonight, I shall hold that question for another time."

She sat back down, and Jane ducked her head in embarrassment.

Later, when they paused to refill their tea and biscuits, Jane screwed up her courage and approached Miss Featherstone, promising to pay the poultry bill herself as soon as she could.

Then she sought out Mrs. Klein. "I was sorry to hear about your husband. He was our piano tuner back at Fairmont House."

"Yes, I remember. Unfortunately, your father was not willing to continue on with me after Mr. Klein died, though I tried to assure him my husband had trained me well."

"I did not realize you shared his skill," Jane said. Her father had begun bringing in a man from Salisbury—an expensive proposition, and Jane had continued with him after marrying John. Perhaps she should reconsider.

The woman nodded her understanding. "Many doubt my ability."

The door burst open, and the vicar's wife bustled in, out of breath. "Sorry to be so late."

"Mrs. Paley, must we remind you again?" Bridget Barton mildly chastised. "You do *not* operate a business."

Mrs. Paley tossed her hat on a chair, her hair beneath askew, her face flushed. "Do I not?" she challenged, her voice rising in uncharacteristic exasperation. "I am about God's business every day, not to mention church business. True, my husband is the head and I the helpmeet, but he can't do it all—or as he says, not much of anything—without me. Who manages the charity guild and donations of clothing for the parish poor? Who keeps Mr. Paley's vestments snowy white, his sons in line, and his hair from looking like a wild bush? Who deals with unhappy parishioners and struggles daily to meet their sometimes unrealistic expectations? Why, I am more than a woman of business. I am politician, teacher, physician, editor, budget stretcher, manager, and feather smoother."

She looked from startled face to startled face and flopped into a chair, spent. "Forgive me. Beyond my home, this is the only place I can be my true self and not have to bite my tongue at every turn. But I am sorry to sound the martyr. I am blessed, I know. It has just been the most trying week."

Mercy said gently, "We understand, Mrs. Paley."

The vicar's wife turned to Jane, eyes downcast. "And Mrs. Bell. I am doubly sorry. What an initiation by fire at your first meeting! I hope it shall not be your last. Not on my account."

It might be Jane's last meeting, but certainly not because of the vicar's wife, whom she liked very much indeed.

As the meeting continued, Jane again looked at the assembled women of varying ages, wearing dresses of various styles—none very fashionable. And their hands—oh, the hands of some of these women! Their professions ranged from the learned like Mercy, to the artisan like the candlemaker and piano tuner, to the humble dairywoman and laundress. Could she be like these women? Capable and independent, hardworking and hands worn? Did she want to be?

Mrs. Bushby rose and reported that her greenhouse had been vandalized—shot at and glass broken—by drunken poachers, she guessed, as hunting season had yet to begin.

"Have you talked to the magistrate?" Mercy asked.

"Yes, but there's nothing he can do without evidence. In the meantime, the glazier requires payment up front to replace the glass, and I won't have sufficient funds until later in the growing season. He wants six pounds!"

"Six pounds!" The women were scandalized.

Mrs. Paley tried to bite a biscuit, then discreetly set it in her saucer. She said, "The vicarage garden is out of control. Perhaps you could do some work for me toward that amount?"

Mrs. Bushy shook her head. "I don't want charity, ma'am."

"Charity? Hardly. You have not seen my garden."

Mrs. Klein rose. "My horse is ailing, and without him, I can't travel very far. Heaven knows there are not enough pianos in Ivy Hill and Wishford alone to keep me busy."

"You can borrow my mule, now the planting's done," Mrs. Bushby offered.

"Or I can take you as far as Codford and Wilton on my weekly route," the carter, Mrs. Burlingame, added.

It crossed Jane's mind to offer Gabriel Locke's services, farrier and self-taught veterinarian that he seemed to be. But in the end, she remained silent, not sure her help—or interference—would be welcome.

"I have a question," one of the Cook sisters asked. "Do you think it's wrong that Miss Morris leaves her father's name on her card and advertisements, as though he is actually still doing the work?"

Becky Morris, the daughter of a deceased painter, protested, "At least I have some work to do this way!"

"Ladies, we are here to help one another, not judge."

Miss Morris added, "She's not the only one criticizing me lately. Mrs. Prater gave me a dressing down just last week. Said climbing ladders to paint houses and signs is unladylike and indecent. Indecent! When she has never complained before. Well, come to find out, young Delbert Prater had been seen looking up my skirts, the rascal!"

The women tutted sympathetically, and a few giggled.

Mrs. Shabner asked, "You do wear drawers, I trust, Becky?"

Becky flashed her a look. "I do now."

Jane bit her lip to stifle a laugh of her own. She smiled at Becky Morris. In the next moment, she felt a stab of guilt. She had seen the fine calligraphy and painting on the Praters' storefront and assumed a man had done it. Apparently, Jane had a lot to learn. In more ways than one.

After the meeting, Mercy and Jane walked out together as far as the High Street.

"What did you think?"

"I don't know, Mercy. I admire how the women help each other, and how hard they work. But I still wish I could return to my old life."

"Your old life? Which life is that?"

"You know what I mean." Jane gestured to the inn across the street. "I wasn't raised for this. I feel so ill prepared."

"Is the 'old life' you idealize really so ideal?" Mercy asked. "Look at Rachel Ashford. Her father disgraced and on his deathbed. And her to lose her home as soon as he dies. Would you trade places with her?"

Jane sighed. "No."

"That old life doesn't exist any longer."

"Not for me," Jane agreed. "Not here."

"Do you think if you moved away somewhere you would be happy?" Mercy asked earnestly. "Sitting alone in some rented room, reading and playing your pianoforte all day for your own amusement? Would you not grow bored? Not to mention lonely?"

That was basically how Jane had been living for the last year. And she had been both bored and lonely since John died. And even before, if she were to admit the truth.

Mercy went on, "And don't think that living with Aunt Matty and me is the solution either. I have to keep my parents' bedchamber available, though they visit but rarely. And I have already offered the spare room to Rachel, for when the time comes. You know she is proud and hates to ask for help. But even if we had another room available, would you really want to retreat back into your hermit-like existence now that you've finally begun to emerge?"

Would she?

Mercy pressed her hand, her eyes bright by lamplight. "Manage the inn, Jane; save it. Have a mission in life. Discover that work worth doing is about more than profit and toil. It's about using the gifts and ability you've been given to serve your fellow man and please your Maker."

Jane stood there, stilled by Mercy's entreaty. She swallowed, "My goodness, Mercy. You ought to be a reformer."

A slow smile transformed Mercy's face. "And who says I am not?"

They parted ways, each to her own home. Nearing the lodge, Jane glanced through The Bell archway and saw Gabriel Locke sitting on the bench outside, whittling something.

He looked up at her approach. "Hello, Mrs. Bell. You're out late."

Jane walked closer. "I attended my first meeting of the Ladies Tea and Knitting Society."

"Tea and knitting?" he asked, forehead furrowed.

"Can you keep a secret?"

"Yes."

She lowered her voice. "Its members are all women in business."

His dark brows rose. "Are they indeed? So you've decided, then."

"I have not deci—"

"I am glad," he went on, not hearing her demur. "I've been dreading what would happen to Ivy Hill if it lost its only coaching inn—its communication point with the outside world and employment for so many who live here." He spread his hands expansively. "Not only the staff itself, but also the baker, the butcher, the chandler who supplies our candles and those long tapers for the coach lamps. The farms that supply our carriage horses. The wheelwright, the carters who deliver goods, not to mention the acting troupes and revivalists The Bell has hosted over the years. And all those employed by or benefited by the inn, in turn patronize the remaining businesses and give to the charity guild and poor fund."

He circled his hand. "Village life is like an ivy vine climbing a great oak. You cut off the vine at the root, and all the way up the tree, the leaves wither. We're all connected."

For a moment Jane stared at him, taken aback by his long and impassioned speech, when he was usually a man of few words, even standoffish in her company.

"My goodness—that was almost poetic."

"No. It is a hard truth. I understand that in some ways it would be easier for you to sell out or hand the reins to Patrick. But you have more than yourself to think of in this situation."

"And that was *not* poetic but a lecture," she said coldly. "One I did not ask for." Who did this man think he was to speak to her so critically?

He grimaced. "I know it isn't my place, but with John gone, I—"

"Please tell me you don't presume to take his place."

"Of course not. But set aside your injured pride for a moment and consider this. John could have left The Bell to Patrick. But he did not. He left it to you. For a reason."

"Because he was duty bound to provide for me."

Gabriel shook his head. "If that were the case, he could have increased your settlement or made your upkeep a stipulation of any bequest to Patrick. But he did not. He left it to you because he thought you were the best person for the job."

"I doubt that," Jane said, thinking, *He left it to me only because he wanted the inn to go to his children eventually, through me. But there are no children.*

As if reading her mind, Gabriel lowered his voice and said, "Remember, John could have rewritten his will at any point."

"Perhaps he meant to but ran out of time," she said, then sighed. "Listen. I know John considered you a friend. And he offered you a place of employment here, I presume, because of that. But *I* do not know you well enough to . . ."

"Trust me?" he supplied.

"Can you blame me?"

He rose. "No. You are a wise woman, Mrs. Bell. For your husband *did* trust me. And look where it got him."

She shot him a look. "What do you mean by that?"

He ran a work-worn hand over his face. "Never mind. Forgive me. That was a callous thing to say."

"But what did it mean?" Jane repeated.

He turned toward the stables. "It means it's time I said good night."

Jane returned to the lodge, her thoughts in a tangle. She set aside her gloves and sat at John's old desk. It was time—past time—to make her decision.

She thought again of the pending loan, the loss of stage lines, the new competition from James Drake. It would be easier to give up. Or give over to Patrick.

But then she considered the words Gabriel Locke had spoken. *"All those employed by or benefited by the inn, in turn patronize the remaining businesses and give to the charity guild and poor fund. Village life is like an ivy vine climbing a great oak. You cut off the vine at the root, and all the way up the tree, the leaves wither. We're all connected."*

When he'd said the words, she hadn't fully understood them. But now, as she sat there and thought again of vines and leaves, she didn't think of the villagers and shopkeepers she recognized only in passing, people she didn't know personally and who were not her concern. Now she thought of Mrs. Bushby, Mrs. Klein, and Miss Morris. She thought of the baker and chandler and cheesemaker. The carter and laundress and poulteress. And of course of The Bell staff. They all supplied the inn or served those who passed through its doors. Would she close the door on all of them? Or risk Patrick doing so?

No. She would not. Not if she could help it.

The next morning, Jane crossed the yard to the inn, determined to tell Thora her decision. She wasn't certain how her mother-in-law would react but knew Patrick would not be pleased. She swallowed her dread and entered the office. Thora was alone inside.

Before she could say a word, Thora launched in, "Jane, have you decided what to do about selling? Or about allowing Patrick to assume the debt? You've had your head in the sand long enough. It is time to face reality."

Emotions washed over Jane—irritation, anger, hurt. She bit back the defensive words that sprang to her lips. Instead, she steeled herself and said, "You are right. As a matter of fact, I have decided to keep the inn myself."

"Good."

Jane reared her head back. "I am surprised. I thought you would like the idea of Patrick owning the inn instead of me—or instead of some stranger."

"Patrick is my son, and of course I want what is best for him. But there are many ways he can earn his livelihood. Other places he can live. Where will *you* live if we lose The Bell? Which could still happen, you know."

"Yes, I know. Still, I hope Patrick won't be too disappointed when I tell him."

"Tell me what?" Patrick asked, appearing in the doorway with the fare book in hand.

"Jane has decided to try to save the inn herself," Thora explained.

Patrick's eyebrows rose. "Has she indeed?"

"Well . . . not *by* myself," Jane quickly interjected. "I hope you two will help."

"I see . . ." Patrick set the book on the desk and crossed his arms. "Well. Good luck."

Jane studied him warily, but it was difficult to tell whether or not he was sincere.

"Now that you've decided," Thora said, "how will you proceed?"

Jane replied, "I think we should all sit down together and discuss what is best to be done."

Thora shook her head. "You don't want me there."

"Yes, I do, Thora. I value your experience and opinions." *Most of the time*, Jane added to herself. "And you too, Patrick."

Thora said, "Then I think we ought to include Walter Talbot as well. He knows more about managing this inn that anyone."

Patrick's brows rose again. "More than you, Mamma?"

"He was far more involved with the transport side of things than I ever was." Thora added, "And what about Gabriel Locke? For any improvements needed in the stable yard."

Jane hesitated. "I doubt Mr. Locke knows much about innkeeping, beyond shoeing horses and caring for their ailments."

"On the contrary, he seems to know a great deal about horses and managing ostlers," Thora said. "Both key to a successful coaching inn."

"Very well. If you think he can contribute. And what about Colin?"

Thora pulled a face. "If we must. Though perhaps someone ought to remain at the reception desk, just in case."

Jane acquiesced. "I suppose you are right."

She wondered again what Thora had against Colin McFarland but pushed the thought to the back of her mind. Right now, she had a meeting to plan.

CHAPTER
SIXTEEN

After Jane left the office, Patrick and Thora remained. Patrick picked up the overdue butcher's bill and looked over it, and Thora stepped to the window.

A few minutes quietly passed, then Thora asked, "How much do you know about Gabriel Locke?"

Patrick shrugged, eyes remaining on the paper. "Not much. Why?"

Thora turned again to the window, looking across the yard where the farrier stood talking to Jane, a chestnut horse tethered nearby. She had seen them speaking together several times recently, and it raised questions—and suspicions—in her mind.

"Where did he work before coming here?"

"I don't know. He was here when I came. Was he not working here before you left for Aunt Di's?"

"Yes. But I thought it was only temporary. I didn't think he'd stay on so long."

Patrick glanced up. "Oh? Why?"

Thora thought back. "He was a friend of John's. They met in London, I believe. I had heard John speak highly of him but did not meet him myself until after John was killed. Mr. Locke was with John when he died."

Patrick frowned. "Was he indeed . . . ?"

"Yes. They were in Epsom together when the accident happened. He accompanied the coffin back to Ivy Hill personally." Pain sliced Thora's heart at the thought. The awful, black memory. The shock and horror and grief of losing her firstborn son.

She swallowed. Her grieving period was over, she sternly reminded herself.

She took a steadying breath and continued, "Talbot is the one who told me Mr. Locke would be staying on as farrier for a time. Cabot had deserted us for a better offer, at the Crown in Wishford, and we'd yet to find a permanent replacement. Jake Fuller filled in when he could, and Talbot tried to manage the stable yard along with the rest of his duties. But it was too much. He called Locke's arrival a godsend."

"Old Cabbage went to work at the Crown?" Patrick asked incredulously. As a boy, he had misunderstood Cabot's name as *Cabbage*, and had never referred to him by anything else.

Thora nodded. "I recalled John mentioning Locke's knowledge of horses, so I didn't question it at the time. With John gone, horses were not uppermost in my mind."

"Of course not, Mamma. Again, I am sorry I wasn't here."

She nodded. "I did try to get word to you when it happened. But my letters were returned."

"I should have been more diligent in letting you know my changes in direction."

"Well. You are here now."

"Yes, I am."

Thora squinted in memory. "I think I even mentioned something to Talbot before I left. Asking him to find out how long Locke planned to stay and allow plenty of time to find a new horseman. Good farriers are difficult to find."

Patrick nodded. "You asked too much of Talbot. Always did."

"Well, I knew Jane would not think to do so." As Patrick's words sank in, Thora tilted her head, regarding her son closely. "What do you mean by that? About asking too much of Talbot?"

Patrick lifted a shoulder and pursed his lip. "Just what I said.

You asked a great deal of the man. Piling on responsibilities be-yond those of any other manager or head porter that I know of. No wonder he left."

"Are you saying it was my fault he left?"

"Not exactly. But when he got the chance, he took it, didn't he? And sharp-like."

"Walter Talbot inherited the family farm after his brother died. That is why he left."

"If you say so. Never imagined our learned Mr. Talbot a yeoman farmer. Thought he'd lease the land to tenants. Especially with his brother's wife still living there in the farmhouse. Or perhaps that's why he moved in. . . ."

"Don't you start on that, Patrick. Those rumors are unkind and untrue."

Patrick lifted a hand. "I wouldn't hold it against him either way. In some cultures, a man is expected to marry and support his brother's widow, not forbidden to, as is done here." He gave Thora a cheeky grin and waggled his brows. "I empathize."

"Don't," she commanded. "In the eyes of the law and the church, Jane is your sister."

"I know, Mamma. I only like to tease you. Anyway, why are you asking about Locke now?"

"I see him talking to Jane quite often lately."

Patrick nodded. "Very opinionated, our Mr. Locke. Horses never rested long enough or fed well enough for our fastidious farrier. He's always complaining about something. I don't give his grumbling much heed, so he must be taking his grievances to Jane now."

His words trailed away and she felt him study her profile. "What has you worried? An irritable farrier seems the least of our troubles at present."

He walked over and stood next to her at the window, following the direction of her gaze. In the stable yard, the farrier groomed an impressive chestnut horse while Jane talked. Thora couldn't hear the conversation, but Locke nodded at whatever she'd asked—

agreeing to come to the meeting perhaps. Jane smiled her thanks, her gaze lingering on the man.

Beside her, Patrick murmured, "Ah . . . I see."

Thora asked, "How much are we paying this esteemed farrier?"

Patrick pursed his lips. "I don't know. I've only been here two months. Haven't paid quarterly wages yet." He returned to the desk. "Let me look."

He opened the wage log and began paging through it. Finding the page, he ran his finger down a column of numbers . . . and frowned, peering closer.

"What?" Thora asked.

Instead of answering, Patrick turned back several pages to the previous quarter. "That's odd."

"What is?" Thora stepped to the desk and bent to see what had caused Patrick's surprise.

"Locke's wages are listed as the same as the ostlers," he said. "Far less than what we used to pay ol' Cabbage."

Thora felt her brow furrow. "Let me see that."

He turned the wage log toward her.

"That *is* strange. . . ." Thora noted that the most recent *paid by* column had been initialed by Jane, since Talbot had already left by then. She flipped back a few pages more. "I would say Jane made a mistake, but the same amount appears for the previous quarters—initialed by Talbot."

"And Talbot is infallible, is he?"

"Evidently not."

Patrick asked, "But why didn't Locke complain when he wasn't paid his due? He complains about everything else."

"Perhaps he did."

"There's no record of Talbot making any adjustment or addition. I could ask Locke about it, but considering our current situation, I am not keen to suggest higher wages to anyone."

"I see your point," Thora said. "I think I will ask Talbot myself. I need to invite him to the planning meeting anyway, and want to see how Nan is faring."

Thora walked out to Talbot's farm that very afternoon. She saw no one in the yard, and the barn doors were closed, so she let herself in through the low gate and approached the house.

Walter Talbot himself answered her knock, wearing trousers and shirtsleeves, a dishcloth in his hand.

"Hello, Thora. Didn't expect to see you today."

"Have I come at a bad time?"

"Not at all. Come in. I was just tidying up." He held the door for her.

"I thought Sadie did that."

"She does. But she has her hands full with Nan. Thought I'd do the washing up today."

"Is Nan worse?"

"I am afraid so." Talbot led the way into the small dining room off the kitchen.

"Then I will not stay," Thora said. "You have more important things to attend to."

"Never mind. You're here now. Nan's in good hands, and the dishes will wait."

They had been waiting, apparently. Through the open door, she could see into the kitchen. The sideboard was stacked with plates, and the stove with a splattered mess of pots and pans. Come to think of it, Talbot was not looking very tidy himself. Not his usual spit-and-polished appearance.

"I'd invite you into the sitting room, but Sadie has taken to sleeping there now, so she can hear Nan in the night. I would offer you tea, but, um . . ." He glanced over at the cluttered stove.

"No, thank you."

He pulled out a chair for her, wiped the cloth over it, and gestured for her to sit down. She did so, and he sat across from her.

"What is it?" he asked. "Problems with McFarland?"

"Always. But that isn't why I've come. We would like you to join us for a planning meeting at The Bell." She told him the particulars, then added, "And while I'm here, I also wanted to ask you about Gabriel Locke."

"What about him? I can't imagine him causing any trouble."

"No trouble. Patrick and I just noticed something odd in the wage log. Mr. Locke has been in The Bell's employ for over a year now. And we noticed that his wages are remarkably low for a farrier."

Talbot lifted his chin. "Ah. I hardly think a man willing to work for low wages would be cause for complaint."

"I am not complaining, Talbot. Only curious. Why did you offer him such a modest salary? Were you planning to increase it after he proved himself? Otherwise, why would he work so cheaply?"

"He didn't want to take any at all." Talbot leaned back, entwining his hands in his lap. "He was a friend of John's and felt terrible about what happened. He knew the hole John would leave and how the inn would struggle without him. So he offered to stay on to help. I don't remember if he knew we were limping along without a full-time farrier or if I told him. But I wasn't about to turn down his offer. You know how difficult it is to find skilled horsemen since the expansion of the turnpike trust."

"But . . . surely he must have left a better-paying position. I am surprised he would just up and leave to work here. I do recall him wanting to help out during those early awful days, but I never expected him to stay on this long. Now, even less so, seeing what we're paying him."

Talbot nodded. "I don't think he'd worked as a farrier long. Though very experienced with horses in general, yes. Perhaps that is why he insisted he would accept no more than the ostlers. He probably didn't know how poorly we pay those fellows. Or that their wages are supplemented by coachmen who often share their tips."

"I would have given him a wage rise, whether he liked it or not," Talbot added. "But then Bill died, and well . . ." He lifted a hand in a helpless gesture.

"Jane probably didn't know that," Thora guessed. "She simply paid everyone the same rate as the previous quarter."

"Makes sense. Can't blame her for that. It slipped my mind, to tell the truth. Figured if he wanted a rise, he'd ask. Think he felt awkward taking any money from his friend's widow. Working for someone changes the relationship. Can't help but do so, as I know firsthand."

Thora tilted her head. "What does that mean?"

"You know very well. And it's no one's fault—just the way of things."

Thora considered that. She and Walt Talbot had been friends in their youth. Was he saying that had stopped being the case after he'd begun working for her family?

She said, "That reminds me. Patrick told me I depended on you too much—asked too much of you. Is that true? I know a door opened for you when Bill died. But . . . did I push you through it?"

He slowly nodded. "Always did boss me around something terrible. . . ." Then he lifted a placating hand. "You were gone by then, Thora. When a door opened, as you say, you weren't even there to offer a helpful shove."

"I would not have done so, and you know it."

He sobered. "I did not mind that you depended on me. I was happy to help you any way I could. But after you left, I . . . Well, I sure don't miss the round-the-clock coaches to attend to."

Is that what he'd meant to say? Thora asked, "And now that I'm back? I suppose you're all the more glad to be out from under my cracking whip."

"I don't miss your scolding tongue—that is true. But I do miss—"

The door opened, and round Sadie Jones entered, tray in hand. Talbot asked her, "Did she eat anything?"

"I'm afraid not, sir. I convinced her to sip a little broth, but that's all. Oh, excuse me. Good day, Mrs. Bell." The broad woman bobbed a curtsy.

"Hello, Sadie." Thora returned her gaze to Talbot. "Would it be all right if I went in and said hello? Or does Nan prefer not to have visitors?"

Talbot rose. "That is very kind, Mrs. Bell. Um . . . Just give me a few minutes to make sure she's equal to a visit."

"If she's not, just tell me flat. Don't be polite on my account."

He nodded and left her.

Dreading the visit, and not knowing what she might say to Nan, Thora rose and paced the room. As the minutes ticked past, Thora wondered if Talbot was having to convince his sister-in-law to agree to see her. Thora had just made up her mind to leave, when he returned.

"Come, Thora. Nan will see you now."

"Are you sure? You were gone quite a while."

"I am. And more importantly, so is Nan. She wants to see you."

"Oh? Well, good."

Feeling ill at ease, Thora walked forward. Talbot opened the sickroom door for her, and she entered. "I'll leave you two ladies to talk."

Thora looked over her shoulder at him, discomfited. She'd assumed he would stay, not saddle her with the entire burden of conversation. She had never been good at gentling her words to suit a difficult occasion. But he closed the door softly behind her.

Thora steadied herself and faced the bed. She doubted her face gave anything away—Charlie Frazer often teased her about her stoic expression, whether peevish or pleased. Her heart immediately softened upon seeing Nan Talbot frail and weak. After all, Nan was near her own age and a widow like herself, though she and Bill had never been blessed with children. How changed Nan was. How diminished. Her skin an ashy pallor. Her wan face and limbs so thin. Her hair—once a glorious gold even Thora had acknowledged as beautiful—was dull and wispy around the sharp bones of her once-lovely face. But her eyes were open and alert. And in them, Thora saw vestiges of the old Nan. Kind and teasing and full of life.

"Hello, Nan."

"Sorry to keep you waiting, Thora. Walter wanted to tidy up in here. Tidy me up a bit too." Nan smiled. "He knew I'd want to comb my hair and wash my face before seeing you again after all this time. Now I'm sure I look a picture." She spread her hands, eyes twinkling.

"How are you feeling?" It was probably a stupid question. Thora never knew what to say at a sickbed—or a deathbed. It seemed unlikely that Nan would leave this house except to step into paradise.

"I feel worse than I look. Which tells you something!" Nan smiled again, but Thora noticed her lips tremble. She admired the woman's humor and her efforts to put her visitor at ease.

"Is there anything you need?" Thora asked, sitting on the chair near the bed. "Anything I can bring you, or . . . ?"

Nan gestured weakly. "No. I have all I need. If I had any appetite, I might ask for one of your famous veal-and-ham pies. But I haven't."

"I shall send one over directly."

"Don't. Or rather, do if you like. I know Walter misses them."

"Very well, I shall."

Nan tilted her head to one side. "You know there *is* something you could do for me."

"Of course." Thora hoped she would not regret that reply.

"When I'm gone, don't let Walter stew in his sadness as he might do, on his own."

Thora pressed her lips together, then lowered her voice. "I know he has always been fond of you, Nan. No doubt if the worst happens, as you fear, it will lay him very low indeed."

Nan nodded. "We are fond of one another, yes. Like brother and sister. Don't look at me like that—and don't tell me you've heard the rumors too?"

"I didn't need to hear any rumors to wonder. I know he once admired you a great deal. And not as a brother."

"That was a long time ago, Thora. And yes, when I first married Bill, things were awkward between us. But the more we were in each other's company, the more comfortable we became. He came to know me as I truly am with all my faults and foibles and realized I was not as perfect as he'd thought. Now we laugh about it! How ill-suited we would have been as husband and wife. But we are a congenial brother and sister, and true friends. It isn't easy for Walter to form friendships with women. But you two were already friends. And you could be again, now that he is an independent man."

"Did you ever admire him?" Thora asked. "Or was it always Bill?"

"Of course I admired him. Such a tall, striking figure of a man. I think he's still handsome, in his way. But don't mistake me. Bill is the man who won my heart and never let it go. And for his part, Walter admires another woman, and has for a long time now."

Thora blinked, but did not ask who it was. Instead she forced a smile and bid Nan farewell, promising to return when she could.

Thora was seated in the coffee room that evening when Charlie Frazer entered, looking refreshed—face washed and hair combed. As Ivy Hill was the end of his route, he had a layover there every other day, having breakfast, sleeping several hours in the bunkroom, and then driving the upline back to Bagshot, ready to begin again the next day. Since Thora's return, they had resurrected their old custom of eating breakfast together, and then a late supper as well, before he took to the road once again.

He smiled as he claimed his usual seat across from her.

"Thora, my angel, when are you going to marry me and put me out of my misery?"

His eyes twinkled, and she guessed he was teasing her again—at least mostly.

"Add to your misery, I think you mean," she replied. "I have no thought of marrying again."

"Do you not? I think of it a great deal and have for years. We have known each other a long time."

"Not well."

"Better than you knew your husband when you married him, I'd wager. You have seen me morning and night, at my charming best, and harried and irritable when your ostlers fall behind, or your cook serves inedible food to my passengers, which cuts my tips at journey's end, I don't mind telling you. And I've seen your tetchy taskmaster self and been the recipient of your dragon tongue often enough to know what I'd be getting into." He winked.

She said dryly, "Your flattery never ceases."

He laughed. "There, you see? You make me laugh, and I know you are using every ounce of control you possess to bite back a smile of your own." He leaned nearer. "I am charming—admit it."

His dark eyes glinted, and he smelled good. Some spicy shaving tonic, and the masculine aroma of worn leather. When he looked at her like that she felt feminine again. Desirable. Young enough to be flattered but old enough to take his words with a grain of salt. "You are charming, Charlie. I admit it."

His smile widened, and he leaned in for a kiss.

She inserted a hand between them. "So charming that you probably have a wife in Bagshot, where you spend every other night. And an admirer at every inn along the way."

"I do not."

"What sort of life would that be for any woman? Sitting in a pair of rooms at one end of your route, while you drive to the other, probably to another woman, neither of us any the wiser. Waiting for you to return, for a few hours of company and a few hours of snoring, and then off you go again."

He gave her a hurt look. "If that is your estimation of my character, Thora Bell, I am surprised you allow me under your roof, let alone call me friend."

"The Bell cannot afford to be as choosy as it once was," she quipped. She waited until Alwena had delivered their suppers, then lowered her voice. "I do consider you a friend, Charlie. And look forward to your company and our conversations."

"As long as we remain . . . only . . . friends?"

"As things are, yes."

"And what if I . . . left the Royal Mail, or changed professions altogether?"

She stared at him. "Charles Angus Frazer hang up his whip and benjamin forever? I would never believe it."

"I can'na drive forever."

"But I can't see you changing professions. Not until old age or infirmity demands it. You love the open road."

He looked down at his hands. "You know me better than I realized. Do you know, when you moved to Bath, I asked . . ." He hesitated.

"You asked what?"

He cleared his throat and changed tack. "Did you miss me, when you were gone?"

"You know *me* better than to expect any romantic nonsense."

"I could make you happy, Thora. If you'd let me."

She held his earnest gaze, longing beginning to loosen the tight grip she held on her emotions. But she bit the inside of her cheek and said, "That is a task beyond mortal man, Charlie. Even you."

Miss Rachel Ashford sat down to compose a letter she had known for some time she would have to write, but dreaded doing so just the same. With a heavy heart, she dipped her quill into the murky ink and began.

> *Dear Ellen,*
>   *Father has passed. I wish you had been here with me.*

Rachel hesitated. Was that really true? She and her sister did not get on well together and had not been close in years. In fact, Ellen annoyed her, and Rachel no doubt annoyed her in return. So did she really wish her sister had been with her?

Yes, she realized.

Dr. Burton assures me everything was done for him that could be, and that Papa did not suffer in the end. He slipped from this life quite peacefully with a tear from each eye.

Had he been in pain, did that explain the tears? Even though he'd been too far gone to utter a sound? Rachel hoped not. She hoped instead his eyes merely watered from some mild physical stimulus like dryness. The vicar theorized that perhaps her father had seen the Lord as he stepped into eternal life. Or loved ones who had gone before him, like his wife. Rachel had forced a small smile at the notion, not really believing it. Had her father been at peace with God? She was not certain. He was not a perfect man by any measure and had done things that had cost him—cost her—dearly. Had he asked God's forgiveness toward the end? She didn't know. But he had not asked hers.

Rachel supposed his failings—unwise investments, questionable business dealings, losing his fortune, and the resulting scandal— were minor things in the face of eternity. But they had not felt minor. They had shaken Rachel's world. Her assumptions about her father's character. Her preconceived notions about herself and her station in life. Her future prospects with Sir Timothy Brockwell.

Ellen, married and living far from Ivy Hill, had escaped the gossip and diminished circumstances—having to sell the carriage and horses, and let some servants go. She had not had to endure the pity, scorn, or gloating over their misfortune. Rachel hated the pity worst of all.

While Papa was still sensible, I read your letter to him more than once. You know how he liked me to read to him. So rest assured he knew you were thinking of him and wished you could see him again, had not maternal duty kept you away. I understand that having William and Walter to care for makes it difficult to travel. And Papa understood that as well. But I hope you will make every effort to come home to Thornvale soon, while it is still ours to come to. What comfort seeing you and my dear nephews would be at this time.

Until then, may God comfort us all in our grief.

Yours,
Rachel

CHAPTER
SEVENTEEN

Jane sat at John's desk in the lodge, writing notes for herself and listing ideas to improve the inn. Two weeks had passed since Blomfield gave them the deadline. She wished they had more time.

She also made a list of questions she wanted to ask Charlie and his guard, as well as a Wedgwood salesman lodging with them at present. The man journeyed across the country carrying a leather case bulging with sample earthenware tiles. He had no doubt stayed in many inns and could give her valuable ideas.

After an hour, Jane grew restless. She set down her quill and rose, pacing across the sitting room as she thought. She paused before the pianoforte and idly played a few measures. Then remembering the stable hands could hear, grew self-conscious and stopped. A knock sounded, and Jane crossed the room to answer it.

Thora stood on her doorstep. "Sir William Ashford died yesterday. Mrs. Mennell just told me."

"Oh no." Jane's stomach fell. "I am sorry to hear it."

"You knew him well, I imagine," Thora said.

"I spent a fair amount of time at Thornvale as a girl," Jane replied. "Though I knew Mrs. Ashford and, of course, Rachel and her sister, much better. He was always kind to me though."

Thora nodded. "I thought you would want to know."

Jane expected Thora to say something cutting about Sir William's fall from grace, or to bring up Jane's own father, but mercifully, she did not. If things were different, Jane would have gone to comfort Rachel in person. Instead, she said, "Thank you for telling me. I shall send Rachel my sympathies straightaway."

After Thora left her, Jane wrote and posted a heartfelt letter to Rachel, then continued her preparations for the upcoming planning meeting.

Two days later she, Patrick, Thora, Talbot, and Mr. Locke met in the infrequently used private parlour.

Jane had requested a tea tray and a plate of biscuits for the occasion, and Mrs. Rooke begrudgingly obliged, resentful not to be included in the meeting. Jane had overheard Thora trying to placate her, telling the woman her duties were too important, and that the meeting would probably be long, boring, and a poor use of her time. She also promised that she or Jane would discuss any ideas related to the kitchen with her after the meeting.

Jane poured tea for everyone, passed around the biscuits, and then resumed her seat. She opened a leather portfolio—a gift from Mercy. A quill and inkpot stood at the ready to take notes.

Noticing her hands tremble, she lowered them into her lap. "Thank you all for coming—especially Mr. Talbot, who took time away from his own farm to be here."

Talbot nodded in acknowledgment and glanced across the table at Thora.

"As you know," Jane began, "I've asked you here to discuss and settle upon the best course to increase The Bell's profitability by ten percent—enough to prove to the bank we are a good investment and to earn an extension for the outstanding loan."

"Still wish I knew where that money went," Patrick grumbled.

Jane chose to ignore him. "We only have an hour until the next stage is due, so let's begin."

She consulted the page before her and cleared her throat. "I have come up with a list of possible improvements after discussions with Mr. Drake, who owns a successful hotel in Southampton, and with a few frequent travelers, coachmen, and a Royal Mail guard. To learn what they experience in other establishments that we might emulate."

"The Bell has never had to imitate other hostelries," Thora objected. "We have been successful in our own way for decades."

"That was once true. But unfortunately that is no longer the case. The Bell has fallen behind." Hoping to diffuse Thora's defensiveness, she added magnanimously, "It is no one's fault. The times have changed, and so must we."

Thora's lips tightened. "My father and grandfather never believed in chasing after fleeting fashions."

Jane clenched her hands and strived to keep her voice pleasant. "They did not have to. The Bell is the oldest inn in the parish, and for many years, the only one for miles. But with the opening of the Crown in Wishford and soon Mr. Drake's new hotel, our patrons have more options."

"Listen to you, Jane. You sound the seasoned tradesman already. I'm impressed." Patrick gave her a sly grin, but Jane did not like his tone. She needed to gain the confidence and respect of those present, as well as the staff and bankers, if she was to have any chance of succeeding. Patrick's teasing would not help her cause.

"I have simply gleaned from others more experienced than I and have given it a great deal of thought," she coolly replied. "Though, of course, I have much to learn—especially from those of you present."

"You're doing fine, Mrs. Bell," Mr. Talbot said encouragingly.

"Thank you. Now just to give us a starting point, I have come up with several possible changes. . . ." *Fiddle.* She knew Thora hated that word and quickly amended, "Improvements we might make in four categories: to better our services, update our appearance, decrease costs, and increase revenues." She glanced at the list, then licked dry lips.

"First, Mr. Drake says all the major inns are improving the quality of their meals, to cater to frequent and exacting travelers.

So we could serve better cuts of meat—and soup served at the appropriate temperature."

Thora huffed. "Meat is expensive."

"Yes, which is why we shall charge more for it. But that is another category—we'll come back to that. Mr. Drake also suggests we tear down this wall, expand our current dining parlour, and add an indoor washroom."

Patrick raised his hands. "Of course that man is happy to make suggestions to spend our last farthing and put us out of business all the sooner."

Thora nodded. "This isn't Bath or London, you know. This is Ivy Hill. We don't need such hoity-toity ways."

"But our patrons come from London, Salisbury, and Exeter. And the other inns along the route do offer such accommodations."

Thora crossed her arms but did not protest further.

Jane continued, "To improve the inn's appearance, we might paint, have a new sign made, or have the old one professionally painted. Hire the Kingsley brothers to repair the broken balustrades and cracked walls, and Mr. Broadbent to take a look at our leaky gutters and water damage." She took a breath and went on, "We could add small vases of flowers to each table in the dining parlour. Buy a fine Turkey carpet for the entryway and new brass lamps to make the hall brighter and more welcoming. Have our gig repainted now that Mr. Locke has repaired it. Offer its use for a fee."

When she again paused for breath, Talbot spoke up. "Well, I don't know about trimmings and flowers and such, but I think the notion of hiring out that gig an excellent one." He interlaced his long fingers. "Many was the time I had to turn down a traveler who wanted to hire a carriage to finish his journey to some outlying area. And while buying a new carriage would be expensive, refurbishing that old one should not be too costly. And if it proves profitable, then we might justify buying another. Perhaps even hire a flyman to drive it, should the customer not wish to drive himself . . . or herself. One of our postboys might like the extra work, now that post traffic has slowed. Well done, Mrs. Bell."

"Thank you, Mr. Talbot."

Gabriel Locke spoke up. "But we shall need a new horse, or even a pair," he said. "Most of our heavy carriage horses aren't suited to single harness work. But I'm sure I could find a suitable fleet animal."

"Buy a horse?" Patrick scowled. "When we have a whole stable full? That doesn't make sense."

"I have an . . . associate who owes me a favor. Not to mention a tidy sum. He has several such horses, and one of them would settle the debt nicely."

"Someone owes you that much money?" Thora asked. "That is a great deal of shoeing and whatnot."

"As I said, the man has many horses."

"Be that as it may, Mr. Locke," Jane protested. "This associate does not owe *us* anything. You cannot transfer payment on that debt to The Bell. We would have to reimburse you."

Locke shrugged. "If the scheme pays off, you may reimburse me then. And if it doesn't, I shall simply sell the horse and the debt will be settled."

"Well. That is very generous, Mr. Locke. And I am in no position to refuse your offer. Thank you. But we shall at least provide your traveling expenses. Patrick, please see to that from our cash reserves. We should have enough for coach fare and a night or two lodging, I trust?"

"No need for lodging," Mr. Locke said. "I can stay with a friend."

Patrick shifted. "I . . . will have to look. I am not certain there is enough ready cash."

"There had better be," Thora said. "We are due to pay quarterly wages next week."

"I have been meaning to bring that up," Patrick said. "But we can talk about that later. In private."

Thora's dark brows lowered ominously. "If there is any doubt about the payroll we had better discuss it here and now."

Patrick looked at Jane. "May we keep it between those of us in this room?"

"Yes," she agreed. "For now, at least."

"There isn't enough. Not to pay wages and our most pressing bills."

Thora frowned. "How can that be? We have never reneged on wages before. Certainly our income is not down that much."

"It is."

Thora shook her head. "Then we cannot spend money on frivolous things like paint and curtains and special horses. We pay our employees first. Bankers and brewers have their fingers in many pies and can wait with no inconvenience to themselves. But our modestly paid staff . . . ?"

Patrick suggested, "We could make an effort to build up our reserves and pay both quarters next time."

"Pay our maids, ostlers, and postboys nothing for another three months? What are they to live on?"

"They have their room and board provided, don't they?" Patrick said. "No one will go hungry. And if anyone had an urgent need, we could cover those on a case-by-case basis."

Thora sent him a challenging look. "I would like to be there when you tell Bertha Rooke that she will not be paid."

"Oh. I never dreamed of not paying ol' Rooke. I prefer to live, thank you. But I won't draw a salary myself this quarter, of course."

"Thank you. But we must still go forward with improvements," Jane insisted.

Patrick threw up his hands. "It makes no sense to throw good money after bad."

Mr. Locke said quietly, "Sometimes you have to spend money to make money."

Thora's eyes flashed. "And you always have to spend money to land in debt!"

Patrick argued, "Why invest money in improvements a potential buyer may not like or want to change anyway? If we fail, the next owner might even gut the place and start over."

"Gut the place!" Thora echoed. "It is like a knife to my heart to hear you say that, Patrick."

"Oh, don't be so dramatic, Mamma. You left, remember? That cord has already been cut."

"But I am back now. Let's have no more talk of gutting, do you hear me?"

He sighed. "Very well."

"Next owner?" Jane repeated. "Have you discounted our chances already, Patrick? I am disappointed to hear it. We have not even tried yet. It is too soon to give up."

"I agree," Talbot said. "We must make improvements and give them time to take effect. We have less than three months, remember. Go on, Jane," he urged.

Jane felt self-conscious and vulnerable to share her other ideas. Surely they would be rejected as foolhardy, especially given the financial straits they were in. Even so, she went on, "Replace our old mattresses with feather beds. At least in our best rooms."

Thora raised a brow at that, but Jane continued, "Have new towels and bedclothes made to replace our threadbare ones. . . ."

"Where is all this money coming from?" Patrick asked.

"Good question. That leads to the next category—ways to earn more money. My initial ideas include offering a better selection of meals at a premium price, as I mentioned earlier. Also, Mr. Drake says our room rates are low and we could increase them. We could also begin charging for things like fires, towels, and soap."

"That seems wrong," Talbot murmured—his first words of dissent.

"I know," Jane said. "But we could compromise. Perhaps we might offer plain lye soap for free, or for a small charge, sweet-smelling floral soap, made locally."

She turned the page and went on. "I have ideas to save money as well. Though I am not certain they are all feasible."

Thora spoke up. "One thing I've noticed since my return is that we now buy quite a bit of our bread and pastries from Crad-dock's—to free up Mrs. Rooke for housekeeper responsibilities along with cooking while I was gone, no doubt. But now that I am back and can resume my former duties, Mrs. Rooke and Dotty might fire up the bake oven again."

Jane remembered Gabriel's words about how they were all dependent on one another. She briefly glanced at him across the table, then said gently, "Or, we might continue to buy from the bakery, but negotiate a better price. I thought we might even display some of the bakery's easy-to-take-away items for a share of proceeds."

Gabriel held her gaze, dark eyes glimmering with . . . something. Did he approve, or think she'd taken his comment too far?

Patrick made his disapproval clear. "Sell Craddock's goods on our front counter? Shall we invite Mr. Prater to bring in his wares next? And perhaps Mrs. Shabner would like to place her dressmaking form just there."

Mr. Talbot spoke up. "I like the idea of taking our fair share of Craddock's profits. Many travelers dart to the bakery as it is, racing to get there and back with some treat before the guard blows his horn again. I think that notion deserves further consideration."

Jane sent him a grateful glance. "Thank you, Mr. Talbot."

He added, "This would also be a good time to renegotiate with all suppliers and see if you might come to better terms."

"Excellent point. And Mrs. O'Brien is a wax-and-tallow chandler on the outskirts of Ivy Hill. We could buy our candles from her instead of Foster's in Wishford."

"Are we still buying them from Wishford?" Thora asked. "I had not realized. I am all in favor of sending as little Ivy Hill money there as possible."

Gabriel Locke spoke up. "If you can spare me for a few days next month, Mrs. Bell, I shall visit my associate. See what horses he has available."

"There is to be an auction in Salisbury in July," Talbot said. "That would be closer."

"Yes, but I haven't contacts in Salisbury. Besides, I have other business that takes me north and can kill two birds with one stone. Perhaps even three . . ."

"But what if a horse needs attention?"

"I thought I would travel on a Saturday and Sunday, when our traffic is lightest. Mr. Fuller will cover for me."

"What other business takes you north?" Jane asked.

"I have a friend who manages the Marquis of Granby—a coaching inn in Epsom. The ostlers there can change a team in two minutes flat. I thought I might spend a little time with him, and see what I can learn to improve our speed in the yard."

"And why would this man share his methods with you?" Jane asked.

"He is . . . very gracious that way."

Jane felt a prickle of suspicion worm up her spine. "May I say, Mr. Locke, you seem awfully eager to leave us."

Patrick nudged her under the table, and she glanced over at him. He gave a small but vigorous shake of his head. A warning. Why? She noticed him exchange a look with Thora, then smile at their farrier.

"If Locke wants a little time off, we are happy to oblige him, are we not? He has worked very hard these many months and has some time coming to him, no doubt."

"Oh . . . ?" Jane replied, perplexed by Patrick's positive response. "Well then. Of course."

For another quarter of an hour, they debated various ideas, and then estimated the costs and benefits of each, just as the horn blew in the distance, announcing the arrival of the next coach.

Thora caught up with Jane after the meeting. "And where will you begin on that long list of yours?"

"The beds, I think. Mr. Drake mentioned they need attention."

"How bad can they be? Before I left, Alwena and I filled the mattresses with new hay and lady's straw to keep them sweet smelling and bug free."

"And I appreciate that. But we have only old horsehair and flock mattresses over them. Apparently, the better inns have feather beds made of white goose feathers or even down."

"Feathers are expensive."

"Do we not save them from all the birds we pluck here?"

"We do. But we serve far more chicken than duck or goose, and Mrs. Rooke has long been allowed to sell the feathers herself."

Jane said, "Then we shall buy what we need from the poulterer and make the feather beds ourselves."

"Our small staff is stretched thin as it is."

"Then I shall do it on my own."

Thora looked at her askance. "Have you ever done so? I imagine the Fairmont housekeeper paid someone to supply new ticks and mattresses for your family."

"I suppose."

"You have no idea how much work it will be."

"No. But something tells me you're about to enlighten me."

Colin, at the desk, spoke up. "Excuse me, but did you say we need new ticks?"

Jane nodded.

"My mother is a needlewoman," he said. "I'm sure sewing ticks would be easy for her, given the materials."

"Really?" Jane saw the protest forming on Thora's lips but replied before she could. "Very well, Colin. How soon could she make, say, four to start?"

He brightened. "A few days, I imagine. I'll talk to her and let you know."

"Wait." Jane stepped to the desk. "Let me write down the dimensions so you can purchase materials for her." She picked up a scrap of paper and wrote quickly. "Here are the length, width, and depth I'd like for each tick." She handed him the note. "You can calculate the yards needed from that."

He stared at her note as though it were Sanskrit. "I don't know how to figure . . . fabric. I'm out of my depth there. But my mother will take care of it without wasting an inch, knowing her. She's frugal that way."

"Very well; I shall leave it to her. But let me know if she has any questions. And as far as payment, shall we say . . . four shillings a tick?"

"Sounds fair." Colin thanked her and hurried out the back door with the note, eager to share the news.

Thora watched him go, lips pursed in disapproval. "You know any money you give the McFarlands will end up down Liam's gullet in the form of blue ruin."

"Thora, that isn't kind." Jane said. She hoped it wasn't true.

Her mother-in-law changed the subject. "So, will you tell Mrs. Rooke your plans for her kitchen, or shall I?"

"Thora, I overheard what you said earlier, about the planning meeting being a waste of time, so I'm afraid I have little confidence in how enthusiastically you would present the plans."

"I was trying to placate her. As I have done for years."

"Well, I suppose it's my turn now."

Ten minutes later, however, Jane was regretting her decision to face Mrs. Rooke herself.

She had asked the woman to join her in the office and explained the plans as positively as she could.

But the woman rose and planted doughy hands on her hips. "Are you saying my meals aren't good enough? Now I am to devise all new menus? You haven't enough money to pay the butcher or poulterer as it is, but I am to order better cuts of meat? Mr. Cottle doesn't give away joints for free, you know. And who's going to make double the amount of soup? I haven't the time. My cooking was good enough for the first Mrs. Bell, and it ought to be good enough for you. What has Thora to say to all this? She has always agreed old ways are the best."

"That may be. But Thora is no longer the landlady. I am."

"And more's the pity."

"Mrs. Rooke!" Thora sharply interrupted from the doorway.

Jane and Mrs. Rooke looked over in surprise, not realizing Thora was there.

Mrs. Rooke pointed a finger at Jane. "Well, have you heard what she's asking me to do? Telling me, more like! And with what budget,

I'd like to know. Bricks without straw—that's what she wants. Her, what never lifted a finger in her life, except to ring a bell."

"Mrs. Rooke, that is quite enough," Thora remonstrated.

The cook threw up her hands. "You can't tell me you agree with all this fustian nonsense! Next we'll be serving pigeon tongue and eye of newt tarts. La! Never heard such foolishness. Not in my kitchen."

Thora's lips tightened. "While I appreciate your loyalty to me, you work for Jane now. My father would never have allowed any member of staff to show such disrespect to her mistress."

"Oh, I see how it is. You're taking her part now. You've seen which side your bread is buttered on—is that it? Well, I call a spade a spade."

"You forget your place, Bertha," Thora said. "And your manners."

Mrs. Rooke reached behind, untied her bib apron, and yanked it off. "Then perhaps this isn't my place any longer. I shall go and work for Mr. Drake." She balled up the apron and tossed it on the desk.

Jane began, "Mrs. Rooke, there is no call for—"

But Mrs. Rooke stalked out of the office. A few moments later, a door down the passage slammed shut.

Thora sighed. "That went well." She looked at Jane grimly. "I hope you know how to cook."

CHAPTER

Eighteen

Shortly after her ill-fated conversation with Mrs. Rooke, Jane entered the kitchen almost timidly, reminding herself that she did indeed own the place—including the kitchen. But these work-rooms, adjacent scullery, and larder had always seemed off limits before—Mrs. Rooke's domain.

The kitchen was larger than the stillroom Jane had sometimes ventured into growing up, to help with jams, cordials, and cosmetics, or drying herbs and flowers. And it was massive compared to the tiny kitchen in the lodge—a small stove, cabinet, and sink tucked into an alcove on one end of the sitting room where Jane made tea, boiled eggs, toasted bread, and reheated Sunday suppers.

From the first days of their marriage, most of their meals had come from the inn kitchen. John had liked retreating from the inn and having quiet meals with her, but he'd seen no need for a second full kitchen in the lodge. No reason to duplicate the work. He used words like *economical* and *efficient*. Jane, however, had felt like a constant guest in her own home, having all those meals delivered, from menus she herself had not selected. Now and again, she enjoyed making simple suppers of toasted cheese, which she melted with an iron salamander, heated over the fire. But that was about the extent of her cooking experience.

Mrs. Rooke generally prepared plain dishes, like roasted beef and mutton, broiled fish, hearty stews and soups. Sometimes Jane missed the finer cooking from the Fairmont House kitchen. Ragout veal, fricassee chickens, ox cheek and dumplings, vegetables with delicate sauces, fruits and salads, followed by puddings, ices, or cheesecakes. Jane's stomach grumbled at the thought.

Her hunger quickly faded, however, as she looked around the inn's kitchen.

On the large worktable that dominated the room lay four rabbits ready to be skinned, three chickens ready for plucking, and a dozen whole fish, staring at her with glassy eyes.

Jane looked away first.

One wall held a roasting range—a large open fire with meat spits and toast racks. A wheeled warming cupboard waited nearby. Against another wall stood a black iron stove with kettles, pots, and pans for stewing sauces and side dishes. In the corner sat a covered copper steamer for puddings, and urns with spickets to keep coffee and tea hot and ready to dispense. A side table held a pair of scales for measuring ingredients in large quantities, as well as mortars and pestles in several sizes.

Everything was oversized and overwhelming. No wonder Mrs. Rooke had felt a queen of her domain.

In the adjacent scullery, Jane found the kitchen maid, Dotty, staring at the menu posted on the wall. When Jane entered, she turned, face stricken. "I'm sorry, ma'am. But I can't do it all. Not on my own."

Jane sighed. "I know."

"That's why we're here, Dotty," Thora said, marching in. She snatched two aprons from pegs on the wall, tossed one to Jane, and tied the other over her dark dress as she crossed the room. She stood beside the maid and squinted up at the menu.

Jane asked, "What do we do first—the soup?"

"Yes. We've got to get those chickens boiling for stock. The rabbits skinned and in the hot box. The turnips and potatoes peeled, and the carrot pudding in the steamer."

Her mother-in-law turned to her. "Which would you like to do? You choose."

Jane glanced at the furry rabbits and quickly away. She met the gaze of the trout and swallowed. "I'll peel the turnips and potatoes."

Jane started in, the mountain of each root vegetable daunting.

After a few minutes, Dotty glanced over and huffed. "We'll be here 'til midnight at that rate. Why don't you gut the trout instead, ma'am. There are only twelve of them."

"Very well. If one of you will show me what to do." Jane stepped onto the wooden pallet beneath the table to keep her shoes out of the worst of the muck.

Thora handed her a knife. "Incise beneath the gills. Press in. That's it. From that fin to about there."

Jane winced as the knife pierced the skin and blood oozed out.

"Now pull out its innards with your fingers. Cut off the entrails there. . . . Yes, that's all there is to it."

Disgusting, Jane thought. But certainly not as gruesome as skinning rabbits, which Thora did without flinching and with impressive efficiency—at least as far as Jane could gauge from the queasy glances she darted toward that end of the table.

When she finished her task, Jane made haste to the scullery sink and washed the blood from her hands. She decided to save a few fish remnants for the grey-and-black cat that regularly visited the lodge now.

The potboy, Ned, happened in, looking for a bite of something, and Thora ordered him to pluck the hens. Taking pity on him, Dotty offered him a thick crust of bread with butter. He wolfed it down, then sat on the back porch and began plucking—clearly a task he'd done before.

Dotty turned back to Jane. "Ma'am, why don't you peel and chop those onions for the soup? That would help. And spinach, parsley, and sweet herbs there?"

"Very well. How fine?"

Following the verbal instructions sent her way from both Thora and Dotty as they bustled around her, Jane set about making the soup. She added the vegetables, removed the bones from the stewed chicken when it was tender, and skimmed the fat from the surface. It was time-consuming but quite simple, Jane realized. Eventually the time came for the final step—adding the thickening.

When she had finished, Thora came over and dipped out an experimental ladle full. "What is this? You were supposed to add a little hot soup to the egg yolks and vinegar gradually!"

Instead, the eggs for the thickening had boiled into a solid stringy mess.

"Oh no," Jane groaned. "I will have to start again."

"There isn't time. We'll have to serve it as it is."

"But it looks . . . wrong."

"We'll call it . . . chicken and egg soup . . . and no one will be the wiser."

Jane doubted that but was grateful for Thora's quick thinking.

"The next coach arrives soon, and they'll expect hot soup," Thora said.

"Very hot," Jane murmured, sending Thora a wry look.

A short while later, Colin knocked on the doorframe, a wary look on his face as he surveyed the kitchen crew. "Sorry to intrude, Mrs. Bell, but Miss Grove is here."

Jane set down her spoon. "I'll be back in a minute," she assured the others. She stepped into the passage, wiping her hands on a dish towel as she went.

Mercy's eyes widened at the sight of her soiled apron. "I dropped by to make sure you'd heard the news about Sir William, but . . ."

"I did hear, yes, and sent my sympathies to Rachel. I am sorry, Mercy, but I can't stop to talk, as much as I'd like to. Our cook has quit."

"Oh no!"

Jane nodded. "Thora, Dotty, and I are muddling along as best we can."

"So I see." Mercy took the towel from her and rubbed egg from her face.

Jane moaned. "Instead of improving The Bell's food, I am making it worse."

Mercy thought. "Our Mrs. Timmons might help, though she is a very plain cook indeed and rather slow at her age. She would not do well in the hectic environment of a coaching inn. Auntie would bake for you, but . . ."

"We buy most of our baked goods from Craddock's."

Mercy grinned. "Praise the Lord for small mercies."

"Well, if you think of anyone who could help even for a few days while we try to find a new cook, let me know."

"I shall ask the Tea and Knitting ladies."

From the sound of the kitchen came the clatter of pots falling and Thora exclaiming, "Hang the gibbet!"

Jane looked back at Mercy. "Please hurry."

Mercy nodded. "I will. Straightaway."

Jane trudged toward the kitchen early the next morning, resigned to another day of toil, and wondering what dish she would spoil this time. At the door, she stopped short at the sight of Bertha Rooke stirring a pot of porridge. Before she could utter a word, Thora appeared, taking Jane's arm and leading her down the corridor and out of earshot.

"Shh . . . let's not risk angering her again already."

Jane gaped at her mother-in-law. "What did you do to get her back, Thora?"

"Nothing."

"You must have done or said something to placate her."

Thora shook her head. "I didn't. I came down bright and early and there she was. Her threat to go and work for Mr. Drake was bluster evidently."

"But Cadi said she saw her walking down the Wishford Road yesterday in her smartest frock and hat."

Thora nodded. "I know. And Patrick told me he overheard her boasting how much more Mr. Drake pays than we do. Apparently she saw his advertisement for a cook."

"Perhaps Patrick persuaded her to stay," Jane said. "He could if anyone could."

Thora looked at her closely. "I thought perhaps you charmed your friend Mr. Drake into not hiring our cook away from us."

"No. I did not think to try." Jane had not seen James Drake in several days, since he paid his bill and departed for Fairmont House. Had he hired a different cook out of deference to her? She would not put it past him.

Thora said, "Well, whatever the case, I shall not look a gift horse in the mouth."

"Nor I."

Thora joined Charlie in the coffee room for breakfast after all, though she'd thought she'd be unable to until they'd replaced their cook. She said, "Bertha Rooke is back at her post, and I for one am grateful. I'd forgot how much work managing that kitchen can be."

"Hard work is good for us, Thora. Keeps us young."

"Oh? And what do you know about hard work?" Thora challenged, spreading her table napkin on her lap.

Charlie picked up his coffee cup. "A great deal."

"Oh come now. Since when does sitting on a bench for hours at a stretch count as hard work?"

Charlie shook his head. "Thora, you disappoint me. How can you have grown up in a coaching inn and doubt the rigors of a coachman's life? Especially a coachman for the Royal Mail?" He sipped his coffee, then continued, "I do far more than sit. I inspect the team and harnesses thoroughly before setting out—that's extremely important. A broken strap can halt the coach or even overturn it. I have to stay alert, gauge when to rotate the horses to avoid callusing their mouths on one side. I have to know when to push and when to rest them, so as not to exhaust the horses unduly, like my counterpart often does, the scapegrace."

He glanced at Thora. "You don't look convinced. Tell you what—ride with me as far as Salisbury next Tuesday and see me in action. I'll send you home in a sister coach driven by Jeb Moore, and you can compare for yourself."

Thora shook her head, about to turn him down, but something in his expression stopped her. He *expected* her to refuse. "Next Tuesday, hmm? What time shall I be ready?"

It was worth it to see the look of surprise on his face.

Rachel Ashford sat wearily down at the writing desk with its delicate carved legs and highly polished surface. How much longer would she be able to sit on any piece of furniture in this house?

It was only a matter of time now until she would be put out of her own home—the only home she'd ever known. Well, Thornvale had never been hers. Not truly. She had always known it was entailed away to the male line. But that fact had never really bothered her or seemed tragic. It wasn't a fate she had regularly contemplated or fretted about growing up. As an idealistic young lady, she had thought her father would live to a ripe old age. And that she would marry a handsome, wealthy gentleman and be mistress of his fine house long before the entail could affect her personally.

She'd been wrong.

With a sigh, Rachel pulled forth a sheet of writing paper, uncorked the ink, and dipped her quill pen.

Dear Ellen,

The funeral is over. The callers gone home. The will read.

No, I am not angry with you for not coming home for the funeral. Of course you are right that women do not typically attend. But it would have been helpful to have you here during all the arrangements and calls and condolences. I grew weary of making your excuses, but I did so, never fear. And

*you were wrong in assuming Jane and I have reconciled, and
that she and Mercy would serve as my companions in your
absence. Mercy does visit when her school responsibilities
allow, but I don't see much of Jane. That has not changed
in all these years. Not since . . .*

Rachel broke from her usual fastidiously neat writing and blot-
ted out those last two words. There was no reason to explain.
No point in going into the whole mortifying ordeal again. Not
when her sister had a perfect husband, a perfect marriage, and a
perfect home.

*In your last letter, you asked about Papa's will for prop-
erty not tied up in the entail. I trust you were not hoping
for money. Mr. Blomfield has made it perfectly clear that
the little remaining will be used to pay down Papa's debts.
Thankfully, you received your dowry years ago. Papa has
also left you what remains of Mamma's jewelry—her topaz
ring, cameo, garnets, and pearls. They are too valuable to
send by post, but I will put them aside for you.*

Mamma had left no will or instructions, so all of her personal
belongings became her husband's to dispose of as he wished.
They'd had to sell a few of her more valuable pieces over the
years to keep Thornvale limping along, but why had he given all
of Mamma's remaining jewelry to Ellen? Why nothing for her?
Ellen was welcome to the pearls and gems. But might she not have
had the less-valuable cameo at least?

Papa has left me his books . . .

Rachel made no mention of how their father's act had cut her.
She told herself that in his view, he had left her the greater bequest, so perhaps she should be grateful. But the entire collection
of scholarly tomes felt like a weighty millstone around her neck.

She knew what Ellen's thoughts would be. She would probably visit her nearest bookseller to ascertain what the collection might be worth—make sure Rachel had not inherited more than she had. Books were expensive. Especially these. These were no slim volumes on cheap paper. They were thick leather or board-bound books with gilt edges—histories, biographies, science texts, and works of philosophy. Books like these were only valuable if you could sell them, however. And her father had stipulated that Rachel would have his entire library on the condition that she neither sell the books nor give them away piecemeal. They must be kept together, the collection intact. And if, at the end of her life, she had no offspring to leave them to, she could bequeath the collection in its entirety to her father's alma mater, or to whichever institution of higher learning would value them most and agree to keep them together for posterity.

. . . *on the condition that I don't sell them, but keep the collection as is. Keep it where? That is what I would like to know.*

What had her father been thinking? Had his faculties faded before his body? He had to remember that the manor housing his library would become the property of his heir—the son of a cousin he had barely known. And she would have to find somewhere else to live. How was she to afford a house or rooms large enough to hold such a collection? Perhaps this heir of his would allow her to leave the books where they were for now. She hoped so. The thought of the work required to box up and move those hundreds of volumes struck her as daunting, not to mention fruitless. Move them where? Mercy and her aunt had offered her the use of their spare room. But the room was too small to hold a fraction of these books.

Rachel knew their solicitor, Mr. Nikel, had written to Father's heir. She had seen his name in print. But beyond that she knew little of the man who now owned Thornvale.

*We are each to have one of Grandmother Woodgate's
sets of china. I know you prefer the rose pattern, so I will
take the willow. The rest of the china and silver, as well as
the furniture and art, goes with the house to Papa's heir, Mr.
Nicholas Ashford. Have you ever met him? I cannot recall
doing so. If you know anything about the man, please write
and tell me.*

Would he be a tyrant? Rachel wondered. An uncouth money-
grubber with no concept of what the house and furnishings were
worth—or the history behind them? Her stomach churned at the
thought of a stranger taking over Thornvale. Especially if the
stranger had no appreciation of the home or the family that had
once lived and died there.

She thought of Jane Bell's childhood home. Sold out of the
family, and now long abandoned and forlorn.

Which fate would be worse? Rachel wondered. She wasn't certain.

On Sunday, Jane arrived at church early to deliver the requested
flowers—an arrangement of bright calendula, sweet William, and
stocks, with spiky digitalis for height.

She positioned the vase before the pulpit and stepped back to
review her work. Satisfied, she turned and walked down the aisle
and took her usual seat. She looked forward to some time sitting
alone in the reverent silence to think and pray. She gazed through
the chancel arch, where sunlight from three gothic windows gave
the altar a golden glow. *Beautiful.*

The vestry door opened, and she glanced toward it. She expected
Mr. Paley, but instead saw the sexton, Mr. Ainsworth, carrying a
brass candle holder. With the candle, he lit the lamp on the lec-
tern, then started toward the pulpit, clearly unaware he was being
observed. He stopped midstride, attention caught by something
on the floor.

"Oh," he said, in polite address. "Good morning, Jerome."

Jane saw no one. Was he talking to himself? Surely he did not address God by such a nickname. She tried to remember what Mr. Paley had said about the man.

The sexton looked up, and Jane feigned interest in something in her reticule to spare him any embarrassment.

The sound of purposeful footfalls echoed through the nave, followed by Mrs. Paley's voice. "Thank you, Mr. Ainsworth. Now, is it not almost time to ring the bell?"

"Yes, ma'am," he murmured and shuffled on. As he passed, Jane caught the mingled scent of tallow, cigars, and furniture polish.

Mrs. Paley noticed her there. "Ah, Jane. Good morning."

"Hello, Mrs. Paley."

Jane waited until Mr. Ainsworth had disappeared into the bell tower, then said, "I just heard the sexton greet someone named Jerome, but I saw no one."

Camilla Paley waved a dismissive hand. "Oh, he was probably talking to the church mice again. He makes pets of them. I hope he didn't frighten you?"

"No."

"Good. I can't tell you how many times I've thought I was alone in the church, when suddenly he appears and scares me half to death. But he's harmless." The vicar's wife turned toward the pulpit. "How lovely your flowers look, Jane. Well done."

"Thank you. It was my pleasure."

"By the way, I trust you heard Sir William passed on early this week?"

"Yes, I did hear that sad news." Rachel's only reply to Jane's letter of condolence and offer of help had been a cool note acknowledging her sympathies, but saying there was nothing she needed.

"Sad, yes, but not unexpected," Mrs. Paley said, then studied her face. "I . . . imagine your friend's loss reminds you of your own father. You don't talk about him, I notice. I suppose it is a painful subject."

Jane met her speculative eyes a moment, then looked away. "Yes."

She felt Mrs. Paley's gaze rest on her a moment longer, then the woman drew herself up. "Well. I had better go and see if my husband is ready. Thank you again for the flowers."

Jane nodded, and as Mrs. Paley's echoing footfalls faded, Jane closed her eyes to savor the reverent silence once more. Then she bowed her head and prayed for wisdom, guidance, and favor. She prayed for Rachel as well.

CHAPTER
Nineteen

On Monday, Jane stood on a chair in the hall, taking down the curtains for the laundress, hoping a good cleaning would brighten them up until they could afford to replace them.

Patrick stepped out of the office. "I need John's keys for the wine cellar, Jane. Do you have them?"

"They're in the lodge. I'll get them for you in a few minutes."

He ran his hand over his face. "I'm in a bit of a hurry. Would you mind if I ran over and fetched them myself?"

"I suppose not. They're on the desk in the corner." Jane hoped she had not left out anything personal, or any undergarments lying in the open.

"Thanks." He hurried out, intent on his errand.

A few minutes later, Mercy walked in the front door and stopped abruptly at seeing Jane upon her perch. "Jane . . . may I help you?"

"Yes, actually. Could you unfasten that end? It's caught on something."

Mercy reached up and, being taller than Jane, easily loosed the trapped edge.

"Thank you." Jane laid the curtain into a mounding basket.

Mercy said, "I've just come from Thornvale."

"Oh? How is Rachel bearing up?"

"Rather well, actually. Sir William suffered such a long illness, she's had plenty of time to prepare herself."

Rachel had even attended church the day before, Jane had noticed, though she'd left immediately after the service without speaking to anyone except the vicar.

Jane said, "I was surprised to not see her sister in church yesterday. Did Rachel say why Ellen has not come?"

"Only that she is busy with her two small children. Speaking of busy, I'm afraid I haven't made any progress in finding you a new cook."

"Oh, I should have told you yesterday. Mrs. Rooke came back."

"I am relieved to hear it. By the way, there's another meeting of the Ladies Tea and Knitting Society tonight. Will you come with me again?"

"Another meeting?" Jane suppressed a frown. "I'm afraid I'm busy here at present. When I'm through with these, there are rugs to beat, and after that I am making feather beds."

"Are you indeed?"

Jane nodded. "Mrs. McFarland is sewing the ticks. And Julia Featherstone is providing the goose feathers." Remembering the last meeting, Jane added sheepishly, "And fear not, I paid her in advance this time."

Mercy nodded her understanding. "When are you planning to fill them?"

"Tomorrow afternoon. If the ticks are ready."

"I would come and help you," Mercy said, "but I am administering examinations all day."

Jane gave her a saucy grin. "Mercy Grove, have you ever filled a tick in your life?"

"No. But a woman can learn anything she sets her mind to."

Jane pressed her friend's hand. "That is exactly what I am counting on."

Thora walked through the inn archway on her way to market, basket and list in hand. She hesitated near the lodge, her conscience niggling her. She realized she ought to ask Jane to review her shopping list before spending Bell money. It grated to have to ask permission to do what she had done by her own authority in the past, but she knew she should. Jane was in charge now, for better or worse.

The lodge door was slightly ajar, so Thora knocked once and let herself inside, stopping abruptly at the sight of Patrick bent over the desk in the corner. He whipped his head around, quickly shut the drawer, and if she was not mistaken, shoved something into his coat pocket.

"Patrick? What are you doing in here?"

"Just fetching John's keys." He turned and dangled them in the air. "Jane was busy—taking down curtains, if you can believe it."

He smiled, but something in his eyes sent a prickle of alarm through her. What had he really been doing nosing through the desk? Should she demand to search his pockets, like a mother of a child hiding candy? Or was she jumping to conclusions again?

"And you, Mamma?" Patrick asked, customary humor returning to his expression. "What has you marching in unannounced?"

Her mouth parted. "I . . ." What had she come for? Finding her son rooting around her daughter-in-law's lodgings had muddled her mind. "I only wanted to ask Jane about the list for market. I thought she was in here."

"No. Just me." Patrick gestured toward the door. "Shall we?"

She gave him a pointed look. "After you."

On Tuesday morning, Jane was sitting behind the front desk when Ned Winkle appeared. The potboy cleared his throat. "Sorry to disturb you, ma'am. But Mrs. Rooke would like a word."

"Of course," Jane said, though inwardly groaned in expectation of another quarrel. She rose from the desk and started toward the kitchen. Ned, she noticed, scurried off in the opposite direction.

At the end of the passage, she saw Mrs. Rooke at the back door, a woman standing just outside with a toddler on her hip.

"You asked for me, Mrs. Rooke?"

The stout cook held a sack in one hand and with the other gestured toward the door. "I already told her we could not pay her today, but she asked to see you."

The thin woman in her early forties wore a cap over faded reddish-brown hair. Her narrow face was punctuated by high cheekbones and shadowed eyes. The child she held looked to be two or three years old—a pretty girl, who stared warily at their cook.

Mrs. Rooke thrust a sack of something at Jane, and with a glance Jane recognized the folded pinstriped material as the ticks she had commissioned. She looked up at the woman who'd made them and gave her an uneasy smile. "Hello. Mrs. McFarland, I trust?"

The woman nodded, eyes full of worry.

Jane would not turn her away empty-handed. She would pay Mrs. McFarland even if she had to sell something, but she had already used the last ten pounds of her own money to pay for the feathers. Old Kelly Featherstone had delivered the sacks in his donkey cart first thing that morning.

Jane looked at Mrs. Rooke and forced a casual tone. "There must be some mistake. There was sufficient money on hand yesterday."

"Well, there isn't enough now, Master Patrick says. Not that and pay the brewer what he's owed."

Jane felt her neck heat, embarrassed to not be able to pay for work as promised. She set down the sack and forced herself to meet the woman's eyes. "Wait here a few moments, if you will, Mrs. McFarland. I shall return shortly."

As she walked away, she heard Mrs. Rooke huff behind her and tromp away into the kitchen.

Reaching the office, she demanded, "Patrick. Give me sixteen shillings, please. I told you I needed that much last week."

"The brewer's bill was larger than expected."

"The brewer gets plenty of our money. Let him wait."

Patrick reared his head back in surprise. "Shall I send the ill-tempered man to you when he comes?"

Jane swallowed at the thought of the burly brute. "If you must."

Patrick clicked his tongue. "Feathers over ale, Jane? And here I'd thought you had the makings of a woman of business."

She lifted her chin. "Mr. Drake says that a good meal and a good bed are the underpinnings of a successful hostelry."

"Mr. Drake this. Mr. Drake that. I grow weary of hearing that man's name." Patrick sighed. "But you are the boss. . . ." He opened the cash drawer and extracted a few coins. "Here is a shiny new half sovereign and six shillings."

"Thank you." Jane turned and swept from the office. She noticed Colin had taken her vacated place at the desk but at the moment was too mortified to meet his gaze.

She returned to the back door and handed the woman the coins. "There you are, Mrs. McFarland. Thank you for waiting." Jane picked up the sack and fingered a hem. "The stitching looks excellent. I will probably request more ticks eventually, though we may have to spread out the buying of feathers. Terribly expensive, I've learned."

The woman nodded her understanding. "I would be pleased to sew or mend anything else, ma'am. Though nothing too fancy, I'm afraid."

"I shall keep that in mind. We will eventually want new bed-clothes, and perhaps curtains and tablecloths as well."

"Yes, ma'am. That I could do. And my Susie's becoming a dab-hand herself, so we'll work double quick."

"Thank you, Mrs. McFarland. Em . . . Colin is just down the hall at the front desk, if you'd like to say hello?"

"That's all right. I know he's busy. We'd better be getting back— her Da is waiting." She bounced the child on her hip.

Jane wondered at the age span between Colin and this little sister. But she said only, "Very well. I'll send word through Colin when I have something else for you."

Mrs. McFarland thanked her again and hurried away.

Jane felt sure she had done the right thing. Even so, she returned to the office and wrote a sweetly worded apology to the pugnacious brewer.

When the time came, Thora was having second thoughts about going for a drive with Charlie Frazer.

She fastened the buttons of her pelisse over her grey carriage dress, put a few candies into her reticule, and walked downstairs, feeling unsettled and distracted. Seeing Patrick and Jane at the desk, she announced, "I had better stay and help you make the feather beds."

"No," Jane insisted. "I can do it myself, and Ned will carry the sacks. You go with Charlie and have a grand time."

"Are you sure?"

"I'm sure."

Deflated, Thora turned to the hall mirror and tied her bonnet strings. "I don't know why I'm doing this," she muttered.

"It's an adventure—that's why," Jane replied. "All these years in a coaching inn. Have you never ridden on the coachman's box before?"

"Not since I was a girl and old Ollie Wakefield let me drive his horses across the yard."

"Well then, you're overdue. Besides, I hear the Red Lion is the finest coaching inn in Salisbury, renowned for its excellent service. You can observe and take notes for me."

Thora humphed.

Patrick crossed his arms and said, "You know, I like Charlie Frazer, Mamma. You could do worse."

"I am not *doing* anything, for better or worse," Thora snapped. That phrase, *for better or worse*, echoed through her mind. Surely they didn't all think this was some strange courting outing? Hopefully Charlie did not see it that way.

"He reminds me of Papa in some ways," Patrick added.

Thora stared at her son. "Does he indeed? How?"

"He's witty, outgoing, charming. Popular with the ladies. Or at least with one particular lady." Patrick winked at her.

Then he opened the side door, and together they crossed the yard to where the Quicksilver awaited.

While Colin assisted passengers and the guard stowed the mail, Charlie walked around his team, verifying that all the harnesses were correctly placed and fastened. He thanked the ostlers, then took hold of the reins, or "ribbons," in one hand and mounted to his box.

Once he settled himself, he reached his free hand toward Thora, assisting her up onto the bench, Patrick offering a helpful push from the rear. At least she was spared the indignity of having to be levered up with the crutch propped nearby for the purpose— usually to push older women or overweight men up onto the roof.

Thora sat on the bench beside Charlie, him looking dapper as usual in his caped coat, his hat at a jaunty angle, a roguish smile on his rugged, handsome face.

"Ready for the ride of your life, lass?"

"Ready as I'll ever be."

Jane came out and stood on the back porch, an amused smile on her face.

"Pray for me, Jane," Thora called. "I am taking my life in my hands."

"No, you are putting your life in Charlie Frazer's hands," Patrick said with a grin. "Even worse!"

Others boarded, the tall coach lurching as passengers climbed in and the guard loaded baggage. Then Jack Gander climbed onto his rear perch and took up his horn to play the start signal and the signal to clear the road.

The ostlers released the horses, and Charlie called "Walk on" and "Get up," and within a few minutes they rumbled around the corner and went barreling down the hill.

"Hang on to your teeth, Thora!" Charlie called over the buffeting wind as their speed increased. At the bottom of the hill, they took the corner at a rapid clip. Thora held on to her bonnet with one hand and Charlie's arm with the other.

He laughed with delight. "I knew this was an excellent idea!"

Behind her on the roof a man lost his hat, and a woman yelped and grabbed onto a sailor.

Thora wasn't sure she agreed.

When the road leveled out, Charlie leaned back and slackened the reins. "On level ground, it's wise to let them take their own speed," he said. The horses settled into a steady pace, and Charlie relaxed, only now and then shaking the reins when the horses seemed inclined to slow down.

"Your turn, Thora." He offered her the reins.

"Are you certain that's a good idea?"

"It's not exactly regulation, but most of us allow an eager passenger to drive now and again, when not in foul weather or on dangerous stretches of road."

She took the reins and felt the exhilaration of being in control, or at least the illusion of it, though each horse outweighed her ten times over. Holding the ribbons gave her a giddy feeling in her stomach—a sense of power and freedom and fun.

Charlie looked over and caught her grinning. "Most first timers white knuckle the ribbons and grimace in concentration. But I should have known Thora Bell would'na be intimidated by something as mundane as driving His Majesty's Royal Mail!" He winked at her, and she smiled back.

He said, "Many wealthy gentlemen pay handsomely for the privilege of driving, you know." He leaned nearer. "All I'm asking from you is a kiss. . . ."

She nudged him back over with her shoulder.

"Heartless woman!" he teased. "Do you know how long I've wanted a kiss from the belle of The Bell?" He leaned near again. "Thought once or twice I might have a chance too. But then you up and left for good. Or so I thought."

She felt his gaze on her profile but kept her eyes on the road and made no reply.

Eventually, Thora returned the reins to Charlie and sat back to enjoy the rest of the drive from the privileged box position.

As they slowed to pass through Wilton, Thora noticed three blond children performing antics along the road, no doubt hoping for a reward. The two youngest turned somersaults on the grassy verge, while their brother wheeled head over heels through the air. Thora pulled a few wrapped taffies from her reticule and tossed them to the youngsters as the Quicksilver passed. In return, the children rewarded *her* with waving hands and broad smiles of delight.

When they reached the Red Lion in Salisbury, Charlie summoned a porter to help Thora down. "Wish I could stay with you, Thora, but we're off again as soon as we change the horses."

"I understand."

"You have time for a nice dinner before the sister coach passes through. I recommend the roast beef."

"Thank you. And thank you for the ride, Charlie. I enjoyed it."

"Enough to earn me that kiss?"

"You never give up, do you."

"Not if I can help it." He tilted his head to one side. "No? Ah well. Perhaps another time. Good-bye, Thora." He smiled and tipped his hat.

"Good-bye."

Thora ventured into the dining parlour and, once seated, watched in impressed silence as the waiter brought out course after course: hot roast beef, cold chicken, green peas, salad, and gooseberry tart. She could not help but compare it to the sparse meals they served at The Bell to rushed coaching passengers. Seeing the spread before her pricked Thora's conscience. Perhaps Jane had a point after all.

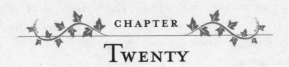

CHAPTER

TWENTY

Ned Winkle helped Jane lay canvas over the back porch, where she planned to work. Ned then spread out the first tick, while Jane opened the bag of feathers.

How hard can it be? she asked herself. Just shove in feathers until the tick is full, then close it up. She shook out some feathers onto her aproned lap for ease of reach, scooped up a handful, and pushed them into the mouth of the tick. Then again. And again.

The cat came over to investigate, drawn by the feathers and the possibility of a bird to eat amongst them. "Don't get any ideas," she warned the tabby. "I paid good money for these feathers—they are not for you."

"Shall I start on a second tick, ma'am?" Ned asked. Not seeing the cat, he tripped over him and landed on the sack, squirting more feathers onto the canvas.

At that moment, wind came whistling through the archway, and sent the feathers flying.

"Oh no . . ." Jane had not expected wind in the sheltered courtyard. In her haste, she forgot the feathers in her lap, and rose, scattering more feathers in her wake.

As if brought by the wind itself, four women strode through the archway—caps, aprons, and pragmatic expressions in place. Jane recognized the carter, Mrs. Burlingame, and the middle-aged

spinsters, the Miss Cooks. They were shepherded in by Julia Featherstone, like a mother hen herding her chicks, though Julia was
the youngest among them.

Jane had no time for a social call. "Hello, ladies. I am afraid
you've caught me at a busy time."

"That's why we're here," Mrs. Burlingame explained in her
lingering Cornish accent. "Mercy told us you were planning to
do this today, and we're here to help you."

"My dear . . ." The younger Miss Cook, Judith, frowned at
the scattered feathers. "I believe the feathers are supposed to go
within the ticking."

"I know, but the wind blew up unexpectedly."

"Could you not have done this inside?" her sister, Charlotte, asked.

"And have feathers everywhere?" Jane said.

"And you don't have that now?"

Miss Featherstone drew herself up. "Well, we shall help you
from here. You go on, Ned." She waved the potboy away. "We'll
take the situation in hand."

Jane hesitated. "Thank you, but I had planned to do it myself
to save expense. . . ."

Charlotte Cook *tsk*ed. "We are not here to earn money, Mrs. Bell."

"Pray, do not be offended, Miss Cook, but have you ever filled
a feather bed either?"

"No. Judith and I deal primarily in lace, as you know. But we
wanted to offer our help, just the same."

Miss Judith sighed. "I adore my feather bed, especially come
the first frost. Charlotte saved and saved, and made me a gift of
one a few winters back."

Her sister nodded. "I cannot abide down myself. Makes me
sneeze. But I am glad you are happy with your bed, Judith."

Jane looked at the woman in bemusement. "If the task will
make you sneeze, Miss Cook, then I am not sure you should—"

"I don't need a feather bed," Mrs. Burlingame interjected. "Mr.
Burlingame gives off more heat than a hot brick, year round."

Jane bit back a smile.

The cat came by again and rubbed itself around Charlotte Cook's hem. She sneezed.

Miss Judith hurried forward. "Poor sister. Let me take puss from you." She lifted the cat and held it in her arms. Jane was surprised the skittish creature would allow it.

"Oh, look at this handsome lad!" Judith purred, stroking its fur. "I do so adore a kitty, but they make dear Char sneeze, so I've never been allowed to keep one. Have you any milk I might give him, Mrs. Bell?"

Charlotte frowned. "Put the cat down, Judy, or you'll be of no help whatever."

Instead, her sister sat on the bench, stroking him. "Pray, what is his name?"

"I don't know," Jane replied. "I've been thinking of calling him Kipper after his favorite treat."

Miss Judith nodded her approval. "Perfect. I'll keep Kipper here from chasing the feathers. He looks ready to pounce."

Her sister sighed. "Very well. Now, let's get these feathers gathered before . . ."

But she spoke too late, for the wind surged again and the feathers scattered, flying up and swirling in the air like snowflakes.

"Not my clean feathers!" Julia wailed, running to catch them before they landed in the muck of the yard. The other women ran about as well, spreading their aprons wide to catch all the feathers they could.

Across the yard, Jane noticed Gabriel Locke standing in the stable doorway, shaking his head.

Jane surveyed the calamitous scene before her and instead of the dread she should have experienced, felt an unexpected bubble of mirth at this odd collection of women, two old enough to be her mother, running about like girls chasing white butterflies, or trying to catch snowflakes as they fell. A laugh escaped Jane and she ran to join the chase.

They rebagged what feathers they could and separated those soiled in the day's misadventure, which would need to be rewashed.

Then the women filled two ticks and promised to return the next day to help Jane finish the rest. A kindhearted Dotty brought out tea for them without being asked and, Jane guessed, without Mrs. Rooke's blessing.

They sat sipping tea and talking, the older women on the bench and wooden chair, and Miss Featherstone on one of the filled ticks, looking as comfortable as a broody hen on her nest.

Charlotte Cook began, "Do you know what Mrs. Barton said when Mercy announced you were making feather beds, and asked if any of us might help? She said, 'No feather beds for me, thank you. If straw bedding is good enough for my bossies, it's good enough for me.'"

Mrs. Burlingame chuckled. "Sounds like Bridget. She certainly loves those cows of hers."

Julia Featherstone lifted one of the empty ticks and studied the seam. "This stitching looks fine. Eileen McFarland's work, is it?"

"Yes. Her son, Colin, works here and mentioned his mother does piecework, mending, whatever she can to earn extra money."

"And hopefully she'll buy food with that money before her husband drinks it away."

"Shh . . . Colin might hear you." Julia nodded toward the door.

Miss Judith sighed. "I wish we could help her somehow."

"What can we do?" Phyllis Burlingame asked in a lower voice. "Her husband is cup-shot daily by noon and blames everyone else for his problems. And Eileen is a proud woman, for all that, and doesn't like accepting charity."

Charlotte sipped her tea. "Can her girls not find work to help out?"

"What can they do?" Miss Judith asked. "They're young yet, are they not?"

Phyllis nodded. "Eileen had Colin when she was newly married. Then Liam took a stonework commission at a church—in the north, I think it was—and was barely home for years. When he returned, they had three more children. I believe the girls are sixteen, thirteen, and ten—give or take. And then there's the baby, who's not quite three. A surprise to them all, I imagine."

The toddler she had seen on Mrs. McFarland's hip. Jane was glad she had heeded Mercy's advice several months ago and given Colin McFarland a chance.

Charlotte Cook took the matter in hand. "Well, for now let's at least see if we can find more needlework for Mrs. McFarland."

When the conversation began to dwindle, Jane thanked the women for their help, then said, "But no need to return tomorrow. You have done more than enough. I shall finish the others. Thanks to you, I think I have the way of it now."

Mrs. Burlingame shook her head. "We'll come anyway. There's something satisfying about seeing a task through to the end."

"Only if you allow me to give you something for your time," Jane insisted.

"Mrs. Bell," Charlotte Cook admonished, "we already told you we didn't help to earn money."

"True." Miss Featherstone's eyes twinkled. "But I have always wanted to dine in an inn."

"Oh, that would be grand," Miss Judith breathed. Around the circle, the others nodded.

Jane felt a slow smile quirk her lips. "I think that can be arranged."

After her meal in the Red Lion, Thora thanked the proprietor, paid her bill, and then found a comfortable chair in the public parlour to wait. She flipped through a selection of newspapers and magazines left there for passengers to peruse—all with recent publication dates. Another thing The Bell lacked.

When the arrival of the sister coach was announced sometime later, Thora rose and strode into the yard. Ahead of her she saw a maroon vehicle with the name *Exeter* emblazoned on its side. A few outside passengers disembarked, and the coachman clambered down and pushed his way in front of his guard, holding out his hand with none of the tact or good humor she had seen Charlie display when "kicking" the passengers for the usual gratuities. This must be the Jeb Moore Charlie referred to. He scowled when the proffered coins were not as plentiful as he thought they should be and grumbled complaints loudly enough for all to hear.

While the ostlers changed the horses, the coachman disappeared into the inn instead of staying to oversee the process. He came out a short while later, wiping the back of his hand across his mouth as though he had just finished eating or drinking. He stumbled over the uneven cobbles, swore under his breath, then belched. Noticing her watching him, he tipped his hat. "Madam."

Thora nodded curtly in reply, already dreading the return trip with this man at the reins.

Charlie had purchased a seat on the roof for her, specifically so she could observe a different coachman in action. The position felt far more precarious than the box seat had. She noticed the coachman did not inspect the harnesses as Charlie had done before taking the reins. The coach swayed under his ponderous weight as he mounted the bench, crowding the scrawny dandy who had paid for the privilege of sitting beside him.

"Like to drive, would you, young sir? Half a crown for the thrill of your life."

"Would I ever! But shall we wait until the road straightens?"

"Where's the fun in that? You want excitement, don't you?"

"Well . . . Might it not be dangerous?"

"Of course it will be! That's where the thrill lies!"

The coachman got the horses moving, then handed over the reins. The young man gripped them, shoulders bunched, head forward and alert.

Several miles passed without mishap. Then the coach approached a sharp curve in the road and swayed perilously. Thora held on to the roof bar for dear life.

The coachman seemed unconcerned, sitting there slouched on the seat, head bowed, chin against his chest. . . .

With a start Thora realized the man was sleeping! He swayed as the coach rounded the bend too fast, two wheels lifting a bit from the road. The guard on back must have realized it as well, because at that moment he blew his horn in a loud, jarring honk that wasn't one of the standard signals Thora recognized. But it was too late. The coachman lurched to the side and toppled off onto the verge of the road, rolling twice before he stopped. The young dandy cried out in alarm, the reins fluttering slack in his hands.

"Stop the horses!" Thora called.

"I don't know how!"

Thora heaved a sigh, then poked the elderly cleric beside her. "Give me your hand," she ordered. He did so, and holding to his steady arm, Thora climbed from the roof to the box.

The coach swayed, and she grabbed the bench to keep her balance, then commandeered the reins from the scared-useless gentleman.

"Whoa!" she called, pulling on the reins. "Whoa now!" she boomed in her deepest, most authoritative voice.

The horses slowed and eventually halted. The roof passengers cheered. The guard hopped down and ran back to help the fallen coachman to his feet, shaken and bruised but otherwise unhurt.

Regaining his seat a few minutes later, the coachman swore at the dandy as though it were his fault, and avoided Thora's eyes.

"You take my seat on the roof," she told the young man. "I'll remain here. Just in case."

The dandy nodded and complied without a murmur of complaint.

The coachman scowled. "Now we shall have to make up for lost time."

They started up the first hill, the horses struggling under the weight of the fully loaded vehicle. Reaching the summit at last, the coachman did not pause to allow the horses to rest or catch their breath but continued on, down the other side. The horses strained and jigged against their bits. Irritated, the coachman pulled a short whip from under his seat and slashed their hindquarters in punishment. With a sickening feeling, Thora recognized it as a short tommy, a whip forbidden by the Royal Mail for its cruelty. Reputable coachmen cracked long whips over their horses' backs—the sound alone spurring the horses forward—without physical pain or whip marks. Short tommies inflicted both. Thora looked back and saw the guard's mouth tighten in a disapproving frown, but seeing her looking, he diverted his gaze, pretending not to see any wrongdoing. If he would do nothing, then she would.

She said, "If you don't stop that this instant, the deputy post-master shall hear of this."

"Hear of what?" the coachman glowered.

"Your diminutive friend, Tommy," she said coldly.

"I have no idea what you are talking about, madam."

"Oh, but I think Hugh Hightower will know very well when I describe what I saw today, Mr. Moore."

She did not like dropping the deputy postmaster's name but decided in this instance it might be useful.

He lowered the whip and narrowed his eyes at her. "Who are you? Besides a devil sent to torment me?"

"Not a devil. An angel."

Later, when they reached The Bell at last, Thora gratefully clutched Tall Ted's hand and climbed down. She thanked him and started across the yard.

Stopping before the porch in surprise, she surveyed the filled ticks and the assembled women sipping tea. She looked at Jane and slowly shook her head. "What happened to 'I can do it my-self,' hmm?"

"We offered to help, Thora," Charlotte Cook insisted.

"Well, so did I," Thora said. "But you are welcome to it. Now, if you will excuse me." She walked into the inn, head held high, hoping no one could see that her legs trembled like jelly.

The ladies rose and departed. Seeing a few passengers enter the inn after Thora, Jane followed behind to see how she might help.

Two men stepped into the dining parlour for refreshment, while a third gentleman perused the few newspapers they offered for sale.

Selecting a copy of *The Times*, he handed Jane a coin, then looked at her again, his eyes lingering on her hair. "Quite orna-mental," he said.

"Hmm?" Jane murmured, unsure of his meaning. Cadi had dressed her hair in its usual style that morning, had she not? Jane ran a hand over her coiffure and felt nothing save pins.

The man only smiled and went on his way.

A few minutes later, Gabriel Locke opened the side door for Colin, as the porter carried in two valises.

Mr. Locke looked her way and raised a hand in greeting. Then he walked toward her, humor in his dark eyes and quirked mouth.

"What?" she asked, self-conscious under his scrutiny.

He slowly lifted a hand and reached behind her ear. She stilled, unsure of his intention. She felt something brush her hair and a moment later he brought his hand back, showing her a feather he had extracted. For a moment longer, he held her gaze.

Embarrassed, she took it from him. "Th-thank you," she murmured.

"A souvenir from a job well done," he said, and turned and walked away.

The next day, after Jane and Ned Winkle lugged the new feather beds up to the best rooms, Jane could not resist testing one, stretching out on a guest bed and sinking into its warm embrace. *Ahh . . .*

Thora stopped in the doorway, hand on her hip. "What are you doing, Jane?"

Jane patted the space beside her. "You have to try this, Thora."

Thora hesitated, then shook her head. "One of us napping in the middle of the day is quite enough."

Jane sighed, and then grumbled to her feet. It was time to get back to work anyway. She had already hung the freshly laundered curtains back in the hall, and today planned to start on those in the dining parlour and guest rooms. Since they were already in arrears with the laundress, Jane decided to try to wash them herself.

But when evening came, she was still scrubbing away on the dining parlour curtains and those for the bedchambers were not fully dry. Her hands felt raw and her back ached from leaning over the tubs for so many hours. Perhaps she ought to have paid Mrs. Snyder to do them after all.

As darkness fell, Thora came outside and found her by the clotheslines behind the inn. "Jane, two guests have complained. They are ready to go to bed but have no privacy to undress without curtains on their windows."

"I'm sorry, Thora. Everything took longer than I guessed it would." Jane wiped a stray hair from her face with the back of her hand. "Can we not . . . hang a sheet or something?"

Thora rolled her eyes. "Oh yes. That would look very smart." She reached for a damp curtain. "Come, let's get these up in the bedchambers at least. They will dry with fewer wrinkles that way."

Jane trudged behind Thora, and together they hung curtains in the guest rooms, finishing the task well past their usual bedtimes. Jane's arm shook. She had never been so exhausted in her life.

The next day, they hung the dining parlour draperies as well. Some of them had not fared well in the wash. Jane hoped she would be able to replace them eventually, as well as the inn's shabby bedclothes and stained tablecloths.

With this in mind, Jane walked over to Prater's and perused their fabric choices, wishing the quality were higher and prices lower. An idea struck her. She crossed the street to Mrs. Shabner's shop and asked the dressmaker if she had any remnants she would be willing to part with at a reduced price. Mrs. Shabner seemed pleased with Jane's humble request and offered her several yards free of charge. When Jane protested, the woman waved her away, saying her reward would be to see Jane in the lavender half-mourning dress.

Jane returned to The Bell, arms full of her new acquisitions. Patrick raised a brow when he glimpsed the colorful, feminine fabrics—so different from the plain, muted bedclothes they'd always had.

Thora fingered through the folded material with a frown. "Printed cotton, sprigged muslin, linen . . . Are these to cover the beds or be worn while sleeping in them?"

"Beggars can't be choosers, Thora," Jane said, an edge of defensiveness in her tone.

Her mother-in-law picked up a length of cambric. "Good heavens. Our curtains shall look like petticoats."

Young Ned touched the sheer fabric with a dreamy grin. "Yes, they shall . . ."

Thora smacked his hand. "Close your mouth and go wash some tankards."

Jane walked away, determined not to take the criticism to heart.

She wished she could go to the linen drapers in Salisbury and buy bolts of the best fabric. But the inn coffers would not allow it. She reminded herself that even if she'd received her settlement money, her father had intended it to provide for her future security, not to buy curtains for a coaching inn.

CHAPTER

TWENTY-ONE

The next quarter day arrived—St. John's Day, also called Mid-summer Day, the 24th of June. As in many great houses and establishments, it had always been Bell tradition to gather the staff on quarter days and pay their wages. Jane had gleaned over the years that it was a day anticipated with happiness by all. But not this time.

Jane dreaded the task ahead. After discussing the situation with Thora and Patrick, she decided to return to the quiet privacy of the lodge to prepare and plan the right words to say. And to pray she did not lose every one of her staff that very day.

Gabriel Locke caught up with her as she crossed the yard. He said quietly, "Give mine to whoever needs it most. But don't say anything. I have a bit put by, and it's no inconvenience for me to forgo wages for a time."

"But—"

"I am in earnest, Mrs. Bell. I am not being gallant."

Oh, but I think you are . . . Jane thought, but said only, "Thank you, Mr. Locke."

Jane continued to the lodge and jerked to a halt at the sight of a dead mouse on her doorstep. Kipper, the grey-and-black cat, sat there proudly with his offering, the second just such "gift" in the last few days. Jane thought of the sexton and his fondness for church mice—a fondness she did not share. *Ugh*. She would have to deal with the mouse later. For now, she stepped over it, retreating inside to gather a few things—including her composure.

A short while later, Patrick came to the door. "Everyone is waiting in the hall," he told her.

"Already?"

"They know it's quarter end. Most have been counting the days."

Jane sighed. "Wonderful. . . ."

Patrick looked into her face, his expression full of compassion. "I'll tell them, Jane. You should not have to."

"Why should you do it? It wouldn't be any easier for you than for me, I don't imagine."

"No, but I'm made of sterner stuff. Your heart is too soft."

"Is it?" She was tempted. Oh, how tempted. She would love to avoid saying the dreaded words. Seeing the disappointed faces. Hearing the complaints and rebukes . . .

Jane stiffened her spine. "Thank you, Patrick. But it is my responsibility. I shan't shirk it."

She reached for the door latch, but he caught her wrist.

"Jane. Why are doing this to yourself? You know you are not cut out for this life. You never wanted this place or its burdens and demands. Let me take it off your hands. I understand you have money coming to you. A settlement, was it? What a godsend. I hate to see you slaving away here, losing your bloom. Look at your hands!" He held one up, and while it wasn't the pruned appendage of a seasoned laundress, it was certainly not as smooth and lily-white as it had once been.

"You needn't become a drudge, Jane," he went on. "Or a coarse, aproned innkeeper. You are a gentlewoman. Raised for better. Let me spare you all this. I could understand if you felt you had no choice. But soon you'll have the means to set up a household for yourself somewhere. Some genteel cottage with flower gardens to tend and peaceful hours to play your pianoforte without carriages rumbling past your door at all hours."

For one moment Jane allowed herself to imagine it. Then she

reminded herself that she had already made her decision. She blinked away the last vestiges of that dream and tugged her hand from his. "Who told you about the settlement?"

He pursed his lips. "I heard it somewhere."

She studied him through narrowed eyes. "Only two people at The Bell knew about it. And I doubt either of them would mention it to you." She shook her head. "I did not realize you and Mr. Blomfield were such good friends."

"Bah. We are not friends. He sees me as a possible business partner. A means of recouping his losses."

"Is that all?"

"Yes."

Was that a flicker of hesitation in his blue eyes? Was he hiding something? She hadn't the time to find out. Her staff was waiting for her.

A few minutes later, Jane walked back across the yard with damp palms and beating heart, dread filling her top to toes.

They will understand, she told herself. They would have to.

As she entered the lion's den, the crowd inside quieted, conversations breaking off one by one as they faced her expectantly. Solemnly. They had probably heard rumors. The Bell's financial difficulties were not a well-kept secret. Not when everyone knew Mr. Prater and Mr. Cottle had cut back their orders, and now the greengrocer was refusing to make any more deliveries until his bill was paid in full.

The ostlers and postillions stood at the back nearest the side door, Gabriel Locke behind them. Clustered together near the front stood the maids, Alwena, Cadi, and Dotty. Beside them were Ned Winkle and Bobbin, the barman. Colin lingered near the front door, anticipating, perhaps, the need to make a hasty exit. Mrs. Rooke stood alone to one side, a hand fisted on her ample hip, an aggressive jut to her jaw, and Jane had not yet said a word.

Patrick positioned himself beside Jane near the office door, and

Thora stood on her other side. Pillars to hold her up. Jane was grateful for their display of support.

She took a deep breath and began, "As you are probably aware by now, we are in a difficult season here at The Bell. Income over recent months has fallen below expenses, and that coupled with an overdue loan has put us behind with our creditors and suppliers. As you know, we are making improvements, cutting costs, and adding new services to help us become profitable again. But in the meantime, I am deeply sorry to say that, for the first time in the long history of The Bell, we have insufficient funds to fully meet our payroll."

Mouths dropped open. Groans and muttered complaints rumbled through the room—and if she was not mistaken, an epithet as well. Jane held up a hand. "I know it is not fair or right. I agree. I realize it will come as small consolation, but none of the Bell family are taking any wages for the quarter." She forced herself to look straight ahead and not glance at Mr. Locke. "Instead of choosing to pay some and not others, we—I—have decided to pay each of you a portion of your normal wages. A small amount for now, hopefully enough to tide you over. And we have every intention of paying the remainder as soon as may be. If any of you have urgent needs, please tell me privately, and I will do all I can to help you. We don't want anyone to suffer."

Thora added, "Please remember that your room and board are provided, so no one will go hungry until we can pay the rest."

Jane nodded. "I hope you will try to understand, and make the best of present circumstances. Together, we can weather this storm and come out the stronger for it." She took a deep breath. "Are there any questions?"

"How much is a 'portion'?" Tuffy, the old ostler, asked.

"Approximately a third of your regular wages."

He winced. "There goes my half pint on my half day."

The other stable hands chuckled.

Colin, she noticed, paled. He opened his mouth to protest, she guessed, but closed it again, looking grimly down at his hands.

Mrs. Rooke stood with a hand on each hip now. "Do you really expect me to work here for a third of my wages, when I could cook for the Crown in Wishford for twice my usual pay?"

"Twice? Surely you exaggerate, Mrs. Rooke."

"I do not. I received such an offer once, and now I am more inclined than ever to accept it. Especially with the larder here all but empty as it is."

Jane didn't know about the Crown, but she had seen Mr. Drake's advertisement for a cook in the newspaper. The wages offered were indeed well above what The Bell paid. Had Mrs. Rooke not applied for the position after "quitting" before, only to do so now?

Not again, Jane inwardly groaned, already dreading having to return to the kitchen.

"Now, don't be hasty, Mrs. Rooke," Patrick crooned. "Here you rule the roost. But at the Crown, you would be under the thumb of Mrs. Phillips. And Mr. Drake wants French cookery. You wouldn't like that."

Jane added, "I am certain we can come to some amicable compromise, Mrs. Rooke."

"You're certain, are you?"

"I hope," Jane gently corrected herself. Thora, she noticed, said nothing.

Jane turned and addressed the assembly once more. "I hope every one of you shall stay on. I realize I still have a great deal to learn. But I promise to work hard and do my best. I trust each of you will as well."

Then she stepped into the office, sat at the desk, and opened the wage log. A wooden tray holding folded paper envelopes sat at her elbow.

She looked at the first name on the list and called, "Ned Winkle."

"Yes, sir. I mean, ma'am." The young potboy stepped inside, hat in hand.

Jane initialed the column and handed him his portion. "Here are sixteen shillings, ninepence halfpenny."

"Much obliged." He backed from the room.

"And the next is . . . Robert Booth."

She leaned forward to survey as much of the hall as possible. No one moved.

"Robert Booth?" she repeated uncertainly, not recalling who it could be.

In the hall, Ned elbowed the barman, and he lurched toward the office. "Oh, sorry, ma'am. I've been called Bobbin so long I almost forgot that was me."

Several others chuckled.

Jane pulled forth the appropriate envelope. "Two pounds, one and sixpence is a third of the sum due to you."

"That's right. I'll make do. Never you fear."

"Thank you, Bobbin."

He stepped out, and she called the next name on the list. "Colin McFarland."

Colin came in, looking agitated.

She began, "And a third of your wages is . . . one pound, eighteen and fourpence."

He looked behind him, then lowered his voice. "I'm sorry, but I need more. The money for the ticks helped, but it's not enough. I wouldn't care for myself. But my mother depends on me—her and my sisters."

"I understand. How much does she need?"

He named a figure, and she penciled it in, more thankful than ever for Mr. Locke's offer to forgo his wages.

Colin accepted it with a sheepish nod of thanks.

One by one, Jane worked her way through the names until she came to Gabriel Locke's. Knowing his desire for secrecy, she called out his name just like every other. He came in, dark brows high in question.

"I have something for you."

"But—"

She lifted a hand to cut off his rebuttal and lowered her voice. "Something of John's." She handed him an envelope with his name in it. It held something weighty, but not wages.

He opened the paper pouch and looked at the items within.

"I found them in John's bedside table."

Gabriel first held up a Roman silver denarius John had found as a boy, with an image of Diana on one side, an ax and ear of corn on the reverse.

"But this might be valuable."

She waved a dismissive hand. "They were once plentiful in the area. Many boys collected them."

Then he held up a copper token engraved with *The Earl's Menagerie* and sent her a quizzical look.

"I thought the two of you might have gone together, for I have never been to a menagerie."

"Ah. John was fond of them, I recall."

Mr. Locke did not, she noticed, confirm or deny he'd attended with him. He returned the items into the envelope. "Thank you, Mrs. Bell," he said, loud enough to be heard by those in the hall.

Last on her list was Bertha Rooke.

With the remainder of Mr. Locke's wages, Jane was able to give Mrs. Rooke the majority of what was owed her. The woman humphed but returned to the kitchen apparently mollified.

Jane closed the book with a heavy sigh, longing for nothing more than a warm bath and an early bedtime.

Rachel had spent the week answering correspondence and packing up her father's clothes to donate to the almshouse. The matron, Mrs. Mennell, had been very appreciative.

At the end of the week, she received a reply from her sister.

Dear Rachel,

Horrors! What you have been through, you poor dear! I should not trade places with you for the world. Though I will say your lot sounds easier to bear than mine some days, what with two little boys underfoot, not to mention one very naughty pug and an equally naughty husband. Nanny can barely keep up with William and Walter, and neither can I! My poor nerves.

Some days I envy you your quiet solitude in dear old Thornvale. Such a pity about the entail, for I'm sure I could convince Mr. Hawley to quit this place for Thornvale, were it ours. And you might have lived with us as beloved aunt to my children! Ah well. Fate has not been kind in that regard. Perhaps I will yet convince dear Robert to send me on my own to Ivy Hill, for I cannot bear the thought of traveling with these young rogues. Trapped for hours with their constant chatter and runny noses? Goodness, no. I love my darlings, of course—don't mistake me. But a respite from the noise and demands of motherhood would be a welcome change, I don't deny. Besides, I should like to meet this distant cousin of ours. Make sure he isn't a greedy old lecher out to seduce you. Pray don't let him dismiss Jemima and leave you without a chaperone!

Yes, I had better come and see what sort of a man he is. I will also help you plan the party Papa always said he wanted after he died. I fear on your own, you will let the thing drop. And of course, I could fetch the jewelry and china at the same time. I hope the dishes won't break. Do be a lamb and ask Mrs. Fife what she would suggest by way of packing and cushioning, will you? And I suppose I shall have to hide the jewels within my unmentionables should we be besieged by highwaymen. How thrilling that would be! Life as mother to wild scamps has prepared me for such an encounter, I assure you. I shall stare them down, take away their favorite guns, and send them off without their tea and biscuits!

I joke to cheer you, my love. I hope you know that. I am not such a ninny to forget you are no doubt unhappy and fearful as you face an uncertain future. If only our snug house were larger! But we have such little space. Especially with Robert's mother living here and another child on the way— Oh! But I meant to wait and tell you in person, so you could be the first to congratulate me. I will purr myself into Robert's good graces and write again when I have a date for a visit. Sooner than later, in my condition. My maid hates to travel, but it can't be helped. She will sigh upon the hour, but at least she will not tug on my skirts and repeat "Mamma, mamma!" until I go mad.

> *Until then, I send my love,*
> *Ellen*

Rachel was surprised to find tears in her eyes, even as she shook her head at her sister's dramatics. She had not cried at her father's death. Not even on the day of his funeral. But now, tears heated and overflowed. Strange. She would not have guessed her sister's chatty letter could evoke such a response. But it was the closest thing to sympathy she had received from family—annoying sister or not. Ellen's words touched her. . . . Well, some of them. There would be time later to read between the lines, to bemoan her sister's self-absorption and petty concerns. To feel the sting of rejection that Ellen would not at least offer, however halfheartedly, to make room for her at their house. But for now, Rachel held the letter to her chest and let the tears come.

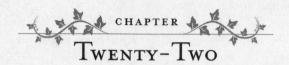

CHAPTER
Twenty-Two

As the summer days passed, sweetened with sunshine and rising temperatures, Jane spent more time working in the inn than she ever had before. Slowly, the burden of ownership warmed to excitement as she carried out improvements and planned more for the future, all the while wishing she might implement every one now. Though a layer of doubt lingered, hope began to sprout through it.

One of Jane's favorite moments from those long days of toil came when she walked past the open door to a guest room one afternoon, then backed up and looked again. There lay Thora atop one of their new feather beds, sound asleep.

A floor board creaked and Thora jerked awake, sputtering, "I was only testing the new beds. . . ."

Jane grinned. "And apparently, they are quite effective."

On the first Sunday in July, Jane and Thora attended church together. Ahead of them, Rachel sat alone in her pew, head held high, profile serene—by all appearances perfectly composed.

After the service, Sir Timothy and his sister paused to speak with her. Justina impulsively embraced her, and Sir Timothy quietly reiterated his sympathies. Rachel stoically thanked them and assured them both she was well. Lady Brockwell coolly inclined her head but otherwise passed by without a word.

A few minutes later, as Jane waited her turn to thank the vicar, her attention was drawn into the south aisle chapel. There, the sexton, Mr. Ainsworth, bent and picked up something from the floor. He held up a wooden trap pinning a dead mouse.

He sucked in a breath, staring at it aghast.

"Poor Jerome . . ." he moaned.

Hearing the mournful words, sadness crimped Jane's stomach.

Beside her, Thora turned to see what had arrested her attention. Jane expected some critical remark, but instead Thora shook her head, a regretful downturn to her lips.

"Pitiful creature," she murmured.

And Jane wasn't completely certain if she referred to the mouse or the man.

Jane turned away from the disheartening sight, thanked the vicar, and started down the churchyard path. But the image of the sexton's grieving face remained with her the rest of the day.

Rachel sat in the drawing room Sunday afternoon, still puzzling over a letter she had received the day before. The maid stepped in and announced that Miss Mercy Grove had arrived. Rising, Rachel felt her spirits instantly buoyed. "Please show her in, and bring tea when you can."

Mercy entered, a smile warming her lovely brown eyes. She wore a simple blue frock, and in her hands she held a curiously lopsided cake streaked with icing of an indeterminate shade of puce-brown. Rachel suspected Mercy's aunt had sent the confection.

"Rachel, my dear, how are you keeping?" Mercy's kind voice was a balm as she leaned near and kissed her cheek. Stepping back, she inspected Rachel with the practiced eye of a schoolmistress.

"I am well," Rachel answered, motioning for Mercy to sit. "Certainly better now that you have come. I have sent for tea."

"Thank you." Mercy set the cake atop the table and slanted Rachel a playful glance. "Aunt Matty sent this with her regards. I think, with a little tea, it shall be edible."

Rachel smiled. "Be sure to thank her for me."

"I shall. And . . . I know Jane has wanted to visit as well."

"Oh. She did write to offer, but I told her not to bother. I know she is busy."

"Not too busy for you . . ."

Mercy paused as the maid entered and set a tray before them. She cut and served the cake before taking her leave.

Mercy noticed the letter on the table. "Have you heard from your sister?"

Rachel nodded and poured tea. "I received a letter from Ellen last week. But this one is from Nicholas Ashford, the heir to Thornvale."

Mercy's eyes widened above the rim of her cup. "Oh?"

Rachel picked up the letter, her gaze once again roving the bold, elegant script. "Shall I read it to you?"

"Yes, please."

Rachel cleared her throat and began:

"My dear Miss Ashford,

I was sorry to hear of the passing of your father. Please accept my sincere condolences. And believe me when I say the news brings none of the self-interested anticipation, which would be so distasteful and rightly disdained by you and anyone of feeling and conscience. Having lost my late honoured father two years ago, I understand at least in part your grief. I confess that knowing I was next in the entail of Thornvale has given me much uneasiness. Not because of your father's recent misfortunes, but because I realize the entail must be a source of vexation and added grief for you and your sister.

I have been so fortunate as to become financially successful in my business and am in a position to maintain Thornvale. So perhaps there is some happy fate at work here after all, though I realize that is easy for me to say, and probably difficult for you to see at present. I take no pleasure in being the means of injuring you or your sister, but especially you, as I understand your sister is settled and lives elsewhere.

I hope it is not presumptuous of me to ask. But may I beg leave to call upon you, to assure you of my readiness to make you every possible amends for the present circumstance? If you should have no objection to receive me, I propose myself the satisfaction of calling on you on the 8th of July, by four o'clock. If that is not suitable, please write to me at the following direction and suggest an alternate arrangement.

Until then, I remain
madam, yours sincerely,
Nicholas Ashford"

When Rachel finished reading, she looked at Mercy over the top of the letter, awaiting her reaction.

"The eighth?" Mercy began. "That is less than a week from now. Will you receive him?"

"I suppose I must."

Mercy considered, then said, "The letter is well composed, and his sympathies are kindly expressed."

Rachel folded the letter, pressing and re-pressing the seal. "He seems a conscientious and polite man," she allowed.

Mercy nodded, and added, "Perhaps he will prove a valuable acquaintance. Especially if he is disposed to make you and your sister any amends."

"Ellen would like that, and I shall not be the person to discourage him. Though it is difficult to guess how he can make us the atonement he thinks our due . . ."

"Is it so difficult?" Mercy asked gently.

Rachel looked at her. "What do you mean? He cannot help being next in line in the entail. He owes me nothing."

"The gesture does him credit. I am predisposed to like him. How old of a man is he, do you know?"

Rachel shook her head. "No. If I ever met him, I don't recall doing so."

Mercy observed, "He has already made his fortune, lucky man. So he cannot be very young, I don't suppose."

Rachel shrugged. What did she care about Nicholas Ashford's age? The crux of the matter was that he was the legal heir and she would have to find a new home and a way to support herself. She supposed it was kind of him to offer to make some amends. A few pounds, perhaps, to help her settle elsewhere? But she had always hated the thought of accepting charity. Her pride smarted at the thought of doing so now. To have this stranger offer to give her some token of what had always seemed hers already. Or was he thinking of giving her some annuity from his proudly vaunted financial success in his trade—whatever it was? She shivered at the thought.

Rachel decided it would be best for everyone if she had her plans worked out by the time he arrived. He would not find her sitting here forlornly—a solitary figure in unrelieved black, hunched over clasped hands, awaiting his knock with weeping and worries, ready to play the helpless victim or grateful recipient of his benevolence. No. Her fate was not in his hands.

For a fleeting moment, she thought of Jane and wished she could go to her for comfort and advice. Instead, she turned to Mercy and forced out the humbling question.

"Mercy, you have offered before, and if the offer still stands . . . might I come to live with you and your aunt? I could pay a little something toward room and board. Well, a very little. Do you need any help in the school? I am not terribly well read, but I know a little French and my mother often praised my fine embroidery. And I am well versed in the rules of precedence, if nothing else."

Mercy smiled apologetically. "My dear Rachel, most of our pupils are bound for lives as shopkeepers or farmers' wives, not as genteel, accomplished ladies."

"Oh . . ." Rachel's spirits plummeted. Was Mercy rejecting her as well?

Instead, her friend leaned forward and pressed her hand. "You are welcome to move in with Aunt Matty and me—don't mistake me. But we will work out the particulars later, all right?"

Rachel nodded in relief, and Mercy raised a forkful of cake high. "At least you know what you are in for," she said with a smile.

Rachel smiled back and nibbled another oddly chewy bite. She realized that if she were going to honor her father's request to hold a party in his honor at Thornvale, she would have to do so soon. Dare she do so while in mourning?

She asked Mercy's opinion. "Do I honor my father's request? Or the social rules that prohibit such entertainments during mourning?"

Mercy considered her dilemma. "Tongues will wag, true. But honoring your father takes precedence over honoring social conventions, in my view."

Rachel nodded. "Ellen agrees with you. But how I dread the inevitable gossip and even more censure from my neighbors."

"Perhaps ask Mr. Paley's advice."

"Thank you. I believe I shall."

On the appointed day, Rachel Ashford waited in the drawing room, hands clasped tightly in her lap. She had never been one to fidget, but she fought the urge to do so now. Nicholas Ashford would arrive soon.

She wondered again what he would be like. Perhaps he would be as kind in person as he seemed in his letters, but doubt lingered. She ached to be sure Thornvale would be left in good hands. Smoothing her black silk skirt, Rachel glanced at the clock. Any moment.

Minutes later, footsteps sounded and the maid announced, "Mr. Nicholas Ashford."

The gentleman who entered was younger than she had expected, and for a moment Rachel thought it might be his valet come in before him. But then she took in his fine striped waistcoat, pristine cravat, and tailcoat and readjusted her opinion.

He was above average height and thin, making him appear perhaps taller than he was. He had light brown hair and bluish-green eyes.

She rose, and he seemed to falter. He paused a few yards away, mouth ajar. His gaze made a quick sweep of the room, and he bowed deeply.

She curtsied.

"You must be Mr. Ashford," she offered helpfully.

"I am. And you are . . . Miss Ashford?"

"Yes. Though I suppose you may call me by my Christian name. We are cousins of a sort, after all."

"Only distantly."

She felt a sting at his words. "Only distantly, yes. Please, be seated. I shall ring for tea. I hope you don't think it presumptuous of me? It is your house and your staff now, after all."

"Not at all."

Rachel rang the bell. "I suppose you might wish to engage new servants? The few retainers we have are worried about that, as you might imagine."

"I have no plans to replace anyone at present."

Rachel nodded in relief. "I had hoped my sister would be here in time to meet you, but she won't be able to visit until next week. She wants to see the house one more time. You understand."

"Of course."

They waited in awkward silence. Him clasping and unclasping his bony knee. Alternately looking at her and around the room.

"Is something wrong?" she asked. "Is the drawing room not to your liking?"

"Hm? Oh no, it's lovely. Lovelier than I expected or was led to believe."

"Perhaps you would prefer a tour of the house instead?"

He rose abruptly. "I would, yes. I don't mean to be rude. But I would like to walk. I have been sitting in a coach for a long time."

"Of course."

"Please don't misunderstand me. It is not that I am so eager to survey my new domain or anything like that."

"It would only be natural if you were. But if you would be more comfortable without me, I would be happy to ask the housekeeper to show you around. She has lived here since before I was born and knows its history better than I do."

"No, no. You are fine. That is . . . please do show me. Or we might simply walk around the grounds first. I noticed a nice little garden and hedge maze . . . ?"

"Yes. My mother loved her flowers. And designed the maze herself."

He looked down, face mottled red and white.

"I did not say that to make you feel guilty, Mr. Ashford. Truly."

"You are very good, madam. Very . . . understanding."

"I have accepted the situation. There is nothing for you to feel bad about."

He slowly looked up and met her gaze. She smiled at him. "Now, let me show you the grounds in hopes you might come to enjoy them as I did."

As she led Mr. Ashford down the corridor and through the conservatory, Rachel felt her chest tighten. How many times had she walked this way to her mother's garden? She pushed the thought aside.

They emerged from the house and stepped onto the cobbled path. She glanced at him to measure his reaction. His arched eyebrows satisfied her pride in the landscape—she had always believed it to be Thornvale's best feature. Today, with sunshine spilling over the lush green lawn, it looked especially beautiful, from the ornamental hedge maze to the garden blooming with all the flowers of summer.

She said, "We've had to cut back on the gardener's time, so it isn't as well kept as it once was. But it's still wonderful, isn't it?"

Mr. Ashford's gaze wandered to her, then away. "Indeed," he murmured.

As they neared the garden archway framed with cascading white clematis, he cleared his throat.

"I must say, Miss Ashford, that you are not at all what I expected."

"No? You expected a bitter and resentful old harridan?"

He winced. "At least a woman of a certain age. Your father was several years older than mine, so I assumed you would be quite a bit older than me."

"He married my mother later in life."

"Ah. I see."

She regarded his smooth boyish complexion. "Though I imagine I am a few years older than you are."

"A very few, if you are."

"Well, what does age matter?" she said.

"In this instance, a great deal."

"How so?"

"In your reply to my letter, you kindly invited me to stay here at Thornvale during my visit. And I accepted, thinking little of it."

"Why should you hesitate? It is your home now, or soon will be."

"Yes, but . . . we are of an age, Miss Ashford. You are no elderly spinster aunt. You are . . ." He paused, his cheeks reddening again. He rushed on. "It would not be proper for me to stay alone with you."

"My goodness, Mr. Ashford. Are you worried about your reputation?"

"Not mine, but I would never forgive myself if you were to become the object of gossip because of me."

Rachel opened her mouth to protest, but paused. Perhaps he had a point. Inwardly, she sighed. "Then I shall leave at once."

"No! Heavens no! I did not mean that you should leave. I meant that perhaps I ought to stay at the inn for now. The coach stopped at a place called The Bell when I arrived in Ivy Hill, and—"

Rachel held up her hand. "I really don't think that is necessary, Mr. Ashford. It is not as though I am without chaperone—not with my lady's maid close at hand, and the housekeeper and housemaid about at all hours. However, if you think it best, I will concede. But tonight you must stay for dinner, at least. Cook would be heartbroken to see all of her haricot mutton go to waste. Not to mention her royal torte."

"Very well."

"And you needn't worry—I plan to have left by the time you return to move in permanently."

They walked on, and Rachel pointed out a stand of tall hollyhocks, a profusion of climbing roses, and a bush bursting with orangey buds. "It is a bit early for a few of the roses yet. But in a few weeks, you will see my mother's favorite peach-colored blooms just there."

"I shall bring you a bouquet of them."

She looked at him in surprise. "I . . . thank you."

After weaving through the rest of the garden and the hedge maze, they returned to the house. Rachel led him through each floor, pointing out her favorite rooms and portraits of common ancestors on the walls.

Later, as they savored their haricot mutton and the rest of the fine meal, Rachel glanced with approval around the dining room. Mrs. Fife had obviously heeded her instructions to impress their guest, having spread a snowy tablecloth and meticulously placed the ornate china and silver reserved for special occasions.

In the flickering candlelight, Rachel studied the man across from her with fresh interest.

"Tell me about your business, Mr. Ashford. You mentioned you have been successful?"

"I hope that wasn't terribly boastful of me. I only meant to assure you that I have the resources to maintain Thornvale as it deserves."

He discreetly referred to the fact that her father had lost his fortune. Without private means of his own, Nicholas Ashford would have had the estate but no way to keep it up.

He said, "So many property-rich and cash-poor aristocrats these days. Not that I am an aristocrat . . ."

Rachel nodded. "My father made his fortune in business. But after he was knighted, he liked to gloss over that detail. We all did."

She sighed and looked around her at the expensive wax candles, the platters of food, and the attending servants. "Yes, without money of your own, you would have to marry a rich heiress to keep up such a place."

He swallowed and set down his wine glass, coughing a little. "Well, I suppose that is often done . . ."

Rachel's neck heated. "Forgive me. Perhaps you plan to do precisely that in any case. It is none of my business."

He did not, she noticed, insist that he had no plans to marry anyone at present. Her curiosity about the future residents of Thornvale overcame her usual polite reserve.

She said, "I am sorry to pry, but may I ask, do you have plans to marry? Perhaps you are engaged already."

"No. I am not engaged . . . as such. Though I do hope to one day marry." He hesitated, then asked, "And you, Miss Ashford? Do you hope to marry one day?"

Her stomach twisted. "I . . . once hoped to, yes. But at my age . . ." She let the words trail away on a shrug.

"But we are close in age, don't forget."

"Perhaps, but you are a man, and men may marry at any age, as my father proved. But women at my age are usually married or on the shelf."

"Ridiculous. You can't be what, five and twenty?"

"I can be, yes. And a few years more. And it is not ridiculous, I assure you. But please, let us leave this tiresome subject."

"If you like."

Thankfully, the bustle of dessert being served came to her rescue, and Mr. Ashford did not press her further.

After they finished their torte, Mr. Ashford sipped his coffee and gazed at her with a wisp of a smile on his lips. "Thank you for today, Miss Ashford. You have been most gracious."

"You are welcome, Mr. Ashford. It has been a pleasure."

"I look forward to introducing you to my mother, when we return in a fortnight."

Rachel dabbed her lips with a napkin. "And I look forward to meeting her." It was true, she reasoned, though the prospect of a new mistress of Thornvale stirred a bitterness in her she would rather not admit.

"I hope that interval will give you sufficient time to . . . prepare?" he asked.

Rachel forced a brave smile and assured him it would.

As he took his leave by the door, Mr. Ashford thanked her again, praised the meal, and pressed her hand. "Good-bye, Miss Ashford."

"Good-bye."

Despite her weariness, Rachel smiled at him with genuine warmth. From all appearances, Nicholas Ashford was the kind man she had hoped him to be. And in her last weeks at Thornvale, she would find comfort in that thought.

CHAPTER
Twenty-Three

Thora awoke on a bright July morning to see a man outside her window.

She bolted upright. *What on earth . . . ?*

Rising quickly, she tied her dressing gown around herself and walked closer to see what was going on. She saw the ladder then, and watched as the man's legs climbed from view. From the glimpse and the position, she guessed it was stout Mr. Broadbent, the plumber. True, repairing the gutters was on the list of future repairs, but finances being what they were, Thora thought they'd decided to put that off for the present. Apparently she'd misremembered, or some new leak had sprung forth since yesterday.

As Thora made her bed, Alwena delivered hot water and left again. Thora washed and dressed herself, having long ago insisted on wearing fasten-in-front stays and dresses she could get into and out of without help. She brushed and pinned her hair in its usual severe coil at the base of her neck and went downstairs.

She made her way to the kitchen for her morning cup of tea and to see how Mrs. Rooke was getting on with her limited larder. In the threshold, she drew up short at the sight of a worktable overflowing with crates of produce and boxes of foodstuffs.

"My goodness," Thora breathed. "The greengrocer have a change of heart?"

Dotty nodded. "Looks like it, ma'am. Mr. Prater too."

Mrs. Barton came in with a large wheel of cheese. Mrs. Rooke poked her head out of the larder. "Right in here, Bridget. Thank you."

Out in the yard, a youth pushed a wheelbarrow of coal to the woodshed, and Colin McFarland directed another man to stack cans of paint near the back door.

Thora turned on her heel and marched to the office.

Inside she found Jane with a stack of new invoices, entering and summing numbers in the ledger.

Thora snapped, "What did you do?"

"Hm?" Jane murmured, without looking up.

Thora said, "Mr. Prater, Mr. Holtman, and Mrs. Barton delivered our orders this morning when they refused to last week. The coal merchant is here, the ironmonger brought the rest of our paint, and Mr. Broadbent is working on our gutters and drain pipes as we speak."

"I wondered what that clanging was," her daughter-in-law said casually. Too casually.

"Jane . . ."

"I merely brought our accounts up to date," she explained. "We cannot operate without coal for the stoves, feed for the horses, and groceries for Mrs. Rooke."

"As I am very well aware. But—"

"And you were in the meeting when we decided on refurbishments and repairs."

"Yes. But Patrick insisted the bills could not be paid. Not and pay even partial wages, let alone fund refurbishments."

Jane glanced up at her, then away again, unable or unwilling to hold her gaze.

"I repeat—what did you do? Tell me you did not withdraw your entire settlement and sink the lot of it into this old place."

"We will be able to pay the rest of the wages now," Jane said matter-of-factly. "And complete our plans for improvement."

"But not pay off the loan?"

"No. There was not nearly enough for that."

"But, Jane, that was your future security. Your nest egg. We could still lose the inn, and then where will you be? What will you live on?"

Jane rose abruptly. "We shall cross that bridge if and when we come to it."

Her bravado did not fool Thora. She saw the uncertainty flash in her eyes.

"And if that bridge collapses?" Thora asked quietly.

"Let's pray that doesn't happen."

When Thora told Patrick what Jane had done, a parade of emotions crossed his face in rapid succession: surprise, irritation, reluctant admiration. Then he tilted his head as a new thought struck him. Smug acceptance?

He pursed his lower lip and crossed his arms. "How kind of Jane to sink her money into our family business. Very manorial of her. The dutiful dowager investing her settlement into her husband's crumbling property. Quite the self-sacrifice. Well, her loss is The Bell's gain."

"She could still lose the inn—lose it all," Thora reminded him.

"Exactly."

Thora frowned. "Patrick . . ."

"That is what makes it a sacrifice, Mamma," he said warmly. "If success were guaranteed, then it would be in her best interests to do so. The risk, the gamble, is what makes it noble."

"You want her to lose," Thora realized aloud, feeling her stomach knot.

"Mamma . . ." Patrick chided, looking like a hurt child. "I would never wish any harm to come to Jane. You know that. I will talk to her and make her see reason before it's too late. She can't have spent all her money yet."

At that moment, a wagon clattered into the yard. From the window they saw the butcher arrive with a side of beef.

Patrick sent Thora an ironic glance. "Or perhaps she has."

Jane stood in front of the inn, head tilted back, watching Mr. Broadbent high on his ladder. She certainly hoped the man wouldn't fall. Unfortunately, he had reported finding several broken roof tiles while repairing the gutters. So they would soon need to have the slater out too.

She became aware of someone behind her and glanced over to see Gabriel Locke—arms crossed—looking up as well. He said, "Patrick is congratulating himself, no doubt. He thinks you'll fail and he'll end up with the place yet, with new paint and gutters in the bargain."

"I think you're wrong about him," Jane said. "He has been nothing but supportive since he returned. He has worked here selflessly to help me, and without drawing a salary."

"No salary, hm? I wonder where he gets the money to buy rounds down at the public house, then."

"Are you saying he is a liar?"

Locke looked at her, and whatever he saw in her face made him change tack. "No, Mrs. Bell. I think he believes himself everything you say he is."

Jane changed the subject, her attention caught by the old roof angel Talbot had mentioned. The carved stone statue depicted an angelic figure in robes, its curled hair giving it a feminine appearance. Unfortunately, a cracked crater marred its face, and it was missing part of its wing.

"I wonder if I should have him take down that broken angel while he's up there. With that damaged face, it looks more like a gargoyle than an angel. Probably struck by lightning once or twice."

"Once," Tuffy said as he hobbled by. "The second strike came from Liam McFarland."

Jane looked at him in surprise. "What do you mean?"

Colin McFarland came out the front door at that moment, and Tuffy put a finger to his lips and shuffled away.

Colin held up a printed Inn Tally form. "Mrs. Bell, would you mind summing this bill for Mr. Wagner? He's ready to depart. I've got to pour the cider for the next coach."

"Of course. I'll be just a moment."

Colin nodded and retreated back inside.

When she looked again, Gabriel Locke still had his head tipped back, considering the statue.

He said, "Probably difficult or even impossible to repair."

Jane agreed. "And I can't see that it would be worth the expense and trouble to do so. Not when the place hasn't been called The Angel in more than thirty years."

He nodded, then sent her a sidelong glance. "Speaking of angels, I hear your adoring cat dropped another *gift* on your doorstep."

She met his gaze, then looked away without replying.

He went on, "Joe mentioned you asked him to dispose of it for you. I'm surprised you didn't ask me."

"I was hoping to avoid being teased about it," she said wryly. "Clearly, I failed."

After that Jane summed the bill for Colin, and Mr. Wagner paid it. Then she returned to the keeper's lodge, feeling unsettled. Had she been rash to withdraw her settlement and use it to pay off the inn's suppliers and finance repairs? She had not yet spent it all but probably would by the time they'd finished all their plans. Was she foolish to do so, as Thora seemed to suggest?

She had thought Thora would appreciate her act, but appreciation was not what had come across in Thora's reaction. Her mother-in-law's words echoed through Jane's mind once again. *"Tell me you did not withdraw your entire settlement and sink the lot of it into this old place. That was your future security. Your nest egg. We could still lose the inn, and then where will you be? What will you live on?"*

Jane's stomach cramped. Would she live to regret her decision? Would she lose the inn to the bank after all? Jane felt suddenly more vulnerable than ever.

Spurred by the notion of being a penniless widow with no roof over her head, Jane thought again of the missing loan money and Patrick's suggestion that John might have hidden it away somewhere. Perhaps with his copy of the loan agreement, wherever it was. She decided to look through their small dwelling just in case.

She supposed it was time to clean out John's belongings anyway, though she dreaded the prospect. Perhaps she should gather John's clothes and see if Patrick wanted any of them, and if not, sell them to the secondhand clothes dealer or donate them to the almshouse.

She had already looked through John's bedside table to find something to give Gabriel Locke in place of his wages. Now she looked deeper, and in more places.

She began by digging through his dressing chest, then looking behind his small collection of books on the shelves, and then behind the framed prints on the walls. She lifted a square box from the cedar chest at the foot of their bed and looked through memorabilia from John's younger days: a few old playbills, calling cards from prominent guests, whist tokens, a Newmarket race bill, and a Roman coin like the one she had given Mr. Locke, this one bearing an image of the emperor. She read a yellowed newspaper clipping announcing him as the new proprietor of The Bell, then picked up a length of pink ribbon, which gave her pause. She reminded herself that he had courted other women before her, including Miss Prater, so it probably belonged to one of them and he simply never discarded it.

At the bottom, she found a piece of stonework, heavy and broken. From the shape and carved feathers, she guessed it had been a part of a wing—perhaps even from the roof angel. Now it was just a fragment of someone's work—of someone's life. Like all these small bits and bobs John had kept. But nothing of monetary value.

Jane rose and looked at the few things atop John's writing desk in the corner of the sitting room, then opened its drawer. She had looked in it before, to extract a quill-sharpening knife or more sealing wax, but had not lingered long. Now she tugged the crammed drawer all the way open and picked up the stack of papers—notes, letters, trade cards, and billheads—she had long ago dismissed as business-related and out of date, and flipped through them again. John had done most of his work at the desk in the office, but here were a few odd pieces of correspondence: a faded reminder from his father to increase the year's order with the coal merchant, a note of thanks from the brewer for their business, a bill from the Salisbury piano tuner, a letter Jane had sent home when she'd gone to London with Mercy, and a folded cover sheet, embossed with the Blomfield, Waters, and Welch seal. She opened the cover sheet, but the folder was empty except for Mr. Blomfield's card. *Strange . . .*

At the bottom of the pile, she found another paper—a letter that had been carefully refolded, and folded in half once again. The handwriting on the outside was scrawled and somewhat smudged, but she made out *Mr. John Bell* and the inn's direction. She unfolded the small sheet all the way and read:

> *Dear Mr. Bell,*
>
> *I was surprised to receive your letter and your offer of help. Especially after the way things ended. Yes, I would be pleased to see you again. If you are serious about wanting to offer some recompense, I will meet you on the 27th as you suggest. You can find me at the Gilded Lily in Epsom. I will be at liberty after 5 o'clock.*
>
> *Sincerely,*
> *Hetty Piper*

Jane frowned and read the brief letter again, thoughts of the banker's card evaporating. In their place, other disturbing thoughts began clanging through her mind like poorly played church bells. Who was Hetty Piper? The name seemed vaguely familiar. A former employee, perhaps? A flicker of an image, a buxom redhead with a winning smile wobbled into memory, then away. Why would John offer to help her? Recompense for what? Surely the first thought that struck her must be wrong. What sort of establishment was the Gilded Lily? A brothel? And finally, the 27th in Epsom. John had died on May the 27th in Epsom. . . .

Jane's stomach roiled, and she swallowed bile. Surely she was reading too much into this. She had to be. John had gone to meet Gabriel Locke to look at horses and attend the races together. A lark, John had said. To keep his friend Locke company. Nothing about a woman, but would not the wife be the last to know? Jane squeezed her eyes shut as another wave of nausea washed over her. Had it all been lies and secrets? Had he been carrying on an affair and she none the wiser? True, their marriage had had its ups and downs—several low periods those last few years. But she'd never thought . . . No. Not John. Not this. He wouldn't.

Would he?

Jane groaned, pain and dread quickly igniting into indignation. *Tell me I did not just invest my settlement into your inn when all the while you were betraying me!* If so, Thora was right; Jane would regret it. Did regret it. Here she was trying to save her husband's inn, his legacy, only to have her loyalty thrown back at her like a bucket of cold water!

Did everyone know? Were they all laughing at her behind her back? *"First her dowry, then her settlement. We sure took advantage of that foolish gentlewoman. . . ."*

Don't jump to conclusions, Jane told herself sternly. She would discover the truth first and then alter her plans as needed. If the worst was true, she would horde every penny she had left, sell every inch of pipe and gallon of paint her money had bought, and leave The Bell to rot without a backward glance. Let the bank have it, or Patrick. Let it burn to the ground.

CHAPTER

Twenty-Four

Jane found Thora seated at John's former desk in the office, wearing spectacles and sorting through papers in the drawers.

"Thora?"

"Hm?" she murmured without pausing her search.

Jane scraped a drop of hardened wax from the desk with her fingernail and attempted to keep her tone casual. "Who is Hetty Piper?"

"Hetty?" Thora looked at her over the rims of her small spectacles.

"Um-hm."

Thora squinted in thought. "Hetty worked here briefly as a maid. Why?"

"Just curious. Was she that ginger-haired girl? The pretty one?"

"Yes," Thora replied. "Too pretty for her own good. Or anyone else's."

"What do you mean?"

"We hired her to clean and change beds, not turn heads. Tempted more than one male, I can tell you."

"Male guests or . . . staff?"

"Both."

Jane dug her fingernails into her palms. Not the answer she wanted. "Why did she leave?"

"I dismissed her—that's why. Gave her the sack, and good riddance. More trouble than she was worth."

"When was this?"

Thora shrugged. "Maybe two years ago. I could look up the exact date in the wage log if you need it for some reason."

"No. That's all right."

Thora studied her, eyes narrowed. "Why are you asking about Hetty Piper now, after all this time?"

"Oh, I . . . ran across her name somewhere, that's all. Just curious. What are you looking for? Still searching for the copy of the loan agreement?"

Thora kept her wary gaze on Jane's face, ignoring the change in topic.

Jane continued, "I just looked in John's desk in the lodge, and unearthed a folded cover sheet from the bank. I thought I might have found the loan papers, but there was nothing inside except Mr. Blomfield's card."

Thora frowned at that, shut the drawer, and removed her spectacles. "That's unfortunate. Patrick seemed to think it might be important. By the way, the greengrocer took advantage of you in Talbot's absence. I found an invoice for a pineapple of all things." She waved the offending billhead.

Jane replied, "I am afraid I ordered that. Delicious. But that was before I realized how expensive such luxuries were."

"I see." Thora set the bill aside.

"Well then." Jane forced a smile. "I shall leave you to it."

Jane thought about asking Patrick what he knew about Hetty. But when she glanced into the taproom, she saw him in animated conversation with several other men and didn't want to spur ribald talk about the apparently infamous redhead.

Instead, she sought out Gabriel Locke. She found him in the stable yard, trimming a horse's hooves.

She leaned her elbows on the gate. "What is the Gilded Lily, Mr. Locke?"

He looked at her over his shoulder in surprise, then scowled. "Not a place I would ever venture into. Why do you ask?"

But John had? she thought. Instead of answering, she asked another question. "You were with my husband the day he died—is that so?"

He grimaced. "You know I was."

"Then do you know he planned to meet a woman named Hetty Piper while he was in Epsom that day? At a place called the Gilded Lily?"

He stared at her a moment, then looked down. "I believe he mentioned something about meeting a former employee, but not the details." He sent her a wary glance. "Where is all this coming from?"

"I found a letter in John's things." She pulled it from her apron pocket. "Miss Piper wrote that she would meet him after five o'clock on May 27th."

Gabriel's face puckered. "Five o'clock?"

"Yes. But John died . . . ?"

"Around four, give or take."

"So this supposed meeting never took place?"

He released the horse's leg, then straightened. "May I see the letter?"

Jane frowned at him, suddenly vexed with the man. "You never mentioned any such meeting before. Or any woman John knew in Epsom. Did he have a mistress? Is that why he was gone from home so often that last year?"

Gabriel looked around to make sure no one was in earshot, then ran a hand over his face. "I never saw him meet a woman. Though, granted, we were not together round the clock. But I don't think so—not when he was married to you."

"I am not such a prize. Our relationship was not all it should have been. But still, I never thought . . ." She fluttered the letter in her hand and turned away.

He called after her, "What are you going to do?"

"I am going to Epsom, apparently," she shouted back.

"Jane. Mrs. Bell. Don't. That establishment is no place for a lady."

She walked on, but he caught up with her.

"Please, don't go. Not now and certainly not alone. I am traveling north later this week to see that associate about a horse, remember? I could inquire on your behalf. Or if you must go, allow me to escort you."

"I think not, Mr. Locke. Something tells me that if I want the truth, you are not the man to give it to me."

He looked pained again, and embarrassed in the bargain. He said, "I am in general an honest man, but I have learned the hard way that those who ask for the truth often wish back their ignorance. Truth, like medicine, is sometimes best in small doses."

"I disagree. And I do not require your protection, Mr. Locke. In deciding how much truth I can handle, or in traveling. I will go by mail, with a maid." She added sardonically, "I believe I may know someone who works in a coaching inn and can help arrange the fare."

Jane turned on her heel and walked smartly away, feeling no satisfaction and weighed down with a queasy dread that he was probably right—it was doubtful she would like the answers she found.

Jane went directly to the reception counter that served double duty as booking desk. Patrick sat there, routes and timetables spread before him.

When she stated her request, he looked at her askance.

"You want to go where?"

"Epsom."

Patrick studied her face, then asked, "Who is in Epsom?"

She went on as though she'd not heard the question. "It's southwest of London."

His eyes remained on her face. "I know where it is."

"Do you?"

"Of course." He slid the route plan forward. "I have the map right here."

For a moment, Patrick set aside his questions and showed her how far she could go on the Royal Mail and where she would have to alight and book passage on a stagecoach to travel the rest of the way.

"The Brighton Road goes right through Epsom, but unfortunately not the Exeter to London route."

She made note of all he said and insisted on paying the fares from her own money.

When they had completed the booking, Patrick rested his elbows on the desk and regarded her again, a strange light in his eyes.

"I'm curious, Jane. Locke was in here last week, asking about the best way to reach Epsom. And now you want to go there at about the same time. Some people might call that a suspicious coincidence. Not I, of course."

"I am glad to hear it," Jane dryly replied. "I would hate to think you know me so little as to suspect some assignation."

"Of course not." He smirked. "Not the proper Lady Jane."

She gave him a sour smile. "Mr. Locke has been planning to visit his associate about a fly horse ever since our planning meeting, remember? While my . . . errand came up rather suddenly. Unrelated, I assure you."

"What is this errand?"

Jane sighed. "Patrick, Epsom is where John died. Can we not leave it at that?"

His smirk fell away, and his appealing eyes turned downward at the corners. "I'm sorry, Jane. I did not mean to upset you."

She so rarely saw him without a playful smile. Far less looking sincerely sad.

She patted his arm. "That's all right, Patrick. I know you like to tease."

He laid his free hand over hers. "True. But I would never want to hurt you, dear Jane."

"I know that, Patrick."

But did she? She thought of Locke's warnings about her brother-in-law, then brushed them aside. Patrick was not the Bell brother uppermost in her mind.

As Jane crossed the yard on her way back to the lodge, she

noticed Kipper waiting for her on the doorstep. Before she could reach him, Mr. Locke hailed her. She reluctantly paused, and in a few long strides he stood before her.

"Still planning to go?"

"Yes. And you—when do you depart?"

"Friday."

Jane nodded. "Excellent. Cadi and I leave Thursday."

He opened his mouth to protest, but she raised her hand to cut him off.

"We have booked the last two seats on the upline, and that is for the best. It is not necessary, nor would it be appropriate for you to travel with us."

He inhaled through flared nostrils, then exhaled heavily. "Very well. But you will be careful?"

"I am always careful, Mr. Locke," she assured him. She opened the lodge door, and with a look of challenge, let the cat inside.

But once the door closed behind her, her smirk faded. She sank to her knees and stroked Kipper, taking comfort from his soft fur. In truth, Jane was nervous about making the trip to an unknown town and about the unpleasant errand ahead of her. But she would hide that fear from Gabriel Locke. And from herself.

The next day, Jane walked down the High Street toward Prater's Universal Stores and Post Office to mail a belated letter to Mr. Coine, thanking him for his help with the settlement and letting him know what she had decided to do with the funds. The Prater's shop had served as post office for years, Ivy Hill being too small to support a separate building for the purpose. Jane recalled John coveting the role for The Bell, but he'd never made any headway with the deputy postmaster toward that end.

As she neared, Jane looked up at the storefront. Brooms and brushes were displayed in one bow window, baskets in the other. Painted in decorative lettering beneath the shop name were the words: *Hardware, Fabrics, Housewares, Haberdashery*. Jane had noticed the sign before, but looked closer to admire the fine lettering now that she knew Miss Morris had done it. Jane planned to ask her to repaint The Bell sign as well.

Ahead of her, a large man—the wheelwright, she believed—opened the shop door. Rachel Ashford appeared from the opposite direction at the same time, letter in hand. Jane nodded to her and together they followed the man into the shop.

Rachel opened her mouth to say something, but the conversation at the back counter silenced her. The ladies there must not have seen Jane and Rachel enter behind the broad man, because after a cursory glance at him striding toward the hardware section, Thora and Mrs. Prater went on with their discussion.

"You would never do such a thing, I trust, Mrs. Bell?"

"Do what?" Thora asked.

"Miss Ashford. Hosting a party—and her father not a month in his grave."

Rachel stiffened and stepped behind a display of copper kettles and pots, shielding her from view. Jane followed suit.

"A party?" Thora asked.

"Yes, a dinner party. Mr. Holtman was just in, boasting of the big order he received for it. And the butcher, no doubt."

Thora asked, "No big order for you, Mrs. Prater?"

Jane heard the wry note in Thora's voice if Mrs. Prater did not.

"No. Not that we'd want to be a party to such a party. During deepest mourning yet. It just isn't done."

"No doubt she has her reasons."

Jane glanced at Rachel, noticing her blush of embarrassment. *Poor Rachel*, Jane thought. At least Thora had not joined in the criticism.

Mrs. Prater finished measuring the coffee Thora had purchased. "Anything else, Mrs. Bell?"

Thora pointed to one of the glass candy jars. "Those lemon bonbons—are they popular with children?"

Mrs. Prater nodded. "Yes, though my grandchildren prefer taffies. But . . . you haven't any grandchildren, have you, Mrs. Bell?"

Jane held her breath.

"You know I haven't," Thora coolly replied.

"My Lydia has three strapping boys, as you may recall. Such hearty appetites already. I do not covet her grocery bill! Thankfully her husband does well as a house agent. When I think how heartbroken she was all those years ago . . ."

Jane's throat tightened. She felt Rachel's gaze on her profile and feigned interest in a gleaming kettle.

"Yes, we can all rejoice that your daughter escaped the dread fate of marrying my son," Thora dryly replied.

"My dear Thora, I did not mean—"

"Yes, Hilda. That is exactly what you meant."

Jane felt the barb personally, having been the one to marry John and then failing to give Thora grandchildren. Ears hot, Jane turned away and slipped out of the shop without completing her business, hoping Thora did not see her leave. She wondered why Mrs. Prater would strike out at Thora. She must know Thora had been in favor of a match between John and her daughter. It was John who chose Jane instead, not his mother. And no doubt, not a day went by when Thora did not lament John's choice.

The shop door jingled behind her, and Jane kept walking, head down, certain it was Thora. Instead Rachel called, "Jane? Wait."

Reluctantly, Jane paused as Rachel caught up with her. "You may not believe me, but I was planning to come and see you after I stopped in the post office."

"Oh? Why?"

"I heard that Fairmont House is to become a hotel and I wanted to—"

"To gloat?" Jane asked.

Rachel Ashford stilled, blinking, and Jane immediately wished back her words. It was the first time Rachel had sought her out in years, and this was the greeting she received? Jane steeled herself for a cutting retort or for Rachel to stalk away.

Instead Rachel said, "No. To commiserate. How could I gloat, when I am losing my home as well?"

"At least Thornvale will not become a hostelry for strangers."

"No. Simply someone else's home, thanks to the entail."

Shame swept over Jane. "I am sorry. I have no right to complain about losing my former home when you are losing your present one."

Rachel looked at her hands. "I suppose you like seeing me knocked down a peg or two."

"No." Once Jane might have felt some unworthy satisfaction, but no longer. "When must you vacate?"

Rachel drew a deep breath. "At the end of next week."

"Will you move in with Mercy? She mentioned the possibility."

"For the time being, yes." Rachel paused to glance back at the shop. "No doubt you heard what Mrs. Prater said—about the party? I suppose you will judge me harshly as well."

Jane shook her head. "It is none of my business."

"Nor theirs. But my father always used to say, 'When I die, don't walk around with long faces. Instead, hold a party in my honor. Promise me; before you're out on your ear, host the grandest dinner you can and clear out the wine cellar!'"

Jane managed a small smile. "You know, I do remember him saying that."

"Well. I wasn't going to do it," Rachel said. "Not when my sister and I are in mourning. But Ellen insists. And I spoke with Mercy and Mr. Paley, and . . . I've decided to honor his last request before I depart Thornvale."

"I understand. And again, I am sorry for your loss."

Rachel lifted the letter in her hand. "I was on my way to post an invitation to Mr. Nikel, Papa's old solicitor and hunting companion. If your father were still with us, I would have invited him as well." Rachel bit her lip. "I . . . don't suppose you would want to come?"

Jane could not tell from Rachel's halting manner whether she had meant to invite her and anticipated a refusal, or if she had not intended to invite Jane but, since she had overheard talk of the party, now felt obligated to do so.

When Jane hesitated, Rachel added, "I am also inviting Sir Timothy and his mother and sister. Mercy and her aunt, whom my father loved to tease. Ellen, of course—though her husband cannot get away. And Mr. and Mrs. Paley. We have far too many females to males, so I've given up thoughts of trying to even our numbers. Unless you think I should?"

"Invite whomever you like, but not on my account."

"Then I will limit the party to old friends."

Old friends . . . Were she and Rachel still friends after all this time and cool distance? She noticed Rachel had made a point of mentioning that she had invited Sir Timothy. Was that her way of warning Jane that it would be awkward if she were there as well? Surely after all this time they could be polite and friendly together. But did Jane want to add to Rachel's anxiety, when she was already uncertain about hosting this party?

"I don't know . . ." Jane said at length. "When is the great occasion to be?"

"The twenty-first."

Jane hesitated, thinking of her upcoming travel plans. Depending on what she learned in Epsom, it was doubtful she would feel equal to a party when she came back. "I am going out of town, and am not certain exactly when I shall return, or if Thora and Patrick will be able to spare me when I do."

"Oh. I see." Rachel nodded. "Well. Have a good trip."

"Thank you," Jane replied, though she doubted it possible.

Rachel walked away, filled with guilt and disappointment. She had not missed Jane's hesitation, the vague nature and duration of her supposed trip—an excuse, no doubt. Well, what had she expected, Rachel asked herself, when she had turned down invitation after invitation from Jane over recent years? She had put off Jane's offers to visit, to come over for tea, to attend a theatrical in Salisbury together. She had turned down Jane's offers of help, of comfort during her father's illness and after his death. Rachel had been polite, but aloof. It was a wonder Jane had tried as long as she had. *What else is Jane to think than I don't want her in my life?*

Rachel wondered if her refusals in the past had cut Jane as deeply as her reticence cut Rachel now. In the strained distance between them, Rachel imagined the worst possible scenarios: Jane hated her. She had no interest in being her friend. She had probably complained to others of how Rachel had treated her. To Mercy, or worst of all, to Timothy.

I am sorry, Jane, she thought. *I did not mean to make you feel like I feel now. I am sorry, God. I know my resentful behavior and selfish superiority cannot have pleased you. I know you love Jane, and that her value as a person has not diminished because of whom she married, or because Timothy loved her more than me. . . .*

Rachel looked over her shoulder, surprised to see Jane still standing there in her black gown, watching her go. The two of them might have been sisters, both of them dressed in mourning. Surely Jane would give it up soon. It had been over a year now since her husband died. Or did she wear it like a suit of armor?

Please forgive me for the way I've treated her, Rachel prayed. *Please help me repair the damage I've done. Help her to forgive me too. Oh merciful heavenly Father, help me not be so full of myself that there is no room for anyone else. And worse, no room for you.*

CHAPTER

Twenty-Five

On the day of her departure, Jane and Thora sat down together to go over a few details and the tasks that would need to be taken care of in Jane and Cadi's absence. She dared not ask Thora to feed a stable cat, but Joe had agreed to sneak treats to Kipper now and again while she was away.

When they finished, Thora set down her quill and removed her spectacles. "Tell me again why you are going?"

"I . . . feel I need answers about John."

"About his death, do you mean?"

That too, Jane thought, but only nodded. She did not want to tell Thora what she really wanted—needed—to find out. She could not bear to reveal it, not to his own mother.

"Again, I am sorry for taking Cadi and leaving you short-handed."

"We'll manage."

But in Thora's glittering gaze, Jane saw questions and suspicions sparking. She wondered again if Thora had any idea that Hetty had moved to Epsom after leaving Ivy Hill. Apparently—hopefully—not.

Thora dug into her apron pocket and drew forth several wax-paper-wrapped taffies. "By the way, give these to Cadi after a few hours. She is fond of them."

Jane accepted them with vague politeness but silently wondered why Thora had sent nothing for her.

Thora stood at the window, observing the scene in the yard. Jane stood in her black bombazine gown and bonnet, a small valise in hand, as forlorn a figure as a new widow. She thought of her own dark, serviceable dresses. Was Jane remaining in mourning for her sake? She hoped not.

Beside Jane's sedate form, Cadi could hardly stand still, all joggles and hand gestures, eager for her first trip out of Wiltshire and her first journey with the Royal Mail, well beyond the means of a chambermaid. *More of Jane's money spent. And for what?*

Across the yard stood Gabriel Locke in the mouth of the open stable, leather apron over his trousers and shirt, leaning his forearm against the doorframe. His eyes were trained on Jane. Jane looked up and for a moment held his gaze. He did not smile or wave. He simply stood there, watching her. Jane looked away first.

What made Jane so ill at ease? And what was really behind this sudden excursion of hers? As far as Thora knew, Jane had not traveled much at all in the last eight years, except a trip or two with her friend Mercy. And not with John since their wedding trip, even though he had traveled often in the last few years of his life. She wondered anew why Jane had not gone along. At the time, Thora had smugly assumed their marriage was not the bed of roses John had been certain it would be. But now she wasn't so sure. Had Jane refused to go? Or had John not asked her to accompany him?

Their conversation of a few days before ran again through Thora's mind—Jane's unexpected question about Hetty Piper. Thora had not thought about that girl in months. The redhead had worked at The Bell quite briefly, and as far as Thora knew, she and Jane would have seen each other only in passing, since Hetty worked primarily upstairs and Jane had so rarely left the keeper's lodge. Had Jane's unexpected question been somehow related to this trip? How could it be?

But standing there, looking at her daughter-in-law in black, thoughts of Hetty quickly faded and Jane's destination returned to the fore. Epsom. The place where John had died, and in such a senseless manner.

Thinking of it now, as she rarely allowed herself to do, a suffocating lump rose in her throat, burning her chest and making it difficult to draw breath. Her son. Killed like that. In a strange city so far from home. She should have been there. Someone he loved should have been with him. Gabriel Locke was a friend of sorts, though not of long standing. That was some comfort. But he was not family.

Thora swallowed. Yes, she could understand Jane's questions. Her desire to see the place where John had died. If Jane had asked her to go along instead of Cadi, she would have. But Jane had not asked.

And that was for the best, Thora told herself, inhaling and squaring her shoulders. If the landlady was going to go gallivanting about the country, some level-headed, experienced person needed to remain behind to oversee things. Especially with their lead horseman leaving for several days as well.

Patrick had mentioned the coincidence with a suggestive smirk, but Thora didn't believe it. She could read Jane well enough to know she was hiding something, yes. But no matter Patrick's theories, she was certain Jane's plans had nothing to do with Gabriel Locke.

But what Mr. Locke might have in mind . . . ? She was far less certain about that.

Jane was very fond of Cadi. She really was. But after an hour in her company she had to stifle the urge to grasp her hand to stop her constant gesturing out the window at this sight or that, and to ask her to *please* be quiet. The girl, understandably excited about her first journey, chattered and exclaimed and asked questions nonstop, giving Jane a headache, and probably their fellow passengers as well.

Suddenly Jane remembered the taffies in her reticule. At the time, Jane had slightly resented that Thora had sent something only for Cadi. Now Jane understood. She smiled to herself at Thora's unexpected thoughtfulness and humor, and offered Cadi a chewy candy. The girl accepted with pleasure, and since she was too polite to talk with her mouth full, they all enjoyed several minutes of blissful quiet.

After the first leg of their journey by Royal Mail, they alighted and ate a meal in a coaching inn on the route. Then they had another hour to wait for the stage to Epsom. They sat in the parlour on a padded bench side by side, biding their time. Cadi's chatter slowed to the occasional question or comment about the inn's fine food, "the best I ever ate—don't tell Mrs. Rooke," to her assessment of the inn's cleanliness, to wondering what the rooms were like.

When Jane ceased replying, Cadi finally drifted into silence. Jane did not mean to be rude, but her thoughts were consumed with the encounter ahead—hoping she would be successful in locating Hetty Piper. Would she be able to find her at the seedy establishment a year later? If not, might someone there tell Jane where she could be found? How would Jane answer any questions about what business she had with the girl?

Soon after settling into the stagecoach to Epsom, Cadi, exhausted at last, nodded off, her head bobbing and finally resting against Jane's shoulder. Jane breathed a sigh of relief and prayed for the strength and grace to face whatever lay ahead.

When they reached Epsom and halted before the Marquis of Granby, a two-story red-brick coaching inn, it was quite late. Jane secured a room for her and Cadi, and the two prepared for bed. Cadi fell asleep almost instantly, but Jane slept fitfully in the strange room, plagued by unsettling dreams.

In the morning, they rose, dressed, and went downstairs. Jane found a porter and asked him to direct her to the Gilded Lily, and how far it was. The man looked at her askance, surveying her top to toe, no doubt assessing her fine, if outmoded, widow's weeds.

"Not far at all, ma'am. Only a short walk. Though it isn't a place for a lady like you."

She thanked him without explaining herself, and then led Cadi into the coffee room.

"You wait here for me, Cadi. I shan't be long." *I hope.*

"But, madam, I am supposed to accompany you."

"And you have done, most capably. But you heard the porter. It is only a short walk."

She glanced around the cheerful coffee room, busy with chatting couples, well-dressed gentlemen, and a mother traveling with two children.

"You will be perfectly safe here until I return."

"But will you be safe?" Cadi asked. "I heard the man say it isn't a proper place for ladies."

"No one will harass a widow like me." She forced a grin and handed the girl several coins. "Have breakfast. Order whatever you like. You're on holiday!"

Cadi's eyes widened at the sight of the coins, and Jane pointed out the menu board, which the girl instantly began to peruse. She was glad the maid could read. Not all could. On her way out, she stopped the innkeeper's wife and asked her to keep an eye on her young friend while she ran a brief errand. After Jane assured the woman Cadi would be ordering and ordering well, the woman agreed.

Following the porter's directions, Jane walked up the High Street. Reaching the tobacconists, she turned right down a narrower lane. At its end she found a surprisingly well-kept, half-timbered building with a small, discreet sign in far better repair than The Bell's.

The Gilded Lily.

Jane took a deep breath, and pushed open the door. It took a moment for her eyes to adjust to the dim interior. Inside she found a parlour richly furnished with upholstered chaise longues and velvet sofas, red draperies on the windows, thick carpets on the floors, and a grand curving stairway leading to the upper floors. Near the bottom of the stairs, at a large gilded desk, sat a stout, heavily rouged woman, bent over a page of fashion prints in a ladies' magazine. Behind the chair, newspapers and magazines were stacked four feet high.

Jane took a deep breath and said, "Pardon me. I was hoping to see Hetty Piper?"

"You and a dozen gents, love."

"Excuse me?"

The blowsy woman glanced up, and looked again, regarding Jane with a frown line between her penciled brows. "Who are you?"

"A . . . friend from home," Jane lied with a feeble smile. *Lord, forgive me.*

The woman stared at her a moment longer, then jerked a thumb toward the stairs. "She's up there, cleaning rooms. Or she should be. If you find her lollygagging, tell her Goldie says get to work, silly baggage."

Jane nodded and started up the stairs, lifting her hem to avoid tripping. Reaching the landing, she walked slowly down the corridor, the smells of pipe smoke, French perfume, and body odor heavy in the air.

At an open door, she stopped and peered warily through the threshold. Inside the room, an aproned figure bent low with a carpet broom, housemaid's box nearby. Jane spied several strands of red hair peeping out from under her cap.

"Hetty?" she called quietly, hoping not to startle her.

Without pausing, the woman muttered, "Who's asking?"

"Mrs. Bell."

The carpet broom stilled, and the maid's capped head looked sharply over her shoulder, mouth O'd. Then she straightened and turned to face her.

The young woman pressed a hand to her significant bosom. "'Bout scared the stuffing right out of me. For a moment I thought you meant Thora Bell." She sighed in relief.

It wasn't the reaction Jane would have expected. She asked, "Do you know who I am?"

"Of course I do. I saw you now and again across the yard or out with your flowers. Though I am surprised you knew who I was—greeted with just that view of my backside." She chuckled.

Jane didn't respond to that, guessing several men would easily identify that view.

Hetty asked, "What are you doing here? In a place like this?"

"I might ask you the same thing."

The young woman shrugged. "Thora Bell sent me away without a character reference. None of the respectable places would take me. I am only a maid here—don't worry—not a doxy. Not for lack of requests, mind, but I refused in no uncertain terms. In the end, old Wigglebottom decided to hire me anyway, just to clean. Likes to have me sweep the walk and polish the front windows just about opening time. Lure the gents in and then hand over one of the other girls. Poor things. Better them than me. I know that's terrible to say, but . . . well, there it is."

The girl hesitated, looking Jane over again, head to toe, as if just noticing her black attire. "Someone die?"

Jane stiffened. "As a matter of fact, yes. My husband."

The girl stared at her, mouth ajar. "What? Mr. John—dead? It can't be."

Was she grieving someone she had cared about, Jane wondered, or just shocked?

Hetty sank onto the made bed. "Knock me down with a feather, I'm blowed. When was this?"

"Last May, on the very day he was to meet you—at least, according to this letter." Jane lifted it from her reticule to show her proof. Would the girl try to deny it? Offer some alternate explanation for the meeting, hopefully a plausible one?

Hetty gently took it from her and glanced at the direction. "Where did you get this?"

"I found it among John's things."

"Mr. John kept it?" Slowly shaking her head, Hetty unfolded

the letter and read its contents, reminding herself of what she had written.

"So that's why he never showed up that day."

"Had he . . . come to see you before?"

"No. I had not laid eyes on him since I left Ivy Hill."

Suddenly the girl sucked in a breath, eyes wide. "Was he the man who was struck by a runaway carriage that day?"

Jane nodded.

"Ohhh . . . I am sorry, ma'am. I heard a man was killed but never guessed it could be Mr. Bell."

Jane steeled herself, then forced out the question. "Were you with child, Hetty? Is that why you needed John's help?"

Jane stood there, every muscle tense, dreading the answer.

Hetty stepped to the door, looked both ways down the corridor, and then closed it, whispering, "Goldie doesn't allow talk of children here." She turned back toward Jane, lowering her eyes, the first sign of shame Jane had seen her display. "Yes, I was."

She looked up. "And you will think me greedy, I suppose, but I welcomed any help Mr. Bell saw fit to offer me. Stuck here as I am."

"Where is the child now?"

Hetty ducked her head, hands clasped. "I had to give it up, didn't I? I had to work. Especially when Mr. Bell didn't help me after all—though now I know why."

Jane drew in a shaky breath. "Mr. Bell was . . . responsible?"

"He wrote that he *felt* responsible." The girl waved a vague gesture. "Especially after his mother sent me away like that, without a shilling or a character."

Jane thought she might be ill but swallowed bile and asked, "Did you . . . love each other?"

"Me and Mr. Bell? Naw. But he was terribly good looking and so devilish charming, you have to admit."

"I . . ." Jane should think her own husband charming, she supposed. How awkward and humiliating to discuss his appeal with another woman, and his lover in the bargain. Hetty, however, seemed

not to feel any qualms about it. Jane faltered, "John was always
. . . very . . . good to me, yes." *Or so I thought.*

Suddenly, Hetty's animated face fell slack and her bow lips
parted. "Bless me! You didn't think I was talking about Mr. John,
did you? Heavens, no! Not *that* Mr. Bell. Patrick Bell." She stepped
nearer. "Mr. John replied to my letter and told me his brother had
left the country but that he felt responsible and wanted to offer
some recompense in Patrick's stead."

She gripped Jane's hand. "Glory be! No wonder you looked so
pale and pinched. No, ma'am. Mr. John might have felt duty bound
to help, but he was not the man who put me in that predicament
in the first place!"

"Oh . . ." Jane exhaled deeply, relief quickly followed by embarrassment. "How foolish you must think me."

"Not at all. Looking at this letter now, I can see how you might
have thought that. But it wasn't Mr. John, I swear it! He was about the
only man who didn't ogle me like that. Well, him and Mr. Talbot."

Jane's relief was soured by this disappointing revelation about
Patrick's character. Is that why he'd left the inn—and the country—around that time? "I feel I should apologize on my brother-
in-law's behalf."

"Oh . . ." Hetty hesitated. "It wasn't his fault. Not really."

"He must share the blame at least, even if he shirked the responsibility." Jane considered, then made up her mind. "I will
write you a character reference myself, Hetty. And give you what
money I have with me, though I'm afraid it isn't much. Or . . . why
don't you come back with me? I shall give you a place at The Bell."

Hetty nibbled her lower lip. "Is Thora Bell still there?"

"Yes. But I am the landlady since John's death."

"And Patrick?"

"He has recently returned."

Hetty shivered theatrically. "I could face the old lioness again
if I had to. Working for Goldie has toughened me up. But I don't
know that I dare put myself in Patrick's path again. He hasn't
gained several stone and lost his teeth, has he?"

Jane shook her head.

"Just as devilishly handsome and charming as ever?"

"I'm afraid so." Though less charming in Jane's estimation after learning of his behavior with someone in their employ.

Hetty said, "Then I had better take my chances with a character reference here."

"Very well. But if you are not able to find a decent situation, promise me you will come to the inn. Write, and I will send the fare myself."

"You are very good, Mrs. Bell."

"I wish I deserved that praise. My husband intended to help you on the last day of his life. How could I do any less?"

A short while later, when Jane stepped out of the Gilded Lily, she paused, disconcerted to see a man loitering on the street, leaning against a lamppost.

He was looking down at his pocket watch, his hat brim shadowing his face. A prospective customer this early? He was well dressed, but that might be a ruse. He could be a footpad. Whatever else he was, he was probably up to no good, especially in front of this particular establishment. She felt embarrassed to be seen leaving the place, and hoped no one thought her associated with what went on there. She raised her chin and determined to look ladylike and unconcerned.

The man glanced up, and she saw his face. His familiar face. Gabriel Locke.

She stopped where she was and scowled at him.

He was better dressed than she usually saw him, with trousers, coat, neckcloth, and beaver hat. He might have looked handsome, were he not scowling back.

He shut his pocket watch with a snap. "In one more minute, I was coming in after you."

She narrowed her eyes. "What are you doing here? I suppose you followed me—how did you get here so quickly?"

"I left earlier than planned."

"And not by stagecoach, apparently."

He made no answer.

She said, "I told you I didn't need you to chaperone me, Mr. Locke. I am a grown woman."

"Yes. One who has grown up in a protected nest and has little concept of the dangers of a town like this, teeming with gamblers and rakes."

"Actually, I thought you were a footpad when I first saw you. Though a well-dressed one, to be sure. Are those your Sunday best?"

"Something like that, yes. Makes little sense to wear good clothes while shoeing horses and mucking out stables."

"This must be a nice diversion for you, then, spying on your employer."

"Did you learn what you came for?"

"I did. And then some."

He stiffened. "What do you mean?"

"I will say only that John was not involved romantically with Hetty Piper."

"I am glad to hear it. Then, may I ask why he offered to help her? Was it only kindness to a former employee? Or for some . . . mistreatment while she worked at The Bell?"

She mimicked his vague reply, "Something like that, yes." She saw no reason to disparage Patrick's reputation further when Mr. Locke already esteemed him so little.

"And you, Mr. Locke? Have you talked to your associate about a horse for the gig?"

"Not yet. I'll see him later. First, I plan to spend some time with my friend at the coaching inn—after I escort you back there."

"Very well."

He gestured down the street and fell into step beside her.

Struck by a sudden thought, Jane turned and gripped his sleeve. "Since you are here, show me where it happened."

He held her gaze, his dark eyes wary and sharp, but did not need to ask what she referred to. "Are you certain?"

"Yes. Please."

He nodded, and when they reached the High Street, he turned right instead of left toward the inn.

As they walked, she said, "I know you told me some things when you first came to Ivy Hill with the news. But I confess, it's a bit of a blur. The shock, the disbelief. I was almost . . . angry with you, I recall." She gave a self-mocking chuckle. "Ready to shoot the messenger, as though it were your fault somehow."

"I felt as though it were my fault. At least in part."

She felt her brows rise. "Did you?"

"I was with John when it happened. I felt responsible."

"You were not driving the coach that struck him," she reminded him.

"No. Thank God for that. Or I would never be able to live with myself."

He paused in front of a newsagent's shop. "We were walking along here. The streets were very crowded that day—the races had just let out. I looked up and saw a carriage careening toward us. John stumbled, or was nudged by the jostling crowd . . . I don't know. Someone nearby must have seen the carriage a second before I did and pulled me out of the way. But not John. I tried to shout, but it was all over in a flash."

"Did they never find the driver?"

"No. He sped off without stopping."

Jane sighed. "I still feel guilty."

"You? Why?"

"Because I wasn't here with him when he died. I've wondered so many times . . . Might I have prevented it somehow? Insisted on traveling with him? I try not to, but I find myself imagining the scene. I vacillate between hoping he died quickly—with little time to feel pain or fear—and hoping he had a few moments to prepare to meet his Maker. I believe you told me he said he loved me. Is that correct?"

"Yes."

"Mr. Locke, please tell me everything again. Everything you

remember. You stayed with him, right to the end. He wasn't alone . . ."

"He wasn't alone." Gabriel Locke looked down at his gloved hands. "He wasn't in great pain. I think he was numb with shock. John lived for several minutes. I called for someone to find a doctor, a surgeon, anyone. And the newsagent went running. But I stayed, knelt beside him, and held his hand."

"What did he say?"

Mr. Locke's voice grew hoarse. "He said, 'Tell Jane I'm sorry. Sorry about leaving her alone so much.'" He hesitated. "'And . . . may God forgive the rest. But I love her. I do. Tell her.'"

"The rest? I don't recall that part. Do you think he meant the loan?"

"I don't know."

Tears filled Jane's eyes and her throat tightened. "I loved him too. The last year or two . . . things were not good between us. It's such a relief to hear he still loved me."

Gabriel nodded. "He did. Your name was first and last on his lips."

Jane reviewed his words in her mind. "I'm glad John asked for forgiveness. I would like to think he'd grown closer to God toward the end of his life. What a comfort that would be."

Gabriel hesitated. "I would like to think so too."

When they returned to the Marquis and entered the coffee room, Jane saw a man seated across from Cadi. A soldier. So much for the innkeeper's wife agreeing to watch over her.

Jane marched forward, but before she reached the table, the officer rose and turned to Jane. "I was only keeping your fair companion company. Someone needed to." He winked at Cadi, bowed, and strode smartly away.

Cadi waved good-bye, dimples blazing. Then she looked back at Jane. "Oh, don't look daggers at him, ma'am, he was only being friendly. Saved me from boredom, I can tell you. Oh! Mr. Locke. I did not expect to see you."

"I came to town earlier than planned and ran into Mrs. Bell on the street. Thought I would escort her back."

"I'm glad of it. She would not let me go with her." She asked Jane, "How was the place? As scandalous as the porter let on?"

"Not . . . too bad. The point is I've done what I came for and we can go home."

"Will you be joining us for the return journey, Mr. Locke?" Cadi asked, a speculative gleam in her eye as she looked from him to Jane.

"No, I still have business to attend to here, and another few errands to complete. But I shall see you both soon."

He gave them a brief bow and took his leave.

Cadi watched him go, eyes still twinkling. "What a coincidence that you should meet someone from The Bell here in Epsom."

But Jane knew it was no coincidence at all.

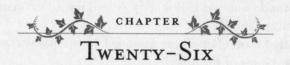

CHAPTER
Twenty-Six

On her way to the office, Thora passed by the hall mirror—placed there so arriving gentlemen and ladies might tidy their windblown hair—and paused at the sight of her own reflection. She wasn't upset about anything, and yet, a slight frown creased her face. She stepped nearer and looked again, and the frown only deepened. Her husband had described her as handsome, and Charlie often complimented her looks. But that was not what she saw.

The "neutral" expression she wore as she went about her day-to-day activities was . . . grim, Thora realized. She lived, it seemed to her, in expectation of disappointment. Her eyes guarded, her mouth slightly downturned at the corners. It was her penchant for efficiency, she told herself. No need for her face to transform from one extreme expression to the next. She was ready to frown at all times. Life had taught her to expect little else.

Thora could think of a few women who went around with equally forbidding expressions who, in her view, had little right to wear them. Lady Brockwell came to mind. And she'd caught her daughter-in-law wearing a similar expression. Yes, she had lost her husband. But not a son. Thora had lost both. And more.

Thora also knew a few women who walked around smiling incessantly for no good reason. Living in expectation of pleasure around every corner. It was annoying, really. She supposed, if they'd never experienced anything else, why wouldn't they smile, naïvely assuming life would always hand them whatever they wanted, tied in a bow. She thought of young Miss Brockwell. Pretty, well-to-do, and not yet twenty. She'd never known how cruel fate could be. Mrs. Paley, the vicar's wife, also came to mind. She probably felt duty bound to always look happy. A walking advertisement for God and the church.

No, that wasn't fair, Thora amended. Mrs. Paley was sincerely contented most of the time.

And then there was the rare woman who had every right to look forlorn, yet did not. Women who lived in expectation of pleasure against all logic. Like Mercy Grove, whom Thora admired most of all. Mercy did not walk around like a ninny with an inane smile splitting her mouth wide. But her long gentle face seemed always on the verge of a soft smile—just waiting to be given a reason to brighten a little more. Her eyes, when she looked at you, shone with inner light. As though hearing whatever you had to say carried the promise of pleasure, whether you were itemizing your laundry list or granting some dearly held wish.

Mercy was plain, had few prospects, and worked tirelessly to teach those who could never fully repay her. Yet that brimming anticipation of finding good wherever she looked added brilliancy to her complexion and made her more beautiful in Thora's view than any so-called "diamond of the first water." Fortunately, men did not often notice and value that deep, beneath-the-surface beauty Mercy possessed. So she'd had no suitors and would probably avoid the pitfalls of marriage.

Thora thought about Jane. Perhaps she should warn her. She had seen the attentions paid to her by Mr. Drake, Sir Timothy, and Mr. Locke, and she didn't want Jane to make the mistake of remarrying.

If Jane did so, the inn would become the property of her husband, unless she engaged a whip-sharp lawyer to draw up another marriage settlement. So warning Jane—protecting her—would be protecting the inn as well, to some degree. The only way marriage would be beneficial was if Jane happened to marry an experienced innkeeper determined to make The Bell successful—or a wealthy man willing to pour funds into the old place. None of her current suitors would do, in Thora's estimation. It was more likely Mr. Drake would sell The Bell and divert the proceeds into his new hotel. A farrier wouldn't have the experience or money to improve the place, and Thora doubted a baronet would marry an innkeeper, but if he did, the first thing he'd do is pluck his lady love out of anything resembling *work* and either sell the place or appoint some fussy dandy to manage it in her stead. Horrors.

Yes, Thora would try to find a good time to offer Jane some friendly advice and hope she wouldn't resent it—and that she would listen to her more than her sons ever did.

On the journey back to Ivy Hill, the coach passed Fairmont House along the new turnpike. Jane glimpsed James Drake outside with Mr. Kingsley, heads bent over a paper spread wide. A wagon loaded with lumber arrived, and James gestured the driver around the side of the house.

Jane pulled her gaze away to find Cadi watching her. She met the maid's questioning look with a reassuring smile.

When they reached The Bell, Cadi offered to take her valise to the lodge, knowing Jane was eager to check on things in the inn. Jane nodded her appreciation and thanked Cadi again for accompanying her on the trip.

Kipper appeared and wound himself around Jane's ankles, mewing his protest of her absence. Jane bent to scratch his head. "Miss me, did you, Kip? I shall find you a treat as soon as I can."

She went inside and found Thora talking with Patrick as he lounged at the front desk.

Her mother-in-law looked up, eyes measuring. "How did it go?"

"Better than I expected, actually."

"How so?"

Jane glanced over the desk at Patrick. "I learned I was wrong about something."

Patrick laced his fingers behind his head. "And that is a good thing?"

"In this case, yes."

Thora asked, "Did you find the answers you were looking for?"

"I did. And then some. I happened into Gabriel Locke while I was there, and he showed me where the accident happened."

She noticed Patrick raise a brow and send his mother a knowing look, but Thora ignored it.

Jane explained, "He was in Epsom to talk to a friend who works at the inn there, remember?"

Patrick smirked. "Whatever you say, Jane."

Jane hadn't decided whether or not to say anything about what she'd learned about Patrick in Epsom but found she couldn't remain silent in the face of his smug innuendo. "While I was there I also saw someone who used to work here. I think you remember her. Hetty Piper?"

His smirk fell away instantly.

"She certainly remembers you."

Thora looked from Patrick to Jane, lips parting to speak. Jane expected her to say something derisive about the girl again, but instead Thora closed her mouth without a word.

Jane said, "I learned that John had gone to Epsom with a view of helping Hetty, but he died before he got the chance."

"Helping her?" Thora asked. "Why would John help Hetty Piper?"

"That is what I wanted to know. Rest assured, there was nothing untoward between them, but we can take comfort in knowing he intended to do a good deed the day he died."

Thora jerked up her hands in exasperation. "Then why did God not spare him?"

Jane shook her head. "I don't know."

"'The good die first . . .'" Patrick murmured, quoting Wordsworth.

Thora sent him a frown, then turned back to her. "Did you learn anything else about John?"

Jane wanted to clutch what she had learned to herself and treasure it. But seeing the unusually vulnerable expression on Thora's face, Jane realized she was not the only woman who needed reassurance about John's death.

Jane drew a deep breath and chose her words carefully. "Most of it we already knew, though I liked hearing it again. John wasn't alone when he died. Gabriel Locke was with him—held his hand, stayed with him until . . ." She swallowed. "He assured me John was not in much pain, but rather, numb with shock. A blessing, in this case. John lived for several minutes. Long enough to apologize for being gone so much. And to say that he loved me."

Thora nodded. "Of course he did."

Jane looked at her in surprise. "He loved you too, Thora, I know. He thought the world of you and respected you highly."

Tears brightened Thora's eyes, but she blinked them away.

Jane thought back, then added, "John also said something like 'May God forgive the rest.' So I'd like to think he made peace with his Maker before he died."

Thora nodded. "I would too."

Talbot and Colin emerged from the office at that moment and hesitated at seeing Thora, Jane, and Patrick deep in serious conversation.

"Pardon us."

Thora drew herself up, glad for the interruption. She'd had more than enough emotion for the time being.

"That's all right. We were just hearing about Jane's trip."

"Ah." Talbot nodded. "And was the Marquis of Granby everything Locke claimed it was—fast turnouts, excellent service . . . ?"

Thora looked to her daughter-in-law. She doubted Jane had paid much attention to the coaching inn itself, focused as she had been on the details of John's passing.

Jane replied, "I . . . thought it very nice. It hasn't the character of The Bell, but the rooms were comfortable and the food excellent. I am sure Mr. Locke will have more specific details to report about their turnouts when he returns."

"And when will that be?" Patrick asked.

"I don't know exactly. He mentioned other errands, including acquiring a horse, so a few days, I'd guess. How is Mr. Fuller doing in his stead?"

"Excellent question." Patrick looked at their porter. "Colin, why don't you and I go out and talk with Jake. See if he has everything he needs."

"Good idea, Mr. Bell."

"I think I will slip out as well," Jane said. "Wash off some of this travel dust. But I will return to relieve you soon."

Thora shook her head. "It's growing late, Jane, and you've had a long day. Go to bed. I'll see you in the morning."

"Are you sure?"

"I am."

After Jane left, Thora wandered to the window. There, she watched Patrick and Colin crossing the yard. With a touch of irony, she asked Talbot, "How is Master McFarland doing?"

Talbot's lips tightened. "He works hard, Thora. And he is not his father—no more than Patrick is his."

Thora gaped at Talbot, the wind knocked from her lungs. It was one thing for her to privately criticize her husband or doubt her son, but Talbot . . . ?

"But you think he is, don't you?" she asked a little breathlessly. "You see Frank in Patrick and mistrust him because of it."

His eyes downturned. "Thora, I had no intention of saying a word against anyone. I only want you to give Colin a chance."

Heart heavy, Thora whispered, "'The apple doesn't fall far from the tree.'"

"Then let's hope for an exception to that rule. In both cases."

Thora inhaled deeply—time to change the subject. "How is Nan?" she asked.

Talbot shrugged. "The same, mostly. I know she'd enjoy another visit from you. You caught us at our worst the last time you were there. Me in my work clothes and Nan in her nightcap. The house a mess. It's only fair you should come again and let us improve your impression. Come after church. See us in our Sunday best. I shall give you a proper tour of the place. You and Jane are not the only ones planning for improvements, you know. And I shall, um, put a roast in the oven and muster up a little something for our dinner."

Thora shook her head. "No."

His brows lowered. "No?"

"Don't go to so much bother. Roast a chicken. Beef is too dear. And I shall bring a few things to go with it. Mrs. Rooke still lets me use her kitchen, and I remember my way around it."

"Thank you, Thora. We would enjoy that."

"Is there anything special Nan likes? Or anything she isn't supposed to eat?"

"The doctor has placed no restrictions on her diet, beyond avoiding anything stronger than a few sips of hot elder wine, which eases her cough. Sadie and I have tried everything from invalid meals to fare worthy of country miners, but little tempts her these days."

Thora frowned in thought. "I see . . ."

"But then," Talbot said, "she has never been offered one of your famous pork-and-veal pies."

"That's right. Nan mentioned you were partial to them."

"Very true." His eyes shone as he grinned at her, and Thora found herself grinning in reply. It was a foreign yet oddly pleasant sensation.

The next day, on her way down the corridor, Jane noticed Thora in the kitchen. "Has Mrs. Rooke recruited you again?"

Thora gestured toward the larder. "Fetch me the sugar loaf, will you?"

"Of course." Jane crossed to the larder, startled to find Colin inside, perusing the shelves. He turned sharply at her entrance.

"Did you need something, Colin?" Jane asked.

A flush crept over the porter's face. "Ah, well, I thought I might help Dotty with the inventory."

From behind Jane came Thora's acerbic voice. "How kind of you, considering Dotty is away visiting her sick aunt today."

Colin's blush deepened. "Beg your pardon, Mrs. Bell . . . and, er, Mrs. Bell. I'd better get back to the yard." Stepping past Jane and Thora, he quickly exited.

Jane reached for the sugar loaf and handed it to Thora, who stood looking after Colin with narrowed eyes. "What did I tell you. You can't trust a McFarland."

"We don't know that he was doing anything wrong, Thora."

Thora huffed. "If you say so."

Jane followed her back to the kitchen table and asked, "Are you ever going to tell me what you have against the McFarlands?"

Thora glanced at her in surprise. "Did John never tell you?"

"Not that I recall. Though Tuffy mentioned something about the roof angel. Did Liam McFarland give her that . . . unfortunate face?"

"Not exactly." Thora kneaded a mound of dough, explaining as she worked. "She was struck by lightning many years ago. Liam McFarland assured us he could repair the injury, or at least make it less noticeable. He is a mason but had also done stone carving, so Frank agreed.

"But when the man arrived to do the job, he was completed fuddled by drink. He would not listen to reason but insisted on climbing up on the roof anyway, eager for his pay. He started in with hammer and chisel but slipped and fell. He flailed for a handhold, struck the angel's face with his chisel, and ended up breaking her wing in the bargain."

Thora whacked the dough for emphasis, and Jane thought of the piece of angel wing she had found among John's things.

Thora continued, "He caught himself on the gutter, which slowed his fall. It was a miracle the fool wasn't killed. He broke his arm, however. Frank agreed to pay Dr. Burton's bill, and Liam's lost wages during his recovery, but he was not satisfied. He kept coming back for more. Even after the doctor declared him fit, Liam would moan of how his arm ached whenever it rained, blaming that—and us—for his inability to work." Irritation flashed in Thora's eyes.

"He started frequenting our taproom and running up a bill, then refused to pay it, saying we owed him. Finally Frank had had enough and banned him from the premises. There were a few ugly scenes after that. But thankfully, the constable and our regulars took Frank's side in the matter and finally Liam gave up coming here, though he swore revenge."

Jane slowly shook her head. "It's a wonder he even allowed Colin to work here."

"Probably sent him here. A new way to get more from The Bell, or retaliate somehow."

"I can't see Colin doing that."

"No? Then you are not looking closely enough." Thora extended a flour encrusted hand. "Pass me the salt, if you please."

Jane didn't agree with Thora's poor estimation of Colin's character, but at least now she understood its origins.

Jane handed over the dish, then watched as Thora cut leaf shapes from salted pastry dough. Decorative pastry? It seemed rather frivolous from practical Thora.

Although she knew she ought to return to the office, Jane lingered, watching Thora shape dough and thinly slice veal with growing curiosity.

"Goodness. That looks too fine for our dining parlour."

"It isn't for ours."

"No? Are we expecting some august guest I don't know about?"

Without looking up from her work, Thora replied, "Meddling does not become you, Jane."

Thora slid two meat pies into the oven, then paused, fanning herself with her apron. "It's devilish hot in here."

"Is it? Must be because you're working so hard. Shall I open a window for you?"

"Thank you. Seems I am always hot these days. Just wait, Jane. It will happen to you one day as well. For the first time in my life I am eager for winter's return."

Thora grated sugar over cooled raspberry tarts, transferred them into a tin, then retrieved a covered basket from the scullery shelves.

Jane felt her brows rise. "Are you preparing a picnic, Thora?"

She placed the tin in the basket. "This is not a picnic."

"It has every appearance of one."

"I am simply packing a few things I hope will tempt Nan Talbot's appetite."

Jane eyed the rich food. It did not look like a bland, soft meal suited to an invalid, but thought it wiser not to say so.

Thora added, "I am going out to the farm to call on her after church tomorrow."

"That is kind of you. Will Mr. Talbot be there too?"

"Of course. It is his home now as well, after all. Why do you ask?"

Jane shrugged. "No reason. It just seems like a great deal of food for an invalid."

"I trust Talbot and his housekeeper will partake as well. Now. What am I missing . . .?" She wiped her hands and looked around the kitchen.

"Do they expect you, or are you calling unannounced?"

"Talbot asked me to call. To visit his sister-in-law and see the improvements on the farm. But one doesn't like to visit empty-handed."

"No risk of that. I half wish I were invited as well. It all looks delicious."

The hint passed without comment.

Jane was not offended Thora did not invite her to join them. Instead she bit back a secretive smile.

CHAPTER
TWENTY-SEVEN

As Thora brushed her hair on Sunday morning, she noticed something on her face. She rubbed a finger over the mark, but it did not yield. "Delightful," she muttered acidly. A small brown spot now marred her temple. She huffed. *What next?* She should have heeded her mother's advice and been more diligent about protecting her skin from the sun.

Someone knocked and Thora called, "Enter."

Alwena poked her head into the room. The mousy maid delivered hot water in the mornings. But she had already done so, and Thora had not expected her to return.

"What is it, Alwena?"

"Um, I hope you don't mind my asking, ma'am, but I was hoping you might help me with something."

"Oh? What?"

"Well, you know how Cadi has become quite accomplished in dressing ladies' hair? She has been teaching me. Mrs. Bell thinks I ought to practice, and then I could dress hair for lady guests when the need arises. I was thinking I could try my hand at dressing your hair—if you'd let me."

"Very few ladies travel without their own maids, Alwena. Jane should know that. A foolish notion and a waste of time."

The maid's expression fell. "Yes, ma'am. Sorry to bother you." She backed from the room.

"Wait," Thora commanded, a thought striking her. "I suppose it can't hurt. I am only dressing for church, of course. And if you make a mess of it, that won't matter—I shall wear my bonnet. As long as you are careful with the hot iron." She wagged a finger. "And no scissors."

"Of course, ma'am. Thank you." Alwena came forward, barely suppressing a smile of relief. Foolish of Jane to get the girl's hopes up. Little call for a lady's maid in a coaching inn like theirs.

Thora sat in front of her dressing table, and Alwena set to work. The maid unpinned and brushed out Thora's shoulder-length, straight black hair.

"You've pretty hair, ma'am, if you don't mind my saying. And lots of it too."

"Is that part of the service, Alwena—flattery along with a good brushing? Or is the flattery extra?"

"No, ma'am."

From her apron pocket, Alwena withdrew a small pot and removed the lid.

"What is that?" Thora frowned.

"Just a bit of pomatum. Gives a little fullness."

Oh well, Thora told herself. She would wash it out tonight if she didn't like the stuff. She hoped it didn't stink. She inhaled, relieved it didn't have an overpowering fragrance.

Alwena worked deftly, applying pomade to the roots of her hair and brushing it forward, then pinned it to the crown of her head with soft height. She coiled the rest of her hair high at the back of Thora's head, loosening the sides before twisting and securing the coil. Then she stood in front of Thora and combed strands free at each temple and curled them with more pomade and a small curling iron heated over the oil lamp.

"Please don't make me look the poodle, Alwena. Or like mutton dressed as lamb."

"No, ma'am. Not at all."

"And do hurry. I don't wish to be late for church."

Alwena stepped away and stood behind Thora once more, both of them looking in the glass. "Well, ma'am?"

Thora had told herself to be kind, to think of something positive to say. Instead she blinked at her reflection. The height and fullness of the hair framed her face and flattered her cheekbones, while the delicate curls softened her features, downplaying her strong nose.

"I look . . . That is, I . . . like it. Well done."

The girl flushed with pleasure. "Thank you. You look lovely, if I do say so myself. Would you allow me to try one more thing?"

"There's more?"

"It's only . . . I've been experimenting, see, and I've concocted a pot of lip rouge—"

"No. No rouge." Thora lifted her hand. "I am not a trollop. And I am going to church, remember, not a ball."

"Well, you see, that's just it. I made this pot of balm to soften lips. But Mrs. Rooke says I didn't put enough vermilion in it, so it's not dark enough—you can barely tell it's there. But I'd hate for it to go to waste. Could we at least try it? You can always rub it off if you don't like it."

Thora considered. "My lips are dry, I admit. If it will soften them and won't be noticeable, then very well."

Alwena uncorked it and offered it to Thora. "Just dab it to your finger and then to your lips. And here, just one more thing . . ."

Before Thora could protest, the maid dabbed a few dots of the stuff to each cheek and then patted it with a bit of cotton wool.

"Just a hint, you see, ma'am. Even the vicar shan't be any the wiser. But you look five years younger."

Thora studied one side of her face, then the other, then looked at herself full on. The rouge gave only the slightest rosy glow to her cheeks and lips. Nothing showy or tawdry. She did look younger. Prettier.

She held out her hand and Alwena's smile fell. Thora accepted the wad of cotton and rubbed the rouge off her cheeks.

"You did well, don't mistake me. But the hair is enough for

now. We don't want people staring. Or not to recognize me, now do we? Perhaps after church, we might . . . try again?"

Alwena released a relieved breath. "With pleasure."

In the end, Thora decided to forgo her usual mobcap and heavy bonnet and instead wore a smaller one of black straw that sat farther back on her head. With its upturned brim, the front and sides of her hair showed a little. After all, there was no use in letting all of Alwena's efforts go to waste.

After church, Thora went up to her room briefly to lay aside her prayer book and black cape. Alwena scratched on the door, a box under one arm.

"I hope I'm not in trouble, ma'am. Mrs. Jane Bell asked me to deliver this to you a few days ago, but I quite forgot 'til now."

"What is it?"

"A few things you passed down to her before she went into mourning. She thought you might want them back now that you've returned."

Alwena opened the lid. On top lay a Kashmir shawl of purple lilac with a border of yellow-gold in a swirling teardrop pattern. "This shawl is lovely," Alwena breathed. "Such a soft color."

"Yes . . ." Thora fingered the fine lightweight wool, remembering how the colors had once given her pleasure.

"This would look so well with your grey dress, ma'am. If you don't mind my saying. There are a few others things in here as well." She set the box on the chest at the foot of her bed. "I'll leave them with you for now. No hurry to decide."

Thora sat, and Alwena came forward and began reapplying the rouge.

As she did so, she shyly asked, "Did anyone at church notice anything . . . different about you?"

"One attends church to praise God, Alwena," Thora mildly reproved. "Not to seek praise for oneself."

"I know that, ma'am. I was only wondering."

"I did receive one or two compliments, now you mention it," Thora begrudgingly admitted. "Mrs. Paley said something kind. As did Miss Grove."

"I am glad to hear it."

Alwena touched up Thora's hair, and then took her leave.

When the door closed behind her, Thora stepped to the box and lifted out the purple shawl. Spreading its length across her bed, she admired the patterned border on each end, noticing how well it still looked after all this time. Then she experimentally wrapped it around her shoulders, eyeing its effect in the looking glass. She barely recognized herself, what with the well-dressed hair and now this . . . color on her person. She had loved this shawl. It was one of the rare extravagances she had allowed herself. She'd bought it in the market from a man wearing a turban. It had come all the way from Kashmir, down into India, and from thence to England, he'd told her. It embodied fashion and wealth, which meant little to Thora. But it had also seemed to represent all the exotic, beautiful places she would never see. She had worn it often before Frank died.

Should she wear it now? Dare she? Wait . . . Thora Stonehouse Bell lacking courage to wear an article of clothing? Since when was she concerned about what other people might think? She let the shawl slip from her shoulders.

Perhaps she would just carry it, folded over her arm, in case it grew chilly on the way home that evening. Protection against the weather, that's all. Perfectly practical.

Talbot had offered to come and fetch her in his cart, but Thora refused. She did not wish to be seen riding side by side with him as though they were some young courting couple. She had walked to the farm before and would do so again, though the basket would grow heavy.

But when she'd retrieved the basket from the kitchen and passed through the hall on her way out, Patrick stopped her.

"Wait, Mamma. I'll ask Colin to drop you off. He offered to

pick up an order of candles from the O'Briens, and Talbot's isn't much out of the way. He's taking the gig, now that it's repaired."

Thora resisted the urge to curl her lip and refuse. Colin likely planned to go by way of the public house if he was anything like his father. Probably fall off like that drunken coachman, and Thora would be left to take the reins again. She sighed. *Oh well. I've done it before. . . .*

Jane came outside to see her off. "Have a pleasant time."

Thora nodded. "Don't burn the place down while I'm gone."

"I'll do my best."

Patrick handed her in as Colin climbed in the other side and picked up the reins. He looked well kempt, as usual, though his hat was somewhat shabbier than his clothes.

They began the trip in relative silence. When they turned out of town and into the open, the wind picked up, and Thora wrapped her shawl around herself for warmth. She had been wise to bring it.

As they neared the McFarland place, Thora again surveyed the house with a jaundiced eye. Several panes of glass were missing from the windows, the gaps covered with paper. Its green door had more bare wood showing than paint. The stone-tile roof and brick chimney stacks were evidence that the structure had once been the home of a reasonably successful tradesman. The neglect—that the tradesman had fallen to drink.

"How is your mother?" Thora asked.

"Thankful to be busy—several village women have given her sewing to do."

"And your father? Is he in good health?"

"No, ma'am. He is not . . . well."

"Has he any work?"

Colin shook his head. "He has not been . . . able to work."

Hmpf, Thora thought. *Not able or not willing?*

She asked, "What does your father think about you working at The Bell? I suppose he was happy when he learned you got the job?"

"No, quite the opposite. In fact, it was the only time he—" Colin broke off abruptly.

Thora glanced over and noticed his clenched jaw. "He . . . what?" she prompted.

"Never mind. Let's just say he was not pleased. But my mother is glad I have the work."

In the yard, Thora saw three girls in ill-fitting dresses. With a start, she recognized an old yellow gown she'd donated to the charity guild a decade ago, now dingy and faded, so long on the girl that it dragged on the ground. Another girl was barefoot, in a coarse brown dress and tattered apron. The third wore a green skirt too short for the leggy adolescent, showing scuffed boots and mismatched stockings, a red knitted shawl wrapped around her torso, hands tucked inside.

As if expecting the gig's approach, the girls came forward eagerly, then stopped short, one girl running into her sister when they saw Thora. Their smiles quickly faded. Apparently, they had been expecting Colin. And Colin alone.

She noticed Colin try to discreetly wave the girls off, his index finger raised as if telling them to wait. Suspicion pricking her, Thora glanced over her shoulder at the back board of the gig and spied a burlap sack pressed into the corner.

She looked back at Colin and saw that he'd followed the direction of her gaze. His Adam's apple rose and fell.

Was he stealing from The Bell? Is that what he'd been doing in the larder? She'd suspected as much.

"Your sisters seem to be expecting you," she said. "Or something from you."

"Oh, that's all right, ma'am. I shall see them later."

"No, by all means, let us stop now," Thora insisted, a note of challenge in her voice.

"Please, ma'am. I . . . Let me take you where you're going. I can stop on the way back, or . . . not at all, if you prefer."

"Heavens, no. Don't keep them waiting on my account."

Colin halted the horse, tied off the reins, and stepped down, reluctantly waving the girls forward.

Thora stepped down as well and followed him to the back of

the gig. He picked up the sack, preparing to hand it over to the girls, unopened.

"Go on. Open it," Thora urged. She stepped to a nearby barrel head and tapped its top surface. "Let's see what you brought for them. Some of The Bell cutlery, or a silver spoon? I hope it fetches a good price. Or perhaps some rashers of bacon or smuggled tea?"

Colin obeyed and dumped out the sack onto the barrel.

But instead of the silver spoons and costly meat or tea she had expected, all that rolled out were bread rolls as hard as rocks, several wrinkled potatoes, and shriveled apples from last year's harvest that Mrs. Rooke had cleaned out of the cellar the day before.

Colin avoided her gaze. "It's only a few things put by from my own meals, ma'am. Or things Dotty said would go to waste. I didn't steal anything, I promise."

Shame swamped Thora. Shame and guilt over her suspicions and humiliating accusations.

Thora looked at the girls' thin, frightened faces, and for the first time, noticed the hollows in Colin's embarrassed cheeks as well. She turned and strode purposely back to the gig.

"Please don't dismiss me," he called after her. "I won't do it again."

"Yes, you will," Thora commanded, turning back. "And moreover, take this." She handed over one of her pies. "We don't need two. Talbot would only grow fat. And it's not charity—you've got it coming, since you had to wait for your full wages."

Colin held her gaze a moment, and she guessed he was about to refuse. Then one of his sisters clutched his hand.

He cleared his throat. "Well, then, thank you, ma'am. I know they'll enjoy it." He turned to his sisters. "Girls, thank Mrs.—"

"No." Thora held up her hand. "You owe me no thanks. Just get me where I need to go and that'll be an end to it." She climbed back into the gig and waited for him to follow suit.

The pie had been a lot of work, Thora reflected, but it was far easier to give than an apology. Besides, apologies did not fill bellies.

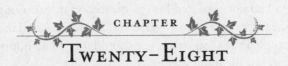

CHAPTER

Twenty-Eight

When Colin urged the mare up the farm drive, Walter Talbot came out to greet them, dressed not unlike Colin in a dark coat, waistcoat, cravat, and trousers, his hair well groomed. The polished Talbot of old.

"Hello, Thora. Colin."

Colin nodded. "Sir."

Talbot held out his hand and helped Thora down, taking the heavy basket from her.

"Thank you, Talbot." Was she supposed to call him Walter now that he no longer worked for the inn? She would find it difficult to do so.

She turned to Colin. "No need to return for me. I shall walk back. Once this basket is empty it shall be no trouble at all."

"Are you certain, ma'am? I don't mind."

"No. You go on. You have more important things to do."

Thora waved him on, and Colin urged the horse forward.

"By the way," Thora said, as they watched him go. "I still don't think Colin is the man for the job, but I was wrong to suspect him of taking advantage as his father did."

Talbot studied her, then nodded solemnly. "That's a start."

He led the way up the walkway and opened the door for her.

"Hopefully this wind will die down. I wanted to show you around the place after we eat."

"I'll not blow away, Talbot."

His gaze swept over her again. "You look . . . well," he said. "I have not seen that shawl in years. The color suits you. And you've done something different with your hair."

Thora had not expected him to notice, or at least not to comment. She felt her neck grow warm and, as they entered the house, quickly pulled the shawl from her shoulders. "I had not intended to wear it, but the wind was brisk."

"Here, put down your things. Something in here smells good." Talbot set the basket on the table, while she peeled off her gloves.

"Nan is awake but still in her bed," he said. "I thought we would help her to the table when all is ready."

Thora nodded her understanding. "May I go in and greet her?"

"Of course." He stepped to the partially open door, knocked, and stuck his head into the room. "Thora is here and would like to say hello."

"Send her in" came Nan's muffled reply.

Talbot turned and smiled at Thora, opening the door wide. "I'll get started in the kitchen."

On impulse, Thora took the shawl in with her.

Nan was sitting upright atop the made bed, bolstered by pillows, a lap rug over her legs. She looked a little brighter than during Thora's last visit, her complexion displaying a bit more color. She wore a pert, frilly cap, a daydress, and a smile.

"Hello, Nan. It is good to see you sitting up and dressed."

"I am grateful to feel well enough to do so."

"I thought you might like this shawl," Thora said, holding it forth.

"Oh no, Thora. It's too fine for me."

"Not at all. It's an old thing. I left it with Jane when I went into mourning, but I don't think she ever wore it. Someone should. It will keep you warm when the wind blows, as it seems to do out here."

"But it's yours."

"Nan, I know I have not been good about visiting, so it would mean a great deal to me if you would accept it."

"Very well, then. I shall." Nan winked. "If it makes you feel better."

She allowed Thora to help her wrap it around her shoulders and straighten its length across her bodice and onto her lap. Nan stroked the smooth wool and silky fringe. "Ah yes. I shall sit here in fine state to greet my visitors. I daresay Dr. Burton shall declare me cured when he sees me in this!" Nan grinned. Then she leaned toward her bedside table.

"What do you need?" Thora asked, stepping over to help.

"Hand me that hinged box there, will you?"

Thora did so, and from it Nan extracted a cameo brooch. She crossed over the two sides of the shawl and used the pin to fasten them together across her chest. "Now let the wind howl all it likes—I shall not feel it." She fingered the brooch. "This was a wedding gift from my husband." She looked up at Thora's bare neck and wrists. "You don't wear jewelry, do you? Besides your wedding ring, I mean?"

"Not often. It is not that I disapprove. I simply don't take the time to bother with it. I've been given a few trinkets over the years, but I rarely wear them." Thora looked down at her hand, the plain thin wedding band, the unadorned wrist, and a memory struck her. She said, "Frank gave me a gift once—a fine gold bracelet with a blue enamel heart dangling from it. He said it was to remind me that I was more than his helpmeet and housekeeper, but also an attractive woman. I was sure I'd break the delicate chain, and the heart clacked against the desk whenever I wrote in the ledger. So I put it back in its box, and there it has remained ever since."

Nan said gently, "We've all been given gifts, Thora, and ought not hide them away. They remind us that we are blessed and loved. They give pleasure to those who see them—especially to the one who bestowed the gift in the first place."

Thora formed a thin smile. "Well, Frank isn't here to see it."

"No, but his son is. And you are." Nan reached over and lightly pressed her arm. Thora willed herself not to pull away.

"I think it is time to bring your blue heart out of hiding, Thora. Let others see it and appreciate it. And you as well."

"Well. Thank you, Nan," Thora said stiffly. "I shall try to remember your advice."

Nan relaxed back against her pillows. "No, you won't. Always were stubborn . . ." Her eyes looked suddenly heavy, ready to close.

"Nan?" Thora asked in concern. "Are you all right? Do you need anything?"

"Just to rest awhile. Such weariness settles on me. Often at the most inconvenient times."

"But I thought you were going to eat dinner with Tal . . . Walter and me?"

"I don't think I shall after all, Thora. Just set aside a few bites of your famous pie, will you? I shall have a tray in my room later. But for now, I fear I must sleep."

Thora rose. "Then perhaps I had better go as well. We can eat together another time."

Nan's eyes flew open again. "No, Thora. Walt has gone to such trouble to clean the place and find a good hen. Don't disappoint him because I am such a weak ninny, please?"

"I don't know . . ."

Nan said, "I was not good about visiting when you lost Frank and then John, so it would mean a great deal to me if you would dine with Walter."

Thora realized Nan had echoed her own words back to her and managed a small grin. "Very well, then. I shall," she said. "If it makes you feel better."

"Yes . . . much better . . ." Nan's eyes drifted closed.

Thora left Nan's room, disappointed and a little uncomfortable at the notion of dining alone with Walter Talbot in his home. She wasn't exactly sure why she felt ill at ease. She was not overly concerned about propriety and doubted anyone would think twice about her dining with a former employee while his ailing sister-in-law slept in the next room. Though she would probably omit that last detail if asked to recount the visit later.

Thora had never been skilled in making small talk and anticipated the meal would be awkward and the conversation stilted. Over the years, she and Talbot had had hundreds of conversations—brief and professional, or sometimes curt when tensions grew high or carriages late, but never awkward. She hoped she could think of something appropriate to say.

He looked up when she entered the kitchen, his gaze flickering over her unrelieved grey gown. "Did you forget your shawl?" he asked.

She shook her head. "I gave it to Nan. Thought it might help keep her warm."

"That was kind of you. Is she ready to join us?"

"No. She wants to sleep, but insists we go ahead without her. She says she will eat in her room later, and asks that we save her some pie."

"Of course." He sighed. Disappointment and something else crossed his face.

"Can you be trusted not to eat it all?" Thora teased, to cheer him up.

He looked up at her, the sadness in his eyes falling away. "For Nan's sake, I shall exhibit a modicum of self-control."

He gestured for her to precede him into the dining room. Thora wondered if they would sit formally at head and foot like a married couple. Where had that thought come from? She inwardly chastised her foolishness.

Instead Walter had set two plates on the table—one at the head, the other to its right. He pulled out the chair for her at the head of the table.

Thora said, "This is your place, surely."

"There is no need for formality between us. Besides," he said with a grin, "I know you like to be mistress of all you survey."

She did not return his grin. Did he think she aspired to be mistress of his home? She had never given such an impression, surely. She felt herself grow increasingly uncomfortable. What was she doing there? What was *he* doing?

She was tempted to leave then and there. But then she recalled Nan's plea, and sat down. Besides, she would not want this fine meal to go to waste. She was eager to see how the pie had turned out.

Thora reached for her table napkin, but Talbot clasped his hands. "Shall we give thanks for the food?"

"Oh. If you like." It was the Sabbath after all, she supposed. Though she was not accustomed to praying before meals.

Talbot closed his eyes, and in his low voice said, "Heavenly Father, we thank thee for this food and for our health. Please have mercy on Nan in her affliction. Strengthen and relieve her. Thou knowest the infirmity of our nature, and the temptations that surround us. Give us a thankful sense of our many blessings; that we may not deserve to lose them by discontent or indifference. Amen."

Thora studied his face as he looked up. "Were any points of that prayer aimed at me?" she asked, feeling unaccountably defensive.

He held her gaze. "Not intentionally. But if something pricked your conscience, then perhaps—"

"If the prayer fits, wear it?" she finished for him, adapting the old adage.

"Something like that. In all truth, I was thinking of my own blessings, failings, and temptations, but like it or not, you are human too, Thora. So I daresay you may have a few of those yourself."

Of course she had failings. But she didn't like him pointing them out. She said, "Surely the reliable Talbot doesn't struggle with temptation?"

He served her a chicken leg, thoughtfully remembering it was the piece she preferred.

"I can think of one temptation quite easily," he said with a lift of his knife. "She is sitting directly across from me. Or perhaps *affliction* is more accurate."

He was teasing her, she knew, and told herself not to let him bait her. If he saw her as an affliction, he would not have invited her over. A temptation? Surely not.

She helped herself to a wedge of pork-and-veal pie and shoved a forkful into her mouth to keep from saying anything she might regret.

Talbot followed her example and took a bite of the layered pie. "Delicious, Thora. Just as I remember it." He closed his eyes to relish the taste. "No. Better."

"I am glad you think so."

She took another bite, pausing to savor the combination of flavors, savory and salty and even sweet. It *was* delicious. She hoped the McFarland girls enjoyed theirs.

They kept the conversation light after that, talking of the inn, favorite regulars, and Colin's progress and continuing struggles. Their conversation was well seasoned and comfortable. Like the rich, nurturing food.

Afterward, they tidied the kitchen together, though Talbot insisted he would do the washing up later on his own. He wanted to have time to show her around the old homeplace before Thora had to leave.

They began with a tour of the house, talking in hushed tones to avoid waking Nan.

"I would like to build on," he said. "A small study or conservatory with windows overlooking the garden."

"What garden?" she asked, and quickly wished she'd bitten her tongue. Why was criticism her first response?

"Nothing much yet, beyond a small kitchen garden. But I am planning one. Let's go outside and I'll show you."

They did so, and when they reached the plot, Talbot said, "Mrs. Bushby has come out to advise me, and has even offered to share cuttings from her own perennials. She says the soil is fertile, though could use more manure. . . ."

"Sounds like plenty of manure has been unloaded already," Thora murmured.

"Hm?"

"Never mind."

Mrs. Bushby was a widow as well, Thora knew. Was she really so helpful, or did her interest in the bachelor-farmer extend beyond his . . . fertile soil?

Talbot gestured her forward. "Come, I'll show you the rest."

They strolled around the farm's perimeter, Thora noticing the stone walls and wooden fences were all well maintained. He had been busy. Talbot pointed out the barn, explaining his plans to add a forge so he could keep his horses shod and equipment in good repair.

As they passed the farm's main gate, Thora observed, "The place needs a name. Most farms and cottages around here have them, as well as estates, of course. Ivy Cottage, Fairmont, Thornvale, the Grange, Lane's Farm . . ."

He shrugged. "We've always just called it the farm. Or the homeplace."

"Not very original."

"Perhaps I ought to have a sign made to hang there on the gate?"

She nodded. "A good sign is important, my father always said."

"Then I shall add that to my ever-mounting list of tasks."

They reached a rise and together stood overlooking the surrounding countryside. He pointed out the borders of his property.

She said, "You could let part of this land to tenants, you know. Or hire more help to increase yields, and then use the money to buy Lane's Farm. He's thinking of selling, I hear."

He gave her a crooked smile. "That's the Thora I know. Never satisfied. Always looking to conquer more territory."

"And you, Talbot? Are you satisfied being a yeoman farmer? I have seen you manage a large staff and dozens of passengers from thirty carriages a day, with income and expenses to match."

"Money and success aren't everything, Thora. I want to make improvements, yes, but have no need to become some powerful landlord. I want to have time to fish. Read. Spend time with the people I care about."

He looked at her. "What about you, Thora? What is it you want out of life, now that The Bell is in Jane's hands?"

"What do I want? You make it sound as if I can pick from a lengthy menu."

"Well, do you plan to return to your sister's?"

She blinked up at him. She'd forgotten how tall he was. "I . . . suppose that depends on what happens with The Bell."

"Does it?" He stepped nearer and lowered his voice. "Thora . . ."

He broke off at the sound of an approaching horse and carriage.

They walked to the front of the house in time to see the Paleys arrive. They exchanged greetings, and Thora noticed the vicar and his wife send curious looks her way.

Talbot explained, "I was just showing Mrs. Bell around the farm."

Mr. Paley nodded his understanding. "Don't stop on our account. We have only dropped by to visit Nan for a bit."

Mrs. Paley added, "You two go ahead with your tour."

Talbot tied up the horse, showed them inside the house, and then returned to Thora. "Where were we?"

They walked on.

"I would like to plant trees as well," Talbot said. "Maples, I'm thinking. For color in the autumn."

"Trees? My goodness. You are thinking ahead. How long do you plan to live?"

"See me as ancient, do you? I am only a year your senior, Thora. Don't forget."

"I don't forget. I feel every one of my years. And I have no plans to plant trees I shan't be around to see."

"Thunder and turf, Thora. You speak as though you have one foot in the grave already. You are only one and fifty—"

"Hush."

"And in robust health, as far as I can see. You will live for another twenty or thirty years."

"Just to spite you."

"Nothing would please me more. I hope you live to see your ninetieth year. And I see it with you."

She shot him a look. "Oh, I shall I outlive you, you old codger, make no mistake about that."

"That's my Thora. Out to win every contest she enters."

It was on the tip of her tongue to retort, *I am not your Thora.* But she bit back the words just in time. A common turn of phrase— that's all it was. But . . . the invitation, the meal, the care for his appearance, the pride in showing her his farm, and his anticipation of her reaction . . . ? *No, no, no.* Surely she was reading too much into it.

When she remained silent, he went on. "Mrs. Bushby said flowering trees would give the place charm. She said it could use a woman's touch, and I have to say I agree."

Her again. Was Martha Bushby offering herself for the job? Thora said, "Nan has lived here for years, and if she hasn't added to the farm's charms in all that time, I doubt anyone else could do so."

"Nan has been sickly for most of those years. But I wasn't thinking merely of feminine decorations. You know I have long admired your abilities in managing property and staff, Thora." He sent her a sidelong glance. "Not to mention your pie-making skills."

"You want to hire me as your housekeeper?" she said tartly. "If the inn fails, I just might take you up on that. I'll be needing a way to earn my keep."

A flash of irritation crossed his face. "No, I don't want to *hire* you, Thora, I—"

The farmhouse door opened, and the Paleys came out.

Thora forced a smile and walked toward them. "And how did you find Nan?"

"Weak, I'm afraid," Mr. Paley said. "But her spirits are good."

"She is rather proud of that shawl you gave her," Mrs. Paley added. "That dash of color is so warming to her complexion."

Mr. Paley looked from one to the other. "We're heading back to town if you would like a ride, Thora. Or . . . are you not finished with your tour?"

"Oh, I think we're finished, all right," Talbot said flatly. "I will help you gather your things."

CHAPTER
TWENTY-NINE

Rachel surveyed the Thornvale dining room, lit by candelabra, laid with the family china and crystal, and decorated with a tiered centerpiece of fruits and flowers. Her cook had prepared an extravagant dinner, using all the silver tureens and serving dishes for, she was sure, the last time. Even if Mr. Ashford kept her on, the woman mournfully predicted, a young man in trade would not appreciate fine dining and would probably want stew and gruel served in pewter tankards.

They had not hosted a party since before her father's illness and financial problems. They'd had to let their old butler go when their fortunes took a turn, and Casper, already in his sixties, had retired to neighboring Wishford. But he had returned for this special dinner, in honor of his former master. His waistcoat puckered at the buttons, but he still cut an authoritative figure. They had hired two footmen to serve as well.

Rachel returned to the hall to await their guests just as her sister descended the stairs. Ellen looked elegant in a black silk evening gown, far more fashionable—and low cut—than her own. Ellen and her maid had arrived a few days before, in time to pack up her china, jewelry, and a few mementos, and to help plan the seating arrangement for the party. It was good to have Ellen at home one last time. Her sister's blithe conversation had distracted Rachel from the sad removal to come.

"Ready?" Ellen asked.

"Ready."

Ellen studied her face. "Will it be difficult for you with him here?"

Rachel did not need to ask whom she meant. "No. It's all so long ago. I'm fine." She smiled, and hoped it was convincing.

Ellen patted her arm. "Fortitude, my sister. No sadness tonight, hmm?"

When Casper announced the arrival of Sir Timothy and Miss Brockwell, Rachel grasped a nearby chair back to steady herself, and avoided her sister's gaze. How handsome Timothy looked in his dark evening clothes, white waistcoat, and cravat. He bowed and she curtsied, glad for a chance to look down.

"My mother sends her regrets," he said. "She is home with a minor cough she does not want anyone else to suffer."

Privately, Rachel was relieved. Lady Brockwell intimidated her.

Ellen elbowed her and beamed a smile at the brother and sister. "Welcome. Thank you for coming."

Rachel focused her attention on young Justina, so pretty in silk the lightest wash of rose pink. She complimented Justina's finely curled and arranged hair, and the young woman admitted shyly that her mother's lady's maid had done it. That gave Rachel an idea. She wondered if Lady Brockwell would consider engaging Jemima as a second lady's maid for Justina. Rachel doubted she would be able to employ her once she left Thornvale. But there would be time to worry about that later.

Mercy and her aunt arrived. Mercy wore an evening gown several years out of fashion in muted mauve and ivory. Her aunt, in startling contrast, wore a bright purple gown with a dyed-to-match feather in her wispy grey curls. Matilda's happy face was as bright as her dress. Old Mr. Nikel, dapper in evening clothes, took her arm and led her to a chair, and the two talked easily together. It pleased Rachel to see her two eldest guests enjoying each other's company, and congratulated herself on including them in their party.

Seeing Justina, Matilda smiled coyly and said, "Did I hear from your mother that we shall have another reason to celebrate soon?"

Justina ducked her head but made no reply.

In her stead, Sir Timothy answered, "I think that is safe to say." He smiled from Matilda to Justina, but his sister refused to meet his gaze.

"Not now, Timothy, please."

"You are right," he replied. "Today is about Sir William."

"And nothing is settled," Justina insisted, then turned to Rachel. "Now. Miss Ashford, we heard you had a visit recently from a relation of yours . . . ?"

"Yes." Seeing in the girl's pleading look that she wished to change the subject, Rachel elaborated, "My second cousin, Nicholas Ashford. He seems an agreeable—if somewhat shy—young man. But I am certain he will make a fine master of Thornvale. In time."

She was not at all certain, but felt duty bound to present the awkward young man in the best possible light. Usurper or not, they were family, however distantly related.

"Mr. Ashford and his mother arrive tomorrow," Rachel added. "I look forward to meeting her as well."

"As do I," Ellen said. "I have not yet met either of the people who will soon call Thornvale home."

"Speaking of new residents," Mr. Nikel spoke up in his craggy voice. "Have you heard Fairmont House is occupied at last? And soon to be a hotel, of all things?"

"I wonder how Jane Bell feels about that," Justina said. "Is she coming tonight, by the way?"

"I'm afraid she was unable to join us," Rachel replied. "Traveling and busy with the inn, I gather."

"I am sorry to hear it," Justina lamented. "I have not talked with her since I returned from London. Though Timothy has, more than once."

"Only in passing," he added.

Rachel's smile stiffened.

Casper announced, "The Reverend Mr. Paley and Mrs. Paley."
The arrival of the vicar and his wife completed their intimate party.

When dinner was announced soon after, Rachel noticed Sir Timothy look to her for a cue of how to process into the dining room. In lieu of precedence by rank, Rachel selected the lady most distinguished by age instead.

Meeting his gaze, Rachel said, "Sir Timothy, will you please escort Miss Matilda?"

He smiled approvingly. "Indeed I shall, with pleasure."

If Ellen, as eldest sister and *de facto* lady of the house, resented it, she did not show it. It helped that everyone was fond of Miss Matty.

Sir Timothy led Matilda Grove to her place, and seated himself beside her at the head. The others filled in.

How good to see the dining room looking so well and adorned with familiar faces. To have old friends gathered together again. If only Jane were there to complete their party.

How bittersweet to have Sir Timothy seated nearby. Ellen had claimed the foot of the table as hostess. Rachel could have argued, insisted it was her place of honor, especially since Ellen had her own home, and Rachel had been the one to live at Thornvale the longest and the last. But she didn't quibble. With Sir Timothy at the head, Rachel wasn't sure she could manage to look across that long expanse and see him there. As if they were host and hostess. Husband and wife, as she once thought they would be. It would be difficult enough with him there at all, but this way she would not be obliged to hold eye contact for long. To smile easily and hope he didn't notice the quiver of her lips.

She would get through this. For her father's sake and even for her own. She would prove to Timothy and to herself that she was well and truly over him.

When they were finally all seated, Rachel stood on shaky legs, not accustomed to having so many pairs of eyes watching her. Or to giving speeches.

"Thank you all for coming. I look around this table at which I partook of countless meals with my parents and sister, and am touched to see your dear faces. I wish there could be a few more of my father's contemporaries here, but sadly, many of his closest friends have passed on as well, or have fallen out of touch after his . . . troubles. That is why it means so much that you are here, Mr. Nikel and Miss Matilda. I also want to thank Mr. and Mrs. Paley for joining us. Mr. Paley visited my father quite often in those last days, and I shall never forget your many kindnesses to us both. Most of you know that my father was not overly concerned with social convention or niceties. But he did love a party. So please join me in a toast."

Around the table, people picked up their glasses. "We are here to honor you, Sir William Ashford. Beloved father, husband, and master of Thornvale. You were not perfect. But who of us is? And so tonight we celebrate your life and your memory. You will always be missed and never forgotten. To Sir William."

"Sir William" echoed around the table, glasses lifted high.

The footmen removed the covers, and they began the first course of soup and fish with a savory sauce.

Ellen asked, "Remember all those Twelfth Night parties Papa hosted, with dancing and charades—and Papa always playing the king?"

Miss Matilda spoke up, eyes shining. "He always assigned *me* the character of Miss All-Agog or Miss Fanny Fanciful. The imp. How he loved to tease."

Sir Timothy said, "I recall the year an acting troupe passed through. Frank Bell did not invite them to perform at the inn, so Sir William set up an outdoor stage here and hosted a performance of Shakespeare's *A Midsummer Night's Dream*—on the one condition that *he* be allowed to play Puck."

Rachel chuckled at the memory, her heart warm to hear Sir Timothy share it.

"And an excellent Puck he was," Mercy said, then quoted Puck's final line from the play, "'So, good night unto you all. Give me your hands, if we be friends, and Robin shall restore amends.'"

Across the table, she and Rachel shared a smile.

Mr. Paley looked from Ellen to Rachel. "I remember that occasion as well, though a little differently. As I recall it, Sir William knew your mother had her heart set upon seeing the play. And that is why he went to the trouble of hosting it. He would have done anything for her. She was the light of his life, along with you two girls."

Rachel's throat tightened. She glanced at Ellen and was touched to see tears brighten her sister's eyes.

Mr. Paley extended one hand to Rachel, and the other to Matilda, beside him. With a sad smile, he echoed softly, "So, good night unto you all. Give me your hands, if we be friends, and *we* shall restore amends."

Around the table, everyone joined hands. Tears filled Rachel's eyes, turning individual candle flames into blurs of golden light.

Mr. Nikel stood. "To Sir William!" he repeated, again raising his glass, and dispelling the poignant moment before it grew too uncomfortable. Once again glasses were raised and the mood lightened.

At that moment, Casper stepped in and announced, "Mr. Nicholas Ashford, and Mrs. Ashford."

Rachel gave a start, heart lurching. They were not expected until tomorrow! Around the room, heads swung toward the door.

Nicholas Ashford entered and drew up abruptly, as surprised to walk into a room full of people as Rachel was to see him.

Beside him stood Mrs. Ashford, a handsome, buxom woman with a thin nose and sharp, dark eyes. She gazed around the table at all the full glasses and arched one brow. "Emptying the cellars, I see."

"Mother," Nicholas hissed under his breath. He bowed to Rachel. "I apologize for the intrusion."

Rachel rose and stepped forward. "I thought you said you would be returning tomorrow. I . . ."

"Yes, well . . ." He glanced pointedly at his mother. "We decided to come a night ahead of schedule. We never guessed we would be interrupting a . . . social gathering."

Mrs. Ashford pursed her lips. "I can't say I am surprised."

Rachel ignored the comment and pasted on a smile. Since Mr. Ashford failed to introduce her, Rachel did so herself. "Mrs. Ashford, we have not met. I am Miss Rachel Ashford." Rachel dipped a curtsy, then turned to Ellen. "And this is my sister, Mrs. Ellen Hawley."

Ellen rose at her place, dipped her head to the mother, and smiled at the son. "How do you do."

Nicholas bowed again.

Rachel said with more warmth than she felt, "Welcome to Thornvale. I hope you shall be very happy here."

"Not as happy as I might be," Mrs. Ashford said. "I had hoped for a quiet dinner and a good night's sleep between freshly laundered sheets. Are we too early for that as well?"

Rachel noticed Ellen frown and open her mouth to protest. Mercy quickly pressed her hand to forestall her.

"Not at all," Rachel replied smoothly, stepping to the door. "I shall just let Mrs. Fife know you're here."

Sir Timothy rose. "Miss Ashford, please stay. This is your last night in your home, after all. And we are here to celebrate your father. As he would have wanted."

"While in mourning?" Mrs. Ashford asked skeptically, though Timothy had not been speaking to her.

Sir Timothy smiled at the woman, but it was a cold smile. One Rachel had seen before and recognized well enough to be glad it was not aimed at her. Then he turned back to Rachel and said, "Perhaps you would be good enough to introduce us?"

"Of course. Mrs. Ashford, allow me to present Sir Timothy Brockwell, Baronet. Sir Timothy, Mrs. Ashford and her son, Mr. Nicholas Ashford." Rachel would not normally have introduced him in that way, nor included his rank, but in this instance felt she should.

"Mrs. Ashford. Mr. Ashford," Sir Timothy began solemnly. "We are gathered this evening to honor Sir William's last request: that we remember him not with mourning, but with a fine dinner and fine wine. His daughters have very graciously invited a few old friends to see them through this difficult hour."

"You are more than welcome to join us," Rachel added, relieved to have Sir Timothy defending her and observing that his title and gallant address had impressed Mrs. Ashford, and some of the ire had faded from her eyes.

Nicholas said, "We would not wish to intrude on your celebration."

"Nonsense," Rachel insisted. "You are family, after all. And Thornvale is your home." Rachel turned toward the table. "In fact, allow me to introduce a few of your new neighbors. This is our vicar, Mr. Paley, and his wife, Mrs. Paley."

Mrs. Ashford's thin brows rose. "The vicar? I am surprised. You approve of a party so soon after a death?"

Mr. Paley smiled. "In this case I do. You see, I had the bittersweet privilege of visiting Sir William several times during his last illness, and heard him ask his daughter to do this very thing. Not one for tradition for tradition's sake was our Sir William. Or for solemn displays and long faces. Were you acquainted with him, madam?"

"I met him only once or twice. My husband knew him better, and my son not at all."

Ellen suggested, "Well then, do dine with us, and we will each share a few favorite memories of Papa, so you might become acquainted with him, at least in a small way."

Rachel added, "Yes, do join us. Cook has outdone herself, and we have more than enough of everything." Seeing Mrs. Ashford was softening, Rachel gestured to the footmen. "Add two more places, if you please."

Nicholas looked about to accept, but his mother held up a decisive hand. "No. Don't go to any trouble on our account. You

THE INNKEEPER OF IVY HILL

go on with your private soiree. Nicholas and I will turn in early, if you would send up a modest supper?"

"Of course," Rachel replied.

Mrs. Fife appeared and offered to show the newcomers to their rooms.

When they departed, dinner continued with awkward reserve and decorum, and afterward, the party quickly drew to a close. A disappointment for all, and worrisome for Rachel, who had not planned to move her things to Mercy's until the following day. She dreaded a confrontation with either Ashford, but especially with Nicholas's shrewish mother.

Ellen was staying the final night as well, and as they climbed the stairs to their respective rooms, Ellen whispered that she and her maid would gather up the last of her belongings and leave first thing in the morning.

On the landing, Ellen reached out and grasped Rachel's hand. "You'll be all right on your own, won't you?"

"I will," Rachel replied with more confidence than she felt. What other choice did she have?

CHAPTER

THIRTY

The next day, Rachel rose at dawn and roused an exhausted Jemima to help her dress. Ellen's coach was leaving very early, and Rachel wanted to see her off.

When her sister was ready, Rachel walked with her from Thornvale to The Bell—Ellen's poor maid laden with parcels and trudging behind.

In front of The Bell, Rachel embraced her sister and wished her a safe journey. "Give my love to my nephews."

"Of course I will." Ellen gestured toward the inn door. "Will you come in and wait with me?"

"I had better not. I need to return and finish my own packing."

Ellen gave her a knowing look. "Before the she-dragon awakes?"

"Something like that."

Ellen said, "I hope I don't see Jane inside, mopping floors or something. How awkward."

"Ellen . . ." Rachel hissed. "You are haughtier than I am."

Her sister smirked. "And *that* is saying something!"

"Don't forget," Rachel added. "You were the one who encouraged her romance with Mr. Bell in the first place."

"He needed no encouragement!" Ellen retorted. "But if I did, I certainly hoped for a better outcome for both of you."

With that, Ellen kissed her cheek and disappeared inside the coaching inn.

Returning to Thornvale a short while later, Rachel let herself in as quietly as she could and tiptoed across the hall.

Mrs. Fife hailed her as she climbed the stairs. "Mr. Ashford asks to see you in the library at your earliest convenience."

Rachel's stomach cramped. So much for slipping away to avoid a confrontation. She swallowed hard. "Very well. Tell him I shall be there in a few minutes."

She hurried to her room and, with trembling fingers, packed the last of her personal items she had used that morning—toothbrush, powder, perfume, and the like—into a small valise. Her trunk, traveling case, and bandboxes were already packed and waiting out in the porte-cochere to be transported to Ivy Cottage.

She looked around her neat and tidy bedchamber—the high bed with its tasseled bed-curtains, the dressing table, and rose-patterned wallpaper—with a stab of nostalgia. She would miss it. All of it. She inhaled deeply and drew back her shoulders. She was the daughter of Sir William Ashford. His forebears had not been good stewards, and the family's wealth had declined over the generations. So he'd had to go out into the world and make his own way and his own fortune. She would do the same. A fearful inner voice reminded her that her father had also lost his fortune, his good name, and his health, but she would not dwell on that now.

Spine stiffened in resolve, Rachel tied a bonnet under her chin, pulled on gloves, and picked up her valise. She left the room hoping that her outdoor apparel would signal her intention to leave immediately and thereby discourage a lengthy conversation—or reprimand.

Stepping silently into the library, she saw lanky Mr. Ashford standing before one of the windows, hands folded behind his back, spinning his thumbs in impatience or nerves. Was he dreading the setdown to come as much as she was? She had a *little* money. She supposed she could offer to replace the wine from the cellar, though the idea that she had no right to share the bottles her father had collected irked her.

She cleared her throat, and he turned sharply. She waited until he faced her, then purposely set her valise at her feet. *See, I am halfway out the door already. . . .*

He swallowed, his Adam's apple convulsing up and down his long pale throat. "Miss Ashford. Rachel. May I call you Rachel?"

"Of course. If you like." A strange way to begin a reprimand.

"Would you, um, care to sit down?" He gestured toward a chair with an agitated jerk of his hand before clasping both before himself.

"No, thank you. I shall stand. I am on my way out, as you see."

"I do see. But . . ." He pressed dry lips together. "That is what I wished to speak with you about."

"You needn't worry. I shall be out of your way shortly. My trunk and case are already outside, and I have my last few things here. I hope you don't mind if I leave my father's books for the time being, until I find other accommodation for them?"

"I don't mind at all. And you are not 'in my way,' as you say." He winced at his unintentional rhyme, then ran a hand over his face. "For the first time in my life I wish I were better with words."

Rachel endeavored to help him along and end this awkward interview as soon as possible. "I know your mother did not approve of my dinner party last night. No doubt you hoped to give her an excellent first impression of your new home. I apologize that her arrival was marred in such an unpleasant manner."

"Miss Ashford, I did not ask you here to speak of that. As far as I am concerned you did nothing wrong. I am not here to redress any grievances. I am sorry if I gave you that impression."

"Oh. Then . . . ?"

"I asked you here to . . . to ask you to marry me."

Rachel's mouth fell open. She felt her brow furrow. "Excuse me . . . what?"

"I realize it is sudden. We are barely acquainted. But I think it is wrong to put you out of your lifelong home. A woman without protection. How can I live here happily, knowing I am the cause of your . . . unhappiness? Not to mention inconvenience and discomfort and, I pray not, deprivation. When I first visited Thornvale, I thought I could simply allow you to remain in a suite of rooms. Like an . . . elderly spinster aunt. No trouble and no impropriety. But then I met you. A beautiful young woman. And I . . . froze. I had to think. And this is what I have concluded. I pray the notion is not repugnant to you."

Rachel stared at him, dumbfounded, and the longer she did so without speaking, the redder his face became. He looked away from her to his clasped hands. "But I see that it is."

She forced herself to speak. "Not repugnant, exactly, but . . . shocking, yes."

A mirthless laugh escaped him. "Not 'exactly,'" he bleakly echoed.

"We are cousins. . . ." she protested. It was a stupid objection, and she wished the words back as soon as she uttered them.

"Cousins more closely related than we are marry all the time."

She narrowed her eyes. "Did your mother put you up to this?"

"Ah . . . no," he replied with a snort of incredulity and lift of his brow.

"She doesn't like me," Jane said.

"She doesn't know you."

"Neither do you."

"I will come to, and so will she. Whether she likes you or not is immaterial."

"But whether you and I like each other *is* material."

He winced. "I realize I possess not those happy manners to ensure my making friends easily."

"I . . . would not know. I have not had time to sketch your character."

"You reject my offer?"

"I think I must. I have no desire to give you pain. I am sensible to the honor of your proposal. But you need not feel responsible for me. Or bound by duty to—"

"Am I not your nearest male relation?"

"I suppose you are, excepting my brother-in-law. And it is kind of you to want to help me. But to marry me? It is beyond the bounds of what is expected in such a situation, trying though it may be."

He lowered his head, and she saw that she had hurt and embarrassed him.

"Mr. Ashford. Nicholas. You need not worry for me. I am going to live with a dear friend and her aunt. Perfectly respectable people. True, we will not have extravagant dinners like last night's." She chuckled self-consciously. "But I will not suffer. The arrangements are settled. There is a room awaiting me." A small and spartan room, but she did not mention it.

"You will not change your mind?" he asked somberly. "Alter these . . . arrangements . . . and remain here?"

She slowly shook her head. "I think not. It is all too sudden."

His jaw tightened. "I see. And you are right. Since you have a safe and respectable place to go, we need not rush into anything. But will you do me the honor of not rejecting my offer outright? Will you think on it, and allow me to call? Allow our acquaintance to grow before you decide with such finality?"

She saw what it cost him to push out the words. The heat and mortification mottling his pale cheeks, his nervous, darting eyes. She was seven and twenty, and had not yet received an offer of marriage—unless one counted that near-miss, more than eight years ago now. She would be foolish to reject him. A successful man. A kind man. Not to mention the owner of her beloved Thornvale.

She ran her tongue over dry lips. "Very well. I shall consider what you say, and your proposal. Thank you for understanding my reservations."

He looked at her almost blankly, as if afraid to believe her words. Then he drew in a breath. "Good. Thank you. We . . . understand one another, then. I shall give you time to settle in to your new situation, and then call. In the meantime, if there is anything you need, please do not hesitate to ask. It will in no way obligate you to any . . . future obligations." He winced at his fumbled words.

Feeling sorry for the man, she impulsively reached out to comfort him, laying her gloved hand on his sleeve. He stared down at it, mouth loose. Before she could retract it, he laid his hand over hers.

She forced a smile and gently tugged free from his grasp. "Good day, then, Mr. Ashford."

"Good day, Miss Ashford. And good-bye. For now."

Rachel went belowstairs to say her final farewells to the servants, then made her way back upstairs and quietly across the hall. The library door was ajar and Mrs. Ashford's grating voice reached her from within, along with a few lower, mollifying murmurs from her son.

"She would not have you, my own son? Who is she, Miss High and Mighty, to give herself such airs? She who lived in this house with so few servants and no carriage. Her father only knighted for some expensive token bestowed upon a grateful monarch. A man who lost his fortune and his good name, and besmirched hers in the bargain. I should like to know where she could find such another man as you, with such a noble heart. I don't care if I am your mother—I am not blind, as she must be."

Ears burning, Rachel slipped silently through the door, leaving Thornvale and the caustic words behind.

When Rachel reached Ivy Cottage, she thanked the cart driver— a woman named Mrs. Burlingame, who was accompanied by her young son.

Matilda Grove stood waiting in the open doorway, arms stretched wide. "Welcome, my dear." She embraced Rachel warmly, and the kind gesture brought unexpected tears to Rachel's eyes.

She blinked them back. "Thank you, Miss Matty."

"Now, I'll show you to your room and let you get settled. As soon as Mercy is finished teaching for the day, we'll all sit down to tea and a nice long chat."

"I would enjoy that."

Mercy's aunt led the way upstairs and down a narrow passage

slanted with age. She opened a door and said, "Here it is. I wish it were larger, or boasted a better view."

"Nonsense. It's lovely, and I'm grateful."

"No more of that now. You know we are happy to have you."

The Groves' manservant, the quiet, brown-skinned Mr. Basu, helped the cart-driver's son unload Rachel's trunk and packing case and carry them to her room. Rachel knew little about the manservant other than he was from the East Indies somewhere. During all her calls to Ivy Cottage over the years, Rachel had yet to hear him speak more than a simple word of greeting or acknowledgment, though Mercy assured her his English was very good.

When Mr. Basu delivered the last valise and bandbox, Rachel thanked the man, and he departed as silently as he'd come.

Alone for the time being, Rachel surveyed the small room that would be hers. For how long? Forever?

The room held a narrow bedstead, side table, dressing chest, washstand, and one small bookcase that would hold the tiniest fraction of her father's collection.

Perhaps that was for the best.

As she began unpacking her possessions, Rachel felt another pinch of resentment that Papa had left Ellen all of Mamma's jewelry, but she pushed the feeling aside. She set her toiletries on the washstand and arranged her mother's framed silhouette and Bible on her side table, grateful to have these few mementos at least.

Then she returned to the trunk and unwrapped the largest item within. She had taken down the portrait of the three of them—Mamma with Rachel and Ellen as young girls—that had hung for years in her father's bedchamber. She didn't care that it was not itemized in the will. It surely belonged to her, or perhaps Ellen. But not to Nicholas Ashford, and certainly not to his mother.

Rachel looked at the image of the former Lavinia Woodgate—not much older than Ellen was now. Ellen, dark like their father, might have inherited their mother's jewelry, but Rachel had inherited her looks. Her honey-gold hair and bright blue eyes. Even the shape of her face, now that Rachel's had lost some of the roundness of youth.

She would have to ask Mr. Basu to help her hang it. It would dominate the room, but that didn't matter. Having it there would help her feel less alone. Less the orphan she felt herself to be, in her late twenties or not.

"He asked you to marry him?" Mercy echoed, looking as dumb-struck as Rachel herself had been at the time.

Rachel nodded and took a sip of tea in the Ivy Cottage sitting room. "I was shocked, as you can imagine."

"But you only met him the once, is that not right?"

"Well, I met him a fortnight ago and then again last night. If I met him at any family occasion when I was a girl, I don't remember it."

"My goodness," Mercy breathed, slowly shaking her head.

"Do you think he loves you?" Matilda Grove asked, hope warming her voice.

"How could he? Nor did he say he did—which is to his credit, for how could I believe it? Especially after that awful scene at the party."

"You do not believe in love at first sight?" Miss Matty asked.

"Not in this case, no."

"I hope you did not refuse him out of any sense of obligation to us," Mercy said gently.

"No. Do you wish I had not refused him?"

"Of course not. You are more than welcome here. Is she not, Auntie?"

"Indeed. The more the merrier. What's one more girl under our roof? Though we may have to put you to work!" Her eyes twinkled.

"Work?" Rachel glanced at the smear of flour on Matilda's cheek and her splattered apron. Matilda Grove enjoyed baking but was notoriously bad at it—and messy. "Of course, I am more than willing to help. I'm afraid I haven't any experience in the kitchen, cooking or cleaning, but I am a quick learner."

"Oh, we didn't mean that you should clean," Mercy said. "We were thinking more along the lines of lessons for the girls on proper speech and manners? Even shop girls and servants would benefit from that."

"Oh . . ." Rachel expelled a breath of relief. "I have no experience teaching either, but shall be happy to give it a go."

Rachel thought of something, ducked her head, then said, "Mr. Ashford indicated that he might like to . . . call, after I am settled. Would that be a problem? I am sure you have rules here about gentlemen callers, for obvious reasons." She gestured out the door to the girls' bonnets on their pegs. "I can write to him and let him know if it would not be appropriate." A part of Rachel almost hoped for a reason to put off his visits. Would such calls mean they were courting? Good heavens. She wasn't ready for that.

"Of course he may call here," Mercy said. "It isn't a nunnery. Quite." She shared a wry grin with her aunt. "You may receive him in the drawing room, just as our pupils receive guests. I know you will be a modest and ladylike example to our girls. I don't doubt that for a moment."

"Thank you," Rachel murmured, half in relief, half in regret. She certainly hoped she could live up to the Miss Groves' high expectations while living together in close proximity day in and day out. Rachel was not as consistently sweet tempered and well-mannered as they apparently believed. She had her faults, just as anyone did, and they would no doubt become aware of each other's foibles before long. She hoped they wouldn't come to regret asking her to stay.

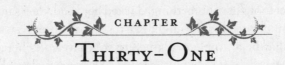

CHAPTER

THIRTY-ONE

Jane was alone at the front desk when James Drake came in wearing frockcoat, beaver hat, and his appealing smile. She had not talked to the man in several weeks.

"Hello, Mr. Drake. We have not seen you in some time."

"Miss me?" he asked, removing his hat.

She had, rather, but did not admit it.

"I have been busy with the Fairmont," he said. "And I see you have been busy too. The new sign and paint look well."

"Thank you. We have yet to make all needed repairs, or enlarge the dining parlour—it seems the Kingsley brothers are too busy at Fairmont House."

He chuckled, looking only mildly sheepish. "Yes. You must come and see our progress. In fact, I insist. Who better than you, who knew the place in all its former glory?"

"Have you changed it so much?"

"Don't worry, the exterior retains all its old elegance. But of course we've had to make changes within. Say you'll come and let me show you around."

She *was* curious. And better to see it for herself than to try to piece together the transformation from secondhand reports.

"Can you get away?" he asked. "It's a beautiful day."

"Very well. Thora has gone to market, but I could come after she returns."

His smile widened. "Excellent."

Jane rode out to Fairmont later that afternoon. She took Ruby, since the boarded horse, Sultan, was no longer there, and Mr. Locke was not on hand to suggest an alternate mount. She was beginning to wonder about the man. He'd been gone over a week—several days longer than expected, although he had mentioned a few errands he needed to take care of before he returned. Mr. Fuller was happy for the work during a slow time at his forge, but the other horsemen were beginning to grumble. They much preferred working with Mr. Locke and worried he wouldn't return. Jane worried too. Patrick laid odds that he'd found a better-paying position.

Ruby trudged down the hill, then managed a bone-jarring trot. Jane missed having a fine-spirited horse a little more with each plodding step. If she closed her eyes, she could still remember what it felt like to ride Hermione. Beautiful Hermione . . .

Jane recalled the day she and John came back from their wedding trip. He had postponed their return a few days, not eager to resume his workaday life.

Her father came to the lodge that very afternoon and broke the news that he had sold her horse the day before.

Eyes plaintive, he said, "I know you would have wanted a chance to say good-bye, but you did not return when you said you would."

Too stunned to protest, Jane had only stared at him as though he were a stranger.

"I'm sorry, Jane. I waited as long as I could. But my time here is short. . . ."

A blackbird called a shrill alarm, startling Jane back to the present.

She rode through Fairmont's gate, and James came out to greet her. He helped her dismount while a young groom took charge of her horse.

"Jane, thank you for coming," Mr. Drake said warmly. "Allow

me to present my new card. You shall be the first to receive one, fresh from the printer." He handed her a white calling card, printed in elegant black lettering:

James Drake
Proprietor
The Drake Arms & The Fairmont

"Do you really mean to call it Fairmont?"

"Yes. Unless . . . do you mind?"

"I suppose not. It is nice to have a bit of the family legacy continue on."

"I hoped you'd like that."

She nodded, and then he lost no time in beginning his guided tour.

"As you can see, we're building a new stable block to accommodate a larger carriage house and more stalls. I thought about masonry, but timber-framed construction takes less time. And we've knocked down the old privy—sad state, that. We've built a new washhouse and privy for the outside staff and are installing running water and water closets inside."

"Goodness. That must be an expensive proposition."

"But worth it, I assure you. Guests will share a commodious bathroom and water closet on each floor, while two of the best rooms will have private water closets."

He gestured toward the garden. "I've had a protégé of Capability Brown come out and look at the landscaping. He plans to move the rose garden from the rear of the house to the side, and transplant the hydrangeas. . . ."

Jane's stomach knotted. Move the garden? Transplant the roses and hydrangeas? When her mother and the late Mr. Bushby had spent years enriching the soil with lime, fighting insects, and trimming trees for optimal sunlight . . . ?

But she murmured simply, "Interesting."

He led her inside the house, where memories instantly assailed her. In the vestibule he began, "We've had to remove the old screen, and the tapestries had been left to fade in the sunlight for years on end, so they've been relegated to the attic."

"I see."

"We will eventually convert this large hall into a reception room, sitting rooms, and a coffee room."

That beautiful open hall . . . Her heart gave a painful thud, but she only nodded her understanding.

"Let's start belowstairs," he suggested. "The inner workings of the place."

Good idea, Jane thought. She was not attached to the kitchens and larders.

She thought wrong.

They descended the backstairs and passed the meat-and-game larder and dairy room without pause. But then James stopped outside the kitchen, gesturing to a pile of rubble being carted away by busy workmen, and the newly bricked-over door to the adjoining stillroom—the stillroom where she and her mother had often spent pleasant afternoons, drying flowers or making preserves, rosewater, and remedies like horehound syrup for Mamma's increasingly bad chest cough.

James explained, "We did away with that ancillary workroom to enlarge and modernize the kitchen with a new stove and spit system to roast enough meat for a grand banquet if need be."

Jane looked into the kitchen. Everything was bright and clean and shining, from the big new steamer for puddings to the dozens of copper pots and jelly moulds on the walls.

"Impressive. By the way, thank you for not hiring Mrs. Rooke as your cook."

He nodded. "I am tempted to allow you to think it was a great sacrifice on my part—a gallant gesture to win your favor. But the truth is, Bertha Rooke was not the person I wanted in my kitchen. No offense to yours."

"None taken."

"I want a finer, more continental style of cookery here. French dishes and French flair."

"Good luck with that. Skilled cooks are difficult to find in this area."

"So I've discovered. I had to advertise farther afield. But I am happy to report Monsieur *Poulet* has arrived and is already preparing meals for me, the few servants I've engaged so far, and the workmen. Though he complains about having to cook amid this construction."

"Monsieur *Poulet*?" Jane repeated. "You must be joking."

James leaned near in a private aside. "Between you and me, his real name is John Poole. But I am trying to come up with a more elegant pronunciation for our 'French' chef."

"Keep trying."

He winked. "Touché."

They made their way back to the ground level.

In the long room where she and her parents had dined together, and friends had gathered to share holiday meals, the table was gone. The room was in the process of being converted into three private dining parlours for august guests who wished to eat without mixing with the common man.

"I want to get all the walls moved and heavy building out of the way before we open to avoid disrupting guests' stays."

"Very thoughtful," Jane said. "Will there be a public dining room as well, or will the coffee room suffice?"

"Ah!" He lifted a finger. "This way . . ." He led her into her father's library, and she stifled a gasp. Mr. Drake had taken down all the floor-to-ceiling bookshelves between the room's tall windows. "It is so much brighter and has a better view, with all these windows overlooking the pond and topiary garden. The old dining room was so dark."

Jane supposed he was right, though it had never seemed dark to her. Filled with candelabra and people and conversations, it had always seemed a bright place.

"I see your point."

He gestured her forward. "Now let's go upstairs and see the guest rooms."

Together they crossed the hall to the stairway.

At its foot, Jane looked up and hesitated. The railing was the same, but the stair treads were newly carpeted in Turkey red. And the portraits were gone from the wall. All those old family portraits in gilded frames. Her ancestors. Gone. The plaster wall had been repainted a bright golden hue.

Noticing her pause, James said, "The portraits are in the attic as well, if you'd like any?"

"Thank you," she murmured. But where would she put them? She swallowed and climbed the stairs without further comment.

At the top, she glanced down into the hall below. The skeletal structure—ceiling beams, outer walls, and placement of windows—was the same. But the view so altered. Gone were the formal tapestries and heavy mahogany furniture. In their place were groupings of brightly upholstered sofas, chairs clustered around tea tables, and inlaid game tables for chess or draughts. She looked away.

He led her next into what had been her parents' room—now unrecognizable. Gone was the massive canopied bed, which she'd needed a footstool to climb into. She wondered for the first time if mattresses of hay, horsehair, flock, or feathers had made it so tall. Oh, the cold winter mornings she had joined Mamma under the covers to talk about the plans for the day, recount some strange dream she'd had, or share dreams for the future. . . .

"The floor here was slanted and sagging on that side, so Mr. Kingsley's men had to bolster it from below. We'll have two fine guest rooms in place of the one here previously."

When she made no comment, he looked at her, the evident pride and excitement in his eyes fading as he studied her face. "Jane? You do not approve?"

"Oh, I . . . It is not my place to approve or disapprove."

"Was this your parents' room?"

She nodded, throat tight.

"Jane, the floorboards were rotting. And the ceiling water-stained. And—"

"I know." She held up her palm to stop him. "I know the place was in disrepair. It was fading when I lived here, and left to disintegrate afterward. I don't blame you for making changes as you see fit—for saving the place from ruin." She forced a cheerful tone to her final words. "In fact, I should thank you."

"Come," he said. "There is one room I know you shall enjoy seeing. I have made no alterations to it beyond repairing the plaster and a leaky window."

He led her down the passage, sidestepping the occasional workman's tool bag, pile of lumber scraps, or pail of plaster. When he reached the door at the end, Jane held her breath.

He opened the door for her. Jane stepped inside and slowly exhaled. She looked at the carved half tester bed with its emerald-green bed-curtains, where Mamma had come to tuck her in and hear her prayers. The upholstered window seat overlooking the fountain was still there. And there—the door to the adjoining dressing room stood ajar, although a glance revealed a gentleman's frock coats in place of the gowns once kept inside. And there—the stuffed chair and footstool near the fireplace where she'd huddled to stay warm while reading book after book, her cat on her lap. Only the dressing table was missing. In its place stood a masculine pedestal desk and chair.

"Whose room was this?" he asked quietly.

"Mine."

"I thought it might have been."

She glanced at him, but he looked away, surveying the room with satisfaction. "It's perfect. I have decided to keep it for myself. The owner's suite, as it were."

"You plan to live here?"

"I do, yes. For the time being."

"And your other hotel?"

"It is well established by now. Steady traffic. Dependable employees. My manager will write if he needs anything, and I will visit now and again to make sure everything is in order. But it's important for me to be on hand here until the Fairmont is established as well."

"How long will that take?"

"Only God knows."

She looked around her old room once more, until she became aware of his gaze on her profile.

He took a step nearer and lowered his voice. "Jane, if you would like to come back here to . . . stay . . ."

Jane's mind, whirling with memories of her parents and child-hood friends, came to a jarring halt. He could not be serious, surely. She pretended to misunderstand him, saying brightly, "I doubt I shall need to stay in a hotel when I live nearby, but thank you so much for the tour, Mr. Drake. And congratulations on your progress. Most impressive. Now, I had better be getting back. . . ."

His expression told her he hadn't been fooled, but he didn't press her, instead gesturing for her to precede him out of the room and down the stairs.

A quarter of an hour later, when she rode through The Bell archway, Tall Ted helped her dismount and led Ruby into the sta-bles. Across the courtyard, Jane saw Thora and Patrick standing outside, looking up at the roof and talking with the slater about the broken roof tiles and damaged statue.

Patrick looked over at her. "How does your old place look? Do we stand a chance?"

Jane summoned up some pluck. "It is most impressive. We shall have our work cut out for us to compete with it. Thank heavens for the Royal Mail or we'd be sunk."

"Wish you could have stayed there?" Patrick teased.

"No. Not . . . quite," she replied.

Thora, Jane noticed, said nothing, her somber eyes studying Jane in disconcerting directness.

Jane looked away to the roof, her gaze lingering on the broken angel. "You know, I've changed my mind about the old angel. Let's not take her down. Let's leave it."

"Are you sure?" Patrick asked.

"Definitely." Jane removed her hatpin. "I'll join you in a few minutes. Just let me put away my things."

Patrick waved and turned back to the others.

Jane entered the lodge, set her hat atop the nearby table, and pulled off her gloves.

Then she stepped into her bedchamber. There, Jane shut the door, leaned back against its solid weight, and let the tears come.

CHAPTER
THIRTY-TWO

After church the next day, Jane returned to the lodge for a short rest, Kipper curled up in a puddle of sunshine beside her. Then Jane played her pianoforte for a time—it had been too long since she had done so. She began with an Irish air, and then a sonata by Pleyel. As the final notes faded, Jane heard horse hooves, and glanced up. From her window, she glimpsed Gabriel Locke ride past—he had come back at last. She rose and looked closer. He rode Sultan, she noticed. *Boarded horse, indeed*. Then she saw the second horse tethered behind—a striking young bay. Good heavens, this was no humble hackney.

Jane hurried outside, in her eagerness forgoing bonnet and gloves.

"Hello, Jane," Gabriel said as he dismounted. "I'm sorry my errand took longer than expected. But I've brought someone to meet you."

Jane slowly walked around the young mare, admiring her glossy russet coat and black mane, tail, legs, and ears. "She's beautiful."

"Glad you agree."

Jane gingerly extended her hand, and the horse snuffled her palm with a velvety muzzle. "Where did she come from? Whose is she?"

"She's yours."

Hope and confusion furrowed her brow. "Mine?"

"Yes. John told me you always regretted losing your horse when you married him. I planned to look for one earlier, but after John died, I—"

"John talked to you about a horse for me?" Jane sucked in a breath. Old assumptions shifted, and a new idea struck her. "Did he ask you to buy her? Is that what the two of you were doing on some of those trips? John was rather secretive, I recall. And that would explain it—if he wanted it to be a surprise." Stroking the horse's sleek neck, Jane said, "You don't know how I've missed having a horse. My Hermione would be quite old by now, but this young beauty reminds me of her."

Gabriel cleared his throat. "Yes, well. I should have acted earlier, but with you in mourning and all . . ." His words drifted away on a shrug.

"How thoughtful of you. And of John. It was John's idea, was it not?" She heard the almost desperate hope in her voice, yet could not stifle the eager smile trembling on her lips. She could not accept such an extravagant gift from Mr. Locke, but if it were from her husband in absentia . . . ?

Gabriel's eyes were distant. "John often spoke of you and asked me about horses."

"He considered you an expert?"

He tilted his head. "I suppose he did."

"Did you intend to find a horse for me when you traveled north?"

"It was one of my purposes, yes."

"You might have mentioned it when we met in Epsom."

"And spoil the surprise? I hope you're not too disappointed that I returned with her instead of a hack?"

"Disappointed? Quite the opposite. Though Thora and Patrick won't approve of the added expense."

Gabriel waved a dismissive hand. "Taking on a horse when one hasn't any is expensive indeed, but when we already have a stable full, and buy feed by the wagon? The incremental cost is not so high."

Jane nodded, hoping Thora and Patrick would see it that way. "What is her name?"

"Athena."

"Athena . . . I like that. Where did you find her?"

"You mentioned the bloodline of your former horse, remember? I asked around until I learned the name of the breeder who bought your mare. It took longer than I expected. However, when I did, I discovered that your Hermione had given birth to a promising foal named Athena, now four and a half years old."

She gaped at him. Looked back at the mare and then shook her head in wonder. "Are you telling me this horse not only looks like my Hermione, but is actually her daughter?" Her voice cracked.

"Yes."

Jane's eyes heated and her throat burned. She turned away so he would not see her tears.

He said quietly, "She is fairly well trained already, but spirited. Let's give her time to settle in. Then I will help you work with her, if you don't mind."

"If I don't mind?" she echoed, half laugh, half sob. "Of course I don't mind, you foolish man."

The thought of The Bell's uncertain future flickered through Jane's mind, and her excitement momentarily faded—tempered by the realization that there might not be a Bell stable for long, and she could not afford a horse's upkeep on her own. But she pushed the thought from her mind. She would not contemplate such a heartbreaking thing. Not yet.

Gabriel cleared his throat and turned toward the stable. "Well, both of these horses have earned their oats, not to mention a good rubdown and grooming, so . . ."

"I will help, if you don't mind."

He gave her a slow smile. "Of course I don't mind, you foolish woman."

Tall Ted, Tuffy, and the young postboy, Joe, came out to greet Gabriel, all three smiling broadly to see him again. So broadly, in fact, that Jane saw Tuffy was missing a few teeth. When the men had exchanged their news, they returned to the bunk room to enjoy some rare leisure on the relatively quiet Sunday.

Jane took Athena's lead and led her into the stables, the mare's ears alert and eyes wary at the sight, sounds, and smells of unfamiliar horses. Jane inhaled a deep breath. She had always liked the smell of stables—hay, leather, horses—though she knew many ladies did not. Now, walking beside Gabriel Locke, she noticed another aroma—his spicy shaving tonic, she guessed. She breathed in the masculine scent, for a moment reminded of John.

Athena whickered nervously, and Jane stroked her neck, murmuring reassurances.

Gabriel led Sultan to his stall, then stepped out to help her maneuver Athena into an empty stall next to it. "At least she is already acquainted with this boy."

Athena resisted a moment, but between the two of them and the lure of a feed bucket, she allowed herself to be cajoled inside. Gabriel stepped gingerly around the horse, his shoulder brushing Jane's as he squeezed by her in the confined space.

"There now, girl. You're all right," he murmured as he passed behind her, and for a moment Jane mistook the words as meant for her.

He disappeared into the tack room, and came out a few moments later with a brush and currycomb for each of them. He handed her a set over the gate, then let himself back into Sultan's stall.

Jane began with the currycomb over Athena's back and sides, loosening dirt and hair, then followed with the brush. Gabriel she noticed, did the same, moving the rough-toothed comb over Sultan's coat in a circular motion.

Jane said, "I take it the man from Pewsey Vale boarding his horse here was you all along?"

"Yes. A recent gift from my uncle. I hope you don't mind."

"You might have said so."

"I thought it might raise questions about where I'd got the money or spur resentment among the other horsemen."

Oh yes, a horse like Sultan would certainly raise questions. Jane had a few of her own.

They worked in companionable silence for several moments, then Jane asked, "Remind me. How did you and John first meet?"

"At a horse market in London."

"Tattersall's?"

"Yes."

"And were you a farrier there as well?"

"No."

"But you did work as a farrier elsewhere?"

"I have worked with horses for years, in several capacities."

"How did you learn the trade? Were you apprenticed at a young age, or . . . ?"

He shook his head. "My grandfather worked with horses, and I was his shadow as a lad. Even had my own toy hammer and mimicked his every move. My uncle joined him in the business, and I helped out whenever I could. Did everything from groom to shoe to worm to shovel manure. I love everything about horses. Their intelligence. Their strength and nobility. The bond that forms when you earn their trust."

His words reminded Jane poignantly of her years with Hermione, and she hoped she and Athena would in time form that same trusting bond.

"Are you from Pewsey Vale?" she asked.

"My uncle lives near there, though my parents live in Newbury. They hoped I might pursue another profession, but I wanted to work with horses like my uncle and grandfather."

"This is a good job for you, then," she said. "Do you enjoy working here?"

He shrugged. "Some days are difficult. Seeing coach horses mistreated or driven to an early death, pulling overloaded carriages up and down hills in all weather . . ." He grimly shook his head. "The life of a stagecoach horse is not much better than a chained slave rowing a ship."

"If you feel that way, then why do you stay on here?"

"I have my reasons."

She paused and looked over at him. "Reasons you'd like to share with me?"

He met her gaze. "No."

Jane studied him a moment longer, weighing the resolve glittering in his dark eyes. She decided to let the matter drop. For the time being.

"Well. I'm glad you're back," she said.

"Are you?"

"Yes." His direct eye contact disconcerted her and she looked away, toward Athena once more. "With such a gift—how could I not be?"

Thora sat at the booking desk early on Tuesday morning, mulling over recent events. She did not like the idea of their farrier buying such a fine horse, let alone making a gift of it to Jane. Unheard of! Jane had tried to justify the gift, saying it had been John's idea—a long-overdue present from him. That searching out a horse for her had been one of the things that had taken John to London and Epsom and Bath all those times. At some point, he had apparently engaged Mr. Locke's help in the quest—a quest that had lain fallow all these months since John's death. Thora couldn't quite credit it. Yes, John had been a besotted fool where Jane was concerned, but not where horses were concerned.

She recalled John mentioning a few years ago that Jane had asked if they might buy a riding horse. But John had discouraged the idea. She was surrounded by horses every day, he reminded her. There was no room in The Bell stables for a horse that didn't earn its keep, unless she wanted to see it harnessed to a post chaise. Jane had not wanted such a life for any horse of hers, so both she and John had let the matter drop, or so Thora had thought.

Now, with a glance at the clock, Thora rose and stepped to the window.

She was looking forward to seeing Charlie Frazer that morning, having missed seeing him the Saturday before. Thora had been feeling a bit low and unsettled since her visit with Nan and Talbot. But she felt certain a talk with Charlie was just the thing to cheer her up.

In a rush of horses, jingling tack, and blowing horns, the Quick-silver arrived right on schedule, ushered into the yard with a cheer-ful tune played by its handsome Royal Mail guard. She'd have to be on *her* guard with that one. She'd already seen Cadi ogling Jack Gander more than once. Although The Bell had only a few overnight guests at present, Thora doubted they would appreciate the private concert at such an early hour. But she did.

Thora returned to the booking desk, feeling a little brighter already.

A short while later, Charlie Frazer entered, removing his hat as he came. He ran a hand through his thick silver-and-black hair.

"Hello, Charlie."

"Thora."

His tone of voice caused her to glance again. His usual jovial smile was absent. He looked down at his hat, as if inspecting the brim.

"What is it, Charlie?"

"May I speak to you?"

"You are speaking to me."

"In private, I mean."

Good heavens. Smoothing his hair nervously, avoiding her eyes . . . and asking to speak to her in private? *What now?*

"Very well. No one is in the office this early." She led the way and opened the door for him. She wondered if she should leave it open, to discourage him from saying anything too personal. Instead she closed the door and turned to face him. "Well?"

Still, he hesitated, and her old impatience returned. She never could abide wasting time.

"Oh, spit it out, Charlie."

"The Royal Mail is . . . pulling out of The Bell."

"What?"

He nodded somberly. "The deputy postmaster is making plans to bypass Ivy Hill in favor of Mr. Drake's new hotel on the turnpike."

Thora's chest tightened, all other concerns evaporating. "You told me nothing like that was afoot."

"I was wrong."

"Charlie Angus Frazer admitting he was wrong about something? The world as we know it is about to end."

He remained sober. "Yes, I'm afraid it is."

Thora sank into a chair. "Can you not put in a good word for us? Use your renowned charm to convince the Royal Mail to award us the contract as usual?"

"Pander to Hugh Hightower, my old adversary? I've despised that man since boyhood." He slouched in the chair opposite and tossed his hat upon the desk.

"What has he ever done to you?"

"He was the devil himself to me when we were lads. When my family moved to Andover from Inverness, he took great pleasure in making certain I knew I was not welcome. My father worked for his, and he never let me forget it. He told scurrilous lies about me to my fellows—and to Eudora Foster, the prettiest girl in the parish. I'd set my sights on her, see. And Hugh was determined to win her regard."

"Did he succeed?"

"No. But she married him anyway."

"Did she?"

"Yes. Apparently I overestimated my charms, as you tell me I often do. And underestimated her father's influence. He wanted his daughter to marry Hugh. Better educated. Wealthier. But no doubt she's come to regret it."

"No doubt," Thora echoed dryly, studying his perturbed expression.

He cleared his throat. "Even if I thought I might be able to influence Hightower, I'm afraid the time has passed. The contracts are up for review as I sit here."

Thora thought. "There must be something we can do. Surely

they won't take the contract away without giving us a chance to prove our mettle."

"I don't know. But I'll see what I can find out." Charlie rose. "I'll start with Jack. As a guard, he's an employee of the post office, and may be privy to more details than I."

"Thank you," Thora said. "And, besides Jack, may we keep this between ourselves for now? I will tell Jane and Patrick, but I don't want the staff to worry."

"Of course. You're the first person I've told." He reached for her hand, taking it in his strong grasp. "I'll do everything in my power to help you, Thora. You know that. I only wish I could do more."

Thora had to leave on an errand, so it was Patrick who delivered the news to Jane about the Fairmont's bid to take over the Royal Mail. He told her, and then walked casually to the coffee room, not nearly as upset about it as he should have been.

When he left the office, Jane picked up Mr. Drake's new calling card from the desk. "Well, he lost no time, did he." Irritation flared through her. "Friendly competitors, ay?" She tossed the card into the dust bin.

Cadi knocked on the doorframe.

"Um . . . ma'am? There's a Mr. Hightower here to see you."

Jane's heart fisted. *Oh no.* Had the deputy postmaster overheard her grumbling? It would not help their cause.

Jane took a deep breath and straightened the piles on the desk.

"Show him in please, Cadi."

A moment later, a tall man who lived up to his surname entered the office, dressed in a fashionable maroon frock coat the color of many Royal Mail coaches. Jane wondered if it was his "official" suit of clothes while carrying out his duties.

He began, "Mrs. John Bell, I take it?"

"Yes. How do you do, Mr. Hightower. Please, won't you be seated?"

He remained standing. "I shan't stay long. I had come out of professional courtesy to inform you of pending changes to the Devonport-London route." He quirked a sardonic brow. "But I take it you've already heard."

"Only just. Quite a shock, as you can imagine. But I am glad you're here. It gives me a chance to show you the many improvements we are making to provide even better service to our customers, especially passengers of the Royal Mail. If you would like to follow me, I will show you what we've done so far, and—"

He raised a hand. "I'm afraid I haven't much time."

Jane swallowed her disappointment and summarized what they had started and what they yet planned. It all sounded rather mundane as she described it. She wished she'd had more notice and time to prepare her case.

"That's all well and good, Mrs. Bell. But speed and efficiency are uppermost in my decision. And the fact is, Mr. Drake's hotel is conveniently located right off the new turnpike. Stopping there to change horses would allow our coaches to avoid the taxing uphill climb, saving time as well as the strain on the horses. I would be remiss not to take those factors into account."

"I understand, but The Bell has a long, successful history with the Royal Mail, and we have undertaken refurbishments with the Royal Mail in mind, whereas Mr. Drake's hotel is untried and unproven."

Mr. Hightower stroked his chin. "The Bell has enjoyed the privilege of servicing the mail for many years, it is true. But it is my duty to look to the glorious future of the Royal Mail and not behind to the past." He replaced his hat. "Well. Thank you for your time and understanding. Good day, Mrs. Bell."

The outer door had barely snapped closed before Patrick popped his head into the office, all eagerness.

"So? How did it go? What did he say?"

Jane rested her head in her hands. "We're doomed."

CHAPTER

THIRTY-THREE

Four days later, Thora sat at the front desk, racking her wits to think of something to save their Royal Mail patronage and the inn. She noticed the Salisbury newspaper lying there, the employment section face up. Had Colin been perusing the Help Wanted notices, already looking for a position in case The Bell failed or was sold? She ran a finger down the advertisements. Perhaps she ought to start looking as well. . . .

Charlie swept in, a spring in his step. Considering the bad tidings he had recently brought them, she was surprised and a little peeved by his cheerful demeanor.

"It is Saturday, Thora," he said. "You know what that means."

She replied flatly, "Everyone will want bath water tonight?"

"That too, no doubt. But more importantly, it is my night off."

Because there was no delivery of letters on Sundays, Saturday nights were an occasion for revelry among many Royal Mail coachmen. Even though clocks might be set by their passing at any other time, on Sundays the Royal Mail coaches returned to London at the drivers' convenience. They would first meet at junction towns such as Andover, Hounslow, and Hockliffe, for an evening of merrymaking.

"Ah yes," Thora replied, turning over the broadsheet. "Your night out with your fellow coachmen."

"Come out with me instead, Thora. Let's live a little."

She paused and looked up at him, surprised by his earnest expression, and the offer. "Your cohorts would miss you."

"You know I would happily sacrifice time with the fellows for time with you."

When she made no reply, he pressed his advantage, leaning against the counter. "Come with me to Andover. I've been invited to a party there—a rout. And I would be proud to have you by my side."

"Considering the bleak news you recently delivered, I hardly think now is the best time to attend some ribald party."

"On the contrary, it is the perfect time. And it is a perfectly respectable occasion. In fact, more than respectable. Fashionable even."

"Oh? And where is this grand occasion to be?" She made no effort to conceal her sarcasm. "The Stag?"

"No. At the home of Hugh Hightower, local deputy postmaster." He waggled his bushy eyebrows for effect.

Thora raised her own eyebrows in reply. "The deputy postmaster? But I thought you told me there was enmity between you. Why would your old rival invite you to his party?"

"He did not. His wife did. I happened to see her yesterday, and she invited me to come."

"Because you and her husband are both involved with the Royal Mail—or because she is still smitten with you?"

"That was years ago, Thora. And regardless, the only woman I am smitten with is you."

Was that true? Thora wondered. She felt winded and a little queasy at the thought.

"Thank you, Charlie. But I cannot go with you. Jane needs me here."

"No I don't," Jane interrupted, poking her head out of the office. She quickly amended, "Of course we *need* you, Thora, but we will manage without you for a night. It is not one of our busy nights after all."

"But all those baths . . ."

"I will ask Dotty and Ned to start heating water early. Don't worry. You just go and have a good time."

Charlie added, "Just think, Thora. It will give you a chance to charm the deputy postmaster, improve The Bell's chances of keeping the Royal Mail."

"If my charm is all that stands between losing and keeping that contract, heaven help us all."

"Nonsense, Thora," Charlie insisted. "You underestimate your charms, as much as I overestimate mine. Between the two of us, we should make quite an impression."

"No doubt. But . . . if there's any chance it will help our cause, I shall go with you."

"How you flatter me," he quipped, holding his hand to his heart and giving her a mock bow.

Then he said, "We'll go in the Quicksilver. In style and speed."

"Is that not against regulations?"

"Not to Andover—it's on the route anyway. But delivering you home after the party? Well, I shan't tell if you don't."

"I could find another way home."

"Nonsense. And deprive me of a moonlit drive back, just the two of us?"

She sent him a sidelong glance. "I thought we were going to help The Bell's cause?"

"That is why *you* are going. I am going to be with you."

Thora rolled her eyes. "You certainly live up to your nickname."

"Which nickname is that?" He struck a pugilist's pose. "Lightning Lefty? Fabulous Frazer?"

"Charming Charlie."

"Ah. That one. I am glad you think so." He grinned at her. "I would tell you to wear something pretty, but I don't wish to press my luck."

She narrowed her eyes. "Wise man."

When Charlie left them, Jane pleaded, "Thora, do wear something pretty. Frank has been gone a long time, and John for over a year. No one will think less of you if you dress in something else. You've been wearing mourning too long."

"That's the pot calling the widow black," Thora dryly replied. "When are *you* going to put off mourning, Jane?"

"I . . . didn't think you'd want me to."

Thora looked at her somberly. "I don't want you to wear black for my sake, but for John's. I don't want you to forget him."

"Of course I won't."

Thora picked a loose thread from her sleeve. "I *was* thinking of my grey-and-black evening gown."

"Very festive," Jane teased.

"At least that is half mourning, rather than full."

"It's a start," Jane allowed.

While Alwena helped Thora prepare for her evening out, Jane settled in to take care of things at the reception desk.

A coach arrived. As Patrick and Colin went out to meet it, Jane stepped to the window, watching the Zephyr passengers alight in the courtyard. One particular woman caught her eye. Her fashionable bright green carriage dress and pert hat made her stand out from the dark-suited gentleman and one elderly woman with a young maid in dark, nondescript traveling clothes. It was fairly uncommon for a female, especially a gentlewoman, to travel alone. So Jane noticed the woman in green, wondering where she had come from and where she was bound.

Curiosity piqued, Jane returned to the desk and observed the passengers as they entered the hall. Most of them hurried into the dining parlour for a quick meal—hopefully with time and at a temperature to actually enjoy it. But this woman walked gingerly, subtly pressing a hand into the small of her back, probably trying to ease the inevitable stiffness from hours of long confinement in a lurching coach. Yard duties done, Patrick returned inside. But seeing Jane at the desk, he waved to her and disappeared into the taproom.

The lady in green broke from the others and approached the reception desk.

"May I help you?" Jane asked, still feeling the newness of her unexpected role.

"I need a room—a private one. And . . . not too many stairs, if you please."

The woman must be in pain, Jane thought, for she looked too young to have difficulty climbing stairs otherwise. She was, perhaps, in her late twenties. "Of course. Just for the one night?"

The woman managed a tight smile. "I don't know."

"May I . . . help you make arrangements to travel on to another destination? I assume you've gone as far as you can on the Zephyr?"

"I . . . am not certain. May I tell you later? I am so tired . . ."

"Of course. You just let me know. The room is yours for as long as you need it. And in the meantime, don't hesitate to let us know if there is anything else you need."

"Thank you." The woman signed the registry and Jane noticed another wave of pain contort her lovely features.

"Are you feeling all right, Mrs. . . . North?" Jane asked, with a glance at the registry.

"A little ill from all that jarring travel, but I trust it shall pass. Quiet rest is all I need."

"I understand," Jane said. "Why don't I show you the way myself. It isn't far." She noticed Colin carrying a pair of freshly polished Hessians for another guest, and called, "Colin, when you're finished there, please see Mrs. North's baggage carried to number three, and ask Alwena to bring up water when she's finished helping Thora."

"Yes, ma'am."

Jane escorted her guest up one flight of stairs. "I've put you in my favorite of our rooms. It has a fine new carpet and feather mattress." She bestowed a warm smile on Mrs. North, and the woman mustered one in return.

Jane led the way to a door not far along the corridor, unlocked it, and gestured the woman in ahead of her. Jane ran her gaze over the airy room with new rose curtains and bedclothes with a strange sense of pride. "We've been doing a little refurbishing."

"It's very nice," the woman said obligingly.

"Here are a few towels, and soap. Alwena will be your chamber-maid. She will be up any moment with warm water for your wash-stand." Jane pointed and said, "There is a commode cabinet there. Or a new privy especially for ladies outside in the garden." She gestured toward the window. "If you are hungry after you rest, dinner is available downstairs. Breakfast tomorrow will be served from six to ten. But let Alwena know if you prefer to have a tray delivered to your room: chocolate, toasted muffins, eggs—whatever you like."

"Thank you, I shall, Mrs. . . . ?"

"Forgive me. I am Jane Bell."

"Are you the innkeeper?"

"Um . . . the landlady, yes."

The woman's eyes sparked with humor. "You don't sound very certain of that."

Feeling self-conscious, Jane explained, "It was my husband's inn. I am still growing accustomed to the title."

"I'm sorry. Has he been gone long?"

"A year." Jane quickly diverted the woman's sympathy, saying lightly, "But we are managing. You may also meet my brother-in-law and another Mrs. Bell—my mother-in-law, in the course of your stay. It is a family business."

A tentative knock sounded on the open door. Colin stood there, valise and bandbox in his hands.

"Come in, Colin."

He set down the woman's baggage and quickly departed. On his heels came Alwena, who bobbed a curtsy and managed not to slosh any water from the can she carried.

Jane stepped to the door. "Well, I shall leave you in Alwena's capable hands. Again, do not hesitate to ask for me if there is anything you need."

"Thank you, Mrs. Bell. I shall."

It was on the tip of her tongue to ask the woman to call her Jane, but she refrained. This was not a social call.

"I hope you feel better soon. Good night."

Duty done, Jane went back downstairs. When Patrick came out to relieve her, Jane slipped away to the stables to visit and groom Athena. She hoped Mrs. Rooke would not miss the three choice carrots she'd helped herself to from the larder.

CHAPTER

Thirty-Four

At the appointed time that evening, Charles Angus Frazer swept into the hall dressed in formal evening coat, white jabot, and . . . kilt. Stockings, black brogues, and sporran. Full Scottish regalia.

Thora shook her head. "Goodness, Charlie. You certainly know how to blend in."

He bowed. "Thank you, lass."

Privately, she acknowledged that he looked extremely handsome in the attire of his homeland. But she would not admit it. The man had far too much confidence as it was.

"You look lovely, Thora." He opened the door for her. "Shall we?"

As she had the last time, Thora sat next to Charlie on the coachman's box. But tonight he seemed in no hurry, allowing the team to trot on at a leisurely pace, content, he said, to enjoy the temperate evening and her company.

It was pleasant, Thora allowed. She was secretly glad the slower pace meant less wind to wreak havoc on her hair, which Alwena had again dressed with care.

When they reached Andover, Thora surveyed the town with new interest. "So this is where you grew up."

"Yes, after my father moved us here from Inverness. He and Mr.

Hightower, senior, had served together, and afterward, he offered my father a job."

"That was kind of him."

Charlie nodded. "He was a good, humble man. But when he died, Hugh inherited most of his hard-earned property and none of his goodness. Puffed-up prig."

"Is that your biased opinion of his character, or the general consensus?"

"Have you never met him?"

"Only in passing. He dealt directly with Frank and later John when contract issues or the occasional delay had to be addressed."

"Then I shall let you draw your own conclusions."

"Too late for that! You might have thought of that before you prejudiced me against the man. How am I to win him over now?"

"Thora Bell butter up any man? This I have to see."

They turned into the yard of the Andover coaching inn, where Charlie was obviously well-known and well-liked. The ostlers greeted him warmly, took charge of the coach and horses, and accepted the coins he handed them in return.

When Charlie helped Thora down, she noticed the ostlers' curious looks and silently rebuked their mothers for not teaching them that staring was rude. Charlie smiled and offered her his arm, and she forgot about the ostlers. She laced her arm through his, and together they walked through town toward their destination.

"Wise not to show up at the deputy postmaster's door with the company vehicle," she said dryly.

"I thought so. No need to raise questions. Or his ire. Besides, tonight I am not a coachman; I am a gentleman escorting a lovely lady to a party."

"Go on with you." She nudged him, then added, "I hope I don't embarrass you. You looking so . . ."

"Handsome. Go on, I know you want to say it."

"Handsome. And me looking so . . . grey."

"*Beautiful* is the word I believe you are looking for."

"In this gown?"

"Well, I would prefer you in Royal Mail red, but I am grateful you are here with me in any case and in any dress. You could wear sackcloth, Thora Bell, and be the most fetching woman in the room."

She swatted his arm. "Enough now. That's going it a bit brown."

"Not at all. I have only just begun."

They reached the stately red-brick house with white trim and door, opened by a footman. Inside the entry hall, they were met by their hostess—a sweet-faced creature with blond ringlets befitting a woman half her age. But she was undeniably attractive in a frothy pink-and-cream satin gown, and a gentle smile on her lightly lined face.

When her benign gaze landed upon Thora's escort, her smile widened and her blue eyes sparkled. "Charlie Frazer!"

He bowed over her extended hand. "Mrs. Hightower. What a pleasure to see you again. You look enchanting, I must say. Have you discovered the fountain of youth? For I declare you have'na aged a day since your eighteenth birthday."

"Oh, go on with you."

Thora recalled responding in similar fashion to Charlie's flattery and hoped she had not sounded as simpering.

"I am delighted you accepted my invitation," Mrs. Hightower said. "Truth be told, I did not think you would." She turned to Thora, her smile resolute. "And who is your companion? I do not believe we've met."

Charlie sent Thora a warm glance. "Allow me to present Mrs. Thora Bell. A dear friend."

"Ah. Mrs. Bell. Frank Bell was your husband, was he not?"

Thora nodded.

"A charming man, and a trying loss, I'm sure. Welcome."

"Thank you, Mrs. Hightower. That is very kind."

"Please, call me Eudora." The woman tilted her head to one side, blond coils bouncing. "Thora . . . That is an unusual name, but I like it. Very strong."

"Yes, it suits her," Charlie remarked. "She is one of the strongest women I know—both in character and brute strength. Do not challenge her to arm wrestle, if you know what is good for you."

Thora dug an elbow into his side.

With an indulgent dimple, Eudora said, "I had not planned to, Charlie, I assure you."

A gentleman hailed Charlie from across the room. "Well, if it isn't Charlie Frazer. Hang me, it is good to see you again, old man. Still cracking the whip for king and country?" He turned to another fellow. "Sedgwick, come and meet the finest whip I ever had the good fortune to meet and the unlucky fortune to fight." The man put his arm around Charlie and pulled him into a circle of men, regaling them with tales of Charlie's exploits, both on the road and in the boxing ring.

She'd forgotten Charlie had been a pugilist in his younger days. So that explained the other nickname he'd mentioned—Lightning Lefty.

Eudora Hightower watched him go, a faraway look on her pretty face. She was clearly still smitten with Charlie.

Then the woman seemed to recall her surroundings and turned a warm smile on Thora. Her gaze traveled discreetly over Thora's grey-and-black gown. "You still grieve your loss, I see."

Thora nodded. "Some losses are difficult to forget."

"Yes, they are. . . ." The woman said softly, her eyes once again seeking out Charlie among the gathered men.

Thora glanced around the crowd and recognized a tall thin man standing near the fireplace. She had not spoken to Hugh Hightower in recent memory, but now that she laid eyes on him again, she recalled seeing him over the years when he'd stopped at The Bell on Royal Mail business or inspections.

Hugh Hightower crossed the room to them, a scowl on his face. He had clearly seen Charlie—and perhaps had noticed his wife's limpid gaze as she looked his way.

"Eudora, what is Frazer doing here? Tell me you did not invite the man."

"I did, my dear. I happened to see him in town and it seemed the right thing to do, what with his connections to the Royal Mail."

"It is hardly a congenial connection." He noticed Thora. "Oh, pardon me."

Mrs. Hightower said, "My dear, may I present Mrs. Thora Bell."

"Ah, Mrs. Bell. From the inn in Ivy Hill?"

Thora was impressed he would remember her. "Yes. The inn has been in my family for several generations. First as The Angel, and then as The Bell."

He nodded. "I remember The Angel. A well-kept establishment. And your parents were . . . ?"

"Harold and Mariah Stonehouse."

"Ah. Mr. Stonehouse. An excellent man and an excellent inn-keeper."

Poignant pleasure ran through Thora at his words. "Thank you, Mr. Hightower. I quite agree with you."

"A pity to see the old place fade. But then age does that to us all, I fear. Present company excluded, of course."

A snappish retort leapt to Thora's lips, but she bit it back. She wanted to speak up in The Bell's defense, but aware of the gentlewoman before her, and of the social situation, she thought the better of it.

A footman approached and offered Thora a glass of ratafia from a silver tray. She accepted it to give her hands something to do, though she had never cared for the sweet cordial, or spirituous drinks in general. But Frank had. Too much so.

From behind her, she heard Hugh Hightower's terse whisper, "A coachman and an innkeeper's wife? Really, Eudora. Think of our reputations."

"We are not so high-and-mighty, Hugh. You work for a living, as did your father before you. . . ."

Thora sipped her drink, pretending not to hear. Pretending the words did not prick her.

Across the room, Charlie was entertaining his eager listeners with swashbuckling tales of highwaymen, recapturing French prisoners-of-war along his route, and plowing through snowdrifts as high as his horses' withers.

Thora felt herself shaking her head and smiling at the true, though exaggerated, accounts. The man ought to pen adventure novels.

The Hightowers moved on, and Thora lingered on the edges of the assembly, not minding feeling out of place but frustrated knowing she was doing nothing to help their cause.

Charlie returned to her side at last. "Sorry—didn't mean to abandon you. May I fetch you another glass of whatever that is?"

"No, thank you. Horrid sweet stuff."

"Any luck with Hightower? Saw you talking to him."

"I'm afraid not. Other than he remembers my father kindly."

Charlie nodded and glanced across the room at their host and hostess, busy greeting more guests. "I know I ought to do something to ingratiate myself, but I can'na stomach the thought of pandering to him."

Thora sighed. "Nor I."

"Then don't," Charlie said. "Your only task tonight, trying though it may be, is to look at me adoringly and laugh at all my jokes. And to look beautiful on my arm, of course, though you do so already without any effort at all."

Thora sent him a sidelong glance. "And why am I supposed to look at you adoringly? So Eudora will be jealous?"

"No," he replied, expression suddenly sober.

"Wish she'd never let you go? Chosen you instead?"

"No."

"Then what?"

"So she'll see at least one woman finds me worthwhile."

Thora's heart went out to him, and she took his arm. "Oh, Charlie . . . of course you are."

The musicians struck up a vigorous reel, and Charlie immediately brightened.

"Ah! A Scottish reel. Say you'll dance with me, lassie."

"I have not danced a reel in years. But for you, I shall try."

"Excellent. Just follow my lead."

By the time Charlie and Thora finished the reel, they were surrounded by admiring and cheering onlookers. Charlie certainly
knew how to entertain a crowd.

Everyone beamed admiration at the handsome man in the kilt.
Everyone except their host.

While they were catching their breaths and drinking cool punch,
Hugh nudged his way into the crowd encircling Charlie.

"Why, if it isn't the son of my father's coachman," Hugh began.
"All dressed up like a gentleman, or rather, gentlewoman. That
skirt you're wearing is several inches too short for decency's sake
and several decades out of fashion."

Charlie replied evenly, "This is the kilt my father wore when he
saved your father's life."

"Smells like it. Never heard of a laundry? Time for the rag man,
I'd say." He smirked as though a joke, but he was the only person
smiling, though one or two people chuckled nervously.

Thora put her arm through Charlie's and squeezed a warning,
and he managed to stifle the angry retort she saw ready to burst
forth.

Hugh's lip curled. "Did you know? Frank Bell attempted to court
my Eudora as you did years ago, but she wouldn't have him either."

Thora blinked in surprise. Frank had admired Eudora before
her?

Hightower went on, "It's somehow fitting that you are here
with the wife of another of Eudora's castoffs. A dour little widow
in the bargain."

Charlie's jaw jutted and his nostrils flared. "Not one more word,
Hugh. Or so help me . . ."

"Mother of a pair of ne'er-do-wells, if memory serves."

Eudora gasped, and Thora stiffened, ready to strike the man
herself.

Charlie fisted his hand. "What's it to be, Hightower. A punch
in the eye, or your most closely guarded secret revealed?"

"You wouldn't dare."

"Which?"

"Either one."

Pop! Charlie delivered a quick punch to the man's face, and the tall man stumbled backward.

"Dash it, Frazer." Hugh recovered his balance and lunged forward, delivering a surprisingly forceful blow to Charlie's jaw.

"Charlie!" Eudora Hightower cried in alarm, her little hands fluttering over her mouth like the wings of a frightened dove.

Her husband sent her a scathing look and swung again. But this time Charlie was ready and ducked, avoiding the blow. Then he grasped Hightower around the middle and shoved, sending both men sprawling to the floor.

Around them the musicians squealed and squeaked to an abrupt halt, and dancers stumbled and turned to see what the fuss was about. Suddenly the other men in their circle broke from their stupefied trance and rushed to intercede, some grabbing Charlie and hauling him off, others helping Hightower to his feet and then holding him back.

Charlie shook off his would-be captors, but Thora took his arm in a relentless grip. "Come, Charlie. We have overstayed our welcome. Pray forgive us, Mrs. Hightower."

Eudora's eyes were still wide and her mouth slack but she managed a shaky nod. Thora had no words of apology to waste on Mr. Hightower, deputy postmaster or not.

Thora pulled Charlie out of the house and down the street. "Well, you certainly won't be invited back there anytime soon."

He sighed. "True."

"Why, Charlie? You knew he was trying to provoke you. Why did you let him succeed?"

"I tried to resist. I bore his slurs about my kilt and country. But I could'na abide hearing him belittle you."

"Oh come, Charlie. Let us be honest. You were defending your own pride. Not mine."

"But he was looking down his long nose at us both."

"Charlie, I realize I am not the social equal of the Hightowers or most of the other people there, and I don't care. I grew up in an inn, catering to the likes of such people, as well as many higher in rank. In fact, the highborn were usually kinder and less demanding than those who'd scratched their way up a mound of their own making. People like Hugh waste no opportunity to let everyone know they are somebody and demand to be treated as such. Hightower may live up to his name in stature, but he is a small man, Charlie. And it would take a great deal more than his few insults to injure me."

Charlie winced. "I am sorry, Thora. I had hoped to improve The Bell's chances, but I have hindered them instead."

"Well, he is an insufferably arrogant man, insecure as well, which are often two sides of the same coin. Just as vanity and insecurity are two sides for many women."

"Hugh Hightower . . . insecure?"

"Wouldn't you be? If you knew the woman you love admired another man? Perhaps even wished she had married someone else? Can you imagine how that must feel?"

"Yes, I believe I can."

She looked at him, surprised by his somber expression. Did he mean Eudora, or . . . ? She wasn't sure she wanted to know. Instead she asked, "Would you really have exposed his most closely guarded secret?"

"No."

She lifted a hand. "Don't tell me what it is, but . . . has it anything to do with Eudora?"

"It might. But I shan't say more."

"I wouldn't want you to."

Charlie shook his head. "He should have known I would'na reveal it. I do have some honor, after all."

"Then why threaten to?"

"To give him a choice."

She lowered her chin and regarded him in disapproval. "To give yourself an excuse to hit him, I think you mean."

Thora felt she had chastised the man enough for one night.

She pulled a handkerchief from her reticule and handed it to him. "Your lip is bleeding."

He paused on the street and dabbed his mouth with it. "I suppose I have lost any chance I had of getting that kiss?"

She looked at the bloody lip and swollen cheek. "Definitely not a tempting prospect at the moment."

Though she *was* just slightly tempted. A part of her wanted to kiss his cheek and soothe his wounded face and his wounded pride. But she resisted. It wouldn't do to reward such behavior, she reminded herself briskly.

They continued on their way.

"It's a good thing you punched him when you did, Charlie," Thora said, sending him a sly smile. "I was about to challenge him to arm wrestle. Then he would have learned the *true* meaning of humiliation."

CHAPTER

THIRTY-FIVE

Later, atop the Quicksilver, they rode in companionable silence back to Ivy Hill, Charlie now and again reaching up with his free hand to massage his jaw. "Hugh has a better arm than I would have credited. I'm out of practice to let him land a blow in the first place."

"You're not a young man any longer, Charlie." She elbowed his slight paunch. "Lightning Lefty is long gone."

"Ach, Thora. Must you always be so blunt?"

She inhaled a long breath, noticing the aromas of freshly scythed grass and lavender in the air. "I have been blunt since I was a little girl, Charlie, and I shall no doubt be blunt when I am old and grey. Or should I say, older and greyer."

"I hope I shall be there to see it."

"Sounds like a fate most men would prefer to avoid."

"I am not most men."

"As I am realizing more and more."

She felt him focus on her profile. "You look beautiful by moonlight, Thora. Your eyes outshine those poor stars."

She turned to look at him. Saw his eyes glimmering as they roved her features. Felt him press his shoulder into hers. His knee . . .

"Lightning Lefty may be dead," she observed, "but I see Charming Charlie is alive and well."

He grinned in reply, then winced at the pain it caused.

They rode the rest of the way in silence, Thora gazing up at a thousand stars, and at candles in every window as they passed wealthy, wasteful Wishford—like a hundred more stars lighting up the night.

When they rattled though The Bell's archway and into the stable yard at last, Thora noticed Gabriel Locke sitting on a bench whittling, a postillion asleep beside him. Gabriel rose and nudged the young man awake, saying, "Go and let the guard know the Quicksilver is here." The lad hurried off to do so, and Mr. Locke walked forward to hold the horses while Charlie dismounted and helped Thora down.

By the courtyard torches, he gave the coachman a second look. "What happened to you, Charlie? Are you all right?"

Charlie blustered, "Oh, ay. I tried to steal a kiss, and Mrs. Bell let me have it, all right."

"Don't pay him any heed, Mr. Locke," Thora said. "Heaven knows I don't. He speaks more nonsense than any man I know."

While Gabriel took charge of the horses, Charlie escorted Thora to the inn door. "I wish I could stay," he said in a low voice.

His gravelly tone, his meaning, startled her, but she kept her expression even, pretending not to hear the desire in his voice.

She said, "But you must be in Bagshot, and the Quicksilver in London by tomorrow, and so off you go." She forced a smile. "In fact, you had better hurry. Here comes your guard now."

Charlie leaned near. "Are you sure I can'na have that kiss? You know I've been longing for one from the angel of The Angel for years . . ."

"That angel has been gone as long as Lightning Lefty has, I'm afraid." She held out her hand instead. "Good night, Charlie. Safe journey. And thank you for a . . . memorable evening."

From the lodge window, Jane watched Charlie and Thora return. She hoped they'd had a pleasant evening and managed to improve The Bell's chances in the bargain.

A few minutes later, when the Quicksilver rumbled back out of the yard after delivering Thora, Jane let the curtain drop and turned away. Something skittered past her feet on the floor.

Jane screamed. She leapt onto a chair, even as she realized doing so was a foolish reaction. She couldn't help it—nor a second scream when the mouse darted from beneath the cupboard into her bedchamber.

Now what should she do? Stay trapped up there like a frozen statue of feminine fear? Well, she was certainly not getting down. The thought of that scratchy, burrowing creature scurrying up her skirts? She shivered. She was fine where she was.

Suddenly her front door burst open with a *pop* and *bang* as it hit the opposite wall.

There crouched Gabriel Locke, eyes alert and hands forward in fighting posture. He swiveled, searching the room. "What is it?"

Slowly, he took in her posture atop the chair. The wary light in his eyes faded and he straightened.

"Don't tell me . . ."

She nodded. "A mouse. A live one this time."

He shook his head, hands on narrow hips. "Thought you were being murdered, woman. What a scream."

"My door was locked. How did you . . . ?"

He turned to it and bent to survey the damage. "Broken." He jiggled the latch. "I can fix it. Not much good as it was. You ought to have a better lock anyway."

At the moment, Jane was glad she had not. She pointed toward the bedchamber. "Please find it."

"How did it get in?"

She nodded toward Kipper, who was sitting on his haunches near the small stove. He looked with casual interest from one to the other, then leisurely licked a paw. "I suppose the cat carried it in."

"Then he can dashed well drag it out." Locke crossed his arms and leaned back against the doorframe.

"Are you just going to stand there?"

"You scared the life out of me. Give me a minute to recuperate."

"You were scared? What about me?"

"Of a mouse? Then I wouldn't advise spending much time in the stables. The ostlers and I are on a first-name basis with several."

She shivered again. "I shan't." But his words reminded her of something. . . .

The mouse scurried across the room again, and Jane clapped a hand over her mouth to stifle another scream. Kipper gave it a playful swat as it passed but didn't pursue it as it disappeared beneath the desk.

Gabriel shook his head, lips pursed. "Playing with his food. I told you not to feed that cat. Now he's useless as a mouser."

"Just catch it. Please."

He sighed and straightened. "Very well. Do you have a broom?"

"Yes, there in the corner. But . . . don't kill it, all right?"

"Then what do you want me to do with it? Tie a ribbon around it and make it a pet?"

"No, of course not." *Not you.* She pointed to a box made of *papier-mâché*. "There's an old glove box. Put it in there."

He rolled his eyes. "It's much more difficult to catch a mouse without harming it."

"I know. But I have a particular reason. Please?"

He sighed again. "You're the boss."

Jane did not sleep well that night, the occasional scratching of the boxed mouse waking her at intervals. "You should be glad to be alive," she muttered irritably, then turned over yet again and pulled a pillow over her head.

In the morning, Jane arose early and dressed herself, making do with less-supportive wraparound short stays, and a gown with a front-fastening bodice, pinning it herself. She donned a long mantle, cap, and bonnet, and set off while the High Street was quiet and many windows still shuttered.

Reaching the churchyard a short while later, she pushed open the swinging gate, walked to the work shed, and left her small offering where it wouldn't be missed.

Her strange errand completed, Jane returned to the inn to have breakfast with Thora and learn how her evening at the Hightowers had gone.

Thora's report was even worse than Jane could have imagined.

"Charlie punched the deputy postmaster?" Jane echoed, incredulous.

Thora nodded.

"That's bad." Jane's mind whirled, grasping at hope. "But certainly he won't hold Charlie's behavior against us. The Bell doesn't belong to Mr. Frazer, it belongs to us, the Bells . . ."

"He doesn't think highly of us either. He referred to me as a 'dour little widow' and to John and Patrick as 'a pair of ne'er-do-wells.'"

"He didn't . . ." Jane breathed.

"He did indeed," Thora said, eyes flashing. "I was tempted to punch the man myself."

"I don't blame you." Jane sighed. "Now what?"

"I don't know. I have to go to the almshouse after church—I promised Mrs. Mennell I would help serve Sunday dinner. But after that I suppose I'll go and talk to Talbot again. See if he has any advice."

Jane noticed reluctance in Thora's voice at the prospect of visiting Talbot again, and wondered why.

"Good idea," Jane encouraged. "While you're there, ask him when he might be able to come back for another meeting in the next few days—as soon as he can. And I'll talk to Mr. Locke. If we all put our minds to it, there must be something we can do to keep the Royal Mail."

"I hope you're right," Thora said. "But in the meantime, I wouldn't get too attached to that expensive new horse if I were you."

After church, Jane and Thora walked home together. How jarring it had been to see strangers in what Jane had always considered Rachel's family pew. Granted, its new occupants were still Ashfords—a Mr. Ashford and his mother—but Jane found it disconcerting even so. Rachel had sat with Mercy and Matilda Grove. Jane wondered if that had been Rachel's choice, or the preference of Thornvale's new occupants.

Jane and Thora parted ways near The Bell sign, Thora entering the inn to gather a few things to take to the almshouse, and Jane returning to the lodge. Inside, she set aside her prayer book and reticule, and found her thoughts shifting to her horse.

Athena had been at The Bell for one week and was slowly growing accustomed to her new environment—and to Jane, who stopped in often to groom her, lead her around the paddock, or bring her an apple or carrot from the larder. Jane's heart sank at the possibility of having to sell Athena, not to mention the entire inn.

She walked out to the stables, eager to spend time with Athena again while she could. And perhaps even to ride, if Gabriel Locke didn't object.

Mr. Locke had no objections, though he asked Jane to begin in the fenced paddock, as she had with Sultan, and wait before riding the untested horse in the open countryside. Jane agreed, went and asked Cadi to help her change into her habit, and then returned.

While Gabriel saddled Athena with a quilted sidesaddle, Jane attempted to insert the bit between the horse's teeth. Athena jigged and jerked her chin out of reach, but a low command from Gabriel stilled her again, and Jane was able to fit the bridle straps over the mare's head and ears.

Then she gently framed the horse's head in her hands and solemnly addressed her. "Your mamma and I were good friends. And I hope we shall be as well."

The big dark eyes regarded her warily, nostrils flaring. Jane reached into her pocket, then opened her palm flat, exposing a lump of sugar she'd broken off the sugar loaf herself. Athena sniffed it, then nibbled it eagerly. Jane reached up and patted the short nap of Athena's shiny coat and stroked her wiry mane.

When the horse was ready, Jane stepped atop the mounting block, and from there Gabriel assisted her up onto the sidesaddle. She hooked her right knee over the pommel, while Gabriel guided her left boot into the single stirrup. Then she adjusted the reins.

When Gabriel unfastened the lead, Athena shied and danced, then submitted to his firm, gentle assurance. "Easy. Easy, girl."

Jane clicked Athena forward in a walk around the paddock, then signaled her into a trot. How much less jarring her gait than old Ruby's! Jane found her seat and settled into a rhythm.

A few minutes later, since all was going well, she urged Athena into a canter, rising and falling with the smooth, rolling gait. A smile tickled her stomach. How she had missed having a fine, fleet horse like this.

After her ride, Mr. Locke helped her dismount and walked alongside her as she led Athena back into the stables. A stagecoach arrived, and the ostlers crossed the courtyard to greet it. Mr. Locke unsaddled Athena for her, but then she shooed him off, saying she would groom the horse herself.

The sound of hooves announced the arrival of a second vehicle. Through the broad stable door she saw a postillion mounted on one of four post horses, followed by a pristine private chaise. The ostlers were still busy with the stagecoach, so Gabriel walked over to the chaise himself. He grasped the leader's rein as the postillion dismounted.

"That's it for me," the young man said, stretching his neck one way, then the other. He jerked a thumb toward the chaise behind him. "This gent's bound for Epsom. Word to the wise: Give him your best horses and best postboy, or you'll get an earful."

"Thanks. Will do."

Curious, Jane let herself from the stall and stood in the threshold for a better look. A well-dressed gentleman alighted. Seeing the man, Mr. Locke hesitated, then turned away.

The man looked at him, then looked again. "Well, I'll be . . . It's Locke, isn't it?"

Gabriel reluctantly turned back. "Yes, who's asking?"

"Jeremy Ford. You sold me a fine pair of Thoroughbreds two years ago. Matched greys. Excellent bit of blood, the both of them. But I say, what are you doing here? You don't work for the place, surely."

Sold . . . Thoroughbreds? Confusion rippled through Jane.

"I am helping out a friend."

"Ah. Going up to the Doncaster meeting in September?"

"No, I'm out of racing. But still working with horses, as you see."

The man nodded, though his brow furrowed. "I had planned to look you up soon. I am in the market for a new hunter, but—"

Mr. Locke pulled a card from his coat pocket and handed it to the gentleman. "See this man. He taught me everything I know."

The gentleman glanced at it. "Thank you. I shall." He tucked it into his waistcoat pocket, started toward the inn, then turned back. "Can I buy you a drink?"

"Thank you, no. Too much to do."

"How long have you been . . . helping out here?"

"About a year. Why?"

"Then you may not have heard about the carriage they found—"

Gabriel glanced over and noticed her standing there. He said abruptly, "Uh . . . yes. Excuse me. I have to go. A good day to you, sir."

He walked away, and the gentleman continued inside.

Jane followed Mr. Locke. "What's this about you selling Thoroughbreds?"

Gabriel blew out a breath and shrugged. "I told you I've worked with horses for years."

"But working with horses and selling them are two different things."

"Perhaps, but they are related. My uncle raises horses."

She studied his face. "Why do I get the feeling there is more you are not telling me?"

His lips parted as though to reply. Instead he turned on his heel and started toward the carriage house.

"Where are you going?"

"I have a great deal of work to do, Mrs. Bell."

She winced at his abupt tone. "About that. We need to have another meeting . . ."

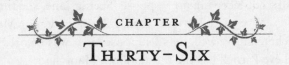

CHAPTER

THIRTY-SIX

Jane returned to the lodge with the hope of a few quiet minutes to rest and think about recent revelations: the probable and troubling loss of the Royal Mail, and now, learning that their humble farrier had sold Thoroughbreds? His owning Sultan suddenly made more sense. Had the horse really been a gift from his uncle?

Jane took off her jacket and sat down at the pianoforte. But she had played only a few soothing measures when a knock on the door pulled her from her thoughts.

Cadi let herself in, her face stretched in panic. "Mrs. Bell, come quick!"

What now? Jane thought in exasperation. "What is it, Cadi?"

"A lady guest has locked herself in her room and won't come out. Won't open the door or answer it either. We heard crying, then a big thump like something—or someone—fell. Alwena's awful scared something bad has happened."

Jane's stomach tightened. "Mrs. North?"

Cadi nodded vigorously.

Jane rose and followed Cadi across the courtyard and into the inn.

As they climbed the stairs, Cadi said, "I tried to find Thora first, but Dotty says she's gone to help at the almshouse."

Jane felt a flash of irritation that the maid had sought out

Thora first instead of her. But in the next moment, Jane wished her mother-in-law were on hand as well. Thora was notoriously level-headed in difficult situations and always seemed to know what to do.

They reached number three and found Mrs. Rooke knocking repeatedly, but receiving no response. Seeing Jane, she threw up her hands. "I've tried. It's your turn. I'd unlock it, but Mrs. Bell has my chatelaine—well, hers I suppose, as it was before."

"I believe Patrick has the master keys," Jane said.

Mrs. Rooke shook her head. "Master Patrick would never enter the room of a female guest without her permission."

Jane was relieved to hear Patrick had some moral standards after all.

Jane knocked on the door. "Mrs. North? It's me, Jane Bell. We met yesterday?"

No response. No sound of any kind. "Cadi," Jane whispered. "Go and get the master keys from Mr. Bell."

"He won't give them to me."

"Then tell him I said to bring them here himself. And sharp-like."

"Yes, ma'am." Cadi rushed off, and Jane noticed Alwena huddled in the passage.

"She were crying something awful before," the skittish maid said. "And now it's so ghostly quiet. I'm afeared something terrible has happened. You don't think she done herself in, do you? Or a highwayman come in through the window and attacked her?"

"No, Alwena, I do not," Jane said sternly. "And I don't want to hear you spreading such rumors. Do you understand me?"

"Yes, ma'am."

Patrick came clomping up the stairs. "What the devil is going on?"

Alwena told him with every expression of woe and doom in her arsenal.

"Thunder and turf." He handed Jane the keys. "Shall I fetch Mamma from the almshouse?"

Jane was tempted to say she could handle it—whatever it was—herself. But she dreaded what she might find on the other side of that door. "Yes, please."

Then she turned back to number three. "Mrs. North? I am going to use the master key and let myself in. It's only me, all right? Here I come . . ."

Please, God, give me strength.

She opened the door and peered in. Seeing nothing right away, she slipped inside and closed the door behind her, in case the woman wasn't fully dressed. Jane surveyed the room, lit by sunlight coming in through partially open shutters. At first glance, it seemed empty.

"Mrs. North?"

Jane stepped forward, and at the foot of the bed stopped abruptly, sucking in a breath. There on the floor lay Mrs. North . . . in a bloodstained nightdress. The chamber pot on the floor overflowed with blood as well. Jane's stomach seized and her chest shrank to a walnut husk. She couldn't breathe. The scene took her back, back, to scenes gruesomely, hauntingly familiar, played over in the lodge. Not once. Not twice . . .

"Mrs. North!" Jane shoved aside the foul churning memories and hurried forward, kneeling on the floor near the fallen woman. She felt for a pulse.

Thank God.

Jane hurried back to the door and cracked it open. "Cadi, send Colin for Dr. Burton and Mrs. Henning. Alwena, bring hot water and rags."

"Yes, ma'am," Cadi said. She turned down the passage, tugging Alwena by the arm behind her.

Jane returned to the woman's side where she lay curled on the floor. Her eyes were closed. Insensible from blood loss, or had she hit her head when she fell? Perhaps both.

"Mrs. North, can you hear me?" Jane asked, patting her cheek. "Hang on. I've sent for a doctor."

The woman's face crumpled. "There's nothing he can do. It's

too late. I've lost it, haven't I? Again! I should never have allowed myself to hope." Her mouth parted, lips stretched in a mask of pain. "Why . . . ?" She rolled to her back and covered her face with both hands. "It's my fault. I shouldn't have traveled. Oh, what have I done? What have I done?"

"It isn't your fault, Mrs. North. It isn't. Shh. . . ." Jane sat on the floor, out of the way of the worst of the mess, but resigned to soiling her skirts. She lifted the woman's head gently onto her lap. "There now, Mrs. North. You will be all right. Hush now. . . ."

And that was how Thora found her ten minutes later when she came in with water and cloths in Alwena's stead. She stared, mouth ajar, looking from the blood, to Mrs. North, to Jane sitting amidst it all, stroking the woman's hair and cooing words of solace over the lump in her throat.

Thora's eyes glistened.

Mrs. North glanced over and moaned, "I've spoilt your new carpet! And your favorite room! I am so sorry."

"Nothing to be sorry for, Mrs. North. Don't give it a second thought."

The woman looked down and plucked at her bloody nightdress. "I don't want anyone to see me like this."

"Then we shall get you cleaned up. The doctor or midwife should be here soon, to make sure nothing else needs to be done."

Mrs. North shook her head, lips trembling. "Nothing can be done. I know that full well."

"There now. You just lie still. I'll be right back." Jane reached up, grasped a pillow, and gently laid it under Mrs. North's head. Then she rose and stepped to the door.

"Miscarriage?" Thora whispered.

Jane nodded, chest tight. "Colin has gone to fetch the doctor and Mrs. Henning."

Thora lifted the basin and rags in her hand. "I found Alwena at the bottom of the stairs clutching these, afraid to come up. But it looks like we'll need a lot more water. Perhaps even the hip bath. Shall I go, or would you like me to stay with her?"

Jane was momentarily tempted to go. A part of her wished to be anyplace besides that red-stained room thick with the iron smell of blood. But she said, "I will stay. But thank you."

Thora returned shortly, and together she and Jane bathed Mrs. North and cleaned the floor. They asked Alwena to bring up a bucket of cold water to soak Mrs. North's nightdress until they could get it to the laundress. Glimpsing the garment, Alwena swore she had never seen so much blood and would not believe Jane when she assured her the woman had not tried to harm herself, nor had some murderous thief climbed through her window and stabbed her, nor any of the other wild theories she spun in her frightened frenzy. The chambermaid was imaginative—Jane would give her that.

Jane sent Cadi to the keeper's lodge to bring back a nightdress and dressing gown for Mrs. North to wear, despite the woman's protests. "I may spoil them yet."

"Don't fret. It doesn't matter." Besides, Jane thought, there was no one to see her in her fine embroidered linen anyway.

As she helped Mrs. North into them, Jane could not help but notice the woman's pale limbs tremble and the slight mound of her abdomen that had yet to subside.

The midwife and doctor arrived on each other's heels, but Mrs. Henning quickly shooed the man away, saying she would tend the poor woman on her own. After examining her and assuring Mrs. North she would heal and be able to try again, Mrs. Henning gave her a soothing herbal tea to drink and plenty of cotton wool to use as padding until her bleeding stopped completely. Before she took her leave, the midwife recommended Mrs. North rest and avoid travel for a few days.

When she had departed, Mrs. North turned her head on the pillow toward Jane. "Again, I am sorry to inconvenience you."

"Hush. It is no trouble at all. And hardly what is important at present."

"You are very kind. Apparently, I will need the room for another few nights."

"Stay as long as you like. We will take care of you."

Jane's gentle words seemed to cause the woman pain, for her face crumpled and tears filled her eyes again. "Thank you," she whispered, voice hoarse.

"Is there anyone I should send word to?" Jane asked. "Or I would be happy to bring up paper and pen if you wish to write a message to whomever is expecting you."

Mrs. North shook her head, sending a tear rolling down her wan cheek. "No one is expecting me."

Jane tucked the bedclothes around her and sat on the edge of the bed, hoping her guest would not be offended by her familiarity. She waited for the woman to explain but did not pry.

"I was going to surprise Geoffrey," she began. "Before he left for the West Indies. He is to be gone a full year at least. I wanted to tell him in person."

"You just found out you were expecting?" Jane asked.

Mrs. North nodded. "I put off seeing a doctor for confirmation. Thinking that if I just let things be a little longer. . . . Not become excited and blurt out the news to my husband prematurely, as I had done before, to my great regret." She shook her head. "I don't think men can care about a child they have never seen. Never held. Or at least Geoffrey could not. He was disappointed, of course. He is not heartless. But he could not understand why I was so upset. Why I could not move past it."

Jane nodded. John had never quite understood either, nor took the losses to heart as Jane had.

"And when I finally sent a note to our family physician, I learned that he was out of town at some medical lecture. So I waited. Geoffrey was not due to leave until the first of the month, so I thought I had more time. But then a letter arrived, asking Geoffrey to come as soon as may be. Some urgent business—I don't recall exactly what—a ship was leaving in a few days' time. As he packed to leave, I thought about telling him what I suspected. But I don't know . . . I felt to do so was to risk things somehow. I will sound as superstitious as your chambermaid."

Jane winced to recall all that Alwena had said. "Heard her, did you?"

Mrs. North nodded and resumed her account. "My physician called on me very soon after my husband left. When he examined me, he seemed so optimistic, estimating my term, and saying he felt quite certain this time would be different. I would soon have a baby boy or girl in my arms, to keep me company while my husband was away.

"That jolted me into action. My husband was about to leave the country for a year. Perhaps longer, especially if he had no specific reason to return earlier. I suppose I thought, if he knew, he might change his mind about going altogether. About leaving me to face confinement and childbirth alone. I haven't much family, you see. And I wanted a loved one with me."

"Of course you did." Jane reached over and squeezed her hand, surprised to find tears stinging her own eyes.

"But I had very little hope of a letter reaching him before he embarked. So I decided to book passage on the fastest coach I could find and try to reach the port before his ship sailed."

She slowly shook her head. "But after all those hours on the road yesterday, I began to dread that I had made a horrible mistake. I began to feel ill, and my back to cramp, and I feared the worst, as has happened before. That is why I decided to stay the night. To rest. And hope the illness and pain were due to the lurching carriage and nothing more. How foolish. How stupid." Her tears flowed again.

"You could not have known this would happen, Mrs. North. My mother-in-law used to boast about how she never missed a day of work during her confinements. Even traveled with her husband to a horse auction in Salisbury a few months before she was due."

Jane had overheard Thora tell the story more than once, when John had attempted to explain to his tireless mother why his young wife would not be helping with the heavy annual spring cleaning, or bailing water from the cellar the year it flooded, or why she remained in the lodge so much of the time. Jane didn't recall

Thora's exact words, but her tone had been rife with exasperated disapproval over John's "indolent" wife. Thora didn't know Mrs. Henning had suggested longer and longer periods of resting in bed—both to hopefully help Jane avoid another loss and then to recover afterward. Like Mrs. North, Jane had decided it was less awkward and disappointing for everyone if she kept the truth of her condition—temporary as it turned out to be—to herself.

"Thank you for trying to make me feel better," Mrs. North whispered.

Jane nodded. "I know I can't, really. Words are scarce comfort. But I understand your pain."

Mrs. North looked at her closely. Too closely. "You do understand, don't you."

Jane nodded again.

"How long has it been?"

Jane opened her mouth to reply, but stopped, seeing Thora in the partially open doorway. Had she overheard? Their gazes met and held . . . then Thora bustled in with a tray as though she'd heard nothing. Perhaps she had not. Perhaps Jane had only imagined that look on her mother-in-law's face.

After Mrs. North had been cajoled into sipping a little broth and tea, she eventually fell asleep.

Thora said, "I'll sit with her a while. You must be exhausted."

"Thank you, Thora. I do need to use the privy."

Thora walked with her as far as the passage, gently closing the door behind her. She said quietly, "You handled that well, Jane."

"I hope so. I wish there was more I could do for her."

Thora studied her. "How did you know what to do?"

Jane hesitated. "I . . . don't know."

Thora said, "I remember Mrs. Henning coming to the lodge a few years after you and John married. Were there . . . other times?"

Jane pressed her lips together, heart pounding. "Yes," she answered dully.

"And . . . were they all early on, in the first few months?"

Jane took a long, slow breath. "No."

"Jane. Were you expecting when I left?"

Jane swallowed. Managed a nod.

"I thought I noticed a change in you. And you did not tell me, because . . . ?" Thora's words trailed away, as she searched for the right phrase.

Jane tensed, expecting her to say something critical like, *"You didn't think I might want to know you were carrying my grand-child?"*

Instead Thora said evenly, "Because you thought I would be unsympathetic."

Jane whispered, "I saw no point in raising anyone's hopes, not when I was sure to disappoint them again."

"How far along were you, when . . . ?"

Jane fidgeted. "Four and a half months. The last time."

Thora winced. "I wish you had written to tell me. Did you tell anyone?"

"Only Mrs. Henning."

"I am sorry, Jane. Sorry I was not here for you."

Jane was surprised at this but told herself not to read too much into Thora's kind words. She shrugged. "Not your fault. You were away with your sister."

Thora shook her head in regret. "But you had no mother or sister. I should have helped you."

Jane's eyes stung, but she said stoically, "Thank you, Thora. But it's all in the past."

Jane walked away, down the stairs, and outside, feeling oddly numb. She had hoped God would spare the child during that last pregnancy, since He had taken John. Jane had carried the babe longer than any of the others, her gowns becoming snug, her bosom and belly filling out a bit. But with the current fashion of high, indistinct waistlines her secret was safe. She had been on the cusp of confiding to Mercy when the bleeding began. She had gone into premature labor, and nothing Mrs. Henning did could stop it. Jane had lain there, tears streaming down her cheeks, as her child came into the world, though he had already left it. No newborn cry. No flailing limbs and squalling little mouth. He just lay curled in the midwife's hand, still and silent. Small and strangely . . . translucent, but unmistakably a baby. Her baby. There had not been much physical pain in the ordeal. But emotionally? Oh yes, the wound had yet to heal. It probably never would.

Jane spent several hours with Emily North over the next two days, then returned to number three one last time after Mrs. Henning had declared her fit for travel. Emily did look a little better, Jane thought, though still somewhat weak.

"What will you do now?" Jane asked.

"Go home, I suppose. Geoffrey will have sailed by now."

Jane nodded. "You mentioned you have little family, but I hope you at least have a friend or two in whom to confide? And to keep you company while your husband is away?"

"I have many acquaintances, Mrs. Bell—"

"Jane," she reminded her.

"Jane. But none I would call bosom friends. Not anymore." She lifted a hand. "No. Don't feel sorry for me. It is my fault. I have never been a good friend. Always too busy, caught up in my own concerns. After I married, I saw my two closest friends less and less. One of them visits now and again, but I feel the distance between us. The other, I lost contact with altogether. Now that Geoffrey has left, I wish I could talk to her. Apologize. But I fear it is too late."

Jane hoped that wasn't true. She said, "Well, you know you are always welcome here if you ever want to visit or write. I can offer you a listening ear if you need to talk to someone who understands."

"Thank you, Jane. I appreciate that more than you know."

CHAPTER

THIRTY-SEVEN

During Mrs. North's crisis, Jane had put off the pressing fact that they were going to lose the Royal Mail unless they thought of a solution and soon. She had less than a month now to present her plan to Mr. Blomfield—and she had no idea how she could prove increased profitability if they lost the traffic and revenue the Royal Mail regularly brought them.

She had called another meeting. But now she expanded her plan. This time, instead of limiting it to only those in positions of authority, she had decided to include the entire staff to help determine what to do.

She shared the plan with Thora, then quickly raised her palm before Thora could say a word. "And no foolishness like last time in assuming I don't want you there. Of course I do."

"It wasn't foolishness," Thora said, a shimmer of vulnerability in her eyes. "John made it clear you didn't want me here long before he died."

Jane stared at her. "I never said that. Never. I may not have wanted you overseeing the way I managed our little lodge, but I never begrudged your involvement here in the inn. Nor am I sorry you are back now."

"Oh? Well . . . good."

Jane lowered her voice. "What about your sister? You've been here two months now. Won't she be disappointed if you stay on much longer?"

Thora shook her head. "Oh, I'm sure her new husband doesn't want a spare wheel hanging about."

"Did he actually say that? Or are you assuming again?"

"Actually, he was quite gracious. But I could not stay there any longer. I am not cut out for idleness."

"And thankfully so—I can think of no better person to help save The Bell."

Thora drew back her shoulders, her cool stoic expression back in place. "Well, then. Let's not fail."

They all crowded into the coffee room, quiet at that time of day. Jane stood and stated the problem, and grumbles of protest instantly arose.

"They haven't even got a proper cook!" Mrs. Rooke thundered. "A Frenchie can't satisfy the hearty appetites of a Charlie Frazer or Jeb Moore. And there's still sawdust and plaster everywhere, I hear."

Bobbin added, "And their cellar and taproom can't match ours. There's got to be some way to prove we're better."

Tall Ted nodded, insisting, "There's no way Mr. Drake's ostlers can complete a turnout faster than we can. We've been at it longer."

Gabriel held up his hand. "Well, I'm afraid it isn't about experience alone, Ted. When I was in Epsom recently, I spent time at the coaching inn there. They can complete a turnout in two minutes flat."

"Two minutes?" Old Tuffy scoffed. "Impossible."

"I saw it myself. They showed me their method."

"Hmm . . . Then maybe you'd better show us."

Jane interjected, "Mr. Hightower did say his decision would be based on efficiency and speed. If we could prove that we are faster than the Fairmont—that it is in the Royal Mail's best interest to stop here instead—then perhaps he would change his mind and award us the contract."

Ted said, "I know two of the fellows Mr. Drake hired down at the Fairmont. Wishford men, the both of 'em. I could take either one of them in any contest you put before me. I'm stronger and faster . . ."

"And taller."

"Than any of 'em. And Tuffy here, well, he's . . ."

"Got experience."

"Right."

"But that don't mean I'm agin learnin' new ways," Tuffy said. "Not if it means keepin' my job. You teach us, Gable, and we'll learn. We'll give them Wishford boys a drubbing."

Walter Talbot leaned forward. "I think you've hit on something there, Ted. Hugh Hightower loves sport more than any man I know. Cricket, boxing, you name it. A contest might be just the thing."

"A contest?" Patrick asked, skeptically.

"Yes . . ." Talbot looked up in thought, warming to the idea. "If Hightower wants speed and efficiency, let the fastest and most efficient hostelry win the contract. How can he have any idea what sort of service the Fairmont will provide when it's not yet open for business? No doubt Mr. Drake has sold him a pretty tale of how the Fairmont will be a *model of modern efficiency within old, elegant surroundings*," as he's printing in his advertisements. But how can he prove he's more efficient when his ostlers have not yet changed a single Royal Mail team?"

"True, but don't forget Mr. Hightower is also keen on Fairmont's location along the turnpike," Jane said. "We cannot compete with that."

"Why not?"

"He says he'd like to avoid the Royal Mail coaches having to make the climb up Ivy Hill."

Gabriel nodded. "That does cause strain on the horses, you can't deny."

Talbot spread his hands. "But remember, my friends, what comes up, must go down. Yes, coaches lose a bit of time on the way up our hill, but can take it easy on the long gentle descent back down. Momentum coaches would be missing if they remain on the turnpike."

"That's going to be a tough argument to sell," Thora said. "Or prove."

"It's worth a try."

"But would Hightower even agree to such a contest?" Jane asked. "It's unorthodox to say the least. He has the authority to make the decision on his own."

"Well, it won't hurt to ask. But who should approach him?"

Sheepish looks were exchanged, but no one offered to take on the assignment.

"Seeing no other volunteers . . ." Jane said wryly, "I will ask him, although I wonder if we should broach the subject with Mr. Drake first. If he is willing, it might go a long way to convincing Mr. Hightower."

"Why should he agree," Thora asked, "when he's all but secured the contract already with his untried staff?"

"Oh, Jane has her ways"—Patrick smirked—"and that man wrapped around her little finger."

Several raised-brow glances turned her way, including Gabriel Locke's. Jane's neck heated. "Patrick, I do not appreciate the insinuation. Mr. Drake and I are friends, colleagues. Nothing more."

Jane went and saw Mr. Drake directly after the meeting. Seated in the new Fairmont reception room, she stated her proposal as positively as she could, while in full expectation of a refusal.

"Sounds like an excellent plan," James replied instead. "Did you think of it?"

She shook her head. "No. I gathered all my staff and asked for ideas."

"But *that* was your idea."

"Well, yes—though I think it was Talbot who actually suggested a contest."

James steepled his fingers. "Good thing Walter Talbot doesn't work for The Bell anymore, because I'd have to try to steal him away from you. Impressive man. Sterling reputation around town and up and down the line from what I hear."

"Yes, we were fortunate to keep him as long as we did."

James pursed his lips. "So what are you thinking? Two coach-and-fours, our ostlers competing side by side?"

"Might be difficult to find two similar coaches not in use during the day. Not to mention two coachmen at their leisure. But if we had one coach, we could take turns, and have an official timekeeper. And you know Mr. Hightower would never approve use of an actual Royal Mail coach and risk any delays."

James lifted a finger. "Except perhaps on a Saturday night."

"Ah . . . good idea! Maybe the Quicksilver, before it returns to London. And its sister coach."

"Yes, that could work. But why stop with the changeover? Why not involve the whole staff, and compare the entire experience from a passenger's point of view: Who has the best porter, the best food, and the most charming innkeeper. . . ." He comically waggled his brows.

Jane rolled her eyes. "Let's not get carried away."

"Why on earth not? Who wants to go through life living half-way?"

"Not you, evidently."

"Ah, Jane. Are you beginning to understand me at last?"

After the staff meeting, Thora and Talbot walked together out of the inn, down the High Street, and over to Ivy Green. It was a place they had spent many hours together during their younger years, playing cricket or tag, or flying kites on its open, grassy expanse. Across the green, a group of lads had gathered to play ball on the early August day—Delbert Prater and two of the Paley boys among them.

Thora said, "Thank you again for taking time away from your own work to come and help us."

"When have I ever been able to say no to you, Thora?"

She sent him a wry glance. "Frequently, as I recall."

"But never when you asked for my help. We have always worked well together, you and I."

"We did, yes, once upon time. Until we left, each for our own reasons."

Talbot nodded. "Your leaving like that came as quite a surprise to me, I admit. It made me realize I'd stayed on too long when I might have worked somewhere else at higher wages—and fewer headaches."

"Glad to have helped," Thora said sarcastically. "No one forced you to stay on as long as you did. Why did you?"

"Because I liked being your right-hand man."

The ball was overshot and rolled their way. Talbot paused to pick it up and tossed it back to the waiting lads.

He continued, "And I hoped that after your mourning passed, our relationship might . . . change. You respected me as a manager but not as a man. Not fully. And privately, I very much wanted you to see me as a man."

She looked at him, and then away again, her heart tripping uneasily.

"But eventually, I realized you would never see me as a potential partner as long as I worked for your family."

She felt her throat tighten. "Do you mean . . . business partner?"

He shook his head, a bitter twist to his lip. "No, I don't."

He meant husband, she knew. But . . . marry Walter Talbot? The young man who had worked his way up from clerk to head porter to manager? Who had butted heads with her and could be as blunt as she was, and as decisive. Whom people admired and liked, where they were only intimidated by her. Who had earned her trust and friendship. . . .

Talbot ran a frustrated hand over his fair, thinning hair. "This is not at all how I wanted to say it. First you put me off at the farm and now here. Dash it, woman. You know how to confound a man."

"And you know how to astound a woman."

"You must have guessed how I felt. What I've wanted to ask you—"

She held up her hand. "Don't. I have no intention of marrying again. I have promised myself that I will never again hand over the reins of my life. I am still reeling from the last time I did so. There is too much to lose."

He frowned. "I understand how you felt about losing The Bell. First to Frank, then to John, and now to Jane. I was there, remember, when it was still called The Angel. When men vied for one of your smiles. But you married Frank, knowing the inn would legally be his one day, after your father passed on."

"He swept me off my feet. Charmer that he was. And I was too young to know better."

"I remember. All too well."

Yes, handsome Frank Bell had swept her off her feet, and their relationship had progressed quickly. He had seemed so confident, and full of plans for the future. And he had seemed taken with Thora and her charms in return. Though in hindsight Thora wondered if it had been The Angel he'd found charming, and the prospect of becoming its owner one day. At a minimum the inn had certainly added to her appeal.

She said, "But you admired Nan back then."

Talbot shook his head. "I admired you first, but you took no notice. Apparently that has not changed."

"I had no idea . . ."

"You saw no one but Frank Bell. And you would not hear a word against him. But that was then, Thora. What are you so afraid of now? What do you stand to lose?"

"Oh, since I don't own anything, I might as well marry anyone, because I have nothing to lose?"

"I did not think I was just 'anyone' in your eyes."

"Of course not. But I still have a great deal to lose—my independence most of all."

"Is independence so important to you? Is there something you fear I would forbid you to do?"

"Forbid me?" Thora echoed. "The very thought that a man would have the right to forbid me anything spurs feelings of rebellion in my heart."

He turned to face her. "Do you trust me?"

"Trust you with what—my life? My heart? My future?"

"Yes, all of those things."

Did she? She considered Talbot a friend, yes. But she was not about to hitch her wagon to anyone else. To wash another man's dirty socks and lose what little independence she had. But nor did she want to lose his friendship. . . .

He stepped nearer and gentled his voice. "Thora. A husband is to be the head of the family, yes. But don't forget he must be willing to lay down his life for his wife."

"I don't need anyone to lay down his life for me."

"No one?" His fair brows rose.

She shook her head. "I don't need saving."

"There I disagree with you. We all need saving. But you're right—you don't need me. Nor, when it comes down to it, do I *need* you. But I do want you, Thora Stonehouse Bell. I want you to be my wife."

Thora swallowed. Hard. Images of Charlie and The Bell and Jane revolved through her mind, not to mention her own warnings to her sister.

It was time to heed her own advice.

She shook her head. "I'm sorry, Talbot. But no."

Thora returned to the inn and was surprised to learn that Mr. Drake had readily agreed to the contest—the contest Talbot had suggested. Thora was both relieved and worried. Now they had to convince Hugh Hightower to agree. Heaven help them.

Mr. Drake had informed Jane that the deputy postmaster was coming to the Fairmont the next day to make an inspection of the new stables. So the following afternoon, Jane took the gig back out to speak to Hugh Hightower there, allowing her to avoid the longer journey to Andover.

Thora waited in The Bell office with Patrick, hoping and praying for a good outcome.

But Jane had not been gone long at all when she returned, looking defeated. She strode into the office and flopped into the extra chair.

"He refused. Point-blank, refused. Didn't even hear me out. 'Ridiculous'"—she mimicked his blustery voice—"'Not regulation. A waste of time.'" Jane pulled out the paper upon which she and James Drake had outlined the terms of the proposed contest and threw it on the desk.

Thora heaved a sigh.

Patrick crossed his arms and leaned back in his chair. "I could say I told you so, but I shan't."

"Now what?" Jane asked.

"Now we pray," Thora replied.

Jane threw up her hands. "What do you think I've been doing?"

Thora glimpsed Charlie crossing the hall toward the coffee room, hair damp and slicked back, fresh from a bath. She rose, deciding to join him. Perhaps he would have some advice. He might know Hightower's Achilles' heel. Or if the man was open to bribes, she thought, half-serious, recalling the man had a secret.

Over a light meal, Thora told Charlie everything that had happened since he was last there—well, almost everything. She left out Walter Talbot's offer of marriage.

Charlie listened intently. His eyes took on a distant light as he searched his mind for solutions, but he offered little advice and little hope. Noticeably absent were his ready smiles and bravado. He made no jesting offers to box with Hightower or challenge him to a duel. Instead the coachman's face was perfectly serious and grimly resolute.

The garden behind Ivy Cottage was surrounded by a stone wall with a gate on one side, and another at its far end, leading onto the village green. The enclosed space held a tree with a swing, a bench, and a kitchen garden. The rest was open lawn, given over to the girls to play games.

During that afternoon's recess, Rachel had agreed to play battle-dore and shuttlecock with three of the girls. Meanwhile, little Alice sat on the swing, the oldest pupil obligingly pushing her. Another girl reclined on the bench, reading a book of poetry.

Thwack. Ping. The shuttlecock flew right at Rachel's face. It was the third time in as many minutes. Fanny was doing it on purpose, Rachel guessed. The girls enjoyed watching her flinch and duck. Oh, if only she had grown up with brothers. . . .

Thwack. Ping. Here it came again. Rachel let out a little squeal and winced, missing the shuttlecock completely. The girls tittered. Worse yet, when she opened her eyes, she noticed a man standing at the gate, witnessing her humiliation.

Nicholas Ashford.

Her face heated.

Rachel handed her battledore to one of the girls. "Here, take my place, please."

Matilda Grove opened the gate, all but pushing the man through it and into the garden, when he was clearly reluctant to do so.

He was well dressed in deep blue frock coat, striped waistcoat, trousers, and a beaver hat atop his head. In one hand, he held a rustic bouquet of roses. Peach roses.

Her smile came naturally then. "Hello, Mr. Ashford."

"Miss Ashford." He bowed over the flowers, and she curtsied.

Around her, the girls buzzed with a rush of whispered curiosity.

Matilda spoke up. "He said he would just leave the flowers, but I thought, what a shame not to see you while he was here. He didn't want to intrude, but I assured him it was no intrusion at all." Eyes twinkling, Miss Matty retreated from the garden. "Well, I shall leave you."

When the gate closed behind her, Mr. Ashford cleared his throat. "I thought you might be in a drawing room or parlour. I did not realize you would be out here, with all of these . . . pupils."

What had he meant to say—witnesses? Eavesdroppers? Either of those descriptors would have been perfectly accurate.

"Yes, supervising the girls out-of-doors is one way I can help," Rachel explained. "Though I am afraid I am not very good at their games. I have never been athletic."

"Well, there are more important qualities."

His shy, admiring gaze rested on her, and she felt her face heat anew.

He looked down, and suddenly seemed to remember the bouquet in his hand. "I wanted to bring you these. I said I would, and I am a man of my word."

And that was worth a great deal, as she had learned.

"I hope I chose the right ones," he said. "I thought it would be easy—gather a bunch and off we go, but I'm afraid the arrangement leaves much to be desired."

True, some of the roses were already bowing their heads, and the stems were uneven.

"Never mind," she said. "It was very thoughtful of you. And no doubt the Miss Groves have a vase I can use to—"

"A vase!" With his free hand, he smacked his temple. "You don't have one. Of course you don't. What an idiot; I should have thought of that. I shall bring you another bouquet. A better one. In a Thornvale vase, which you must keep, and . . ."

She pressed his arm to halt his self-reproach. "Mr. Ashford. Nicholas. It is all right, I promise you."

At her touch and the sound of his given name on her lips, he fell silent and held her gaze a bit too earnestly for comfort.

She tentatively held out her hands. "May I?"

"Oh. Of course." He thrust the roses forward and relinquished them at last, and only then did she notice the cloth strip bandages around three fingers and thin red scratches on the backs of his hands.

"Oh, dear," she murmured.

He looked down at them as well. "I know. I should have worn gloves. Again, I misjudged the thorny endeavor."

She smiled at his little joke. "Does it hurt?"

He shook his head. "It was well worth it, if you are pleased."

"I am."

"Good. Oh, you will be glad to know that your gardener has agreed to resume his duties full time. He'll keep everything ship-shape, or whatever the gardening equivalent is."

"I am happy to hear it."

"I hoped you would be." His eyes darted toward the girls. "I . . . know this isn't the proper place. But I had hoped to arrange a time to call on you . . . formally."

Nearby, two of the girls giggled, hands cupped over their mouths.

"Girls, please give Mr. Ashford and me a moment of privacy."

"Oh! Privvv-ah-seeee . . ." Fanny drawled. "He must want to kiss her."

"Fanny!" the oldest pupil hissed in reprimand.

Nicholas Ashford reddened, neck to brow.

The students would never have behaved so inappropriately if Mercy were there.

"I am sorry, Mr. Ashford," Rachel said. "Perhaps you might call again, or write and suggest a better time?"

He nodded, and with a sigh of relief, backed out the garden gate. "Yes, yes. Good idea. I will call again. Or write. Good day, Miss Ashford."

"Good day, Mr. Ashford. And thank you again for the roses."

Two days after Mr. Hightower's rejection of Jane's proposed contest, a note was delivered for her by messenger. She was sitting in the coffee room with Thora and Charlie when it arrived, and she opened it then and there.

"It's from Hugh Hightower."

Jane read it, then looked up from the page, dumbfounded. "He's changed his mind. The contest is on for next Saturday."

Thora's brow furrowed. "What? Why?"

"I have no idea." Jane handed over the note.

Thora slipped on her spectacles, read it, and then looked at Charlie over the rims. "What did you do?"

"Me?"

She narrowed her eyes. "Tell me you didn't threaten to expose his secret?"

He frowned. "What do you take me for?"

"You threatened him once."

"Ach. I threatened him all right." Charlie playfully lifted a fist. "To reacquaint him with my left hook!"

"Charlie . . ."

"I am only teasing you, Thora. You should know me better than that by now. Upon my honor, I did not threaten the man."

"I suppose you charmed Mrs. Hightower into persuading her husband to agree?"

Charlie opened his mouth to refuse but then changed tack. He said, "If I'd thought that would work, I might have."

Jane rose. "Well, whatever the reason, I'm thankful for the chance. Let's make the most of it."

CHAPTER

THIRTY-EIGHT

They gathered in the courtyard that very afternoon to start working with the horsemen. Jane and Thora stood on either side of Charlie Frazer and Gabriel Locke, in a show of support to get them started.

They did not have a Royal Mail coach available to them to practice with, but Jane had swallowed her pride and asked Sir Timothy to lend them his town coach, which was reasonably similar.

Charlie had risen after only a few hours' sleep to join them. To please Thora, Jane guessed.

Colin was late. Again. But Jane knew this time it was because Thora had insisted he move a guest's belongings from one room to another. Apparently, Colin had failed to give the regular customer his usual room. The guest had not complained, but Thora had.

In some ways, things had improved between Colin and Thora, Jane noticed. Thora was not as critical about him as a person—or as a McFarland—as she had been. But she still found fault with the way he carried out his duties.

As they waited for Colin to join them, Tall Ted asked Charlie, "Gable says he saw ostlers change a team in two minutes flat. Is it really possible?"

Charlie nodded. "Quite possible, as I know from experience. I was once challenged by a box passenger to do so. He timed me with his gold watch. I effected the change in two minutes and a half, with only one horsekeeper, assisted by the guard. Though I have heard accounts, as Mr. Locke has, of even shorter times."

Tuffy grimaced, his old face wrinkling with skepticism. "Hardly seems credible to me. Four horses taken from a coach, and four others put into their places, in a blinkin' one hundred and twenty seconds?"

"Yet so it is at many inns nowadays," Gabriel said, joining the conversation.

The old ostler shook his head. "When I first started, a quarter of an hour, or at least ten minutes, was the usual time. And if we done it faster, well then, that was cause enough to celebrate with a pint."

He looked hopefully at Thora, but her mouth tightened. "No pints, Tuffy."

His thin shoulders slumped.

"Not during training at least," Jane said to soften the blow. "Though I'm sure we can provide some refreshments along the way."

Charlie spoke up. "I remember those days as well, Tuffy. But now—unless some business is to be transacted such as taking fares, setting down, getting out parcels, or the like—I would say the average is about three minutes for each change."

"Three minutes?" Tuffy shook his head once more. "What's the world coming to? Next you'll ask us to fly."

Jane could only wish.

For the actual contest the following Saturday, their team would be made up of two ostlers (Tuffy and Tall Ted), Charlie, as coachman, and his guard, Jack Gander. Mr. Hightower insisted the Royal Mail coaches must be driven by experienced coachmen and carry official post-office guards at all times. Bertha Rooke, Jane, Colin, and Bobbin would have roles in the contest as well.

When Colin came jogging into the yard at last, Jane began, "As you know, we have been granted an opportunity to prove our superiority to Mr. Drake's new hotel. Granted, changing a team in the middle of the High Street is not the same as what you do day in and out here, but hopefully the contest is a close enough approximation to showcase our services."

Tuffy scratched his head. "Best speak plainer, missus, if you want us simple folks to understand."

"Sorry." Jane turned to Gabriel in relief. "I have asked Mr. Locke to explain the horsemen's role in the contest."

He nodded and took over. "The Quicksilver and the Exeter will start at our end of the High Street. Each will have a coachman, guard, and four stand-in 'passengers' on board. At Mr. Hightower's signal, the two coaches will advance across a chalk line, and that's when you'll spring into action—change out the four horses for a fresh four, inspect the harnesses and traces, water and groom the horses."

"Meanwhile," Jane added, "two male passengers will dismount from the top of the coach and help the ladies alight from inside. I will transfer the incoming mailbag and parcels from the guard to our local postmaster, and carry outgoing mail back. Colin will remove two forty-pound valises from the boot and carry them to Hightower. Mrs. Rooke will hand a small pie to each passenger, and Bobbin will deliver a tankard to Charlie."

"Oh, sure. *He* gets a pint," Tuffy grumbled.

"Finally, men," Gabriel concluded, "when you've completed the change, stand clear, because Charlie will snap his whip over the leaders and bound for the finish line. The first coach to cross wins."

"Sounds easy enough," Tall Ted said, all eagerness. "We'll show those Wishford boys how it's done."

"Let's not grow overconfident," Jane cautioned. "Those 'Wishford boys' are being trained as well."

Gabriel turned to Ted and Tuffy. "To begin with, let's go through a change as we do things now, and I will time you." He pulled out his pocket watch, and for the first time Jane noticed how fine it was—a newer design with a smaller seconds dial inset in the face.

The Brockwell town coach was brought forward and the horses readied. At Gabriel's signal, the ostlers lurched into action. In their hurry and self-consciousness before an audience, they tripped over one another, got tangled in the harnesses, and had to couple and recouple the leaders twice.

They finally completed the changeover and turned to Gabriel for his verdict, Tuffy all smiles and Tall Ted's head dipped in embarrassment.

Gabriel winced at his watch. "Nine minutes, thirty seconds."

Tuffy raised a triumphant fist. "That calls for a pint!"

Gabriel shook his head and laid a hand on the older man's shoulder. "Well, at least we know where we stand. And how much work we have cut out for us."

He turned to Charlie Frazer. "Any advice?"

Charlie nodded and stepped forward. "Every coachman has his own particular method, and I'll be happy to describe mine. Though mind you, I am not usually out to win contests. To negotiate the changeover quickly, everyone must know his own place, and not be tumbling over one another."

Here, Ted ducked his head again, and Charlie delivered a good-natured cuff to the young man's back.

He continued, "I believe a wise coachman takes his part by instructing the passenger beside him to unbuckle the lead and wheel reins as the coach comes to a stop. The first ostler unhooks the near leader's outside trace and changes the near horse, while the second ostler unhooks the remaining lead traces, uncouples the wheel horses, and changes the offside one. The coachman climbs down as fast as he can and finishes changing the leaders."

Charlie ended with a showy flourish of his hand, and Jane half-expected him to take a bow.

Tuffy stared at him, mouth open.

Tall Ted's face puckered. "Is *that* what we were meant to do every time you arrive?" He looked at his partner in disbelief.

Tuffy said, "I did wonder what you were a doin' half the time."

"Well, I work with several coaching inns along the route and each has its own ways, I realize," Charlie said graciously. "The method I describe is ideal, I believe, though not often achieved."

Gabriel nodded. "The Marquis in Epsom uses a similar method.

It's challenging, but I know you men can do it. I have every confidence in you. We have one week. So let's get to work."

All the following week, the horsemen practiced their drill every spare moment they could, in between their other duties. Under Gabriel's direction, they worked hard to hone their routine on each stage that passed through, and used the Brockwells' coach during lulls. They made the most of the Royal Mail coaches that stopped there, and Charlie and Jack Gander joined them when their schedules allowed.

The day before the contest, Jane paced across the yard, notebook and stubby drawing pencil in hand, waiting for the ostlers to start again. Thora sat on a bench nearby with a pile of mending, now and again looking over the top of her spectacles to observe their progress.

When the horses were properly placed, Gabriel looked down at his pocket watch, squinting at the small seconds dial. "And . . . go."

Ted ran forward to unhook the near leader and changed the near horse, while Tuffy uncoupled the wheel horses and changed the offside one. Joe, playing the role of coachman in Charlie's absence, leapt down and finished changing the leaders.

Gabriel consulted the watch and failed to hide his grimace. "Four minutes and forty seconds."

Jane wrote it down on her pad, then called, "Again!"

Gabriel ran a weary hand over his face. "A rest first, I think."

"We've got to keep practicing," Jane said. "Everything depends on it."

The men groaned.

At that moment, Sir Timothy rode into the stable yard, handsome in a cutaway riding coat and black boots with contrasting tan cuffs. He cut a dashing figure atop his tall black horse. He greeted the others politely, then looked at her. "Hello, Jane. I've come to take you riding."

"I cannot. The contest is tomorrow."

"I know it is. That is why I am here. I know you well enough to know you are driving your staff—and yourself—too hard. A respite is in order."

Jane was tempted, but there was so much to do. "Thank you, but I—"

"Oh, go on, Jane," Thora said. "Sir Timothy is perfectly right. Go expend some of that nervous tension you're inflicting on everyone."

"The lads could do with a rest," Gabriel added.

Jane huffed. "Very well. It seems I'm outnumbered. I would love to show you my new horse anyway."

Sir Timothy's brows rose. "New horse?"

Jane glanced at Gabriel and found him expectantly awaiting her reply. She looked back at Sir Timothy and said, "I . . . shall explain as we ride."

After a quick change into her riding habit with Cadi's help, Jane returned to the stable. There, Gabriel deftly assisted her up onto the sidesaddle. As usual, he guided her boot into the single stirrup. But this time she felt oddly self-conscious with her ankle in his hand—especially with Sir Timothy there, watching the process. As soon as he'd finished, Jane smoothed down her long skirt, making sure her legs were fully covered. Then she adjusted the reins and clicked the horse into motion.

Surveying Athena, Sir Timothy gave a low whistle. "There's a prime bit of blood. And very like your old mare, is she not?"

"Yes, very."

Sir Timothy nudged his horse to come alongside hers. Athena snorted and gave the male a wild-eyed warning.

"It's okay, girl," Jane murmured.

"Take it easy," Gabriel instructed. "She isn't used to this dark horse yet."

Sir Timothy gave him an odd look at that but then urged his horse forward.

Together he and Jane rode at a modest trot through the archway and then down the hill. Green fields dotted with red poppies spread before them, and blue sky above. As the ground leveled, they eased into a smooth canter. *Ah . . .*

She smiled at Timothy. "You were right. I needed this." Her tension and fears drifted away on the temperate summer breeze.

As they rode toward Wishford, Jane became aware of an acrid odor. She sniffed the air. Was someone burning brush? "Do you smell smoke?" she asked.

He nodded, the crease between his eyebrows deepening. "I do."

Nearing the turnpike, Jane looked ahead to Fairmont. Her heart thudded. A column of black smoke spiraled upward. From the house? She pressed a hand to her chest. No. The new stable block.

From somewhere nearby a man's sharp cry of "Fire!" rang out. Then again, "Fire! Fire in the stables!"

One of the builders, Jane guessed. Her heart tripped again. All that hay and straw. The poor horses!

For a moment she remained frozen in the saddle, dread seizing her. Where was James? She looked this way and that but saw no one to call to. Then she unhooked her knee and leapt down.

"Jane!" Timothy called in alarm. He dismounted in a rush and grabbed both sets of reins.

She hitched up her skirts and ran—through the gate and past the manor house toward the new building.

Reaching the stables, she saw smoke and a harried ostler trying to herd the horses from harm. He had bridled a stubborn dun and was all but dragging the terrified animal by the reins.

"Where is Mr. Drake?" she called. "Is he safely out?"

"Don't know, ma'am."

Jane tentatively crossed the threshold. The sound of crackling fire drew her attention to a door at one end of the building. The feed or tack room, perhaps. Smoke ran from under it like a black river.

Sir Timothy caught up with her, rushing in to help with the horses. A panicked grey whinnied and bucked, its hooves kicking the stall gate. Timothy yanked a lead rope from a peg and looped it quickly over the horse's head, then led the frightened horse out to the yard.

Over his shoulder he called, "Jane, come out of there!"

"I want to make sure James is safe. Do you see him?"

Timothy dashed back in and took her by the arm, firmly drawing her out. "Let's go."

Other men came running from the manor and outbuildings, but still no sign of its new owner.

"There!" Sir Timothy pointed upward, and Jane looked to see what had drawn his attention.

Flames shot out from the upper-story loft. Through its open loading door, she saw James, trying to beat out flames with a horse blanket.

Seeing them below, he yelled, "Get help!"

Jane nodded, yelling to the gathering men as she passed, "There are ladders and buckets in the coal cellar. Fetch them!"

Jane ran back through the yard, jumped over a pile of lumber, and hurried to her horse, tethered near the gate. Timothy ran beside her. Reaching Athena, he bent and cupped his gloved hands. As she had done so many times over their long friendship, she placed her boot into his interlaced fingers, and he gave her a leg up.

Then he mounted his own horse. "I'll summon men from Brockwell Court and alert Wishford on the way."

She nodded. "I will bring help from The Bell and Ivy Hill."

Jane galloped back up the hill, while Timothy diverted down the Wishford Road. Cresting the rise several minutes later, she turned Athena through The Bell archway.

There was Gabriel emerging from the stables, leading Sultan by the reins. He turned at the sound of galloping hooves. Seeing her, he called, "What is it?"

"Fire!" she yelled, pointing back the way she had come. "At Fairmont House."

Jane noticed Tuffy, Ted, and Joe working in the courtyard. Mrs. Rooke and Dotty sat on the back porch, plucking hens.

Gabriel frowned in thought, then looked around him. "Tuffy, hitch up the wagon. You lads, load every can and bucket we have. We'll have to start a water brigade."

Mrs. Rooke said, "Why should any of us break our necks to help the man trying to put us out of business?"

Gabriel mounted Sultan. "Tomorrow we're rivals. Today we're neighbors."

The horsemen hurried to do as Gabriel asked, and Jane continued on, riding through the village, shouting a call for help. At the churchyard gate, she spied the sexton and his shovel. "Ring the bell! There's a fire at Fairmont House!"

Mr. Ainsworth tossed his shovel aside and loped toward the church.

Then Jane galloped back to the Fairmont, the clanging of the bell fading as she went. When she reached her old home, she was relieved to see Gabriel had arrived before her and had joined the builders and Fairmont staff already forming a line to the pond behind the manor. James stood on a ladder propped against the stable, awaiting the first bucket. Wagons from The Bell and Brockwell Court rumbled through the gate, and people came on foot from Ivy Hill, huffing and puffing down the slope, carrying pails and cans.

Through the crowd and smoke, Jane saw Sir Timothy, Thora, Talbot, and Joe. And there was Patrick at the pond's edge, filling buckets with surprising energy and speed. Her heart warmed to him. She recognized a few regulars from The Bell, as well as Mr. Paley, Mrs. Bushby, and Mr. Cottle, the butcher. And several other villagers she knew by face if not by name. Other people ran over from the direction of nearby Wishford and began filling in the line.

Her heart filled to see people from both villages laying aside rivalry and self-interest to help a neighbor in need. Her eyes heated, but she blinked away tears before they could fall. It was probably just the smoke. It was certainly not the time to become sentimental.

Jane picked up a bucket and took her place in line.

Within an hour, they'd managed to put out the fire. By then, the stable's west end—the tack room and hayloft—had been all but destroyed.

She overheard Sir Timothy, ever the magistrate, ask the Fairmont's head ostler, "How did it start?"

"I don't know. One of the builders with a careless cigar, I'd wager."

"Or a spark from a lamp," Mr. Kingsley rebutted.

Considering it was daylight, Jane doubted lamps had even been lit.

James Drake, she noticed, said nothing. He stood staring at the ruined stable building, jaw tense and face streaked with soot. Jane's heart went out to him.

Eventually the staff retreated inside and the builders and villagers departed for their own homes and businesses.

When only he, Jane, Gabriel, and James remained, Sir Timothy said, "Considering your contest tomorrow, it is difficult to believe this fire was an accident."

"You think someone started it intentionally?" Jane asked.

"Wouldn't you think so, if you were Mr. Drake?"

"But who would do such a thing?" Jane asked. "I hope you don't think I had anything to do with it."

"I would never believe it of you, Jane. Though perhaps someone who works for you."

One possibility flickered through her mind, but she dismissed it. "I am sure you are mistaken."

Beside them, James inhaled and drew back his shoulders. He glossed over Sir Timothy's suspicions, saying, "I agree. An accident is far more likely, and won't stop us from competing tomorrow."

"But, James, look at this." Jane gestured toward the partially charred building. "If you want to postpone for a few days, I—"

"No, Jane," he said, his unflappable confidence reasserting itself. "The contest shall go forward as planned. And setback or no, the victory shall be ours."

After the fire, Thora walked back to the inn. She washed her grimy face and hands at the pump, and then trudged inside, ready to recline in the office chair and rest for a few minutes. But when she entered, she was irritated to find Colin McFarland already seated at the desk.

She asked, "Why did you not come out and help with the fire?"

He rose. "I didn't hear about it until after it was over."

"Didn't hear about it? Everyone in the village heard. Ah . . ." Thora realized, with a lift of her chin. "Out at your folks' place again, were you? I understand that you wish to help your family, but I sometimes think you spend more time there than doing what you're paid to do here." She ran a finger over the dusty desktop. "This office was never this untidy in Talbot's day. By the way, *he* managed to find time to help with the fire."

Colin sighed and muttered, "Of course he did . . ."

"What was that?" Thora asked sharply. "I will not hear a word against Walter Talbot."

"I would not dare, believe me." Colin shook his head. "You save your criticism for me. 'Colin, you charged Mr. Sanders the wrong fare. Talbot always charged him the lower rate.'" He repeated her words in an uncomfortably familiar tone. "'Colin, why must you make two trips? Talbot could carry half a dozen valises at once.' 'Colin, why on earth did you put Mr. Peterson in room four? I've told you we always put him in number six.'"

"Well, it's true," Thora defended. "He snores unbelievably, and there's a linen cupboard there to muffle the sound. That was Talbot's idea too."

Colin threw up his hands. "Talbot this. Talbot that. I get it. He was the perfect head porter and manager. And I will never be half as good. No one shall. You will never be happy with any other man."

Thora blinked, taken aback by the outburst from the usually mild-mannered young man.

Colin stalked out, and a moment later Bertha Rooke appeared in the doorway, a knowing light in her eye. She'd no doubt over-heard everything.

She leaned her bulky shoulder against the doorframe and said, "He's right, you know. You're too hard on him. Isn't his fault he's not Walter Talbot. God made only one, and we are not likely to see his equal again."

Thora rose. She'd had enough. But before she could send the impertinent cook away, Bertha held up a beefy palm and cut her off.

"I know it's not my place, but I also know from Sadie and Martha Bushby that you've been spendin' a fair deal of time with our Mr. Talbot lately. Gettin' his hopes up again. If you're never going to accept him, tell him so in no uncertain terms, so he'll give up waitin'. Then someone else might have a chance with him. There aren't enough men to go around since the war, and certainly not good, hardworking, respectable men like Walter Talbot."

"I did tell him."

Bertha frowned. "What? You refused him?"

She nodded.

"Thora Bell! I thought you were cleverer than that."

"Bertha Rooke, watch your tongue."

"Go ahead—give me the sack if you want. None of us will have a job here for long, so why not speak my mind if it might do some good? Though it appears I spoke too late."

"Yes, you are too late, so go about your own business and leave me to mine. We don't want supper to be late as well."

The cook went off in a huff, but Thora felt no triumph for putting her in her place.

Instead her stomach soured and churned with the realization that Colin and Bertha were probably right. *Is it too late?*

CHAPTER
THIRTY-NINE

They were not ready, but Saturday morning dawned anyway. As the sun spilled its light over the inn rooftop and into the courtyard, Gabriel Locke and the ostlers were already up and practicing again.

Jane came out to watch, antsy and nervous as the contest drew closer. The men completed another change and looked expectantly at Gabriel.

He frowned down at his pocket watch. Tension emanated from his taut stance and dark glower.

Jane waited, fists at her sides, fingernails digging into her palms. "Well?"

"Still not good enough." He looked at the men. "You have improved—don't mistake me—but we still have not mastered it."

Tuffy rubbed the back of his scrawny neck. "Show me again, Gable. If I see you do it just one more time, maybe I'll get it right."

"Very well."

They ran through it again, Gabriel demonstrating Tuffy's role. He worked with impressive speed. Tuffy watched, head bobbing, eyes alight trying to follow his every move, knobby hands mimicking his actions.

Afterward, Gabriel called to his team, "Take a rest, lads. We'll start again in ten minutes."

Tall Ted and Joe nodded and slogged across the yard to the water pump.

Jane planted her hands on her hips. "Now is not the time to rest. The contest is this afternoon!"

"I know it is, Jane," Gabriel snapped. "Your reminding us of that fact every five minutes is not helping."

Jane reared her head back at his sharp tone. Clearly nerves and tension were running high all around.

"Gable, why don't you take my place in the contest?" Tuffy said, walking near. "I don't mind, and you're so much faster. I'm getting too old for sport like this."

Gabriel clapped his shoulder. "You're the ostler, Tuffy. You can do it."

Jane said quietly, "You are a Bell horseman, Mr. Locke. It wouldn't break any rules."

Gabriel shook his head. "I am only the trainer."

The Royal Mail arrived, and as the men hurried to change an authentic mail coach, Jane backed out of the way, wishing there was more she could do to help. The roles she, Colin, Mrs. Rooke, and Bobbin would play were relatively easy, and their times were already good. It would all come down to the horsemen.

Patrick came out, and after taking care of his duties, approached Jane and handed her a letter. "This came for you."

"Thank you." Jane did not recognize the feminine handwriting. The sender had written the direction very poorly indeed. But her own name was clear enough.

Jane unfolded the page, and unfolded again. Secured within was a small newspaper clipping, accompanied by a few handwritten lines.

After your visit, I began digging through Goldie's piles of old newspapers (She doesn't throw anything away!) to see what, if anything, had been reported about Mr. John. Here's all I found. I thought you'd want to see it.

—Hetty

Jane held up the clipping and read.

Fatal Carriage Found

A carriage matching the description of one involved in a collision in May, which resulted in the death of one man, a John Bell of Ivy Hill, Wilts., was found abandoned in the woods near Epsom. Authorities traced it to a local inn. The driver had hired the carriage earlier that day, paid cash in advance, then failed to return the vehicle. He has not been found or identified. Authorities suspect he may have given the innkeeper a false name. Anyone with information about the driver is asked to come forward.

Jane's stomach twisted, her thoughts confused and alarmed. She looked up to find Gabriel watching her.

"What is it?" he asked.

She walked toward him and handed him the clipping. "They found the carriage that killed John. Abandoned in the woods."

He said nothing as he read the clipping. His silence drew her attention, and she studied his face with growing suspicion. "You already knew, didn't you."

"I . . . heard something about it in Epsom, after you left."

"Why didn't you tell me?"

He shrugged. "They still haven't found the driver. There really wasn't anything new to tell."

"Nothing new?" she asked incredulously and snatched back the clipping. "It says the driver hired the carriage under a false name that *very* day."

He nodded. "Several witnesses had described the coach, and after it was found, they were able to identify it as the one involved in the accident."

"Accident? You want me to believe that a man hired a carriage under a false name and then just happened to run into my husband at speed sufficient to kill him?"

He momentarily met her gaze, then lowered his eyes. "He may

have hired the coach for some other nefarious purpose and John simply got in the way when he made his escape."

She slowly shook her head, temper sparking. "No, that isn't what you think happened. I can see it in your face. You think someone intentionally killed John, don't you."

He winced. "No one knows for certain. But it is possible."

"How long have you suspected? This clipping isn't dated, but it's not recent."

"I heard rumors shortly afterward, but nothing concrete."

"Then why did you let me believe otherwise?" She waved the clipping. "Why must I learn this now, more than a year later, from a relative stranger?"

Gabriel glanced across the yard and noticed the ostlers were looking their way. "Shh . . . lower your voice, Jane."

"I will not! I find out my husband was *not* killed in an unfortunate accident but may have been intentionally run down, and I am supposed to be quiet?"

He laid a hand on her sleeve. "Hush."

She jerked her arm away. "Don't hush me, Mr. Locke. You have no right. I thought I could trust you. Why didn't you tell me?"

"It wouldn't have brought John back. And I thought it would only add to your pain."

She remembered in Epsom, when he'd said he felt guilty about John's death, as if it had been his fault. Surely Gabriel had nothing to do with it. She narrowed her eyes at him. "What else aren't you telling me?"

His jaw tensed.

"Who would want to hurt a small-town innkeeper, and why?" she demanded, her eyes locked on his.

He looked away, rubbing a hand over his face. "We don't have time for this now, Jane. Let's deal with it later. At the moment, you should be making sure you, Colin, and Mrs. Rooke are ready to do your parts."

Jane shook her head. "Has this something to do with John's

loan—the missing money? Are you keeping secrets about that too?"

"There is no missing money!" Gabriel growled.

Jane recoiled as though she'd been slapped. Across the yard, Tall Ted, Tuffy, and Joe turned abruptly and gaped at them.

Gabriel grimly led Jane into the stable block and lowered his voice. "Jane, I don't know where you got the idea that John hid that money somewhere, but it isn't true. He spent it. Every last farthing. Gambled it away on horse races."

Jane sucked in a breath. "What . . . ?"

He nodded tersely. "That's what took him to Epsom. As well as Newmarket and Brighton and Bath."

"But . . . he came to see you. About buying horses."

"Initially, maybe. But then we decided to attend the races together. John knew I had a good eye for horses, and bet as I did. We both made money at first, and it went to our heads. After that, John kept seeking me out at different races, wanting my help in picking the horses to bet on. Some of my picks won, some didn't—I am no fortune teller. John began losing money. A lot of money. I lost too, but eventually stopped wagering. I tried to convince John to stop as well. But he was certain he would recoup his losses if he just had more funds, and neither you nor his mother would have to be any the wiser. When the loan money was gone, he borrowed more from the wrong man. A man who does not forgive unpaid debts."

"Are you saying this man killed John?"

"I can't prove it, but it seems likely."

"Who is this man?"

"I don't know his name. Just his type."

"But why kill John? Now he will never get his money back."

"My guess is, when he realized he would probably never get paid, he retaliated. To send a message to other debtors, I imagine. Pay up or pay fatal consequences."

"But you were John's friend. Could you not help him?"

Pain flashed across his face. "I tried, but John would not heed me. I warned him not to return to Epsom. That it was dangerous. But he went anyway. I asked for the name of the gullgroper who'd loaned him the money and how much he was in for, but John refused to tell me—refused my help. He was a proud man."

"Proud?!" Jane bitterly spat out the word.

"Jane . . ." He laid a consoling hand on her arm. "John was not a bad man. He was just . . . weak in this one way."

Jane shook her head. "And you knew all the while, and didn't tell me? All this time, questioning Blomfield, and searching, and wondering, and trying to save this place for John's sake, when he was ready to gamble it all away?"

"You're not saving it for him, Jane. You're saving it for yourself, and all those who work for you."

Jane jerked away from his hand. "You should have told me the truth. Instead you lied and pretended to be someone you're not. A simple farrier with his own Thoroughbred, a fine watch, and a bank account in Wishford? How stupid I am."

"You were already grieving. I thought the truth would make things worse. Why do you think I've been wracked with guilt and got out of racehorses altogether? Why do you think I came here to help?"

"Help?" She snorted, shaking her head. "You're too late to help—John is dead. And if your help comes in the form of lying and deceit, I don't want it. I don't want a man I can't trust living on my doorstep." Another thought struck her. "How do I even know any of this is true, when you lied about everything else?"

Jane whirled and ran to the lodge, slamming the door behind her and securing the new lock Gabriel had installed himself. Irony struck her, for one brief second overriding her shock and grief. *Thing probably doesn't even work. . . .*

Then in the next moment, another wave of horror washed all other thoughts aside. She sat on the edge of her bed and hid her face in her hands. Emotions pummeled her. Betrayal. Disappointment. Anger. Humiliation. Her husband—a gambler. A liar. A deceiver. What was wrong with her that she was drawn to the wrong men? Men she could not or should not trust? She'd been on the cusp of trusting Gabriel Locke, only to discover he was a liar too.

Someone knocked at her door, but Jane didn't answer. Instead she lay down and pulled a pillow over her head.

Sometime later, Jane awoke, realizing she had cried herself to sleep. She rose and washed her face. As she patted it dry with a towel, she resisted the urge to bury her face in it and go back to bed, to stay hidden in the lodge and avoid everyone, especially Mr. Locke.

But now that the worst of the shock had faded and heated anger had cooled, she admitted to herself that Mr. Locke's revelation about where the money had gone was all too believable.

Jane inhaled deeply and steeled her resolve. She didn't need to hide her face, she told herself. Hopefully no one had overheard what John had done, and the likely truth of how he had died. She would deal with Gabriel Locke later. How, she did not know. But first, they had to get ready for the contest.

Mr. Locke had been right about one thing. She wasn't trying to save the inn for John. Apparently, she had to save it *from* John, for the sake of all who depended on The Bell.

Jane walked outside and looked around the yard, frowning at the lack of activity. Why were they not practicing? Where was Gabriel Locke?

The men stood around, Tall Ted leaning against the stable door. "Gable's gone, ma'am."

"Gone?" Jane asked, heart skipping a beat. "What do you mean he's gone?"

"After you and he had your . . . em . . . disagreement, he packed up and left."

"Dash it," Jane breathed.

Young Joe shook his head. "Not like Gable to run off. Musta been some fight."

Ted pulled a face. "I don't see how we're going to win without him."

"We can't," Tuffy said. "We've got no chance without him."

"Of course we can," Jane said desperately. "You're the ostlers."

Ted's eyes downturned. "But he's our leader."

Oh, what have I done? Jane silently lamented, gripping her hands. *He's the one who lied or at least withheld the truth*, she reminded herself. *I won't go chasing after him. I won't.*

Patrick came out of the inn and stood on the back porch, arms crossed. "The contest begins in one hour, Jane."

"Thank you, Patrick, for that helpful report." She gave him a sour smile, then turned to Tuffy. "Did you see which way he went?"

"Aye, ma'am. Toward Wishford."

Jane huffed. Of course. It was always Wishford.

She had not intended to send Gabriel away. She had been shocked and angry, but primarily with John. She had not really meant it when she'd said she did not want him there.

Jane paced. Through the archway, she noticed activity in the High Street. The Fairmont team was beginning to assemble. Around her, the ostlers and postillions stuffed hands into their pockets or shifted, exchanging grave looks.

Jane turned to the slight postillion—young, but an excellent rider. "Joe, take our fastest horse, and use the bridle path to cut across the meadow to reach the Wishford Road. Find Gabriel and ask him to return directly."

The young man's eyebrows rose. "I couldn't. Our fastest horse is Athena, and she don't like me."

Tall Ted stepped forward and said gently, "Why not go yourself, Mrs. Bell, and ask him soft-like? I know he'll come back then. Gable is a true gentleman that way."

A gentleman? Jane inwardly fumed, *who lies and pretends to be someone he's not?* But she stifled the words, remembering these men looked up to Gabriel as their leader. To win, he would need the full confidence of his men.

She paced again, thinking, *I will not beg him.*

"Forty minutes, Jane," Patrick said with a sly, satisfied smile. "Unless you prefer to concede now and have it over and done."

Jane bit her lip to stem the tears burning her eyes. She was tempted to throw up her hands. Why bother to try with so many men against her: Mr. Drake, Mr. Blomfield, Mr. Hightower, Patrick, and now Gabriel as well?

Out of the inn stepped a timid Alwena, followed by Cadi, Dotty, and Mrs. Rooke, face lined in concern. Then came Ned, the potboy, and Bobbin. They all stood, solemnly. Looking at her. Waiting for her to make a decision. To save them.

"Oh, very well!" Jane exclaimed. "I'll go. Saddle Athena quickly."

"Yes, ma'am!"

The ostlers leapt into action. Even old Tuffy moved with surprising speed to help saddle and bridle the horse. They clearly believed their fate rested in Gabriel's capable hands. And at the moment, Jane could not disagree.

A few minutes later, Tuffy led out Athena, her ears back and eyes wide at the gathered crowd and commotion. Jane briefly held her head and whispered, "Don't fail me now, girl."

Ted gave her a hand up, and Jane landed ungracefully on the saddle, jerking the fabric of her daydress and petticoat out from under her to cover her legs as best she could. There was no time to change into her riding habit.

"Godspeed, missus," old Tuffy said, hand on his heart.

Jane took up the reins. "Get up, girl. Hyah!" She urged the horse from trot to canter to gallop in rapid succession, out the gate, past the lodge, and onto the road. She sped down the hill, scattering gravel in her wake, before turning onto the bridlepath, hoping with every breath that she would catch up with Gabriel in time.

As she crossed the meadow and neared Wishford, she spied a mounted figure riding sedately up the road.

Even from a distance, she recognized the chestnut horse and Gabriel's confident posture as he sat tall in the saddle.

No doubt hearing thundering hooves, he glanced over his shoulder.

She lifted a hand. "Gabriel! Wait!"

He paused and turned Sultan toward her, and sat there waiting as she approached.

As she neared, she tried to gauge his expression. He did not look hurt or angry as she feared, nor self-satisfied. Though wary, yes.

She called, "Not exactly racing away. Were you betting I'd come after you?"

"I am no longer a wagering man, Mrs. Bell."

She rode closer. "Why are you leaving?"

"You made it clear you wanted me gone."

She halted her horse beside his. "I was shocked and angry. But I am sorry I spoke to you so harshly."

"And I am sorry I wasn't completely truthful with you before." He tilted his head to one side. "You must care a great deal about the contest to come after me and apologize."

She nodded. "I will have to think about the rest later, but for now, I want to win. I want to keep the contract and save the inn. But we can't do it without you. *I* can't do it without you. Please don't leave me, Gabriel."

His eyes darkened. And for a moment she feared she'd said the wrong thing. Angered him somehow.

She tried to think of what else to say to convince him. But he shifted his weight, and his well-trained horse started moving.

Gabriel lifted his chin in the direction of Ivy Hill. "Let's go."

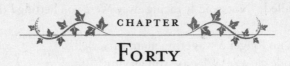

CHAPTER

FORTY

When Jane and Gabriel Locke came riding up the hill together, Thora released a long breath and murmured a prayer of thanksgiving. She had almost given up hope.

She had been prepared to perform Jane's role in the contest, if necessary, but doubted their chances of victory without Mr. Locke leading the ostlers.

The rest of the inn's team had gathered along the High Street, waiting anxiously. At the arrival of their leaders, cheers went up. Charlie looked over and met Thora's gaze with a small smile, but it did not quite reach his eyes.

Tuffy approached Mr. Locke as he dismounted. She didn't hear what the ostler said, but Gabriel replied, "Are you sure, Tuffy?"

The older man nodded. "We've got it all worked out. I'm to be a passenger. That I can do and do sprightly."

"Very well."

Both sides of the High Street were filled with onlookers and noisy hawkers peddling refreshments. Opportunistic Mr. Prater had swathed bunting over his storefront and set up a long plank table bearing candies, parasols, and bamboo fans, to ward off the heat of the summer afternoon. His daughter weaved her way through the throng, passing out printed advertisements. The Craddocks sent out their adolescent son with a tray of iced buns and small pies to sell from their bakery. The public house rolled out barrels of ginger beer and ale to offer the thirsty crowd.

Royal Mail guard Jack Gander played festive melodies on his long horn to entertain the crowd while they waited for the contest to begin. At the appointed hour, Mr. Hightower caught his eye, and Jack blew a signal to gain everyone's attention.

The deputy postmaster stood atop a mounting box and announced the contest terms to the crowd. "Today's contest between The Bell and the Fairmont will proceed as follows. Each team will perform a complete turnout of horses, hand off mail, unload and load baggage, feed the passengers, and, em, water the coachmen."

Laughter erupted at that.

Thora was surprised at Hightower's jollity when he had not wanted the contest in the first place. Apparently he enjoyed having an audience.

Hightower turned and pointed to the end of the High Street. Thora noticed a man wave from an upper-story window. "Mr. Gordon there will call the race from his vantage over the finish line. Are the competitors ready?"

As planned, the Quicksilver and the Exeter were situated at the other end of the street, their first four horses harnessed and ready to go. Jack Gander jogged down the street to catch up with Charlie.

Thora recognized the coachman driving for the Fairmont team as the nasty Jeb Moore she had ridden with from Salisbury. That was a point in their favor, she thought, knowing the slovenly coachman couldn't keep up with Charlie, assuming he didn't wield his forbidden short tommy.

The coachmen, guards, and those portraying passengers boarded the coaches, while the ostlers, cooks, barmen, porters, and innkeepers waited at the chalk line near the center of the street, where Hugh Hightower stood as judge over the proceedings.

Behind him, Thora noticed Patrick leaning against a shop wall, arms crossed. She did not see Talbot anywhere about, which surprised her.

Hightower raised a white flag in his hand, and when a hush fell over the crowd, he brought it down with a flourish.

The guards sounded their horns in reply, and the coaches lurched forward. Thora pressed a hand over her heart and murmured a prayer. From the corner of her eye, she saw Patrick straighten to see over the heads of the crowd.

Nearby, each pair of ostlers urged a second quartet of horses into proper position, the wheel horses on each side of the street, and the leaders coupled together.

As the coaches neared the chalk line and began to slow, Tuffy, now playing the role of a box passenger, unbuckled the lead and wheel reins at Charlie's command. Gabriel Locke ran forward to unhook the near leader's outside trace, and as the coach stopped, drew the lead rein through the terrets and changed the near horse. Ted worked feverishly on the offside, unhooking the remaining lead traces, uncoupling the wheel horses, and changing the offside one. Charlie, descending faster than she had ever seen him, finished changing the leaders.

Thora shifted her gaze to the Fairmont team; The Bell team was ahead!

Meanwhile, the "passengers" began to move. Tuffy climbed gingerly down from the bench, while young Joe slid easily from the roof and opened the door to help Cadi and Alwena alight from inside.

At the same time, nimble Jack Gander jumped to the ground and opened the lid of the boot. He lifted the twenty-pound mailbag and handed it to Jane, who carried it with effort to the mounting block. There, she picked up an "outgoing" mailbag and lugged it back to the guard, nearly dropping it, and having to pause to heft its bulk higher to keep it from dragging. Was her daughter-in-law so weak, or had someone piled bricks inside?

Thora glanced nervously to their opponents, seeing Mr. Drake carrying his bags with ease and sending a cheeky smile to Jane as he did so.

Jack then unlocked the box under the coachmen's bench, where parcels were kept. Jane made a show of signing for them, and then carried them to Mr. Prater, the official local postmaster, who stood beside Mr. Hightower.

Meanwhile, Colin hurried to unload two heavy valises and carry them to the mounting block. Mrs. Rooke lumbered forward with a tray, handing a pie to each passenger, while Bobbin delivered a foaming tankard to Charlie. Charlie tossed it back, then climbed onto the box. The ostlers stood clear, and Charlie whisked his whip over the leaders. The horses lurched forward and bounded toward the finish line.

Thora looked over at the Exeter. Charlie had managed to get his horses moving ahead of his rival's, but now the Fairmont team was building speed and gaining ground. Would the vile Jeb Moore pull out his short tommy from its hiding place? Apparently he did not dare in front of Mr. Hightower, but that didn't stop the man from lashing his horses' backs while Charlie merely whipped the air. The Exeter narrowed the gap, and then caught up with the Quicksilver.

Thora clasped her hands over her heart. *Please, please . . .*

Among cheers and shouts and thundering hooves, both teams galloped toward the string finish line. Five yards, three, one . . .

Thora held her breath.

Perched in his upper-story window, Mr. Gordon shouted, "The Quicksilver wins!"

Cheers erupted. Thora blinked. They had won! The Bell had won? It seemed too good to be true.

More cheers rose. Cadi and Alwena hugged one another, Cadi squealing and bouncing up and down. Sir Timothy, she noticed, moved toward Jane, but before he reached her, Mercy stepped over and embraced Jane, smile bright.

Caught up in the excitement, Bobbin threw his arms around Bertha Rooke—at least as far around as they could go. The woman hugged him back, and in her exuberance, lifted the man several inches off the ground. Boyish Joe launched himself at Gabriel's back, and was carried in an impromptu piggyback ride, while Tall Ted and Tuffy danced a celebratory jig.

Three of the men who'd ridden with the coaches across the finish line returned on foot: the opposing coachman and guard, heads bowed in defeat. And Jack Gander, beaming and waving to the crowd like a conquering hero, tipping his hat to the ladies, and leaving several females swooning and simpering—Cadi included.

Thora craned her neck, looking for Charlie. But he failed to appear.

James Drake crossed the street, hand graciously extended to Jane. Thora could almost start to like the man.

Still atop the mounting block, Hugh Hightower consulted his pocket watch, then waved a hand to the opposing guard to gesture him over. Whatever he said to the guard was swallowed by the cheering crowd, but a moment later the guard blew a loud blast on his horn, interrupting the cheerful melee. People turned toward the sound, and voices quieted.

Mr. Hightower snapped his pocket watch shut and lifted his hand to silence the crowd. "Although the team from The Bell crossed the finish line first, they did not win with the margin required to compensate for the greater distance from the turnpike and the climb up Ivy Hill. I therefore declare the Fairmont the winner and recipient of the Royal Mail contract."

That condition had not been stated before. Thora's heart sank. She'd known it had been too good to be true.

"Yes!" Jeb Moore raised a fist in the air.

But no one else cheered, not even the staff of the Fairmont. And many others protested.

"What?" Ted shouted angrily.

Tuffy said something best not recorded.

Mr. Locke frowned darkly, hands on hips. And Jane just stood there, mouth parted, staring in disbelief.

Amid the groans and grumbles, James Drake walked toward the mounting block, his expression difficult to decipher, but not, to his credit, triumphant.

He said, loud enough for all to hear, "I'm afraid, Mr. Hightower, that we at the Fairmont must concede the contest. We will not be prepared to serve the Royal Mail creditably in time to fulfill this year's contract after all." He looked at Jane. "But if my lovely colleague would like a rematch *next* year, she need only say the word."

Mr. Drake reached for Jane's hand and lifted it in triumphant pose. "The winner! Fair and square!"

Yes, Thora would definitely have to start liking James Drake.

More cheers rose. Hugh Hightower opened his mouth as if to protest, but seeing the overwhelming support of the crowd, including Sir Timothy's own applause, and receiving Mr. Drake's concession so publicly, he seemed to realize it was time to accept the outcome graciously, even though it meant that his old rival, Charlie Frazer, was the winning coachman.

Where was Charlie? Again, Thora looked for him among the crowd but did not see him. Why had he not returned to celebrate?

Eudora Hightower appeared out of the crowd and walked toward her. Thora had not realized she had come to Ivy Hill with her husband.

"Congratulations, Mrs. Bell," she began, pausing to stand beside her.

"Thank you, Mrs. Hightower. Though I had very little to do with it."

"Somehow I doubt that."

The woman then gave her an apologetic look, incongruent with her congratulations of a moment before. "I am sorry about Charlie. Were you two close?"

Thora frowned. *Sorry?* Why? And why the past tense? Her stomach dropped. Surely nothing had happened to Charlie.

She said evenly, "We were and continue to be good friends. Why?"

"I hope he made you no promises?"

"Promises?" Thora echoed, feeling befuddled. "No."

"Good." Eudora sighed in relief.

"Mrs. Hightower, what are you talking about? Is something wrong with Charlie? I saw him during the contest, and he seemed well enough."

"You don't know?" Eudora pressed a hand to her fichu-covered chest.

"Know what?" Trepidation seeped through Thora.

"I am sorry to be the one to tell you. But he is leaving—the area and the Devonport-London line."

Thora blinked, struggling to comprehend the woman's words.

"He came to see my husband last week," Mrs. Hightower explained. "Never could I have imagined Charlie Frazer coming to Hugh, hat in hand. He apologized for his behavior at the party, and in his youth, and for any attention he once paid me that might have led to unjustified rumors. He meekly—if you can imagine Charlie Frazer behaving meekly—asked Hugh not to hold his conduct against you or The Bell. He beseeched Hugh to sanction this contest, and give The Bell a fair and fighting chance to prove itself. In return, Charlie said he would leave the county altogether. Take a transfer to another line far from here, out of Hugh's jurisdiction."

"Did he?" Thora breathed.

"Yes. Manchester, I believe it was. He had applied for a transfer to Bath last year. But he retracted that request a few months ago."

After I returned to Ivy Hill, Thora guessed, heart thudding dully.

"At all events, Hugh accepted his offer," Eudora said. "You know he has long been eager to see the back of Charlie Frazer."

"I can imagine." So that is why Hugh had changed his mind and agreed to the unorthodox contest, Thora realized. The chance to rid himself of Charming Charlie once and for all had proved too great a temptation.

Eudora added, "Charlie spoke very highly of The Bell, the Bell family, and all its staff. But especially of you, Thora. I thought you should know. He thinks a great deal of you."

"And I of him," Thora allowed, her chest tight and her pulse pounding to realize what Charlie had sacrificed for her. His pride most of all.

She asked, "Do you know if the transfer is effective immediately or if he will remain with the Quicksilver until they replace him?"

"I assume he has left already. In fact, I believe he's traveling by stagecoach this very day."

"What a pity," Thora said. "I would have liked to thank him. And say good-bye."

Eudora Hightower briefly pressed Thora's hand, her cornflower blue eyes bright with tears. "He is a difficult man to say good-bye to."

Thora was surprised to find answering tears sting her eyes, but she blinked them away. She thanked the woman for telling her, squared her shoulders, and strode back to The Bell.

Jane and Patrick caught up with her on the way.

"Where's Charlie?" Jane asked. "I wanted to thank him for his part in the contest."

"So did I. He left right after crossing the finish line, I hear. Probably on his way to Bagshot by now." *To pack his belongings before moving away and out of our lives,* Thora added to herself. She wished she could tell Jane what he'd done for them, but if Charlie hadn't told her, he probably didn't want anyone else to know either.

"Why didn't he wait and travel back with the Royal Mail?"

Thora inhaled and said simply, "Hightower's orders. He is traveling by stage."

Patrick gave his mother a long look, then said, "You know, the only stagecoach going to Bagshot at this time of day is the Flying Fiddle. That coach leaves from the Crown in Wishford in"—he glanced at his pocket watch—"forty minutes."

Thora stopped and looked at Patrick, surprised by his perceptive suggestion. "Are you trying to get rid of me?"

"Not at all, Mamma. But regret is a hard thing to live with."

"Know something about that, do you?"

His blue eyes, so much like hers, glinted. "A bit, yes."

When Thora left them and disappeared through the archway into the stable yard, Jane barely resisted the urge to follow her. She wanted to find Gabriel and the whole team and thank them again. But Patrick lingered, surprisingly eager to rehearse the details of the contest and The Bell's victory.

"I thought old Tuffy would have an apoplexy! And did you see Hightower's face when your Mr. Drake conceded? That was rich. . . ."

So the two of them stood talking in front of the inn for several minutes, now and again accepting the well-wishes of passersby still drifting home after the big event.

Talbot approached them. "Sorry I'm late—one of the ram lambs caught his horn in a fence, or I would have been here sooner. I heard the good news on the way and want to offer my congratulations."

"Thank you, Talbot," Jane said. "And thank you again for suggesting the contest in the first place."

"Oh, I think it was Ted's idea," he said modestly. "I merely recognized its potential."

"Yes, you are good at that," Jane said with a smile.

Talbot didn't return it. "Is Thora here?" he asked. "I'd like to congratulate her as well."

"Oh, um. She was, but . . ." Jane looked toward the archway, debating what to say.

At that moment, Thora rattled through it in the gig, urging Ruby to "Come on, old thing, get up." Focused on the horse and her destination, Thora didn't notice the three of them standing there.

Talbot asked, "Where is Thora going in such a hurry?"

Jane hesitated. "She, um . . ."

Patrick said bluntly, "She is going after Charlie Frazer."

Jane stole a glance at Talbot's face as he watched Thora disappear down the hill. His lips slightly parted, his eyes . . . Oh, the pain written there nearly broke Jane's heart.

"To thank him," Jane hastened to add. "For the contest, you know. He drove, and had to leave right after. That's all."

Was that all? Jane wasn't certain, but she had to do something to try to staunch the wound.

"Of course. Well . . ." Talbot cleared his throat. "All the best to them both."

Fifteen minutes later, Thora entered the Crown for the first time in her life, a place she'd forsworn decades before. Her gaze traveled over the dim taproom. *There* . . . She expelled a relieved breath at the sight of a familiar figure at a back table.

She walked forward. "Sneaking away without saying good-bye? That isn't like you."

Charlie looked up in surprise. "Thora . . . ?"

She lifted a staying palm, not wanting to raise his hopes. "I've come to say good-bye in person. And to thank you. Eudora told me what you did. I can only guess what that cost you. And I deeply appreciate it."

"I did nothing so great. I had been thinking of transferring for some time, even if I let Hightower believe it was a great sacrifice on my part to do so. You see how eager he was to be rid of me— insisted I leave this very day, and booked my passage himself."

"Would you have come to tell me good-bye if he had given you more time?"

Charlie shrugged. "I don't know. I thought it would be easier not to."

"Easier for you or for me?"

"Both of us, I imagine."

Thora sat down beside him. "I suppose you're right. But difficult or not, I need you to know that I will never forget what you did for us, and you will always be welcome at The Bell, as long as I have anything to say about it. And I know I speak for Jane as well."

"Thank you, Thora."

She took a deep breath and forced herself to continue. "I know things didn't turn out between us as you might have liked. But I will miss you, Charlie, and always consider you a close friend. And . . . I've come to give you something." She swallowed. "Something you told me you've wanted for years. Though I don't know if you still do . . ."

His brows rose. "If it is what I think it is, then the answer is yes, definitely."

"Even though it means good-bye?"

He hesitated, a sad smile creasing his handsome face. "Must it?"
Tears heated her eyes. "I am afraid so."

"Very well," he said, a roguish grin overtaking his features.
"Then I shall take what I can get. Beggars can'na be choosers."

Thora recognized his bravado for what it was and admired his
courage.

She leaned forward to plant a kiss on his cheek, but he turned
his head and gave her a sound smack on the lips instead.

Her eyes widened in surprise.

He sighed theatrically. "I suppose you shall now feel duty bound
to deliver a slap to that cheek instead of the kiss you intended?"

"Yes," she quietly replied. "Will you turn the other cheek?"

He turned his cheek toward her and she surprised them both
by leaning in close and delivering a second peck.

"A good-bye kiss," she said, in benediction.

He leaned back, a satisfied grin stretching his mouth. "At last!
A kiss from the belle of The Bell and the angel of The Angel! I
can die a happy man."

"Don't die, Charlie Frazer. Live long and be happy."

"I shall if you shall, Thora Bell."

She held out her hand to him, a woman of business, ready to
make a deal. "You strike a hard bargain. But I shall do my best."

He pressed her hand, then brought it to his lips in final farewell.

Later that night, Jane sat on the doorstep outside her lodge,
petting Kipper beside her. She was exhausted, yet too restless to
sleep. What a day it had been.

The courtyard was quiet, and only the lamp illuminating their
repaired sign still flickered. They were not expecting any more
coaches that night, and inside the inn, candles were doused one
by one.

Jane looked up at the stars, more visible now that the yard was
dim. She thought of John. She had struggled all these months to
come to terms with his death, and the news she learned earlier that

day had rocked what little peace she had, yet at the same time, it answered lingering questions. Filled in missing pieces. Laid to rest other doubts and theories.

Jane had not told Thora. And wouldn't, she decided, at least until circumstances forced her to. Thora idealized John, and Jane knew what a cruel blow it would be. And as her thoughts formed and her decision to say nothing solidified, Jane realized she was doing the exact same thing she had blamed Gabriel Locke for doing. She knew that didn't justify her decision to shield Thora, but it did help Jane understand why Gabriel had withheld the information. And allowed her to forgive him. She wasn't certain she could yet fully trust the man. But hopefully, in time, that would change.

The creak and slide of the stable door caught her attention, and Jane looked through the archway. Gabriel Locke walked out, leading Sultan, saddlebags bulging, and valise in hand.

Her heart lifted to see the man who had helped win the day, but a moment later she realized what the saddlebags and valise foretold.

She rose and stood there, conflicting emotions wrestling within her, and waited as he neared. "You're leaving?" she asked.

"Yes."

"But, I . . . I didn't mean it when I said I didn't want you here. I'm sorry. I thought you understood."

He nodded. "I came back to help with the contest. And you won."

"We won."

"But now it's time for me to leave—amicably this time." He managed a small grin. "I have unfinished business in Epsom, and in Pewsey Vale. I already spoke to Fuller. He will fill in again until you find another farrier."

"But you're so much more than a farrier."

He strapped his valise handle to the saddle and then turned back to her. He slowly reached out and took her hand in both of his. How large, how callused, how strong.

"You'll be all right, Jane Bell," he said, voice low. "I know it."

Her chin trembled. "Will I?"

He nodded. "I have every confidence in you."

CHAPTER
FORTY-ONE

Thora offered to remain at the reception desk for most of the following week, allowing her daughter-in-law to work on her written plan for Mr. Blomfield. Thora read over sections and gave her opinion when asked but otherwise said little. She tried to remind herself that this was her future too, but her heart was not convinced. After all the recent excitement with the contest, she felt oddly deflated.

Jane stepped out of the office and showed her the projected increase in income, resulting profits, and a proposed timeline for paying down the loan.

When Thora removed her spectacles, Jane asked, "Do you have any suggestions? Anything to add?"

Thora shook her head. "Looks fine to me."

Jane sent her a skeptical look. "Are you all right, Thora?"

"Of course I am."

"Is there . . . anything you want to talk about?"

"No." Thora looked around. "I think all is in hand. The bills and staff are paid. Menus set. Repairs progressing."

"I don't mean about the inn. I mean, is there anything *else* you want to talk about. Anything . . . bothering you?"

A dear face passed through Thora's mind, wearing a disappointed look—one she had put there. "What would be bothering me?" she said. "Now, go and finish that plan."

Jane's gaze lingered on her a moment longer. Then she turned and went back into the office.

A coach arrived, and Patrick and Colin went out to meet it. Thora stepped to the window to count how many passengers they could expect to feed. She noticed how grey the day was. It would start raining any time, she concluded, already dreading the wet, muddy footprints they'd have to deal with later.

She returned to the desk with a sigh.

Mr. Paley entered through the front door. "Hello, Thora. I stopped by to tell you. Nan Talbot died this morning."

Thora's heart fisted. "What?"

"Nan Talbot died," he repeated. "Mrs. Paley is still there, helping Sadie for a while, but I had to get back. I just thought you would want to know."

For one moment, Thora sank hard onto the chair, the breath knocked from her. But in the next instant, she was on her feet, striding across the hall.

"Thank you, Parson."

"Thora? I can take you out there, if you would like. It looks like rain."

But Thora made no reply, her steps growing more rapid, out the door, down the High Street, gaining speed. Making the turn out of the village, her walk became a jog.

Talbot.

The rain started as a gentle drizzle and grew heavier, seeping through her gown.

Thora reached the farm at last, damp, side aching, and winded. She paused at the gate to catch her breath, bending over, hands on her waist. When Thora straightened, she saw it, and her heart lurched.

A new sign hung on the gate, identifying Talbot's homeplace.

The Angel Farm

Thora stilled, staring at it. Her eyes and cheeks became wet, and she swiped a hand across her face. *Only the rain. . . .*

Pushing open the gate, she ran through it toward the house, expecting he would be inside, grieving. As she neared, she heard the discordant sound of someone chopping wood in the rain. Thora paused, craning her neck toward the woodshed to see who it was, wondering who would be out working in this weather. Surely not Talbot, not at a time like this.

Sadie stepped outside, a grey shawl tented over her head, and followed the direction of her gaze.

"He's been at it for an hour." The woman shook her head. "He won't stop. I tried. Mrs. Paley tried . . ."

Thora turned and strode toward the woodshed.

Sadie called after her, "Take an umbrella at least!"

But Thora paid her no mind.

She rounded the house and there he was, his head bare, in his shirt-sleeves and trousers, his boots a muddy mess. She would recognize his profile anywhere, the long, aquiline nose, sharp cheekbones and chin.

"Walter Talbot," she called. "What are you doing?"

He glanced over, and a rivulet of rain coursed down his forehead, between his eyebrows, and ran off his nose. His hair lay plastered to his brow, his shirt clung to his shoulders and arms.

With a determined expression, he turned back to his task. He lifted the ax high over his head and slammed it down on the chopping block with a solid *thunk*, splitting the log with ease. Again, he set up a log, split it, and tossed the pieces onto the pile.

Thora strode forward. "Talbot!" she repeated as she neared, but he either did not hear her over the pelting rain or chose not to respond.

She waited until he'd bent to pick up another log—the ax out of harm's way—and then stepped close.

"Stop," she commanded, gripping his arms to still his movements. "Nan is gone. Work is not the way to handle this."

"Ha. It's what you've done all these years."

She blinked. "I know."

Grasping his taut shoulders, she felt them tremble, and slowly turned him toward her.

"I'm sorry," she said. "I know it hurts."

He tried to avert his face. His grief. But she saw, and understood.

Thora Stonehouse Bell was not one for displays of affection. Never had been. But she wrapped her arms around Walter Talbot and held him tight. For a moment he stood there, stiff and unyielding. Then he put his arms around her in return, and slowly, tentatively pulled her close. They had never touched like this before, never touched at all except in passing, and certainly had never embraced.

Thora gingerly laid her head on his shoulder. He, in turn, laid his cheek atop her head. They stood there in the rain for several achingly sweet moments, then Thora pulled away first.

"What are we doing standing out here like a couple of daft ducks? Let's go inside before we catch our deaths. Sadie has enough to deal with as it is."

"You two look worse than wet cats," Sadie muttered as they bustled, dripping, into the house. "Sit by the fire and I'll bring hot tea to warm you. Add another log, Mr. Talbot. By the looks of that pile, we've got enough to last us 'til the second coming."

Talbot complied.

Later, after they'd dried off as best they could with towels and left their shoes to dry by the fire, Talbot slipped away. He returned a few moments later and handed Thora something.

Her purple shawl, folded neatly.

Thora protested, "But I gave that to Nan."

"I know you did. But she asked me to give it back to you after she passed. And her brooch with it." He pointed to the cameo, still pinned to the shawl. "She said, 'Tell Thora to remember what I told her about gifts.'"

Thora wrapped the shawl around her shoulders and fingered Nan's cameo. Warmth and memories instantly enveloped her.

Excusing herself, Thora tiptoed into Nan's room. Sadie and Mrs. Paley had bathed and dressed Nan in fine satin and carefully arranged her hair. She looked as though she were sleeping peacefully. But when Thora approached the bed and viewed her inanimate form more closely, it was perfectly clear to Thora that the real Nan—her soul, her spirit, her essence—was not there any longer. She had gone somewhere far better.

Thora reached out and touched Nan's cool hand, then once again touched the brooch. "Thank you, Nan," Thora whispered. "I will remember."

Rachel Ashford lay atop her bedclothes, hoping for a mid-afternoon rest. Since her arrival the month before, she had endeavored to make herself useful at Ivy Cottage—mending, knitting mittens for next winter, and overseeing the girls' recesses in the garden—but she knew it was not enough. She could not take advantage of Mercy's hospitality much longer. She needed to find a way to secure her own livelihood.

Out in the passage, girls hurried past, as they seemed to do in a near-constant stream—calling out questions, arguing about borrowing another's hair comb without asking, or giggling over some girlish trifle. Had she been just as loud and frivolous at their ages? Ellen certainly had. Rachel and Jane *had* talked a lot as girls, though their conversations had mostly been whispered dreams and softly shared secrets high atop those evergreens. . . . But all that was a long time ago.

Life in Thornvale had been a quiet affair—at least for the last several years. Rachel was not yet accustomed to sharing a house with so many people, with all the accompanying noise and activity. She would get used to it, Rachel told herself. She would.

As often happened, Rachel found her gaze drawn to the mother-daughter portrait, which Mr. Basu had quietly and efficiently hung for her. In the pose, Mamma was seated with a young Rachel on her lap, her long, graceful hand affectionately holding Rachel's small one. Ellen stood beside Mamma, leaning against her shoulder.

Their mother had been gone a long time, but Rachel still missed her. It was something else she and Jane had in common. She wondered for the first time in years how Jane had felt, moving from the grand expanse of Fairmont House to that tiny innkeeper's lodge—a mere two or three rooms Rachel had secretly disdained. Yet now here *she* was, with her belongings crammed into only one.

And unlike Jane once had, Rachel had no husband to share her snug second home.

Rachel had been with Jane when she first met John Bell all those years ago. Rachel, Jane, and a newly engaged Ellen had traveled to Bath together to visit the modistes and milliners of that larger, fashionable city. Ellen had sought wedding clothes, and Rachel a gown for her coming-out ball, which might have been planned earlier had Mamma lived.

While out shopping, Jane had pulled them into a book shop "just for a minute," she promised, knowing Ellen and Rachel would far rather look at hats.

Inside, the three of them had been intrigued by the sight of a strikingly handsome man perusing a novel. He had looked slightly familiar to Rachel, though she could not place him. She had a few acquaintances in Bath, but did not think he numbered among them. Perhaps she had met him at a ball or dinner given by a mutual friend, she guessed, not recognizing him out of context.

Ellen had whispered none too softly, "Who is that handsome man? My goodness, Jane, how he looks at you! I think it must be love at first sight!"

Perhaps if they had known who he was from the beginning, things might have turned out differently. For all of them.

Sometimes Rachel still found it difficult to believe proud Jane Fairmont had married an innkeeper. Had she lived to regret it?

Rachel wondered again if Sir Timothy had ever asked Jane to marry him. Or only wished he had. Did he regret not marrying at all? Or did he thank God he had escaped with his family's reputation intact? She doubted she would ever know.

With a sigh, Rachel looked once more around her small room, her single bed, and the still-empty bookcase. Then, remembering, she turned her head toward her side table, her gaze lingering on the bouquet of peach roses Nicholas Ashford had so thoughtfully given her from Thornvale's garden. The blooms were fading now and the petals falling. Perhaps she ought to consider his proposal more seriously. And soon.

The following week, after Nan Talbot had been laid to rest, many friends and neighbors called to express their sympathy and see how Walter was getting along. Thora had spent time at the farm as well, helping to clean Nan's room and the sitting room, and catching up on household tasks that had gone undone while Sadie had rightly focused on Nan.

The visitors had gone home now, though the table still overflowed with offerings of food. Talbot had given Sadie a few days off to rest and spend time with her family. She had worked such long hours over recent months, caring for Nan, and deserved some time away.

When the Paleys took their leave, Thora alone remained. She had kept busy the last few hours offering food and drink to Talbot's guests and refilling platters. Now she continued to bustle about, gathering soiled cutlery and wiping up spills.

Talbot said, "You've done more than enough, Thora. Leave it for now and come rest a minute."

"I am not tired."

"Well, watching you is making me tired."

"Very well." She dried her hands and sat down on the sofa next to his chair.

"How is Jane's plan coming along?" he asked.

"She is presenting it to Blomfield this afternoon."

He nodded. "Will you go with her?"

"No, she has it in hand. Though I would like to be at the inn when she returns to learn how it went."

"Of course." He glanced toward the clock on the mantelpiece. "Leave whenever you need to."

"I have some time yet."

"Good."

They sat there a few moments, looking everywhere but at each other. The ticking clock seemed suddenly loud in the room.

Thora clasped her hands in her lap. "May I bring you anything to drink or eat?"

"No, thank you." He glanced through the dining room door to the table. "How is one man to eat all that?"

"Sadie will help when she returns. An excellent appetite, that one."

"Yes, but it won't all last that long. Take some food back with you to the inn."

She nodded. "Or perhaps I . . . could take some to the McFarlands on my way back."

He looked at her in surprise. "That is thoughtful of you, Thora. An excellent idea."

Thora shrugged off his praise. "It's the least I could do. I've spent too long blaming all McFarlands for something one of them did. I was wrong, and you were right."

"Those are words I never thought I'd hear you say." His eyes twinkled. "I should warn you, though—Eileen McFarland may try to refuse the food as charity."

"If she does, I shall remind her that it is not kind to disappoint a grieving man."

Talbot's eyes dimmed. Thora had been trying to tease him to lighten the mood but had instead reminded him of his loss. She regretted her thoughtless words, and again the room fell into awkward silence.

Talbot looked around, his gaze lingering on the door to Nan's old room. "How quiet this house is. How empty it feels."

"Sadie will be back soon," she reminded him.

"Yes. Though we've talked about it, and she may cut back to half days. Cook the main meal for the men and me. Do a bit of cleaning and laundry. I don't know that I need her full-time now that Nan is gone. Sadie's getting older and wouldn't mind having more time with her family."

Thora nodded. "I see."

Eyes distant in thought, Talbot inhaled deeply. "I've never been on my own, really. I've lived with my parents, with other boys at school, with all of you at the inn, and lastly here, with Nan and Sadie. Don't misunderstand me—I'm not feeling sorry for myself. I've simply grown accustomed to having people about. Living alone shall take some getting used to."

"You don't have to."

He looked at her, a little frown line between his eyes. "Don't have to—what?"

"Live alone."

He studied her face, and then a tentative grin crooked his mouth. "Thora Bell, that is quite a forward thing to say, if I don't mistake your meaning." His grin faded. "Or *do* I mistake you?"

She looked down, pulling a loose yarn from the blanket folded over the sofa.

When she made no reply, Talbot frowned. "Don't tell me you are offering to work for me again, or I'll—"

"That is not what I was . . . offering."

Flushed at her own words, Thora rose in agitation. She picked up a stray water glass and turned toward the kitchen. "I suppose I will begin packing up some food for the McFarlands . . ."

He rose as well and gripped her wrist, halting her when she would have escaped into the other room. She looked up at him. Way up. How tall he was. How . . . masculine. She swallowed.

He slowly extracted the glass from her hand, bent to set it back down, and then turned to face her. She blinked, not sure what he intended. He lifted his hand and cupped the side of her face. For once, the gesture of affection did not make her stiffen or wish to pull away. Rather it made her want to draw closer.

Talbot looked into her eyes, then leaned down, slowly, until his lips touched hers. For a moment, she just stood there, uncertain how to respond. She had not been kissed like this in so long . . .

He pressed his lips to hers, firmly, warmly. She found she rather liked it, and kissed him back.

Talbot pulled away far enough to look into her face. His voice rough with emotion, he began, "We've got a lot of history between us, you and I, and—"

"Shh." She laid her fingertips over his lips and whispered, "You've never been given to speeches, Talbot. Don't start now." She raised up on her toes and kissed him again.

CHAPTER

FORTY-TWO

Jane set the written plan, neatly bound, on Mr. Blomfield's desk, proud of herself for completing it one week ahead of schedule. She sat across from him to await his review and verdict, hands anxiously clasped, praying their plans would be enough to convince him—grateful to know others were praying too.

Instead he pushed the folder away, unopened. "No."

Jane blinked, stunned. "You haven't even read it yet. And we've secured the Royal Mail contract, so . . ."

"It's a moot point."

"I have invested a great deal of my settlement into refurbishments and plan to fund more, as you will see." She tapped the leather-bound plan, adding, "Though I could pay a few hundred toward the loan now, in good faith, if that would help."

"It will not. Nor will I change my mind. Not with your license about to expire."

"What?"

"The victualler's license was in your husband's name, and without one The Bell cannot operate."

Jane's heart plummeted. "I don't understand—the inn has continued to operate after John's death, and no one has mentioned it."

He nodded. "The license transferred to you as his heir, and

the parish grants a three-month extension in the case of a license holder's death. You could apply for a new one in your own name, but women are rarely granted licenses in their own right." The banker gave her a patronizing smile.

How did he know about the expiring license when she did not? Had the banker known all along? He clearly took satisfaction in delivering this blow. She wanted to rail, *"You might have mentioned it earlier,"* but dared not anger the man again.

What a shocking disappointment, especially after their victory.

Jane squeezed her hands and held her emotions in check. "I did not realize the license was about to expire. Thank you for informing me. I will take care of that oversight immediately."

"You may try, though it isn't as easy as all that. I am sure Thora Bell can fill you in on all the particulars. In fact, I am surprised she has not done so already."

Me too, Jane thought. She rose and turned stiffly to go, biting the inside of her cheek to keep tears at bay.

He slid the folder to the edge of his desk. "Don't forget your plan."

She turned back. "You keep it. Show it to your partners and assure them the license will be in order as soon as may be." She hoped she sounded more confident than she felt.

Jane walked back to The Bell and trudged into the office. How she hated to be the bearer of such bad news when everyone had worked so hard!

"Well?" Thora asked. She and Patrick sat together, awaiting her return.

Jane gave a terse shake of her head. "He said our license is about to expire, so he didn't even read it!"

Thora pressed her eyes closed. "Dash it. How quickly the time has gone."

She looked significantly at Patrick, but he raised both hands in self-defense. "It completely escaped my notice."

Jane stifled her exasperation. "Well, how do I apply for a new license?"

"You have to appear before the magistrates at the petty sessions," Patrick said. "And prove you are of good character."

"Why is my character an issue?"

"Because travelers put themselves and their belongings under your protection. More than one unscrupulous innkeeper has been found to be in league with highwaymen or local thieves."

Jane groaned. "Mr. Blomfield said women are rarely granted licenses."

"Married women are *never* granted licenses," Thora replied. "Even if they are the ones truly doing the work, as is often the case. Only widows, and occasionally single women, are granted licenses in their own right."

Jane frowned. "Then why did Mr. Blomfield say I have little chance of succeeding? He knows I am a widow."

"Arthur Blomfield believes it's in his best interest if the inn is sold or ownership assumed by a male landlord." Again she glanced at Patrick. "Either that, or he truly feels your chances of proving yourself competent are slim to none."

"And you, Thora. Do you agree with him?"

Thora shook her head. "I don't think a male is naturally superior to a female innkeeper."

She did not, Jane noticed, say anything about the particular female innkeeper in question.

Thora added, "But I am not a JP. It is Sir Timothy you should be asking that question."

Jane nodded. "Very well, I shall."

Jane knocked on the front door of Brockwell Court, as she had so many times in her younger years.

The butler opened the door, and Jane smiled at the old retainer.

"Good day, Carville. I would like to speak to Sir Timothy on a legal matter, if he is at liberty."

She expected the man to ask her to wait, but instead he gestured her across the hall. "Right this way, madam."

"Do you . . . not need to announce me?"

"No, madam." The butler did not expand on his reply.

Jane was surprised but relieved Timothy could see her without delay. She slipped the mantle from her shoulders and handed it to the man, but kept on her smart hat. It gave her added height and confidence.

Carville led the way to Sir Timothy's study on the ground floor, which she knew also served as his office for carrying out his magisterial duties, incumbent on him as the parish's leading landowner—like his father, Sir Justin, before him.

Carville opened the door and said, "A caller to see you, sir."

Timothy reluctantly looked up from his correspondence, an expression of mild irritation immediately transforming to pleasure.

He rose to his feet. "Jane. How good to see you. What a nice surprise."

Jane glanced at the door as the butler closed it, then said, "I was surprised Carville did not first inquire if you were busy before showing me in."

"I gave Carville standing orders years ago that you were to be shown in directly without ceremony. Man has a better memory than I credit him for. Of course, that was back when you used to call . . . quite often."

He held her gaze, and Jane felt her neck grow warm.

She looked away first, taking a seat and feigning interest in the papers on his desk. "I hope I am not interrupting something important?"

He looked down at them as if just recalling their existence and reclaimed his seat. "Oh, no. Nothing critical. Reviewing cases for the next sessions."

"That is what I wished to speak with you about."

Confusion or perhaps disappointment creased his brow. "Is it? Why?"

"Our license is expiring."

"Ah. Of course. I should have guessed." He formed an unconvincing smile.

"Can you help me navigate the steps, or does that constitute a conflict of interest on your part, or something like that?"

"I will happily tell you what is required and how to go about it. But I wish you had come to me weeks ago. The docket for tomorrow's petty sessions is already filled."

"But . . . the license extension expires in two days."

"Hm. I will send a message to Winspear and see what I can do. In the meantime, have you given any thought to who would vouch for you—your two bondsmen?"

"No. Who spoke for John?"

"George Phillips from the Crown and Harlan Godfrey from the public house."

"Competing publicans?" Jane asked.

He shrugged. "Collegial business, these regulations. John served as one of their bondsmen as well."

Jane frowned. "I have never met George Phillips. And I only know Mr. Godfrey by his less-than-sterling reputation. Does it have to be a fellow publican?"

"No. But it helps. A fellow in the same line understands the regulations you are being asked to uphold."

"Who would you suggest?"

"*Would* Mr. Godfrey speak for you?"

"Do I want him to?"

"The JPs are accustomed to him speaking up for The Bell. Unfortunately, you don't have time to foster an acquaintance with Mr. Phillips on such short notice."

"What about . . . Mr. Drake?" she asked. "He owns a successful hotel in Southampton."

"Risky. He is a newcomer, unknown to the magistrates. But his status as a hotel proprietor might help. Would he speak for you?"

"I think so. I shall have to ask him. What about someone like Mercy Grove? She isn't an innkeeper, but she does keep her own school and is a descendant of one of Ivy Hill's founding families."

"But she's a woman."

"So am I!"

He lifted a consolatory palm. "I know. And bondsmen can be women, but considering your case is already irregular, I would advise against it. Lord Winspear is not the most enlightened of men and does not believe the fair sex have any place in business."

"What about the vicar? I am certain Mr. Paley would give a good account of my character."

"I am sure he would. But I expect he knows little about managing a hostelry, or how well you would carry out your specific responsibilities as a licensed innkeeper."

"Does anyone? I am still so new at it."

He said patiently, "I realize it may seem like an unnecessary formality, Jane, but it is important. Anyone who serves intoxicating beverages is responsible to see that they are handled wisely. We must also assure that an innkeeper will not allow, say, gambling or—if you will forgive me—prostitution to occur on the premises." He opened a drawer and pulled out a printed sheet. "Here is a list of the obligations you must agree to, as well as pledging to maintain good behavior at the inn. Landlords who fail to adhere to these requirements could be charged with keeping a disorderly house."

Jane sighed. "I shall look these over. And perhaps ask Thora's advice as well."

"Yes, she has a great deal of experience, but don't forget that she has never held a license herself. And Jane . . . " He hesitated. "I would not advise asking your brother-in-law. He got into a few scrapes in his youth, and Lord Winspear has a long memory. His appearance as a bondsman would not help your cause. Besides, as family, he could not be viewed as objective."

"I understand."

Sir Timothy explained the Victualler's Recognizances, the questions she and her bondsmen would be asked, and how they were customarily answered.

"That all sounds fairly straightforward," Jane observed.

"Don't become overconfident. I, of course, will be on your side. And Bingley is an easygoing fellow, but Lord Winspear? He is a stickler for regulations and seems to take pleasure in being difficult."

Jane had been acquainted with the man when she was young

but had not seen him in years. "I will bear that in mind." She rose. "Well. Thank you for your time and assistance."

He rose as she did and walked her to the door. "Jane, I have to ask . . . Do you really intend to continue on as innkeeper? Manage The Bell yourself?"

Something in his tone made her look up into his face. "I am as astonished as you are."

"Are you certain this is what you want?"

"What I want? Not at all. It is certainly not what I expected to become."

"Then I wish I . . ."

"You wish what?"

He hesitated. "That I could be of more help."

"You have helped. A great deal. And I count on your continued help at the petty sessions—without compromising your position, of course. I would never ask you to do anything unethical."

"I know you wouldn't. But I have no doubts about your good character. I have known you too long and too well for that."

At the front door, they paused, and Sir Timothy took her gloved hand in his bare one. "Jane Fairmont Bell. A licensed victualler. Who would ever have guessed?"

Jane smiled and shook her head. "Not I."

CHAPTER
FORTY-THREE

The next day, Jane dressed with care for the petty sessions. She chose a walking dress of somber grey half mourning, hoping to look the competent, respectful widow.

"Don't let Winspear intimidate you, Jane," Thora advised. "For I have no doubt he shall try."

Jane nodded, then asked, "Will you be there?"

Thora avoided her eyes. "I . . . have something else to do this afternoon. But you will be fine on your own."

Jane felt a stab of rejection. Did Thora really have something she had to do, Jane wondered, or did she think attending would be a vote of confidence she wasn't prepared to give?

Patrick would not be there either. He had, for some unknown reason, gone to Salisbury. So Jane would be the sole member of the Bell family present at the license hearing that day.

The petty sessions rotated between Ivy Hill's village hall, the Crown in Wishford, and the Pelican in Stapleford. That day's meeting would convene in the council chambers in the village hall. Lord Winspear, Mr. Bingley, and Sir Timothy Brockwell presiding.

Jane arrived early, as did Mercy and Mr. Drake. She hoped Mr. Godfrey would join them soon. The Miss Cooks entered, Charlotte suitably reserved for the occasion, while Judith waved vigorously to Jane, wearing a dimpled smile.

Lord Winspear, as senior magistrate, sat in the center chair at the table on the raised dais, flanked by Sir Timothy and Mr. Bingley. As more people filed into the room, occupying its few chairs, standing, or leaning against the back wall, Lord Winspear grumbled, "What are all these people doing here?" He raised his voice and said, "This is a formal meeting, not a theatrical performance. Keep your peace or I shall oust you."

Jane resisted the urge to bounce her knee or tap her foot as they sat through several other matters of business. She grew more agitated by the minute—Mr. Godfrey had yet to appear.

Finally Lord Winspear consulted his notes and announced, "And now we come to the licenses due for renewal. First on the docket is Mrs. John Bell. A last-minute entry." Here he glowered at Sir Timothy before looking at Jane. "State your case, please."

Jane rose and faced the trio of magistrates. "As you may know, my husband, John Bell, was the previous license holder of The Bell, but he died last year. So I am here to apply for a new license in his stead."

"It is your intention then, to carry on the role of innkeeper?" Lord Winspear asked, his eyes as black as her jet brooch.

"It is, my lord."

"Why?"

"Why?" Jane echoed in confusion. "Because the license is about to expire, and—"

"No—why do it at all?" he challenged. "Jane Fairmont, an innkeeper? Remember, I was acquainted with your parents. Your good mother would be turning in her grave if she knew what her daughter proposed to do with her life."

Jane's chest tightened until she feared it would cave in on her. She stared at the man. He had been a guest in their house when Fairmont had been a gracious home, and she the daughter of gentry. Was he right—*would* her mother turn in her grave? She could certainly not approve. Jane felt her eyes heat and willed away tears. She could not cry in front of these people. She would not. Remembering Thora's words, Jane lifted her chin, forcing herself to meet the man's onyx gaze.

Sir Timothy said, "Lord Winspear, Mrs. Bell's motivations for carrying on her husband's business are outside the scope of this hearing."

"Oh, let her speak for herself, Brockwell. I know you two were childhood friends." He returned his hard stare to Jane. "Again I repeat, why?"

Jane inhaled, grasped at her composure with both hands, and answered, "It is true, my lord, that being an innkeeper was never among my cherished childhood dreams. But these are the circumstances fate has thrust me into."

"Fate? Did fate force you to marry an innkeeper?"

Jane swallowed. "No. I made that choice for reasons of my own." She stole a glance at Sir Timothy, then continued. "But I did not choose that my husband would die at such a young age. And I was as surprised as anyone to learn that he'd left the inn part and parcel to me. But I have decided to honor his decision and do my duty to The Bell staff, suppliers, and patrons."

"Very noble," he said dryly.

Again Sir Timothy spoke up. "This being your intention, who is your first bondsman?"

"Mr. James Drake."

James stood, finely turned out in a dark blue frockcoat and patterned waistcoat, looking confident and at his ease.

"Drake? I do not know any Drake," Winspear said. "Who are you, sir, to speak in this matter?"

Sir Timothy interjected, "Surely, my lord, you have heard of Mr. Drake's new hotel being fitted up in the former Fairmont estate?"

"Turning the family home of old friends of mine into a public hostelry? Am I supposed to congratulate him? I don't know anything about the man, or any reason I should value his testimony."

"Mr. Drake may be a newcomer here, but he has owned and operated a successful hotel in Southampton for several years."

"If Mr. Drake is so successful in the thriving city of Southampton, pray why would he be interested in the inconsequential knoll of Ivy Hill?"

It was an interesting question, Jane agreed, though what bearing it had on her license, she couldn't see. Did he question the man's business acumen, or his judgment in general?

James remained calm, taking the JP's sharp words in his stride. "I first saw the name Ivy Hill while reviewing plans for the new turnpike trust," he began. "It struck me as a place of . . . opportunity."

Lord Winspear eyed him skeptically. "Something tells me there is more to the story."

"There may be. Though nothing that bears on the issue at hand. But let us share a bottle of Chambertin some evening and I shall tell you all the stories you like."

"Yes, I believe you would," Lord Winspear archly replied. "So, Mr. Successful *Hôtelier*, you feel you can vouch for Mrs. Bell in her capacity as innkeeper?"

"I do, my lord."

"On what grounds?"

"Jane Bell may not have a great deal of experience, it is true. But she does have a great deal of intelligence and, in my estimation, natural talent. When she learned of my background, she asked excellent questions, and both absorbed and challenged my advice in an insightful way I found most impressive. She may not know everything—yet. But she is a quick study, and experience will soon teach her the rest. I had not known Mrs. Bell long before I considered her one of the keenest women of my acquaintance. I think she will be a worthy competitor, as the recent contest for the Royal Mail proved. I, for one, look forward to a long and mutually profitable relationship."

"Are you married, sir?"

James reared his head back. "No, my lord. I have not had that privilege. But if you mean to imply that I flatter Mrs. Bell in hopes of earning her favor, you are mistaken."

"You do not wish to earn her favor?"

Jane noticed her knee bouncing up and down and wished Sir Timothy might object again, but he did not.

"Of course I would," James replied. "But that is not why I am here."

Sir Timothy cleared his throat. "You speak very . . . warmly on Mrs. Bell's behalf."

Lord Winspear smirked. "Yes, he does."

James nodded and pulled forth several folded pages from his pocket. "If I may, my lords. Here are my licenses, regularly renewed as you can see, without blemish or fail. I hope that adds some credence to my testimony if my word here does not speak for itself."

Lord Winspear waved away the offered papers. "Thank you, Mr. Drake. But not every council upholds regulations to the same exacting standards that we do here. Speaking of which—where is your license for this new establishment you speak of? I don't recall issuing one."

"He's last on today's docket, my lord," the clerk interjected. "Which we shall get to by midnight, at this rate."

"Very well. Let's get on with it. Your second bondsmen is . . . ?"

"Mr. Godfrey." Jane looked around the room, stomach sinking. Where was he? He'd agreed to come, though reluctantly.

"Ah. Our old friend—and I use that term loosely—Mr. Godfrey." Lord Winspear peered over the top of his spectacles at the assembled company. "Did he fail to appear? Imagine that. Well, without a second bondsman, we cannot proceed."

Mercy Grove rose. "I shall stand as her bondsman, or woman, in this case. I may not be an innkeeper, but I can vouch for Mrs. Bell's character unequivocally."

"Thank you, *Miss* Grove. But please sit down. A bondsman is called a bonds*man* for a reason."

Timothy began, "There is no regulation against a female—"

"There is a prejudice, Sir Timothy. A strong prejudice. Besides, Miss Grove may keep a bit of a school, but that does not qualify her to vouch for an innkeeper."

"Then I shall stand as bondsman," Mr. Paley said, rising.

Lord Winspear sighed heavily. "Mr. Paley. You are a man of God, not a man of business."

❖ 417 ❖

"I disagree, my good fellow. Do I not oversee a church, several charities, parish clerk, and sexton, all while striving to keep a group of—if not patrons—parishioners happy?"

His words reminded Jane of what Mrs. Paley had said at the Ladies Tea and Knitting Society meeting. Perhaps his wife had written the little speech for him.

"An excellent try, Mr. Paley," Lord Winspear said. "But we shall leave ecclesiastical matters to you if you will leave legal matters to us."

Bile soured Jane's mouth. She felt her future falling away, sick at the thought of disappointing so many who depended on her.

"So without a second qualified bondsman, we have no choice but to decline the license, and perhaps that is for the best. A gentlewoman is bred to sew cushions and play the pianoforte. She has no idea how to manage an inn. How to negotiate with brewers and stage lines, and deal with customers, coachmen, drunkards, and worse—"

"My lord, if you'll forgive me," a voice from the back of the room interrupted, "it sounds as if you do."

Lord Winspear scowled. "Who said that? Who interrupts so brazenly?"

Thora walked forward, the crowd parting to make way. "Perhaps you would like a job at The Bell, my lord." She glanced at Jane. "Do you think we might find him something?"

Lord Winspear slowly shook his head and leaned back in his chair. "Thora Bell. I should have known. Your tongue has always been too sharp for your own good."

Thora stood before the magistrates, hands casually clasped low over her skirt. "My lord. Good to see you again."

"And you. Are you here offering to serve as bondsman as well?"

"No, my lord. She did not ask me."

"Ah . . . because she fears you would not speak highly of her?"

Thora shrugged easily. "I have certainly given her reason to fear that. Would you even allow me to speak for her, considering she is my daughter-in-law? Would you not reject any testimony I might give as biased and untrustworthy, as I have a personal interest in today's proceedings?"

"I see your point. And were you any other woman—or any other family member—I would definitely rule you out. But I know your plain speaking too well. And I cannot imagine *you* approve of a gentlewoman managing your family's inn?"

Thora hedged, "I can certainly vouch for Jane Bell's character."

"But it is not only her character that concerns us today, but her ability to manage the conduct of her staff and patrons."

"If anything, my lord, I imagine a gentlewoman like Jane, with all her fine, ladylike manners, will expect a higher level of conduct from both staff and patrons than any other Bell would ever have done."

"Are you saying you have no concerns about Jane Bell's suitability as an innkeeper?"

For a moment Thora and Lord Winspear locked gazes. And Jane held her breath, thinking of all the disapproving looks and words Thora had given her, and their many disagreements. Oh, Thora had her concerns, all right. And her doubts. And probably relished the chance to express them.

Thora considered, then began, "There will never be another innkeeper like my father. He was gentlemanlike and fair, yet firm. Wise and generous. He knew how to encourage everyone from the lowliest potboy to the most cantankerous cook to do their best and be proud of a job well done. He served the poorest, frightened servant-girl on her way to a new post, to the most exacting highborn dowager, with humility and warmth. In many ways, Jane reminds me of him. She is wise enough to know when to ask for help and when to make an unpopular decision on her own. She is kindhearted and willing to make sacrifices, and not too proud to get her hands dirty to help her staff and serve her patrons. All marks of a good leader. I believe Jane Bell will be an excellent innkeeper. And I pledge to do all I can to help her succeed."

For a moment, silence hung in the chambers.

Jane stared, disbelieving, at her irritable, disapproving mother-in-law, as if she didn't recognize her. As if she were seeing her for the first time.

Even Lord Winspear seemed momentarily transfixed. Then his glittering gaze returned. "A very pretty speech, madam. Do you mean it?"

"Of course. You know I never praise anyone if I can help it."

"I do, indeed."

Lord Winspear studied her for a moment longer and then threw up his hands. "Well. I see you are all in league against me. And so I will object no further. I hope, rather than believe, Jane Bell will be the successful landlady you all seem to think her."

Jane exhaled, and her heart lightened in relief. "Come, my lord," she cajoled. "Why must it be us against you? How well I remember when you used to come to Fairmont House at Christmas to share a toast and roasted chestnuts. And sing 'God Rest Ye Merry, Gentlemen' in your fine bass voice. I shall never forget it."

He cleared his throat. "This is not the place for such remembrances."

"Then come to the inn sometime, and we'll rehearse those dear memories of Christmases past, and of my father and my mother."

"Your mother was an excellent woman. You are very like her."

"Am I? There is no greater compliment you could give me." Jane doubted she was much like her mamma any longer, but was pleased the man thought as highly of her mother as she did.

"Yes, well." Again Lord Winspear cleared his throat and put on a severe look. "Enough now. We have not finished yet. There are regulations to uphold. Are you ready to make your pledge, Mrs. Bell?"

Jane bit back a smile. "I am, my lord."

He led her through the formal, legal pledge of recognizance and ended with a stern warning. "Remember, Jane Fairmont Bell, that if you fail to adhere to these regulations, I will not hesitate to summon you before us again on charges of keeping a disorderly house." He shot Timothy a dark look. "Family connections or no."

Jane nodded earnestly. "I will remember, my lord. And thank you."

When the sessions ended, the crowd began dispersing, many lingering to congratulate Jane. She thanked James and Mr. Paley for speaking up for her, but thought it wisest to keep her distance from Sir Timothy while in the council chambers.

Others came forward, including Mrs. Klein and Miss Morris from the Ladies Tea and Knitting Society, though Jane saw no one else from The Bell. She was polite in her thanks but craned her neck to see over the heads of the others, looking for Thora. She spotted her across the room, cornered by the Miss Cooks.

Mercy came over and embraced her, and then excused herself, saying she would talk to her later, but had to hurry back to Ivy Cottage to see how Rachel was getting on with the girls. Jane said good-bye, and when she looked again, Thora was gone.

Jane made her way through the crowd, accepting well-wishes as she went. Finally, she exited the village hall, and with a little unladylike burst of speed, caught up with Thora halfway down Potters Lane, striding back alone.

She wanted to ask if Thora had really meant what she'd said about her but held her tongue. She reminded herself that she, too, was quite familiar with Thora's plain speaking. To save the inn, her mother-in-law might have spoken more confidently than she felt, and if so, Jane would not blame her.

"Thank you, Thora," she said instead.

Thora nodded without pause, and Jane fell into step beside her. On impulse, Jane linked her arm through Thora's and held her breath, waiting to be rebuffed. Instead, Thora briefly pressed a hand to Jane's.

She said, "I used to shake my head and wonder what in the world John was thinking to leave The Bell to you. But now I see the truth of the matter. John knew you better than anyone—perhaps even better than you know yourself. And he somehow knew you were the very person to oversee The Bell after he was gone. To save it."

Jane felt tears prick her eyes at her mother-in-law's unexpected and astounding praise. They were not in a license hearing now.

"Thank you, Thora," she repeated over the lump in her throat. "I hope you are right."

Thora slanted her a look. "I usually am," she said. "Don't prove me wrong this time."

Jane stopped on the corner, instead of crossing the street to the inn. "You go ahead, Thora. I'm going straight to the bank with my license."

Thora hesitated. "Very well. But don't be long."

Jane nodded. She turned up the High Street and strode smartly to the stone-and-brick building at the end. Reaching the door of Blomfield, Waters, and Welch, she let herself in.

The young clerk rose. "I am sorry, Mrs. Bell, but Mr. Blomfield is not—"

Jane did not pause to listen to excuses. "Never mind, I will show myself in."

"But—"

Jane pushed open the door to Mr. Blomfield's office and drew up short at the sight of the man behind the desk.

Not Mr. Blomfield. A man she didn't recognize. And in the guest chair? Patrick Bell.

"Ah. Jane," Patrick drawled. "We were just talking about you."

"Oh? I thought you were in Salisbury."

"I was." He gestured toward the man behind the desk. "You two have not met, I don't think. Jane Bell, allow me to introduce Mr. Welch, of the former Blomfield, Waters, and Welch."

"The former? I don't understand."

Mr. Welch rose. "Mrs. Bell. I wish we were meeting under happier circumstances. Please, do be seated."

"But . . . I gave Mr. Blomfield our plan and am here about an extension for a loan. I have just come from the petty sessions and have my new license to show him. Where is he?"

"Honestly, I don't know," Mr. Welch said. "Far from here by now, I should guess."

"What do you mean?"

"He has absconded."

Jane gaped. "What? Why?"

Patrick handed her a sheaf of papers. "Here is John's copy of the loan papers. Take a look."

Jane looked from him to the papers, brows high. "Where did you find them?"

"In John's desk drawer. I'm ashamed to say I, em, borrowed them." He pointed to the top page. "Notice anything . . . odd there?"

Jane glanced over the summary page. John's signature. Blomfield's. Then a figure caught her eye and she looked again. "*Five* thousand pounds? But it was fifteen."

"So Arthur Blomfield led us to believe."

She stared at him. "But I saw the original loan paper myself, and John's signature."

Mr. Welch said, "My theory is that Blomfield embezzled money from the firm. To hide the missing funds from us, he tacked on the sum to your husband's outstanding loan."

Patrick nodded. "Blomfield was always dabbling in risky ventures, and my guess is he 'borrowed' money to invest, intending to pay it back, but instead lost it all. After John's death, he thought he was free and clear—as long as a copy showing the original amount didn't turn up. When I first confronted him, Blomfield denied any wrongdoing. Said it was John's word against his. Called this a forgery. But we all know it is far easier to add a number one before the five, than the other way around. Later, Blomfield asked me to hand the copy over to him, hinting that in return, he would make me The Bell's owner by summer's end. And I admit I was tempted, but only briefly. Since then I've been trying to work out how best to proceed. I thought about going to the magistrates, but in the end, I took this to his partners in Salisbury."

Mr. Welch nodded. "We had suspected Blomfield of mismanaging funds for some time, but never had any proof. Now we do."

Patrick grimaced. "Unfortunately, I revealed my hand too soon, and Blomfield cleared out and left before his partners could react or involve the law."

"Is he really gone?" Jane asked.

Mr. Welch nodded. "His apartment upstairs has been vacated and he gave no forwarding address to his housekeeper. The possessions he left behind in his haste will be sold for what we can get, but it will not nearly make up for what we've lost. Be glad you demanded what was left of your settlement, Mrs. Bell, or he would probably have taken that as well. Mr. Waters and I will make what restitution we can to those who lost money, but it will take time, and may drive us to insolvency if we're not careful."

"I am sorry to hear it, Mr. Welch."

"Thank you. But that is our problem, Mrs. Bell. Not yours. Allow me to congratulate you on the progress you have made on The Bell so far, and your excellent plan." He tapped the folder on the desk before him. "On behalf of Mr. Waters and myself, I am happy to grant the requested extension on the *five* thousand you owe."

Two-thirds of the weight lifted from Jane's shoulders.

She managed a shaky smile. "Thank you, Mr. Welch."

Patrick rose. "May I walk you back, Jane? We have a lot to talk about."

"If you like."

They left poor Mr. Welch to sort out the mess of Arthur Blomfield's making.

They stepped out of the bank and started down the High Street. Jane sent Patrick a sidelong glance. "How long have you known?"

He shrugged. "I've suspected something was afoot ever since Blomfield hesitated to tell us the loan amount, at least until he verified we had not seen John's copy of the papers."

"Does Thora know?"

He shook his head. "Though she saw me looking in the desk in the lodge and no doubt suspects the worst."

Jane shook her head, disgusted. "You went through John's desk and then didn't tell me what you'd found? When was this?"

"When I offered to fetch John's keys for the wine cellar. I am sorry, Jane. I took something that didn't belong to me and was tempted to use it to my advantage, or at least to enjoy watching Blomfield squirm. It was wrong of me, I know. I hope you will forgive me."

Jane studied her brother-in-law's face, then drew a long breath. "Well . . . I suppose I understand. Which of us has not been tempted to act selfishly? But you did the right thing in the end, and that counts for something. For today, let's focus on the fact that we have the license and the extension, so The Bell is safe for now."

"Hurrah."

She looked at him closely. "Are you being sarcastic, or are you really happy for me?"

"I am. Truly."

"Then we shall talk more about the rest later." She wagged a finger at him and said sternly, "But stay out of the lodge."

He held up his palm. "I promise."

"And no more secrets. And no more . . . sneaking," Jane added. "Thora has had enough heartache. She wants to trust you. And so do I."

"I know. Which reminds me—we had better hurry back to The Bell."

"Oh? Why?"

He grinned. "You'll see."

CHAPTER

Forty-Four

When they returned to the inn, commotion from the courtyard drew Jane's attention. Instead of entering through the front door, Jane and Patrick walked past it, through the archway. Jane halted abruptly at the sight of the beehive of activity before her.

Noticing their arrival, Thora walked forward to meet them.

"What's going on?" Jane asked her, taking in the hodgepodge of mismatched tables, chairs, and benches, and streams of bunting strung from one side of the courtyard to the other. Ostlers and maids worked together, carrying out platters, spreading cloths on makeshift plank tables followed by vases of flowers. Mrs. Rooke stood at the center of it all, ordering people about in good-natured firmness.

"Why, Jane, can you not tell?" Thora replied. "We're throwing you a party."

Jane looked at her in wonder, then surveyed the scene once more.

Mrs. Rooke had performed a loaves-and-fishes miracle with food for the spur-of-the-moment gathering. She had cleared out the larder and bought out Craddock's bakery shelves by the looks of a buffet table filled with cakes and biscuits along with her own jam tarts. There was also a ham, a joint of cold beef, and a chicken with actual meat on its bones. What the cook lacked in variety of side dishes, she made up for with an abundance of potatoes, cabbage, and pickled cucumbers. To drink, there were jugs of lemonade and pots of tea and coffee.

"My goodness, Mrs. Rooke, you have outdone yourself," Jane said. "I am astounded at this bounty, and at such short notice."

"Oh, I collected a few favors. . . . It's a great day for all of us, and I wanted to do my part."

Bravely, Jane put a hand on the woman's stout arm. "And you have done—and then some!"

Mrs. Rooke smiled, and it might have been the first time Jane had ever seen the woman look genuinely kind.

Finishing their tasks, three musicians began to warm up their instruments. Tall Ted on fiddle, Colin on pipe, and Tuffy on sweet mandolin.

Thora pressed Jane's hand. "Now go and change out of those drab widow's weeds, Jane. It's time to celebrate."

A few hours later, as twilight settled its dusky mantle over the courtyard, the straggling parade of arriving guests finally slowed to a trickle. Jane, in her lavender dress, sat back a moment, her gaze moving over the courtyard, lit by torches, lanterns, and the twinkling lights of stubby candles in glass jars. Her heart felt full. Almost painfully so.

Patrick was in the office, she knew, but there were Thora and Talbot—a black mourning band over his sleeve in honor of Nan. And Jane's staff: Mrs. Rooke, Tuffy, Tall Ted, Joe and the other postboys. Cadi and Alwena. Colin, Bobbin, and Ned. Old friends from the village, like Mr. and Mrs. Paley, and new friends like James Drake, and Mrs. Klein and the Miss Cooks from the Ladies Tea and Knitting Society, sitting and sipping and laughing together.

And there was dear Mercy along with her aunt. If only Rachel had come to complete the trio of longtime friends. Mercy must have noticed Jane's disappointed expression when they had ar- rived without Rachel, for she'd sent her a sad, understanding look.

Neither Mr. Bingley nor Lord Winspear had come, which did not surprise her. But Jane's heart lifted to see Sir Timothy ride through the archway as evening deepened. Tall Ted set down his instrument and hurried over to take his horse.

"Just tether and water him, if you don't mind. I won't be long." From his saddlebag Sir Timothy withdrew two carefully wrapped bottles.

Jane walked forward to greet him. "Hello, Timothy. I wasn't sure you would cross Lord Winspear again by coming."

He smiled. "I shan't stay long, but I did want to congratulate you. I've brought along a few bottles of good champagne for the well-deserved celebration." He glanced around the crowded court-yard. "But I see I should have brought more. Half of Ivy Hill seems to be here."

"Thank you. That is very kind." She hailed the potboy as he passed. "Ned—please take these to Bobbin and ask him to open them."

Ned nodded and darted off to do so.

"I was proud of you today, Jane," Sir Timothy said. "You han-dled yourself well."

"Thank you, though Mr. Drake and Thora saved the day."

"But you earned their good opinion in the first place, don't forget. They only gave testimony to the excellent character you have always had, and your growing competence as a woman of business."

Warmth flooded Jane at his praise. "Thank you, Timothy. That means a great deal, coming from you."

He removed his hat. Glancing down at it, he said, "Jane, tell me if I am being impertinent, but . . . is there something between you and Mr. Drake?"

Jane hesitated, surprised at the question, though after Mr. Drake's effusive praise, what else was he to think? "You are right, Timothy," she said on a laugh. "You are terribly impertinent."

She turned and thanked Ned as he returned with two glasses. "Here, have some champagne." She handed a glass to Timothy. "It was a gift from a wealthy old friend of mine. It's probably not his best, but . . ." She shrugged, then grinned at him.

He returned her grin, but his sober tone did not match his expression. "Only the best for you, Jane. You deserve every good thing life has to offer." He lifted his glass. "To Jane Fairmont Bell. An excellent woman and an excellent innkeeper."

Jane felt unexpected tears prick her eyes and blinked them away. Today was a day for celebration and plans for the future, not to linger on past regrets. "Thank you." She forced a smile and touched her glass to his. "To old friends."

She thought again of Rachel. The old friend missing like a piece torn from a family portrait. Incomplete. Was Timothy aware of her absence as well?

The champagne tingled warmly down her throat, the sensation more pleasant than the taste itself. Sir Timothy, she noticed, set down his glass, untasted. He bowed to her, then made his way through the crowd, at his ease as always, confident and comfortable in his role as village squire, known and respected by all. Jane watched him over the rim of her glass as he greeted Thora, spoke politely to Mercy and Matilda, shook Mr. Drake's hand, joined in the applause as the makeshift band of musicians finished a song, and then with a general wave to the assembled company and another to her, strode back to the stables to reclaim his horse. A few moments later, he rode away through the archway as regally as he'd arrived, and Jane watched until he'd disappeared from view.

Mercy appeared at her side. Her gentle, understanding look threatened to bring tears to Jane's eyes again—so many emotions swept through her!

"All right, Jane?" she asked softly.

Jane inhaled deeply. "I am more than all right." She smiled, realizing it was true. "In fact, I am an excellent innkeeper," she added, echoing Timothy's private toast.

"I am glad to hear it. It is your night, after all."

"It's a night for all of us. Well, almost all of us. . . ." Her heart pricked again. But what had she expected, when she had not attended Rachel's party at Thornvale?

Mercy said gently, "I did ask Rachel to join us, but she was expecting a call from Mr. Ashford, so . . ."

Jane nodded and asked, "Then who is watching the girls tonight?"

"Martha Bushby offered."

"Ah. That was kind of her." Jane handed Timothy's untouched glass to Mercy. "Champagne from Brockwell Court."

"I've never cared for it, but Auntie will enjoy it." Mercy accepted the glass, squeezed Jane's free hand with her own, and returned to her aunt.

Watching her walk away to join the others, Jane suppressed a sigh. She looked around the crowded courtyard once more, reminding herself of all those who *had* come. She looked again at Thora, her heart warming anew to think of how she had spoken up for her so staunchly that day. She was not only her friend, but her family. At the thought, Jane felt another relaxed smile lift her mouth.

Gabriel Locke was not there. He had gone back to his uncle's horse farm, she guessed. He should be celebrating with them, since he had helped them win the contest. They would not have beaten Mr. Drake's team without his hard work in training and admirable skill in leading others. She wished she had more of that skill herself. She would need it to carry out the remainder of their plans and lead The Bell staff in the weeks and months ahead. They had been given a second chance, and she did not mean to waste it.

Gabriel might be absent, but James Drake was there, just across the courtyard. He had been her rival in the contest for the Royal Mail, but her supporter and her bondsman in the licensing hearing. She thought again of what he had said, his warm praise of her as a woman and an innkeeper, and felt a little flutter of . . . what? Happiness? Attraction? Hope? She wasn't completely certain how she felt about the man. But she felt *something*. She glanced over and found him watching her, a private smile on his face as his eyes met hers, the grooves in his cheeks emphasized by the flickering candlelight. He looked relaxed. Content. A little removed from the general clamor and conversation all around him, sipping from his glass. She walked over to join him.

"Enjoying yourself?" he asked as she approached.

"I am. You?"

He smiled deeply into her eyes. "I am now."

Together they found seats at one of the tables and settled in to savor the good food, good company, and merry music. They watched with pleasure and amusement as old couples and odd couples began to dance. Mrs. Shabner and Aunt Matty clapped side by side as young Joe performed a bashful little jig alone. Cadi and Alwena cajoled him and another postboy to join them in a country dance.

Cadi appealed to the crowd, "We need more couples!"

Ned and Dotty joined in. Talbot asked Thora, but she turned him down to refill the tea urn. Patrick emerged from the office and also tried to convince his mother to dance. He soon gave up and danced with Mrs. Rooke instead. Mr. and Mrs. Paley joined them as well.

James looked at her, green eyes warm on her face. "Dance with me, Jane."

"With pleasure."

He held out his hand to her, and she placed hers in his.

They walked over and joined hands with the others. In time with the music, they circled one way, then the other. Then the couples "gipsied" around each other shoulder to shoulder, James holding her gaze all the while. Finally, they all circled around, right hand, then left, in a revolving chain.

From the corner of her eye, Jane saw a figure emerge from the shadows curtaining the archway. Her heart leapt. For one foolish moment she thought it might be Gabriel returning. But when she recognized who it was, her disappointment evaporated.

Rachel. She had come after all.

Jane excused herself from James and walked over to meet her old friend.

"Rachel, I am so glad you came."

"Are you? I wasn't sure I should."

"Of course you should. It means a great deal to me."

"I'm not too late, I hope."

Jane risked teasing her, "You always did like to make an entrance."

Rachel tentatively grinned in return. "These days my grand entrances are limited to church and the schoolroom. Your party is the highlight of my social season."

Rachel surveyed the assembled company. Was she looking for Sir Timothy? Jane wondered. She said tentatively, "Mercy mentioned you were expecting Mr. Ashford to call . . . ?"

Rachel nodded a little sheepishly. "I sent my regrets. I did not want to miss this opportunity to congratulate you on your success."

"Thank you. We have won the Royal Mail contract and a license, but we still have to become more profitable. Our challenges are not over yet."

"I hope you triumph over each one."

"Me too. Thankfully, I am not in this alone."

"So I see." Rachel surveyed the courtyard again—the filled tables, musicians, and dancers. "My goodness, this is a much more festive party than my attempt at Thornvale."

"And I can take no credit for it." Jane turned, seeking out the people responsible and subtly pointing them out. "Mrs. Rooke, Dotty, Cadi, Alwena, Ned, and Colin, as well as the ostlers, Ted and Tuffy, prepared everything this afternoon, while I was away at the license hearing."

Rachel said, "And you do know it was Thora who went around the village, inviting everyone?"

"Did she?" Jane asked, looking for Thora in the crowd. "I did wonder. . . ." *So that was why she had been late to the hearing.*

When Jane turned back, she was surprised to see Rachel's gaze fastened on her in bemusement. She slowly shook her head. "I can't get over it. You are so changed. A proper employer you are now, on a first-name basis with your staff."

Jane was glad to hear no censure in Rachel's voice. She replied,

"I suppose it's not much different than overseeing menus and servants at either Fairmont or Thornvale once was."

"True." Rachel released a dry puff of laughter. "Do you remember when we were girls, sitting in those tall pine trees, the wind swaying our perches, talking about our dreams for the future?"

"Yes, I do."

"I have been thinking about it a lot lately. Especially since moving in with Mercy. I don't recall exactly what I dreamt then, but—"

"I do. You said you would marry well and live in a fine house with only two children, because you did not wish to increase your risk of death in childbirth or spoil your figure."

Rachel chuckled. "Did I? I wonder how I thought I'd manage that. Seems so silly now."

Jane lifted her chin in recollection. "And I dreamt of playing pianoforte for the king or learning to jump Hermione."

"Well, that too. But I remember you wanted to marry and have several children—a big family."

Jane winced. The words were a painful stab, however unintentionally delivered.

Unaware, Rachel sighed wistfully. "And here we are. Both alone. Neither of us living the life we dreamt of or thought we'd have."

For a moment Jane was quiet, the sting receding behind a growing realization. It rose within her on a bubble of discovery that tickled her breastbone and warmed her heart more than champagne ever could. Yes, she had lost her parents and her husband and her babies. But she was not alone. She looked from dear face to dear face as they talked with one another, teased and laughed, or danced. God had given her the desire of her heart: a big, warm, loving family—in the staff of The Bell and the community of Ivy Hill.

That naïve young girl in the treetops could never have imagined what her life would become. None of it was what she would have expected or chosen. But she wouldn't trade places with anyone.

She smiled at her old friend. "I am not alone, Rachel. And neither are you. And never will be, if Mercy and I have anything to say about it. Now, go and enjoy yourself."

"What about you?"

"I'll join you in a minute."

Rachel crossed the courtyard, and as she approached the table, Mercy beamed at her, and James rose and offered his seat.

The musicians paused for another respite, and after the crowd's applause faded, Talbot stood and gestured for everyone's attention.

"I have an announcement to make." He waited until everyone quieted, then looked at Thora seated on the bench next to him. Her expression was difficult to decipher but increasingly uncomfortable when all those pairs of eyes turned in her direction.

"As you know," Talbot said, "I have traveled through this life of mine unattached, matrimonially speaking—though I am certainly attached to this place, and to all of you."

His gaze sought her out across the courtyard. "I hope you don't mind, Jane, if I trespass on a moment of your party to celebrate something even nearer and dearer to my heart than this old inn." He laid a work-worn hand on Thora's shoulder. "It is with great pride and wonder that I tell you that this woman, Thora Bell, has agreed to make me the happiest of men by becoming my wife."

Jane sucked in a breath of surprise and delight. Around the tables, the stunned silence was quickly replaced by cheers and applause.

Thora pulled a face. "I said I'd marry you, you old coot. I never said I'd make you happy."

Laughter rumbled through their midst.

"Ah, but you already have." Talbot smiled fondly at her, then leaned down and kissed her cheek.

She playfully slapped his shoulder. "Go on with you now. They don't want to see the romantic antics of two old fools like us."

"Too bad." He kissed her again.

More whoops and applause erupted, and the musicians launched into a jaunty tune befitting the joyous occasion.

Again Talbot asked Thora to dance, and this time she agreed. The sight of stern, officious Thora skipping and holding hands with Talbot in a lively country dance brought bittersweet tears to

Jane's eyes. Thora's rare smile lifted her features and chased years from her face. She looked young and pretty and happy.

Jane glanced through the archway to the inn sign, with its freshly-painted placard suspended on two sturdy chains.

No Vacancy.

It was true, Jane realized with gratitude. God had filled her empty heart with love and family and hope for the future.

AUTHOR'S NOTE

If you're anything like me, you probably love village series set in England, whether in books or in film or television. Series like *Larkrise to Candleford*, *Cranford*, and THRUSH GREEN—a series of novels published over many years, which, I understand, partly inspired Jan Karon's MITFORD series. And have you read the GRESHAM CHRONICLES by Lawana Blackwell? I adored it. I think what draws us to these series are their close-knit communities filled with quirky characters, which create an idyllic place to retreat from the hectic modern world. Or maybe it's just the British accents. Whatever the reason, I hope you will enjoy my first series as well.

Ivy Hill is a fictional place, but there are many villages like it in England. I've based Ivy Hill's layout on the National Trust village of Lacock in Wiltshire, which I've had the privilege of visiting a few times. Lacock was used as a film location for scenes in *Pride and Prejudice* (1995), *Cranford* (2007), *Emma* (1996), and recently, a market scene in *Downton Abbey* (season 6). Even though I am using Lacock as a basic model for Ivy Hill, I've placed the village farther south, on the old Devonport-London Royal Mail route, not far from Salisbury and the real village of Great Wishford.

During a trip to England in 2014, a reader who lives in Wiltshire invited me and my old friend and traveling companion, Sara, to visit. Katie Read and her family own a large farm and riding stables called Pewsey Vale Riding Centre and are active in teaching and competing. Sara and I enjoyed meeting Katie, who took us for a pleasant ride on two gentle horses and introduced us to her staff and her handsome horse, Harry. And we loved meeting her mother-in-law, Jacky, who lives with her husband in a five-hundred-year-old thatched-roof cottage, where we relished tea and cake and equally sweet conversation. So, with fond memories of that day, I've placed Gabriel Locke's family farm in Pewsey Vale. I also want to thank Katie for kindly reading the book to check the horse and riding details for me. Any remaining errors are mine.

If you have read my other novels, you probably know that I like to honor some of my favorite authors with little nods to their work. This book is no exception. In it, I've included a few lines that echo Elizabeth Gaskell's *North & South* (one of my all-time favorite books/miniseries), as well as a scene partly inspired by one in *Far From the Madding Crowd* by Thomas Hardy. You may also notice a nod or two to *Pride and Prejudice*, and Talbot's prayer is reminiscent of prayers written by Jane Austen herself. Some readers have written to me, telling me they enjoy finding these hidden treasures in my books. Perhaps you're one of them.

I also want to thank the Reverend Tim Schenck for his blog post entitled "Is Your Sexton Nuts?" which gave me the idea to have my fictional sexton talk to church mice.

The Ladies Tea and Knitting Society was inspired by the women of one of my favorite book clubs, the Tantalizing Ladies Tea: A Christian Book Coterie, who have included me in several of their meetings. Beverly, Kristine, Judy, Sherri, Becky, Phyllis, Tiffany, Shari, Kelly, Julia, and Teresa, thank you for laughter-filled afternoons with savory conversation and savory food. You have spoiled me, and I love being an honorary member!

The talented Anna Paulson worked as my assistant while I wrote this book, and helped research Royal Mail routes, coaches, and coaching inns, among other things. She also helped me keep track of timelines, unsnarl problems, edit, and much more. I'm very grateful for her help in tackling this, book one in my first-ever series.

I also want to thank Cari Weber, who helped me brainstorm the series as a whole and serves so capably as my beta reader and awesome friend.

I am indebted to Michelle Griep, author and master critiquer, who helped me tighten and polish the manuscript. If you haven't read her books yet, I highly recommend them!

As always, I want to thank my agent, Wendy Lawton, and my editors, Karen Schurrer and Raela Schoenherr, for all the ways they champion my work.

And thanks again to Sara Ring, who traveled with me, took photos, and had the difficult task of spending time with me in historic inns around England. To see some of her photos related to the book, visit the research page of my website.

Speaking of the Web, be sure to visit the new Internet home of this series—TalesFromIvyHill.com—for more about the books, including photos, character lists, maps, previews of upcoming releases, and more.

Lastly, I appreciate you, dear reader! Thank you for spending time with me in Ivy Hill. I hope you will come again. I will have a room reserved for you at The Bell, a hot cup of tea waiting, and more stories to tell.

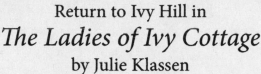

Return to Ivy Hill in
The Ladies of Ivy Cottage
by Julie Klassen

~

Don't miss a moment
as friendships deepen, romances blossom, and mysteries unfold. . . .

RACHEL discovers two mysteries hidden among the books in her possession. Sir Timothy helps her search for answers, but will both find more than they bargained for?

MERCY is perplexed by Mr. Drake's interest in her school. Or is it a resident of Ivy Cottage who has captured his attention?

JANE longs for peace with the past. As her heart heals, she also yearns for something else . . . or perhaps *someone* else.

THORA begins her new life, but then a newcomer arrives in Ivy Hill who could change her world—and Patrick's—forever. . . .

~

Coming
December 2017

In the meantime, visit
www.TalesFromIvyHill.com
for information about the series, including photos, character lists, a map, and more.

Discussion Questions

1. One character relates village life to "an ivy vine climbing a great oak. You cut off the vine at the root and all the way up the tree, the leaves wither. We're all connected." How does the book illustrate this truth in Ivy Hill?

2. What historical details most intrigued you about the book (e.g., the Royal Mail, coaching inns, inheritance laws)?

3. Which character reminds you the most of yourself or someone you know? Why? Which character would you love to spend time with?

4. Describe a moment in the book that sticks in your memory. What made that part stand out to you?

5. Several characters in the story struggle to accept help from others. Describe a time in your own life when you were humbled by your circumstances and had to rely on others. What did you learn?

6. Unexpected gestures of kindness encourage healing and trust between characters throughout the story. When was a time that someone who had hurt you in the past surprised you

with their thoughtfulness? Did it help restore your faith in that person?

7. All three main characters face disillusionment and loss at the beginning of the book. How does each woman handle her grief? How does the way they cope with hardship reveal who they are?

8. Despite the prejudice against women in business at this time in history, many strong female characters run businesses in Ivy Hill. How have specific women in your own life inspired you?

9. Compare the first scene and the last scene of the book. Explain how these scenes capture Jane's journey as a character.

10. What are you looking forward to in book two of the TALES FROM IVY HILL series? Do you have any predictions to offer?

JULIE KLASSEN loves all things Jane—*Jane Eyre* and Jane Austen. A graduate of the University of Illinois, Julie worked in publishing for sixteen years and now writes full-time. Three of her books, *The Silent Governess*, *The Girl in the Gatehouse*, and *The Maid of Fairbourne Hall*, have won the Christy Award for Historical Romance. *The Secret of Pembrooke Park* was honored with the Minnesota Book Award for genre fiction. Julie has also won the Midwest Book Award and Christian Retailing's BEST Award, and has been a finalist in the Romance Writers of America's RITA Awards and ACFW's Carol Awards. Julie and her husband have two sons and live in a suburb of St. Paul, Minnesota.

For more information, visit www.julieklassen.com.

Sign up for Julie's newsletter!

Keep up to date with news on Julie's upcoming book releases and events by signing up for her email list at julieklassen.com

---

More Romance From Julie Klassen

After the man she loves abruptly sails for Italy, Sophie Dupont's future is in jeopardy. Wesley left her in dire straits, and she has nowhere to turn—until Captain Stephen Overtree comes looking for his wayward brother. He offers her a solution, but can it truly be that simple?

The Painter's Daughter

You May Also Enjoy . . .

Lady Ella Myerston is determined to put an end to the danger that haunts her brother. While visiting her friend Brook, the owner of the Fire Eyes jewels, Ella gets entangled in an attempt to blackmail the newly reformed Lord Cayton. Will she become the next casualty of the "curse"?

A Lady Unrivaled by Roseanna M. White
LADIES OF THE MANOR, roseannamwhite.com

When disaster ruins Charlotte Ward's attempt to restart a London acting career, her estranged daughter, Rosalind, moves her to a quiet village where she can recover. There, Rosalind gets a second chance at romance, and mother and daughter reconnect—until Charlotte's troubles catch up to her.

A Haven on Orchard Lane by Lawana Blackwell

Lady Miranda Hawthorne secretly longs to be bold. But she is mortified when her brother's new valet mistakenly mails her private thoughts to a duke she's never met—until he responds. As she sorts out her feelings for two men, she uncovers secrets that will put more than her heart at risk.

A Noble Masquerade by Kristi Ann Hunter
HAWTHORNE HOUSE, kristiannhunter.com